"Crystal Caudill has hit a home run with[...] cal romance. If you like characters who come alive, a hero to make you swoon, and edge-of-your-seat intrigue, you'll love this story. A fantastic debut from an author I'm looking forward to reading again!"

—Misty M. Beller, *USA Today* best-selling author of
the Brides of Laurent series

"*Counterfeit Love* is sure to delight fans of historical romantic suspense. As Caudill immerses readers in the world of counterfeiting rings and the early days of the Secret Service, she weaves a tale that is simultaneously well-researched and action-packed with delightfully flawed characters who will leave readers rooting for their redemption."

—Amanda Cox, Christy Award–winning author of
The Edge of Belonging

"*Counterfeit Love* is a dazzling debut! Caudill weaves a tale of intrigue, danger, and romance. Theresa and Broderick will long live in my heart as deep characters who struggle with relinquishing control to God . . . the same struggle many of us have felt to our core. A story to cheer for and an author to watch!"

—Tara Johnson, author of *All Through the Night*

"A thrilling romance, a gallant Secret Service operative, and a courageous heroine—Crystal Caudill's *Counterfeit Love* is an exceptional tale of tragic loss, healing, and redeeming love."

—Grace Hitchcock, author of *My Dear Miss Dupré* and
Her Darling Mr. Day

"Caudill's debut is a fast-paced tale full of brave and brilliant characters, much skullduggery, and conflict that will have you unable to tear yourself away."

—Erica Vetsch, author of *The Debutante's Code*

"With swoony romance, fascinating history, gripping plot twists, and strong characters, *Counterfeit Love* is one of the strongest debut novels I've ever read! Caudill's writing voice is pitch-perfect and draws readers immediately into the heart of the story, holding them in thrall until the end. And did I mention the swoony romance? I couldn't put it down, and I am already eagerly waiting for the next book!"

—Carrie Schmidt, blogger at ReadingIsMySuperPower.org

"Crystal Caudill creates a world of intrigue in *Counterfeit Love* that will thrust readers into a Secret Service investigation paired with a romance that will have you cheering for second chances."

—Toni Shiloh, author of *An Unlikely Proposal*

COUNTERFEIT
LOVE

HIDDEN HEARTS OF THE GILDED AGE
Counterfeit Love
Counterfeit Hope
Counterfeit Faith

HIDDEN HEARTS
OF THE GILDED AGE
- ONE -

COUNTERFEIT
LOVE

CRYSTAL CAUDILL

KREGEL
PUBLICATIONS

Published by Kregel Publications, a division of Kregel Inc., 2450 Oak Industrial Dr. NE, Grand Rapids, MI 49505.

Library of Congress Cataloging-in-Publication Data
Names: Caudill, Crystal, 1985- author.
Title: Counterfeit love / Crystal Caudill.
Description: Grand Rapids, MI : Kregel Publications, [2022] | Series: Hidden hearts of the gilded age ; book 1
Identifiers: LCCN 2021051717 (print) | LCCN 2021051718 (ebook) | ISBN 9780825447402 (paperback) | ISBN 9780825477973 (ebook)
Subjects: LCGFT: Thrillers (Fiction). | Romance fiction. | Christian fiction.
Classification: LCC PS3603.A89866 C68 2022 (print) | LCC PS3603. A89866 (ebook) | DDC 813/.6--dc23/eng/20211022
LC record available at https://lccn.loc.gov/2021051717
LC ebook record available at https://lccn.loc.gov/2021051718

ISBN 978-0-8254-4740-2, print
ISBN 978-0-8254-7797-3, epub
ISBN 978-0-8254-6948-0, Kindle

Printed in the United States of America
22 23 24 25 26 27 28 29 30 31 / 5 4 3 2 1

First and always—
To God, my Savior Jesus,
may You be glorified always, and may this offering
be pleasing to You. I will trust You, even if.

To the hero of my heart, Travis Caudill—
Everything I've learned about Christlike heroes I've learned from you.
You are and will always be the inspiration for all my literary heroes.
Also, I love you the mostest. One, two, three . . . I win!

"The detection of crime, when entered upon with an honest purpose to discover the haunts of criminals and protect society from their depredations by bringing them to justice, is held to be an honorable calling and worthy of the commendation of all good men."

—HIRAM C. WHITLEY, Secret Service Chief
(May 1869–September 1874)

CHAPTER 1

December 31, 1883

"I DON'T UNDERSTAND WHY WE can't marry sooner. Cincinnati doesn't require your grandfather's consent."

Not this topic again. Theresa sighed as her fiancé tilted the umbrella to shield her from falling sleet and helped her into the closed carriage. She'd spent weeks updating her seasons-old dress with a larger bustle and salvaged lace. Couldn't they simply enjoy the New Year's Eve Ball at Bellevue House and for one evening pretend all was right in the world?

"You know I want his blessing." However, convincing her stubborn grandfather that Edward Greystone was a suitable match would take more time. Lots more.

"I don't see why." The carriage rocked as Edward squeezed into the cramped space. "The curmudgeon hardly gives you anything, much less his approval."

"He's a good man." What other grandfather would sacrifice a beloved military career to raise a fourteen-year-old granddaughter? "And he's all the family I have left. I need him as much as he needs me."

"You're better off without him." Edward turned sideways to allow his long legs room to stretch and speared her with a pointed look. "What did you pawn this week to pay his debts?"

She waved aside the answer as the carriage rolled forward. He didn't need to know the elegant furniture from her parents' bedroom had succumbed to her desperate need. One less creditor on their list of many made the sentimental loss worth it. She owed Grandfather everything within her power to help.

"Can we just enjoy the evening, please? I want 1884 to be the year life takes a turn for the better."

"Then wed me tomorrow." He clasped her hands and rubbed his thumb over the emerald engagement ring she wore inside her glove. "My work at the shipping docks may not afford us a mansion yet, but I can provide for you and save you from Colonel Plane's downfall."

Edward's hopeful expression pricked her conscience. Grandfather would never approve of their marrying, no matter how long she tried to convince him. Edward's vocal southern sympathies earned him no respect from the former Union colonel. Whatever Edward did to cultivate favor, he'd always be the enemy. Would Grandfather ever find any man acceptable? Broderick Cosgrove had shared most of her grandfather's political views, but Grandfather had still objected to him. Of course, he'd been right about that match.

Unbidden, the image of her former fiancé's smiling face filled her mind, and disappointment washed over her anew. She'd waited six years for Broderick to return with an explanation and a desire for reconciliation. Her foolish heart should know the truth by now. He was never coming back.

Edward, though, stayed by her side, whatever the hardship. He loved her. To delay their marriage bordered lunacy. Besides, where her head went, her heart eventually followed.

She smoothed Edward's waxed mustache and offered a tentative smile. "I—"

The carriage halted, and voices rose.

"Stay here. I'll check with the driver." Edward reached for the door, but the handle jerked from his grip.

The smell of stale whiskey and cheap cigar filled the interior as a dark-haired vagrant forced his way inside, lobbying the barrel of a gun at them.

Edward lunged in front of her, blocking her view. "Get out."

"Not 'til I get my money."

Theresa sucked in a breath. No one forgot that raspy voice once they heard it, and she'd heard it coming from behind Grandfather's closed office door more than once. Vincent Drake, the money monger, looked as villainous as his reputation.

"Over my dead body." Edward, the brave fool.

"I can arrange that."

Her heart skittered. "Move, Edward. Mr. Drake is Grandfather's creditor."

He didn't shift.

The gun cocked. "I'd hate for the bullet to go through you and kill her."

Edward eased next to her, fists clenched.

"Now, Miss Plane, where's my money?"

"If you'll speak to my gran—"

"Already did. All I got were excuses. I'll not be put off again. A nice filly like you will make what's owed me in a few nights on George Street."

Edward lashed out with a growl, and the gun blasted.

Theresa flinched, and her ears shrilled as acrid smoke fogged the air and filled her lungs. She blinked at Drake's smug smile, then swung her gaze to Edward. *God, please, no.* He was pressed against the side of the carriage, face pale, jaw slack, hand over chest. With breath held and fingers trembling, she pried away his hand. Nothing. No blood. No hole. Not even a tear.

"Consider yourself lucky. Next one won't miss." Drake gestured to the narrow space between her and Edward.

Theresa swallowed. A bullet-sized circle next to Edward's head gave view to the dark, deserted street outside. *Thank You, God.* For once, He'd seen fit to intervene. Unfortunately, with the miserable weather and New Year celebrations, everyone remained indoors. No one would come to their aid, even if the driver dared to call for help.

"How much does my grandfather owe you?"

"Two hundred twenty."

That much? "Perhaps we can make another arrangement."

"Unless it involves money in my hand tonight, I think not." Drake knocked on the carriage's ceiling and called out "George Street!" The conveyance lurched into motion.

"Even if I had it to give, the banks are closed."

"Not my problem."

At the edge of her vision, Edward's hands flexed. Any more heroic attempts, and he might not survive. She needed a plan of her own. Her gaze dropped to the bump beneath her glove and sparked an idea. It wouldn't settle the debt, but it should help her negotiate payment for the remainder.

"Will you take a valuable item instead?"

Edward shot her a look, but he needn't worry about his engagement ring. Praise God Lydia insisted on a literal funeral for Theresa's past with Broderick. The ritual of burying both his engagement ring and her dreams in the ground next to her parents seemed childish a year ago, but now her novelist friend's dramatic ways proved a godsend.

"I knew I did right comin' to you." Drake's smirk sent shivers down her back as his gaze swept the length of her body. "Where is it?"

"Hidden." She took a shaky breath. "In Spring Grove Cemetery."

The place where her dreams met their death over and over again.

Please, God, not this time.

Decent men dared not venture into Dirk's Saloon, but Broderick Cosgrove wasn't a decent man these days. The dimly lit bar held more than a dozen loyal patrons, both law-abiding and those who sought a more lucrative supplement to their income. Dirk's lookout, more muscle than man, openly scrutinized Broderick from his worn cap to his scuffed shoes. Assured Broderick wasn't a foolish copper, he returned to nursing his pint.

Good. His day had been long enough without fighting for the right to be here. Broderick leaned against the counter and nodded to Dirk. The portly bartender filled a mug with Broderick's usual and then held out his palm for payment. Dirk reserved tabs only for those he personally trusted, which was no one. After examining the twenty-cent coin for any sign of being spurious, Dirk relinquished the mug.

Lager sloshed over the rim as Broderick walked toward the scum of Cincinnati huddled around a three-legged table steadied by an empty keg. This sorry lot of men made for poor friends—they'd betray their grandmothers for the right price—but their wagers made for interesting nights. Based on the odd assortment of valuables in the center of the table, tonight's wins would require a trip to the pawnshop. If he weren't after more than trinkets, he'd go elsewhere. He approached the table as Fitz collected cards.

"Yer late, Smith." Fitz's Irish brogue accentuated his ire.

Known as Brody Smith to this crew, Broderick stole an empty chair and dragged it to the table. "I was busy with Cat." Or rather, busy avoiding her.

The madame was indefatigable in her quest to have him rent a girl along with the room Fitz had arranged for him. Broderick's residence at the brothel supported his cover as a counterfeit wholesaler and strengthened his relationship with Fitz. A necessary evil considering Fitz's position as gatekeeper to the counterfeiting ring the Secret Service sought to eradicate. Even so, other than to sleep, he avoided the place.

"Living with Cat has benefits, sure." Fitz grunted as he shuffled the cards. "Up for another beating, lads?"

Broderick sacrificed a coin to the blind bid as Fitz dealt the cards. Everyone peeked at their hands, and grumbles followed. Fitz stacked the deck better than anyone Broderick knew, and his tardiness hadn't bought him any favors. Five unpaired cards with a high of seven. The lousy hand matched his mood. Worse cards replaced the three he discarded, and the Irish scoundrel smirked. Broderick bit back an exclamation. Calling out the cheat meant an encounter with the bark of iron.

Smoke hung thick as fog over the Ohio River, growing denser as the hours passed. A barmaid well past her prime kept their mugs filled and flaunted her wrinkled bosom barely contained by her low-cut dress. The volume and severity of insults grew with each round of drinks. These kinds of nights wore on Broderick, but perseverance would pay off. It had to.

The magnitude of this counterfeiting ring made any of his previous cases trifling in comparison. The Secret Service had removed $265,000 in counterfeit tens from circulation over the last nine months alone. All of them came from the same imperfect issue, whose origins he'd traced to one man in Cincinnati.

Fitz held his cards close to the chest as the call to raise the bid shifted to Broderick. "If it's a drowning you're after, don't torment yourself with shallow water. Double or nothing."

The gatekeeper showed no mercy at the gaming table, nor did his lips ever loosen with information about his partners. Broderick could arrest the thirty-eight identified dealers and wholesalers, but that would only slow distribution. To end the counterfeiting ring's success, he had to infiltrate the very depths of the production firm.

Broderick pushed his small pile of money reserved for nights at the saloon to the table's center. "I'm all in."

Fitz tsk-tsked. "Never bet against me. You'll always lose." He laid down a royal flush.

From the bar, Dirk shouted, "You there! Grab a bucket and clean up the mess out front."

Fitz tensed beside Broderick and turned his gaze. The rumble of conversation returned after several beats, but Fitz ignored his winnings and focused on the stranger staring at them from the counter.

The announcement must have been a prearranged signal.

Masking his observation by downing the rest of his drink, Broderick noted the new man's stubby build and dark, thinning hair. Gray and black stained the fabric of his clothes except for a clean area where he likely wore an apron. A printer or machinist? "Stubby" gave a curt nod and then passed the bartender a note. With nothing more, he disappeared into the night.

Fitz returned to playing cards until Dirk brought a tray of drinks a few minutes later. He grabbed the lone shot of whiskey, not quite managing the sleight of hand necessary to hide Stubby's note, then quaffed it. After a brief grimace, he stood.

"I'm out, lads. It's been a pleasure." He shoved his winnings into oversized coat pockets, then nodded to Broderick as a signal and left.

Broderick clenched his jaw as he accepted a new hand of cards. One man always left ahead of the other for their rendezvous, but that note could contain evidence—or worse, the revelation of his true profession. Convincing Fitz that he was a wholesaler in search of good counterfeits to sell to his extensive number of contacts had taken months of substantial purchases. If anyone in the counterfeiting ring discovered Broderick marked his initials on each banknote used for payment, they'd know the truth. Only officers marked money.

"Smith must have a terrible hand." Grubber, a usual at the gaming table, ribbed his neighbor. "His finger's tapping as fast as the needle on my wife's newfangled sewing machine."

The possibility of exposure ate at him worse than a swarm of mosquitoes. He needed to know what that note contained. "You're right. I'm out."

Broderick discarded the flush hand facedown and rose. As long as he followed at a distance, he shouldn't raise Fitz's suspicions. He exited through the back door into the night fit only for penguins. Cold drops of sleet slipped down his collar as he scanned the gaslit streets for Fitz, but he saw only a creaky carriage and an off-key drunkard slogging through the slush. Fitz hadn't traveled the direct route to their meeting place off George Street, but he couldn't have gone far.

Growing up in a family of detectives had its benefits. Broderick's father had required all his sons to become walking maps, memorizing every alley and private path that cut through Cincinnati. Few options moved Fitz in the right direction while still providing cover. Broderick picked the most likely choice.

Within three minutes, he spotted Fitz ahead, folding and then shoving the note into his pocket. Lack of information always left Broderick with knots in his shoulders, doubly so now.

Fitz continued to their usual meeting spot without speaking or signaling to anyone. Broderick held back and checked the cylinder of his Colt single-action army revolver. Though costly, the reliable six-shooter never failed him. Whatever Fitz planned, Broderick would be ready.

He waited a few minutes to give the illusion of having followed directions and then ducked into the dark alley, where a pig snuffled through the refuse at the entrance and caused him to stumble. The feral beast grunted its displeasure before moving to another pile, where the dim gaslight failed to penetrate the darkness.

Light from a match flickered, and the orange tip of a cigarette burned to life. "Get in here afore someone sees you." Once Broderick reached him, Fitz removed a roll of bogus banknotes from his pocket. "I brang six hundred."

The note must not pertain to their meeting. Fitz wouldn't move forward with a deal if he suspected treachery. Broderick's muscles eased a little.

"Only six hundred? I wanted twelve." The Secret Service demanded he purchase only the minimum amount required to forge relations with their suspects, but a change to the deal didn't bode well. "Did you sell part of your boodle to my competitor?"

"I didn't. We ran out, but more's being printed. I've a better offer from the big gun."

So Broderick had finally earned the leader's attention. He exchanged his marked money for Fitz's false. "What's better than tens for three each?"

Fitz flipped through the bills as he spoke around his cigarette. "Exclusive rights to the first run o' fifties."

The words landed a punch with the strength of a floorer. How had the production firm created such a lucrative note without arousing rumors? His network of informants would trip over their feet to bring him news of such a large denomination. Fitz's invitation to exclusive rights provided a small measure of solace. Every wholesaler wanted to secure sole purchasing rights so they could control the counterfeiting market. Rarely was it offered.

"Any other buyers know about the fifties?"

"They don't. Yet." Fitz moved toward the street's light and then examined one of the marked banknotes.

Broderick gripped the heart-shaped rock he always carried. May God prevent Fitz's discovery of the initials hidden in Benjamin Franklin's kite. Fitz adjusted his bowler, exposing red curls, and brought the note closer to his nose. Broderick squeezed the rock until it no doubt left an impression on his palm. After a moment, Fitz scrubbed the note's surface with the tip of his nail. His face relaxed, and he shook his head.

"This weather be making me eyes cross."

Fitz tucked the payment into his pocket. When he removed his hand, a paper fell to the mud. Broderick noted where it landed but said nothing.

Fitz took a long drag on his cigarette and stared at Broderick with calculating measure. After a slow release, he flicked the cigarette to the ground. "The big gun's looking to be adding another partner. You pay for exclusive rights, and you're in."

If the leader sought to add another partner, the production firm must be running short on legitimate cash. No surprise considering most counterfeiters spent more than they saved. "Investing sight unseen is risky. Got a sample of the fifty?"

"I don't. The engraver be making a few adjustments afore they go to print, but the same engraver who done the tens be doing these. So what say you, Smith? I'll not be offering again."

"Will I meet the other partners? I don't trust anyone I haven't met."

"You won't. And you won't be seeing where the fifties are made either, so don't be asking. That's my deal, or I take it elsewhere."

Not the answer he wanted, but it wouldn't keep him from uncovering the other members' identities.

"If the notes are as good as you say, I'm in." He extended his hand, and they shook.

"Grand. We'll meet here a week hence, and I'll have a fifty on me." Broderick waited until Fitz disappeared down a side alley before he retrieved the soppy, dropped paper, then shoved it into his pocket and followed. Fitz avoided direct paths. Anytime he crossed a street, he risked his neck to cut in front of a carriage midway down the square. At corners he pivoted at the last second—a tactic employed to expose anyone who shadowed him. Broderick recognized the trick and traveled down the next alley to continue the trail. After three squares of moving into the heart of downtown, Fitz hired a hack.

Unable to follow, Broderick ducked under the canopy of a closed mercantile. Though he should count this as a case-breaking evening, urgency pricked at the nape of his neck. Who was the big gun? What role did he play? Had Fitz been honest about not offering the fifties to other wholesalers and dealers? Should those fifties get into circulation and people found out, panic could lead to another market crash. Businesses already reported a steep decline in profits, and railroad expansion had slowed considerably over the last few years. Families were hurting. The fragile economy couldn't withstand another blow without teetering back into depression.

Lord, I know You care about these people. Help me. Don't continue to allow these men to hide in the dark.

At least tonight's deal gave hope to his stagnant case. He wrapped his hand around the wad of counterfeit money his partner Josiah Isaacs would document. Too bad he wouldn't have something more tangible to add to his report to Chief Brooks, like a name or location. Once the man discovered fifties were nearly ready for production, he'd lose any remaining patience with Broderick and Isaacs.

Broderick tucked the wad into a safer spot and then reached for his rock. Damp paper grazed his fingers. The message. Hope flared in his chest as he peeled the edges apart. Water smeared ink across the page, leaving *midnight* the sole legible word.

A meeting, then, and likely tonight. He shifted into the full light of a gas lamp and squinted at the partial letters.

Sp—— G——

D–xter Maus——

Midnight.

Given the organization and capitalization of words, he held the details to a secret meeting between ring members. *Sp—— G——* could be part of a business or a street name. He'd need a directory to check business names, but Stubby likely referred to a street. Tracing the thin edges of his rock, he closed his eyes and examined his mental map of Cincinnati. No downtown place fit the partial words. Residential areas in the hills had expanded since he left six years ago, but none of the new ones he'd memorized contained anything close. Clifton Heights held no possibilities, but the outskirts of town provided a candidate.

Spring Grove.

The long street covered over five miles with any number of possible meeting places. He referenced the paper again. No street numbers or indication they'd smeared.

D–xter Maus—— could be the name of the leader. Headquarters might match the partial name to a record, but that required time and he would likely return empty-handed.

Or *D–xter Maus——* could be a something.

The thought stilled his hand. He'd learned to rely on God's prompting Spirit over the years. More than once, it had saved his life. Spring Grove Cemetery, home of the Dexter Mausoleum. He must be growing dull not to have immediately recalled the cathedral-like mausoleum near the Plane family plot. First kisses were hard to forget, especially when they occurred on the steps of that cryptic building.

The tip of the rock bit into his hand like the unwanted memory bit into his soul. He shoved both where they belonged—the rock in his pocket and the memory in the recesses of his mind.

Fitz worked seasonally at the cemetery, so the location made sense. He had access, and no one would question his presence if discovered. Broderick flicked open his pocket watch. Under an hour remained to travel through downtown, up the Mount Auburn incline, and past Clifton Heights.

It would be close, but he had to make it to Spring Grove Cemetery before he missed his chance.

CHAPTER 2

CONFOUND IT!

Theresa frowned as lantern light flickered over the locked iron gates and empty gatehouse of Spring Grove Cemetery. Of course, nothing worked in her favor. The unusual absence of Louis, the night watchman, must be another snub from God. Any other night the man would be hunkered inside, away from the foul weather, ready to offer her a cup of tea and listening ear.

She glanced to where Drake held Edward hostage and grit her teeth. "We'll have to break in."

Drake spat, the tar-colored glob striking her gown's hem. "Ain't no *we* to it. I ain't going in there."

"Surely you're not afraid of spirits?"

He sneered, crinkling the scar running the length of his face. "You've got thirty minutes to bring me those valuables or your beau here will need an eternity box."

Ice threaded through her veins. Spring Grove Cemetery covered over four hundred acres. It would take thirty minutes just to reach her family's plot. "I'll never make it. Give me an hour, please. I beg you."

He narrowed his gaze and remained silent for far too long. "Forty-five. Not a second longer."

Not sufficient, but what choice did she have? "I need Edward to lift me over the fence."

"Fine, but try anything funny, and I'll shoot."

To her relief, Edward walked with her to the four-foot fence with no heroic attempts. His hands wrapped around her waist, and he lifted her with no more trouble than if she were a child. Granted, she wasn't much larger than a twelve-year-old boy, but the ease of his effort still startled.

When she reached the height of his mouth, his breath fanned against her neck. "Don't come back."

"But he'll—"

"Go." He eased her over and lowered her to the ground.

As soon as she found steady footing, she faced him. He couldn't seriously expect her to leave him. Before she spoke, the butt of Drake's gun cracked against Edward's skull. Edward staggered. A second blow followed, and he crumpled against the fence.

"Edward!" She dropped to her knees and sought his face in the shadows. Was he conscious? Or dying before her eyes?

"Don't get any heroic ideas. The next hit comes from a bullet." Drake kicked Edward over as though he were a sack of flour. Edward groaned.

No matter what Edward said, no honorable soldier left another behind. She touched his hand through the bars. "I'm coming back for you." Then she rose and ran, Drake's shouted reminder of her deadline overpowered by the thrumming in her ears. She'd reach her parents' gravesite in twenty minutes if she ran. Too bad corsets weren't designed for exertion. She needed to be smart, or she'd waste time in a faint.

Forcing control of her breathing, she slowed to a jog and skirted the edge of an iced pond. Sleet beat against headstones as she wove her way between the familiar rectangular mounds and plot boundaries. Mud pulled at her shoes, and biting cold numbed her feet and legs by the time the Dexter Mausoleum loomed ahead.

A few minutes beyond the Gothic cathedral, she reached her parents' graves. Slush slid down the simple marble of her mother's headstone like a tear. How her parents must grieve to know the trouble their only child faced. She kissed her fingertips and then pressed them to the surface. "Pray for me." If God listened to anyone's prayers, it would be her saintly mother's. Even from heaven, she'd be interceding.

Fireworks exploded in the distance, announcing the end of 1883. Already, 1884 proved no better.

Theresa shook her head and focused on her task. Mud seeped through her petticoats as she knelt by the shared brownstone obelisk where Grandmother Plane long awaited her husband's arrival. At the base, Theresa slid aside a loose slab of limestone and peered into the shallow grave. The canning jar representing the death of her once cherished dreams still lay there. How ironic that the man who'd abandoned her would be the one to rescue her now. She pulled both gloves free, placed her emerald ring in a pocket of her skirt, then twisted the jar's lid.

Memories long buried clawed at her as this ring's weight landed in her palm. The proposal on a tender spring day. Broderick slipping the large opal onto her finger and then gathering her into his arms. The way he'd attributed each seed pearl encompassing the opal's perimeter to a cherished memory. *To help you remember how much I love you whenever we're apart.*

Emotion clogged her throat. His love had proved as fleeting as the rainbow that once gleamed off the opal's surface. Despite Lydia's insistence that burying the ring would bring healing, the pain in Theresa's chest burned with the same intensity it had the day she'd discovered Broderick gone forever. With a shaky breath, she shoved the ring where Edward's should have been, then tugged her gloves onto damp hands. All that mattered was the ring's monetary value—not the man, not the memories, and certainly not the finality of letting the ring go. Edward needed her, and she would not fail him.

When she reached the path again, lantern light glowed from the side of the Dexter Mausoleum. Unexpected relief eased the tension in her body. Perhaps God hadn't forgotten her after all. Louis could go for help while she stalled for time at the gate.

She darted across the footpath and into the light. "I'm glad I found you."

Louis did not return a greeting. Instead, flinty eyes narrowed over the bulbous nose of a short man. Tangled hair draped past his matted beard in greasy strings, and clothes unlikely to have ever seen wash water stretched over thick arms and a broad chest. His taller, cleaner companion brandished a weapon and revealed himself no more civilized.

Was the entire world naught but villains and scoundrels? She pivoted and fled.

Feet pounded behind her, growing louder with each stride. A rancid body crushed her into the ground, and mud filled her mouth and nose. Pinned, she thrashed, but the thug's grip tightened around her throat. Light flashed. Her heart pounded. Try as she might to breathe, air neither entered nor exited her lungs.

"Let herself up, Grimm."

The iron grip released, and she gasped. How many times must she stare into death's face before it claimed her?

The one who'd pinned her—Grimm, apparently—yanked her to her feet. "Scream, and I'll cut out your tongue."

If he believed a scream was the worst she could offer, he was about to get the surprise of his life. She slammed a knee into his groin. A curse exploded from his mouth, and he bent forward without releasing his hold. *If your first shot doesn't work, take the next, and don't hesitate.* For once, she didn't rebuke Broderick's voice in her head. Grimm's nose extended like a tree limb, big and hard to miss. Theresa rammed forward. The crack of breaking bone turned her stomach but granted sweet release. Grimm stumbled, hands trying to staunch the free flow of blood.

She retreated until a cold circle of metal pressed into the nape of her neck.

"Be still, lass."

Really? Heat flared throughout her body, and she clenched her hands into fists. This wasn't fair! Wasn't God supposed to protect His children? She took a steadying breath and raised her hands. Reacting in anger would get her killed, and Edward needed her.

"Better be learning to recognize your boss's kin," the Irishman said. "What Miss Plane done to you ain't nothing to what he'll be doing when he finds you touched her."

The Irishman's words jumbled in her head, jarring her senses. How had he known her name? Were they creditors too? No, they couldn't be. He'd called her the boss's kin, but they couldn't be pressmen from Grandfather's printshop either.

"Then what's she doin' here, Fitz?" Grimm glowered at her as he nursed his nose. "He send ya to spy on us?"

"I'm sure the lass has herself an explanation." Fitz slid into view and gestured toward the tree's shelter with his gun. "That so?"

Not an explanation they would believe. She hardly believed the truth herself. Theresa swiped mud from her face as she moved toward a lantern and ragged carpetbag. Given they were in a cemetery at midnight, the contents of the bag must be illegal. What had Grandfather gotten them into?

"Well, lass?"

If Grandfather were indeed their employer, that had to buy her some power. She straightened into the soldier he'd raised her to be. "I owe you no explanation, and you will let me go immediately."

An amused smirk creased Fitz's face. "Sorry, lass. I can't be doing that."

Theresa held his unwavering gaze. He stood too far away to strike her, but he held a gun. If she ran, would he really shoot? After all, he'd warned Grimm of punishment for touching her. How much more would this man suffer if she were shot?

The Irishman seemed to read her thoughts and cocked his gun. She could call his bluff—

A branch snapped. "There you are, Reese."

Her head jerked toward the all-too-familiar voice, though her heart cried out at the impossibility of it. Only one person called her that. The ghost of her dreams emerged from the shadows. "Broderick?"

He'd grown a full, unruly beard and shaggy hair. An ill-fitted overcoat disguised the slender build that fooled many into thinking him an easy opponent, but it didn't deceive her. Before her stood the man who'd stolen her heart, then pulverized it and abandoned her without a second thought. Punching his handsome face would be so satisfying.

But she wouldn't deny his help. The skunk was her only ally in this situation, and he was the type of man everyone wanted at their side during a fight. Likely, Broderick's sharp appraisal took in every detail and his keen mind formed a brilliant plan of escape.

Fitz shifted next to her. "What do you be doing here, Smith?"

Theresa stiffened. Smith? Broderick must still be a detective, working undercover, and her little slip of his name might cost them their freedom.

"Theresa asked me to escort her to her parents' graves."

Plausible, and if the Irishman knew her family at all, believable.

"Then why weren't you together, Miss Plane?"

He *would* ask her directly. She ran her tongue over suddenly dry lips. "I . . . uh . . ." Her gaze landed on the trees behind him. "I needed to use the necessary."

"In a cemetery?"

Heat flamed her face, and she dropped her gaze. "It was an emergency."

Heaven help her. If she didn't die of a bullet wound, she'd die of mortification. Fitz stood in prolonged silence as if judging the truth of her words. A hand slipped around her elbow, and she dared a peek. Broderick's spring-green eyes looked down on her, concern etching the crinkle of his brow. If he was so worried about her, he should have returned sooner.

When the Irishman bent to retrieve the carpetbag, Theresa crushed the toe of Broderick's shoe with her heel. He jerked, but uttered no sound.

"Shove off, Grimm." Fitz straightened. "We're done."

"What about them?"

"I'll be taking 'em to the boss."

"No, you will not." The words escaped before she'd given them consideration, but it didn't matter. If Grandfather was their boss, she'd see him on her terms. And if their boss was someone else? This mire was treacherous enough. She would go no deeper. As it was, Edward's life depended on her getting back to the gatehouse without further delay.

"Come again?" That infernal weapon reappeared.

If Fitz wanted to play that game, she'd call his bluff. "I said, no."

Had Theresa lost all sense? Broderick pulled her behind him, but the stubborn woman wrenched free, then planted fists on her hips and stared Fitz down as if he held a flower, not a Remington revolver.

If she wouldn't allow him to defend her, he could at least divert attention. "What she means to say is, Do you want to be the one who delivers your boss's kin injured and bleeding?"

Fitz squinted at Broderick, his lips flattening. "Is that so?"

Broderick tensed as he realized his slip. The mention of Theresa's connection to the boss occurred before he'd abandoned his hiding spot to rescue her, not after.

Ignoring the rising tension, Theresa continued to assert her position. "Yes. Grandfather's protective of me, and I doubt he'll accept any excuse you offer. In fact, I'll ensure he doesn't. That is"—she folded her arms—"unless we're allowed to leave of our own free will."

The silence stretched as Fitz's gaze shifted between Broderick and Theresa.

She moaned, swaying and lifting a hand to her head. "I'm starting to see double, and the world is spinning. I think I might have a concussion." The corner of her mouth curled.

It was a good try, but her best artifice wouldn't deflect Fitz's suspicion. They were in trouble.

Grimm burst into the lantern light. "Guard comin'."

Fitz cursed, breaking the silent standoff. "Get herself out of here, Smith, and be sure she don't get caught." He holstered his gun and disappeared into the darkness with the carpetbag probably full of evidence. Grimm escaped in the opposite direction.

Broderick faced Theresa. Clumps of dark hair fell from her once-pinned style, and mud stood in stark contrast to her pale face. Her wrestling match with Grimm rendered her cloak and dress beyond repair. This wasn't the safe, quiet life he'd envisioned for her, but the how and why of her presence would have to wait. Seeing to her immediate safety took precedence.

"Let's go." He tugged her hand, but she remained rooted to the spot.

"The only place I'm going is with that guard."

The woman still had a habit of digging in her heels at the wrong times. "I'm not leaving you behind."

"Not leave—" Her eyes flashed, and her arm drew back.

Before the fist could crash into his face, he deflected it and pinned her against him. The fit of her small frame against his body stirred memories best left forgotten. She wasn't his anymore, and she could never be again. Her breath warmed his face, and he looked down. He should release her, but he didn't dare. "Most women thank their rescuers, not swing a right hook."

"Most men don't leave the woman they supposedly love to fight for her life alone."

His breath whooshed. Love hadn't been the problem. His brother's betrayal had. "It's complicated."

Gravel crunched behind them, and another lantern added to the light from the one left behind. "You're under arrest for trespassing."

There went an escape without discovery. Broderick released Theresa.

Her whole body relaxed. "Louis. Praise God!"

Broderick faced the elderly man in a soaked overcoat and drooping hat and winced at his hobbled step. Louis should be in bed nursing his rheumatism, not policing a cemetery.

"Well, this is something I never thought to see again." Louis shook his head in disappointment. "What will your fiancé think, Miss Theresa?"

Fiancé? Broderick's gaze fell to her gloved left hand where an unnatural bump bulged from her ring finger. He mentally kicked himself. What did he expect? That she'd live as a spinster forever?

"It's not what it looks like." Theresa's face reddened in the lantern light. "Louis, please, I'm in trouble. I need your help."

Louis hobbled toward Broderick. "A night in the cemetery jail ought to teach you to leave Miss Theresa be."

"As much as he deserves it, Broderick's not the issue. Grandfather's"—she glanced at Broderick—"obligations forced me here, and I need to return to the gate with all haste."

"What obligations would force you here at this hour?" Louis peered at Broderick as if trying to sort out the truth.

"The kind where lives are at stake."

The trauma of her encounter with Fitz must have caught up with her. "You're safe, Reese. The danger's passed."

"No, it hasn't." Fear and determination mingled in her eyes before she stepped past him toward Louis. "Please, give me the gate keys and see that Broderick leaves unseen. I don't have time to explain, and you know I wouldn't ask if it weren't urgent."

Louis extended a ring of keys, and Broderick covered her hand as she grabbed them. "Whatever trouble you're in, we can figure it out together."

Her anxious gaze met his. "Not this time. You need to leave and never return." She took the keys and ran.

"Meet me at our spot tomorrow. Usual time!" She gave no acknowledgment of his raised voice. He turned to the elderly man. "I'm sorry, Louis. I can't let her go by herself, and you'll never keep up."

Louis grunted his acquiescence as Broderick jogged after Theresa.

The exertion did little to ease the growing tension in his body. Was she warning him off the case? Surely not. The determination to ferret out justice once pulsed through her veins as strongly as his. How often had she pushed or challenged him on cases deemed hopeless by his father's detective agency? Yet Fitz's words made her connection to the counterfeiting ring undeniable.

Any involvement must be the result of her grandfather's scheming.

Colonel Plane might be a war hero, but the honor transformed him into a self-interested curmudgeon who didn't deserve to be Theresa's guardian. Not that anyone could convince her. The woman was loyal to a fault, and Colonel Plane twisted that loyalty for his benefit. Whether Theresa wanted it or not, she needed Broderick's help.

Halfway to the gate, the unmistakable sound of gunfire echoed in the distance.

"No!" Theresa hiked her skirts and charged forward.

Broderick closed the distance between them. Whatever she'd hoped to prevent, it was too late now. She reached the gate ahead of him, then unlocked it before tossing aside the keys. A man with dark hair and a scarred face waited on the other side. Broderick ducked into the line of bushes and crouch-walked closer.

"I thought that might hurry you," the man rasped. "Where is it?"

"Edward!" Theresa dropped to her knees next to Goliath's blond cousin. Though hunched with his head in his hands, he sat nearly as tall as Theresa stood and twice as wide. A carriage with a clearly distraught driver waited nearby.

"He ain't shot, but that can change."

Theresa turned a murderous glare on the speaker and yanked off a glove. She slid a ring from her finger and threw it at him. "It won't cover the full amount, but I have buyers waiting."

Buyers? Broderick's throat tightened. Was she selling counterfeits?

"I'll make deliveries this week and provide the remainder plus ten percent interest to you by the end of the week."

God, please don't let it be true.

"Fine, but no more chances." The brute retrieved the jewelry from the ground and shoved it into a pocket. "I will get what's owed me, one way or another." Dragging the driver from his carriage perch, the evil man climbed up and drove off.

Theresa waved the driver toward town. "Go to the police, but tell them only that your carriage was stolen." After he left, Theresa turned to Edward. "Come on. We need to go."

"We need to report this." He wobbled as he struggled to stand, and Theresa's attempt to bolster him resembled a mouse supporting a lion.

Edward grumbled when she ignored him, but whatever injury he'd incurred left him unable to withstand Theresa's stubborn will. As they hobbled away, Broderick scrubbed a hand over his face. Had the woman he loved become one of the criminals he hunted?

CHAPTER 3

By the time Broderick reached the Keppler Hotel, the streets were empty of merrymakers and silent. Too bad the tumult of his mind hadn't followed suit. Even if Theresa proved innocent of involvement, Colonel Plane's created its own set of challenges. Once he discovered Broderick's presence, the colonel would expose him to the other ring members or shoot him. Likely both. After all, he'd shot at Broderick before.

Apprehending the production firm and extracting Theresa from its entanglement required strategizing with Isaacs.

He took the hotel's main stairs and rapped the coded signal on the door at the hall's end. No answer. Not that he'd expected one given the late hour. He waited a few extra seconds before unlocking and opening the door.

A low-burning lamp illuminated Isaacs sitting erect in bed, blond hair mussed and revolver ready for trouble. "What the devil, Cosgrove!"

"Afraid a hobgoblin came to snatch you?" Broderick smirked despite the tension tonight had brought. Josiah Isaacs might claim the always-burning lamp an advantage over criminals, but Broderick suspected a fear of the dark the real culprit.

"Of course not." Isaacs shoved the weapon under his pillow. "Kitty being persistent tonight?"

"Cat, and I haven't come from the brothel. We have a problem."

"Worse than this?" Isaacs turned up the lamp, then passed him a telegram from the nightstand.

Broderick accepted it and glanced at the sender's name—James Brooks, Department of the Treasury. A message directly from the chief of the Secret Service never boded well.

SENDING DARLINGTON. ARRIVAL 1:35 TRAIN TOMORROW.

Pressure pulsed in his temples. Darlington's arrival changed everything. The man was as relentless as a starving wolf and about as gentle. Once he identified a suspect, he ran them into the ground without considering collateral. Whether or not she was an innocent victim, he'd attack Theresa with merciless stratagem and ruin any hope of a respectable future. Broderick had to protect her, but if Darlington discovered his connection to the Plane family, he would remove him from the case. "We don't need him."

"I agree." Isaacs stretched. "But with progress stalled for weeks, Chief Brooks doesn't see it that way."

"We're not stalled anymore. I've been offered exclusive rights to the new fifties."

Isaacs gave a low whistle. "They've got brass. Does that give you access to the other partners?"

"Not through Fitz."

Broderick sought the rock in his pocket, but turning it over in his hand didn't bring comfort. Everything hinged on the repercussions of his encounter at the cemetery. The complex nature of his compromised cover shouldn't be hidden, but how much should he reveal? Four years of working with Isaacs had formed a friendship that extended beyond work hours. He trusted the man with his life and career. If he wanted to protect Theresa's reputation until he knew the truth, he needed an ally against Darlington's biased and merciless tactics.

"I've discovered a former friend has family ties to the production firm. It's almost certain her grandfather is involved."

Isaacs leaned forward. "How close of a family friend are we talking? Can you still infiltrate the ring without arousing suspicion?"

"I don't know." Theresa certainly hadn't been happy to see him, and her statement about buyers hadn't stopped haunting him. "But we're meeting in a few hours."

"What's the name? I can look into the family's affairs."

Broderick stopped rotating the rock and examined its perfect heart shape. His next words would either condemn the woman he loved or ensure her protection. "Theresa Plane."

Isaacs knocked the back of his head against the wall. "Of course it is."

Outside of the Cosgrove family, only Isaacs knew the whole sordid story of Broderick's relationship with Theresa and its nearly fatal end. Even now the guilt of not reporting his brother's suspicious activity to their father until too late ate at Broderick. Had he done his duty instead of worrying about besmirching the name of his father's favorite son, Nathaniel would have been in jail long before the betrayal that resulted in Theresa's fight for her life. Broderick's reluctance to do the right thing destroyed his family and his future with her.

"Darlington will remove you from the case the moment he learns of your connection."

"Then help me make sure he doesn't."

His partner's gaze snapped to Broderick's. The request went beyond professional courtesy. Withholding information could get them fired.

"I owe it to Theresa to ensure she and her grandfather are investigated without false accusations to ruin their reputations. You know Darlington can't be turned from an idea once it gets into his head."

"How sure are you the Planes are involved? Darlington may not consider them."

"I'm almost certain Colonel Plane is part of the leadership. Theresa appears to be a victim of his machinations, but I'm not certain."

"If it proves she isn't innocent, are you prepared to turn over all evidence and arrest her?"

He would bring Theresa to justice, but it wouldn't be necessary. She was guilty of nothing beyond having a lousy guardian. "I'll do my job no matter the outcome. I just need time to uncover the truth without Darlington's interference."

Isaacs slipped into pensive silence. Broderick would allow him all the time he needed. Known as "the Charmer" by their colleagues, Isaacs had a soft spot for women in trouble. So soft, he'd managed to be cornered into eight proposals, though so far he'd escaped them all. Yet Isaacs was no fool. Women were just as capable of becoming counterfeiters as men.

Finally, Isaacs nodded, his agreement marking the depth of their friendship. "I'll do it because I'd ask the same thing of you if she were mine."

"She's not mine. Not anymore."

Isaacs harrumphed. "Once you love one, you never love another."

Given Isaacs's number of unfulfilled engagements, truth lingered in the statement, though Isaacs never mentioned the woman who *had* claimed his heart.

"When do you meet her?"

"Just after sunrise." *Assuming she'll come.*

"Need a second nearby?"

Probably prudent, but a precaution he'd forgo. Theresa wouldn't do him any real harm. He knew all her tricks, and if her grandfather showed up? Colonel Plane would receive the same treatment as any criminal.

"No, but I do need you to send descriptions of some new suspects to your Pinkerton friend and headquarters. With any luck, they'll have records and connections Darlington can pursue."

Anyone connected to Theresa required investigation, especially the scoundrel she'd promised money to and the fiancé. Maybe the latter was more personal than case-related, but he couldn't eliminate anyone as a suspect.

After recording the descriptions, they settled into their beds. With the lantern dimmed and the mattress far more comfortable than the one at Cat's, sleep should come quickly. But Theresa filled his mind— the fear she tried to hide, her words to the scarred man.

I have buyers waiting.

People changed, and rarely to the good. Had she? He'd have to tread carefully tomorrow. Her response could make or break his case—and his career.

Theresa shoved her head beneath a pillow as a bugle blared "Reveille," then fumbled for another to help subdue the racket. One day she'd find where Grandfather hid that obnoxious instrument and crush it beyond repair.

Cocooned in warmth and the bugle a dull annoyance, she relaxed into the plush mattress—a luxury she refused to pawn. The edge of a dream with a green-eyed detective beckoned her to return to its story of daring rescues, but cold air smacked her awake.

She sucked in a painful breath as her kittens mewled their displeasure.

"Up and at 'em, soldier." Mrs. Hawking, housekeeper and all-around deliverer of evil, held Theresa's coverlet hostage. She deposited it on the room's opposite side and flung open the curtains. Not that her action added any light. Even the sun had the good sense to still be asleep. "Your rescue animals are to remain outside." She returned and plucked the kittens off the bed by the scruff of their necks, then dropped them into a basket.

"But it snowed last night."

"They have fur." The rail-thin she-devil swatted an escapee back into the basket. "Inspection is at six o'clock sharp, and breakfast follows"—she sniffed in the direction of the muddy pile at the foot of the bed—"for those who pass muster." With a nod of dismissal, she about-faced and marched out of the room.

Mrs. Hawking should register with the army. She'd be a general in no time.

Theresa plopped back on her pillows and groaned. Every inch of her hurt. Muscles she didn't know existed screamed. The sting of a thousand bees pricked her damaged lungs, and her throat burned with each breath and swallow. Her hair wanted in on the protest, knotting into a giant rat's nest. Inspection at six? More like a condemnation for solitary confinement, which at the moment sounded heavenly. Then again, solitary confinement meant no opportunity to speak with Grandfather.

So much for a luxurious day in bed.

She wasted another minute and then forced herself to rise. By the time six o'clock arrived, her coverlet had crisp lines, the ruined dress hung in the wardrobe, her boots shined, and dirt swept from the floor littered the snow outside. All that remained was straightening the required, modified version of a soldier's uniform. She smoothed the light-blue day skirt and straightened the navy bodice with a single row of brass buttons. After she tightened the brown belt and arranged her hair into a tight bun, she felt ready to pass muster.

The morning ritual had become a game between them. A fight to outdo the other in perfection. It was a tinge unfair that Grandfather judged the contest, but most days she enjoyed the challenge. Today, however, she just wanted to pass without reprimand and tackle the secret she'd uncovered last night. To bolster her resolve, she retrieved the engagement ring from her nightstand drawer and wiggled the tight fit onto her finger. Grandfather didn't like to see her wearing it, but she needed the physical reminder of last night's debacle to give her courage.

Grandfather's jerky gait sounded in the hall, warning her to stand at attention by the door. He entered in uniformed glory and arched a brow. "I trust everything is in order?"

"Perfect order, sir."

"We'll see about that." A smirk belied his serious tone.

His double-breasted frock coat with domed double-row buttons creased as he leaned forward to run a white glove over the surfaces in her room. Not a dust mite dared appear. Determined to find imperfection, he lifted the rug and then knelt to check for dust bunnies. Satisfied—or rather disappointed—he rose and turned his attention to her bed. The silver eagle on the epaulet flapped its wings as he smoothed an invisible wrinkle from her coverlet. One point against her, and an extra chore added to her list. He must have something in mind to stoop to such imaginary levels.

Next, he went to her wardrobe and proceeded to check each piece hung exactly a hand's breadth apart. He stopped when he reached the ruined ball gown.

"You left with him after I expressly forbade it, didn't you?" Grandfather turned, all trace of the game lost to a scowl.

"We're to be married soon."

"Do you know what this medal means?" His bony finger pointed to the gleaming surface of his Medal of Honor. "It means I protect those under my care. I can't do that if you disobey me."

She took a deep breath to protest but immediately regretted it. The rattle in her chest echoed throughout the room, and his eyes narrowed.

"And now you're wheezing." He stalked to the door and bellowed for Mrs. Hawking.

The woman emerged before the last syllable left his mouth. "Yes, sir?"

"See to it that Theresa's fire is stoked with extra coals and she is served herbal tea and a bowl of broth."

The housekeeper saluted and marched to do as commanded.

Nothing scared Grandfather more than illness. Both her parents died during the cholera outbreak of 1873. Then prolonged bouts of pneumonia almost succeeded in killing her where drowning failed. At the slightest sniffle, Grandfather turned into the harsh colonel that made him a feared legend and executed an immediate counterattack.

Once Mrs. Hawking's footfalls no longer echoed on the steps, he speared Theresa with a glower. "A mere ball doesn't cause wheezing. I want a full report on last night's activities."

In other words, it was time for her court-martial. It was not the first one, nor would it be the last, but this time Grandfather had his own explanations to give. With raised chin, she focused on the tintype of her father's serious face, taken the day before he left to serve in the

Great Rebellion. If he faced the depravities of war, she could battle Grandfather.

"Edward and I endured an evening fit for dime novels." A story Lydia would no doubt write, given the chance. "Mr. Drake captured our carriage and threatened murder unless I paid your debts."

Grandfather's nostrils flared, and she flinched when he pounded a fist against the wall. "That man has no business coming to you."

"And you have no business borrowing from him."

"How I conduct myself is not your concern."

"When it affects me, it is." Many a man had retreated from his steely eyes, sharp as bayonets, but she would not cower. "Decent men earn their wages honestly and don't take loans from shady characters who threaten and manhandle a woman to get what they want."

"He touched you?"

"Not him." She held his gaze, ready to detect any lie he might give. "Tell me. Who are Grimm and Fitz?"

He reeled back with eyes wide. "Where did you hear those names?"

Vincent Drake scared ghosts to death, and yet it was Grimm's and Fitz's names that struck fear in him? Granted, she'd be happy to never see them again, but why should a boss be afraid of his employees? Unless he feared what she discovered. After a moment, he recovered and cupped her chin in his bony hand.

His breathing was ragged. "Did they do this?"

When she didn't answer, he barked the question again.

"Yes."

Silence stretched between them as his pained gaze roved her face, pausing at each instance of cut or bruise. Then he slumped onto the bed, appearing thirty years older than his sixty-six. "What injuries can't I see?"

She rotated her shoulders and shifted her back. They hurt, but nothing was broken, praise God. Too bad her salvation came in the form of a rotten skunk.

"Nothing more than you see, thanks to Broderick." She bit her lip as soon as the words escaped.

Grandfather jerked upright. "He was there?"

Why had she let his name slip? Only Broderick ranked higher than Edward on Grandfather's list of loathed men. Broderick had saved her, and she'd just returned the favor by alerting the enemy. Maybe if he hadn't recaptured her dreams and disturbed her rest, her tongue wouldn't have released the secret she'd meant to hold tight. Perhaps if she painted Broderick in a favorable light, Grandfather wouldn't hunt him down.

"He stumbled into their meeting about the same time as I and led a successful retreat. Without him, the evening could have ended much worse."

Grandfather stood. "Mrs. Hawking!" The strength of his voice indicated he'd fully recovered, yet she still had no answers.

Footsteps rushed up the stairs and slowed outside the door. After a moment, Mrs. Hawking entered, carrying a tray sloshed with a tea and broth mixture. "I apologize for the delay, sir."

"Theresa is to be confined to her room for the duration of her illness. See to it that she is tucked into bed and monitored closely. No trips to the carriage house."

"But my animals need to be fed."

"Not by you."

She stepped forward. "You haven't answered my question. Who are—"

He silenced further argument with a slash of his hand. "I owe you no explanation."

Grandfather owed her many things. The least he could give her was an explanation of their new predicament. She grabbed his arm, ready to press the issue, but he pivoted free. His defense was as impenetrable as Lucifer's heart. If he didn't give her the answers she required, she'd get them herself.

"Mrs. Hawking, take extra precautions that no one leaves nor enters this room other than you or me."

Drat! Grandfather knew her too well. Escaping Mrs. Hawking's supervision required great skill and creative problem-solving. Good thing she'd always been a creative person.

By the time she finished her tea and broth, she'd formed a battle plan. She squinted at the porcelain clock on her bedside table. If she hurried, she still might catch a skunk.

CHAPTER 4

BRODERICK LEANED AGAINST THE WEEPING willow as light dawned above the trees behind Burnet Woods Lake. Clouds puffed with each breath, white like the rest of the world around him. He rubbed warmth into his hands and took one last look at the initials—BTC and TMP, damaged by six slashes, one for each year of separation.

Senseless hope that Theresa would appear had held him in place for far too long. But no more. Thorny weeds snagged his trousers and cut flesh as he followed the neglected trail through Burnet Woods to Clifton Avenue. Whether or not she was angry, he needed answers from Theresa. He'd wrestled all night with the possibility of her active involvement in the counterfeiting ring, but he couldn't believe it. This was his Theresa, the girl who loved without reserve, defended what she believed, and pursued justice by his side. Had he done a better job years ago, she wouldn't be in trouble now.

Burnet Woods ended across the street from Plane Manor's hedge-fenced yard, where a narrow gap once provided secret entrance. Years of disuse had left it overgrown. By the time he pushed through, he resembled a rogue. Not that it mattered. Theresa wasn't likely to notice the trimming and extra care he'd taken with his appearance that morning.

He searched the yard for anyone who might have noticed his approach, then frowned. Negligence extended well beyond the hedge. Once-shaped bushes had grown wild. Weeds that must have grown longer than one season bowed under the snow's weight. Paint peeled from the sides of the gray carriage house in need of repair. Though stone walls preserved the main house's structure, several wooden shutters hung at odd angles. A weak breeze would dislocate the slate tiles from their precarious rooftop perch. If Colonel Plane led the counterfeiting ring, he didn't spend his profits on upkeep.

Broderick turned his attention to the maple outside Theresa's second-story window. It appeared healthy and presented a better option for entrance than the front door. When he'd attempted to visit her six years ago, Colonel Plane had chased him off with a spray of buckshot. He was unlikely to miss a second time. Theresa, however, wouldn't risk killing him by pushing him from the tree. At least, he hoped not.

He sprinted across the grounds to the cover of bushes and plotted his climb. Thick branches would get him midway, but those thinner ones were questionable.

The window above him slid open, and a pair of boy's boots thudded to the ground inches from where he crouched. If shoes fell, a body was bound to follow. Broderick crept behind an unkempt bush and waited.

Black-stockinged feet and legs protruded from the sill's edge, followed by blue skirts. Delicate hands adjusted the material before the familiar slender body swung from the ledge's safety to straining twigs.

Of all the dangerous stunts! It was one thing for him to climb up, another for her to attempt climbing down. The little imp would get herself killed.

Broderick moved from the bush's safety and resisted the urge to call out. Startling her could end in disaster, but words of rebuke played through his mind as displaced snow plopped around him. She couldn't possibly see her next step beneath those skirts. Making it to the ground without mishap would be—

A branch snapped.

Theresa screamed. Blue and white material waved in surrender to the inevitable as she fell. Broderick lunged for her. The tree limbs cracked like a grand finale of fireworks, stopping moments before she crashed into his arms. His legs buckled, and they dropped to the ground with Theresa landing on his chest.

He lay still, his lungs begging for air but refusing to accept it. Given the force of their impact, a human-shaped crater would exist once he moved—if he ever moved again.

Theresa rolled to her knees beside him and stared in dazed silence.

Pain seared his arms as he pushed to a sitting position. "Are you hurt?"

Confusion creased her face as she blinked at him. She might be sorting through a touch of shock, but no discomfort contorted her features, which was more than he could say for himself. He rotated his shoulders and then flexed his arms. In a few years he might laugh about catching an angel, but right now he felt like he'd caught an anvil.

Theresa's wide eyes dropped into a squint. "What are you doing here?"

"Saving you from a broken neck."

She pinched her lip between teeth, but those coffee eyes churned with a tangle of emotions. The ability to hold her tongue must be a new skill. Before he left, she'd never kept anything from him. Not her thoughts. Not her troubles. Not her love.

He sighed and plucked a twig from the too-tight bun. He'd rather free her soft tresses from their confines, but he didn't dare. Now was not the time to yearn for the woman who should have been his wife.

After rising from the ground, he conducted a visual evaluation—strictly for injuries, of course. Half-moons darkened the skin beneath Theresa's eyes, and several scrapes crisscrossed her ivory cheeks. Her plump, kissable lips were chapped, but he saw nothing in need of a doctor. She leaned on her arms, so they must not be in too much pain. Nothing wrong with her curves either—except they made a man crazy with wanting to hold her. Her legs bent at the right spot, and her exposed ankles didn't appear swollen.

Yep—he swallowed—*she's more than fine.*

The window above them opened and drew both their gazes.

Mrs. Hawking stuck out her head, that still-familiar grimace in place. "March yourself back inside, young lady, before I alert the colonel. And you—" Her gaze swung to his. Whoever she expected to find with Theresa, it hadn't been him. Her eyes widened before settling into a scornful glare. "And you, Master Broderick, best be off the property before I return with my shotgun." The window slammed shut.

Broderick dropped his gaze to Theresa. "I see she's still as charming as ever."

A corner of Theresa's mouth twitched. "Always, and her threats are never hollow."

"Then perhaps we should move this meeting elsewhere."

He passed her boots over and enjoyed the momentary brush of their fingers. She, on the other hand, jerked away as if burned. Green glinted off her ring finger and drew his attention. Another man's engagement ring, not his, claimed her future and her heart. Regret rose like an old friend to greet him.

Oblivious to his thoughts, Theresa loosened her boot laces. "The carriage house should suffice if we bar the door behind us."

"Care to enlighten me as to why you chose the tree instead of the stairs?"

"For the same reason you're at the base of my tree and not at the front door. Avoiding Grandfather."

Why anyone so smart had chosen him evaded logic, but then again, she'd never been logical. He crossed his arms and winced. His pain more than proved her lack in that area.

Theresa's tiny feet slid into the polished boots and provoked a smile. Watching probably bordered indecent, but her sprite-like features never failed to amuse him.

Her nimble fingers worked the laces as she cocked a brow. "The real question is why you're here at all."

"I didn't want to deprive you of a second chance at a right hook."

Her lips scrunched, but her dimple betrayed the suppressed smile.

"Here. I offer it willingly." He crouched and tapped his cheek.

When she didn't swing, he clasped her nearest hand and guided it into a soft punch. Though it pained him, he flailed his arms and rocked back and forth until he fell with an exaggerated thud. A bubble of laughter freed her restrained smile and lit her eyes. If she could laugh, then he could hope for her cooperation.

"Nice try, but I prefer my opponent's defeat to be genuine." A door slammed somewhere inside, and her smile dropped. "Mrs. Hawking's retrieved her gun. I hope you're still fast."

She ignored his proffered hand and fumbled to her feet. Stubborn to a fault. Just because she didn't want his help didn't mean he couldn't be a gentleman. He outstripped her and held the carriage house door open until she brushed past.

Once he closed it behind them, she dropped the bar into place. "There. We're safe for now."

Broderick scanned the carriage house to verify her claim. Dim light filtered through the high windows, casting shadows into near-empty stalls. Gone were the stallions fit for war and the polished carriage. No one greeted them from the hayloft or tack room. Instead, a strange collection of animals peeked through stall doors or wandered the aisle. The only horse-like creature was a mangy mule munching hay in the back, next to a rickety donkey cart. Where had the Plane wealth gone?

Theresa shooed a chicken missing half its feathers. "One minute, Blue."

Blue? The chicken was bright orange.

She shrugged on a dirty coat, and a whiff of mule and muck assailed his senses.

"I love the perfume. It's very"—Broderick sniffed again and tried not to choke—"natural."

"I'd rather smell like a mule than be a skunk."

"At least I know my colors. That chicken is orange, not blue."

Her stony frown bunched and released into a smile when she chuckled. She filled a cup with feed and tossed it toward the chicken. "Her name is Cordon Bleu."

"You named her after a dish?" Broderick eyed the unfortunate bird.

"That's what Mrs. Hawking planned to turn her into before I

rescued her. I thought the name fitting. The other animals are rescues too."

She shared rescue stories as she distributed food to her little menagerie of goats, rabbits, cats, and a raccoon. Even ducks swam in a deep, half-buried trough filled with water. Broderick studied the overly fat raccoon. It couldn't be the same baby she convinced him to give a bath. He rubbed a scar along his forearm, remembering the stitches Dr. Pelton gave along with a stern lecture about being led astray by foolish women.

"This is Tipsy." She rubbed the ear of a three-legged goat. "She's my favorite rescue mission." A mischievous smile indicated a story lurked in those words, but she moved on to the forlorn mule with a patch over one eye. "And this is Captain Blackbeard, the scourge of man and beast. He'll nip and bite anyone foolish enough to get close— unless they come bearing treats." She grinned as she offered the mule a sugar cube from her pocket. "But he's a hard worker and helps me with deliveries."

Deliveries. A stone seemed to settle in his stomach. Evidence around them spoke of hard times and a lack of funds. "What do you deliver?"

"Portraits mostly, but on occasion someone wants one of my landscapes. It's all I can do to stave off Grandfather's creditors." She frowned as she patted Blackbeard's side.

Broderick released his breath. Paintings weren't illegal. "What happened?"

Her head swiveled as she surveyed the carriage house. Creases deepened in her face, and he could almost see her mind comparing the ramshackle building to its former glory. After an extended silence, she dropped to the ground and leaned against a stall door. A black kitten pounced onto her lap and nuzzled against her hands. She gave a mirthless smile and scratched its chin.

"After you left, everything changed." She turned hard eyes toward him. "And not for the better. How could you leave me? Why not a word in all these years?"

He removed his gloves and sat next to her. There was no turning back. He'd made his decision, and he'd make it again. "I told you, it's complicated."

"Then *un*complicate it."

How could he simplify watching his brother betray them both by tossing her into the river to drown? Or the terror of dragging her limp and breathless body ashore? Or the scandal that followed to destroy the lives of all he held dear? A husband should provide for and protect his wife, and he'd failed to do both before they'd managed to say vows. "You're not safe with me. The river proved it."

"That's your complicated excuse? I'm not safe?" She scoffed. "Safe doesn't exist, Broderick. Not then. Not now. We knew the risks when I assisted you on cases, but we faced them together."

"I never should have allowed you to do it."

Theresa's lips parted, but then she turned away.

Lord help him, because this wasn't going well. He grasped her cold hand. She tried to withdraw it, but he held firm until she stopped resisting. "Look at me, Reese." He waited until her eyes, shimmering with unshed moisture, lifted to meet his. "No case is ever worth risking your life. I was selfish to keep you by my side, and the cost was more than I could bear. I can never make amends for the pain I've caused, but whatever trouble you're in, I can help."

She took a shuddered, wheezy breath. "Fine, but only because I need a detective, and you were once the best around."

Not a solid vote of confidence, but it was an opening. "I'm at your service."

Her attention dropped to the kitten nudging her hand to be pet. She complied with a resigned sigh. "Obviously, we're not the wealthy family you remember. By the end of the Great Depression, Grandfather had nearly lost the printshop. He had to use his entire savings to keep it running. When he finally began turning a profit two years ago, his partner gambled away his share to a man named John Whist." Her hands fisted. "He has no business sense. Despite my taking on engraving projects, we're not bringing in enough income."

"You're an engraver?" Broderick clutched the rock in his pocket.

"That's a new skill." One that would place her under Darlington's immediate suspicion.

"Yes. Between bouts of pneumonia, life has been quite boring. Grandfather encouraged the skill as a challenging, useful distraction."

Why couldn't she stick to sketching and painting? Those innocuous hobbies wouldn't give Darlington occasion to froth at the mouth like a rabid dog. "Does the colonel still engrave?"

"Yes, but his latest project has taken a year, leaving me with everything else. He swears whatever it is will end all our troubles."

Broderick cringed. Good banknote plates required a year to engrave, and the fifty-dollar plates were nearly finished. He might not be the leader, but Colonel Plane played a crucial part.

Theresa continued. "And I hope it will end our troubles. When the banks denied Grandfather's application for loans after last spring's flood, he turned to unconventional places for credit."

"Like that man last night?"

"I should've known you followed. Yes, Vincent Drake is one of Grandfather's creditors, but he's no longer the worst of my problems. I fear Grandfather is involved with something illegal."

Broderick searched for any signs she withheld information or could be personally involved, but he saw nothing but fear and uncertainty in her eyes. Illegal activities meant an arrest. As a counterfeit engraver, Colonel Plane could be fined a thousand dollars and spend up to fifteen years in prison. Even at his age, he could be put to hard labor.

"I know you weren't taking a midnight stroll in the cemetery. Who are they, Broderick? Grimm and Fitz."

If she didn't know, he wouldn't tell her. Too much information could be dangerous. "They're criminals."

Her look conveyed a desire to smack him. "I know they're criminals, but what kind?"

"Dangerous ones."

She jumped to her feet, causing the kitten to yowl, then planted her hands on her hips. "Broderick Thomas Cosgrove, stop trying to shield me. How is Grandfather involved?"

She never relented until she had an answer, but he could provide none that would satisfy. He stood. "I can't say for certain, but he is involved, and that puts you in danger."

"Theresa!" Colonel Plane's voice boomed from a side door. "Return to your quarters at once."

Broderick pivoted and shielded Theresa behind him.

Colonel Plane scowled. "I told you what would happen if I ever saw you again. Retreat before I shoot."

Broderick examined Colonel Plane's waist. A hollow threat. He carried no gun, but he *could* hurt Broderick's case. "I'm here at Theresa's request."

"She doesn't need you." Colonel Plane folded his arms as though daring Broderick to contradict him. "I suggest you abandon whatever case brought you here."

Theresa stepped around Broderick and matched Colonel Plane's stance. "I'm hiring Broderick to find out who Fitz and Grimm are. That is unless you want to tell me."

"They're my problem, not yours."

"That's a lie, and you know it. Broderick saved me. You owe the truth to us both."

Colonel Plane closed his eyes and drew a long breath. "They're creditors who offered me a deal." He opened his eyes and swung his gaze to Broderick. "Consider yourself fired."

"Those men were not creditors, Grandfather. Nor were you subject to them. They called you their boss."

"What I've told you is true enough, and it's all the answer you'll get. Now, return to your quarters at once."

"But—"

Mrs. Hawking interrupted at the side door with shotgun in hand. "Sir, Mr. Greystone is in the parlor. He wishes to speak with you privately."

Theresa glanced from Broderick to Colonel Plane. After a moment her shoulders sagged. "Edward's probably here about last night. I'll go smooth things over." Her gaze shifted and lingered on Broderick's face as if memorizing his every detail. "Goodbye."

She pivoted away and plodded out the door with Mrs. Hawking bringing up the rear. Colonel Plane waited until the door shut before speaking again. "For Theresa's sake, I'll pretend you were never here, but you must abandon this foolish pursuit. Theresa's had enough trouble because of you."

"Last night's trouble had nothing to do with me. Your colleagues—"

"Will be dealt with. I've only a few more weeks of associating with them, and then Theresa and I will be free."

It appeared Colonel Plane was a reluctant participant, and those were often the best men to turn into informants. His crucial knowledge could be all Broderick needed to bring down the entire counterfeiting ring. "I can help you."

"No. My poor choices brought Theresa into this situation. I'll do whatever's necessary to get her out. "

"I have the connections and resources to protect her and end your troubles."

"I trusted you once with my greatest possession, but I'll not be such a fool again. Now leave. I've a foul-tempered suitor to contend with before he absconds with my naïve granddaughter."

Rather than turning to exit through the side door, Colonel Plane marched to the carriage house's entrance, then unbarred the door and left.

Broderick scrubbed the back of his neck. Colonel Plane, whether coerced or not, engraved for the production firm. Even if Broderick convinced the man to squeal on it for a plea bargain, Colonel Plane would spend months to years in jail. Theresa would hate Broderick then, if she didn't already.

He needed to bring down the production firm before Darlington discovered her innocent connection. No matter what it took, he would protect her—and see to it she received her happily ever after, even if it wasn't with him.

CHAPTER 5

HUDDLED IN THE OVERGROWN SHRUBBERY, Broderick observed the front of Plane Manor and the side yard leading to the carriage house. Colonel Plane wouldn't tolerate Theresa's mistreatment, no matter if he lacked power within the counterfeiting ring. He would reach out to his connections and retaliate. The trick was not getting frostbite before Colonel Plane enacted his plan.

Broderick shivered for an hour before Mrs. Hawking emerged with a pail in hand. She disappeared into the carriage house, and a few minutes later, bleating and shouts erupted inside.

When she stomped out, empty-handed and skirts wet, she shouted, "When I want milk, you give it, or next time I'll make mutton chops out of you!"

Broderick chuckled. It would be quite the feat to turn those goats into sheep. She returned to the house with no indication of communication to or from Colonel Plane.

Not long after, Theresa appeared on the front porch with her fiancé. Broderick wanted to look away and avoid seeing a lingering goodbye, but he needed to know she was happy. Though Greystone offered a display of affection, she pulled away quickly. That could be the result of the last eight hours, but this resembled more of a pulling into herself and tolerating her fiancé's touch. She'd always clung to Broderick when hurting.

But maybe thinking no one could fill his place in her heart was merely hopeful thinking.

Greystone departed, and Theresa went back inside. Other than the occasional bleat of the goats or clop of hooves on the street, the neighborhood remained quiet. Hours passed with no more foot traffic to or from the house. He stomped his feet, tucked his hands in the crook of his armpits, and stuck his nose into his coat collar, but it did little to keep him warm. A pot of steaming hot coffee and a bowl of the Keppler's stew would do wonders. Skipping breakfast had seemed wise at the time, but now his stomach pinched. He checked his watch—three o'clock. Isaacs should have picked up Darlington from the train station by now and received the cryptic message Broderick had sent about needing to be relieved as soon as possible.

The front door slammed, and Broderick peeked through the hedges. Mrs. Hawking scurried toward the street, a look of determination engraved on her stony features. She broke into a run near the end of the drive and hailed the horse and buggy plodding past Plane Manor.

"Mr. Bramlage! Please, wait!"

Broderick slipped closer until he could make out Mrs. Hawking panting by the back wheel.

"Can you take me to Orchard Street? We have need of a doctor."

Doctor Pelton lived on Orchard Street. Broderick glanced back to the house. Was something wrong with Theresa? Or was this a cover for Colonel Plane to send a message to his colleagues? Mrs. Hawking climbed into the seat beside Mr. Bramlage and urged the man to hurry the horse. Her panic seemed genuine, and if something were wrong with Theresa, Dr. Pelton would be the only man they trusted. He and Colonel Plane had served in—and retired from—the same regiment. For a moment Broderick considered following, but he would never keep up on foot without drawing notice. Besides, monitoring Colonel Plane was his priority and the man remained inside.

Sooner than he expected, a different buggy returned transporting Mrs. Hawking, Dr. Pelton, and his eldest daughter, Lydia. Dr. Pelton and Colonel Plane spent so much time together that Theresa and Lydia had grown up as close as sisters. Lydia must have been visiting him when Mrs. Hawking arrived.

Using the cover of the overgrown landscape, Broderick shifted closer.

Mrs. Hawking stepped down, wringing her hands. "We managed to get her upstairs to bed, but she's started coughing so much she can't catch a breath."

Broderick clenched his rock and squelched the rising anxiety those words brought.

"We'll start with a steam treatment, Mrs. Hawking. Go boil a pot of water."

The woman wasted no time in obeying the man.

Dr. Pelton exited, then turned to give an obviously pregnant Lydia a hand down. "Remember what I said." He retrieved a medical bag from the floor of the buggy before giving Lydia an admonishing look. "I'm here to evaluate Theresa's health, not gather information for your husband."

"But if she should share something—"

"I let you come along to be a comfort to her, not to determine how much she knows." He led the way into the house, then closed the door on their conversation.

Broderick sat on his haunches. Surely the Pelton family was not involved too. He wasn't surprised by Colonel Plane, but Dr. Pelton had a moral compass so strong it turned all those within his influence true north. Perhaps it wasn't Dr. Pelton who possessed a dubious character. Maybe it was Lydia's husband. Her penchant for adventure could have caused her to stray. Broderick knew well how upstanding parents didn't guarantee an upstanding child.

"*Psst.*"

He twisted around and found Isaacs's messenger boy, Gillie, crouched in the bushes behind him. Isaacs had caught the homeless orphan stealing a sandwich to stave off his hunger. Rather than shoo him away or turn him over to the police, Isaacs hired him on the spot. Broderick led the boy a safe distance away before nodding for him to continue.

Gillie whispered, "Your pal Joe says to come back quick."

"I can't. Someone needs to watch the house."

"I'll tell him, but that bloke Joe picked up ain't gonna be happy."

Darlington. Broderick pinched the bridge of his nose. He couldn't afford to start off on the wrong side of Darlington's temper. Dr. Pelton would give Theresa considerable attention, and with Lydia in tow, they could be there for hours. Decision made, he left Gillie to watch the house.

By the time Broderick reached the Secret Service field office on the post office's third floor, a knot kinked his shoulders. Isaacs swung the door open at his knock. The stench of whiskey hit Broderick like a bat. Given Isaacs hated the stuff, there had to be a story.

"Drink much?"

Isaacs shook his head and gestured toward the room's opposite end. "Tread lightly. He's in a foul temper."

Andrew Darlington sat at the office's only desk, scrutinizing months of case notes. He must have perfected that dour expression through drinking vinegar.

When the door shut, he looked up. "Cosgrove. It's about time you showed up." He rose and stalked over.

Stature-wise, he stood neither overly tall nor extraordinarily short. Other than his expression, no feature stood out. Even his clothes were gray and unremarkable. Darlington could easily fall into the background of any location—a perfect quality for their line of work.

Broderick grimaced.

"It's no wonder this case hasn't progressed with you two at the helm." Darlington speared Isaacs with a glare. "First Josiah picks me up smelling like he took a bath in whiskey—"

"I told you, a barmaid created a reason to get close by spilling her tray on me. I didn't have time to change."

"And then he hands me this useless stack of kindling claiming it's all you have. What have you been doing for the last four months? Living a life of leisure at the Treasury's expense?"

Broderick clamped down tight on the rock in his pocket until the urge to give a biting retort passed. "We've been doing our job."

"Then I'm changing your strategy."

"I'll accept your suggestions, but this is my case. My lead."

"Not anymore. Chief Brooks assigned me as lead." He withdrew official letterhead from his coat and passed it to Broderick. "To do business with koniackers, you have to think like them, not make pals of them."

"That's part of the job." Broderick tossed the paper atop the desk rather than wad the official demotion. Were they really debating the foundational support of investigation? "A detective is only as good as his network of informants. Cultivating those relationships takes time and genuine interest in their lives."

"Nonsense. It's all about their wants and needs. If you know those, you can manipulate the situation to your benefit."

This was the man Chief Brooks sent to take over the case? Darlington's hard-nosed methods might finish it, but they would sever ties that could help future cases.

Isaacs shook his head. "They're a skittish group. If you pump too hard or they suspect your intentions, they'll scatter and regroup elsewhere."

Which would force the Secret Service to start all over again while the counterfeiters got their fifties into circulation.

"Then we determine which informants we can rope in without spooking the production firm. Give me every detail of your connections' lives you didn't include in those reports. You've missed something we can use."

This was a waste of precious time. By the point they finished talking, Dr. Pelton and Lydia would be long gone along with Broderick's chance to eavesdrop. "Isaacs can apprise you. I have a suspect to shadow."

Isaacs pushed the desk chair toward Broderick and claimed another chair for himself. "You know more than I could ever share. Piping down another suspect will have to wait. A fresh mind might give us the new perspective we need."

With no other choice, Broderick sat. Thankfully, neither Theresa's nor Colonel Plane's names were recorded in the file. For now, Broderick had the freedom to investigate their involvement and connections on his own, but he wouldn't have long. If the suitcase by the door were any indication, Darlington hadn't even wasted time by getting settled into a hotel before diving into the case.

For hours, Darlington worked over the list of informants and identified counterfeiting ring members. He wrote pages of notes while Isaacs and Broderick spoke, and when they reached the end, he frowned. "Are none of these men competitors of the production firm?"

Broderick chafed under the question. He'd identified a few smaller firms but hadn't considered them in connection to this case. Competitors made great informants as they were eager to destroy the competition or mete out revenge. "None on that list, but I can provide names of a few local ones."

"Good. Meet here first thing tomorrow morning. I'll have a plan and assignments ready by then."

Sunlight poured through Theresa's bedroom window and illuminated the vibrant colors of Mrs. Donahue's portrait. In person, the woman was as wrinkled as a raisin, but the gentle strokes of Theresa's brush smoothed away more than a decade of life. Add the green brocade dress's vibrancy and ivory broach, and the eighty-something great-grandmother of Theresa's client appeared younger than Grandfather. One more layer to bring out the final spark of mischief in Mrs. Donahue's eyes and the painting would be finished.

Catarrh or not, she could no longer delay the completion of her commissions. Vincent Drake would soon require payment beyond the opal ring. Given the cold temperatures and spots of thick paint, the portrait would require at least two days to dry before varnishing, and then another two before she attempted delivery. Delaying Mr. Drake's payment until Monday was probably unwise, but her hands were tied. She had no money until she made deliveries, and she couldn't deliver wet paintings.

She stifled a yawn turned cough. How many naps did a body need in a day?

The door opened, and Mrs. Hawking rushed past her to open the window. "How can you breathe with these noxious fumes filling your lungs?"

Theresa wiped the excess paint off her brush and dipped it in linseed oil. "Better the warm, fresh-paint air than the biting breeze from an open window." The scent of the oil paints might make her feel lightheaded, but the outside air made each breath literally hurt. "Please close it. Removing my supplies from the room and leaving the door open should be sufficient to clear the air while I rest."

Mrs. Hawking lifted the painting from its scaffold and carried it off to one of the empty rooms used for art storage. Theresa finished cleaning her brushes and tucked the unused color tubes into her paint box. From the bottom of her brush compartment, she pulled free the note that had arrived two nights ago, skillfully hidden in an arrangement of red carnations. *My heart aches for you.* Had Broderick realized the flowers' meaning when he selected them? Or had they merely been the only variety available? She flipped the folded sheet open again, but still his words could indicate either of two meanings.

I'm not giving up. If you need me, send a note to the Keppler Hotel.—B

A traitorous twinge of excitement traveled down her spine as she tucked the note back into place. Perhaps she'd read too many of Lydia's fanciful novels, but the part of her heart that hoped for Broderick's return feasted on his words. Still, it was best to douse those would-be sparks of love's renewal before they flamed. In the carriage house, Broderick had made it clear they did not belong together, and the man was too steady to say one thing in the morning and then send a note declaring the opposite the same evening.

Grandfather's voice rose with Edward's in the hall.

So much for a nap. Those two could not enter the same room without fighting. Theresa latched her paint box and left it lying on her coverlet.

Both men looked up and fell silent as she descended the stairs.

Grandfather frowned, but Edward beamed. When she reached the landing, he gathered her into a hug. "You should be resting."

"Says the man with a concussion. How's your head?"

He wrapped his hand around hers and prevented her from reaching the bump still visible on the back.

"Pounding, but there was trouble at the shipping docks this morning, so no rest for the weary."

"Not anything too terrible, I hope?"

"Nothing to concern you. Just a few unruly day-laborers taking liberties with my merchandise, but there will be no more trouble." His soft gaze lifted to Grandfather's, then darkened. "I'm taking care of everything."

"Of everything but yourself." Theresa cupped his face to capture his attention and avoid another argument. "You should have gone home to rest, not come all the way here."

"Colonel Plane wasn't at the printshop to tell me how you fared, and I couldn't rest until I knew. Besides, I wanted to bring you these." Edward released her and retrieved a bag from the foyer table.

She opened it. A dozen paint tubes sat at the bottom. She pulled one out and read the silver-and-black label—Winsor & Newton Watercolor. Bless him. He'd tried. How could she expect him to remember she painted only in oil when he had no artistic ability of his own?

"I thought you might need more considering you're supposed to be confined to your room."

"Thank you, Edward. They're wonderful." Maybe she'd try her hand at watercolor again. It had been years since her last failed attempt. "Let's sit. I confess I don't have much energy at the moment."

"No. I've done what I came to do, and we both need our rest." He winced as he leaned forward to kiss her hand. When he noticed the engagement ring on her finger, he smiled. "May we both recover quickly so we can finish setting a date."

Grandfather snorted behind them but refrained from speaking.

Edward pulled an envelope from his pocket and extended it toward Grandfather. "When I stopped by the printshop, Mr. Whist asked me to deliver this."

Grandfather accepted it without thanks. "You remember the way out."

Edward clenched his hands into fists before giving her a wobbly bow. Thankfully, he left without incident. Grandfather disappeared toward his smaller office at the far side of the house, closer to where his business visitors came through the side yard entrance. He liked the quiet there as opposed to the commotion he might hear from the office off the foyer.

She trudged upstairs for a much-needed nap.

When she woke a few hours later, dusk cloaked her room in shadows. There would be no more painting tonight, and snooping through Grandfather's office for clues wasn't likely either. She rolled over, and a man-sized shadow shifted in her desk chair.

Theresa scrambled to sit up, then reached for the clock to launch at her would-be attacker.

"Peace, child. It's me." Grandfather turned up the kerosene lamp.

The man before her was not the crisp, callous colonel the world knew. Haggard and pale, he slumped in the chair as though his body could no longer hold its own weight, and his thinning hair shot out in wild directions.

"What's happened?" She jumped from her bed to reach for him.

In a rare show of affection, he wrapped his hand around hers and held it. "My sins are catching up with me, and I fear there is no escape."

Such despair coming from the man who declared fear the figment of one's imagination. She kneeled before him and patted her free hand on top of their clasped ones. "Surely it's not as bad as all that. Momma always said sin has power over you only until you confess it. Tell me what's going on. We can figure this out together."

"No. I've not been able to protect you from poverty, but I will protect you from this."

"If you won't let me help, then let Dr. Pelton. He has connections within the police department, especially since Lydia married a detective on the force."

"Precisely the reason I cannot turn to him."

So he *was* involved in something illegal. Theresa dropped her gaze to the weathered and scarred hand holding hers. This was the man who ensured she wouldn't have to finish growing up in a boarding school. He'd attacked her upbringing with military rigor because it was the only way he knew. When any of her adventures turned to disaster—which were most—he'd stepped in, cleaned up the mess, and taught her to do and be better next time. His punishments had been harsh, but they were all meant to guide her back onto the path of righteous living. If he could forgive her mistakes, she could forgive his. Maybe he'd accept her gentle push toward redemption, even if not through Dr. Pelton.

"Broderick's a private detective. Going to him wouldn't be the same as going to the police."

"I trusted him with you once. I'll not do it again."

"He's neither responsible for his brother's choices nor for the fact that I ran headlong into danger." Her gaze strayed to the flowers on her desk. "He's always sought to protect me. No matter what you're involved in, I'm confident he'll help."

Grandfather stared at her for a long time, seeming to weigh her words. At length, he said, "I'll consider it."

That was the best she could hope to hear. "He's staying at the Keppler Hotel."

He nodded, then stood.

"Should I have Mrs. Hawking bring up the chessboard? A good game always helps you think."

"Not tonight, little soldier."

He patted her head in the same distracted manner he had when she was a little girl, then left the room stroking his beard, a sure sign he was forming a battle plan without her.

CHAPTER 6

FOUR DAYS LATER, BITTER AIR burned Theresa's lungs as she waited with Blackbeard to board the approaching incline platform that would transport them from Clifton Heights to the city below. A week of rest may have improved her health, but nothing worked to distract her from the resurrected dreams of a future with Broderick—not Edward, not painting or engraving, and especially not the brief visit from her best friend. When Lydia asked probing questions about her bruises, Theresa had resorted to a coughing fit to end the visit prematurely. After all, as far as she knew, Grandfather hadn't mentioned her run-in with any of the people she'd encountered at the cemetery to Lydia or anyone else.

And if Lydia discovered Broderick's return . . . Theresa shook her head. Enough complications surrounded her without the addition of Lydia's matchmaking schemes.

Blackbeard shied from the steel-and-wood platform as it connected with the headhouse. Drake's threat crinkled in her pocket as she shifted to regain control. At least the ability to tangibly act on a problem soothed where other efforts had failed. Once she delivered the paintings and collected payments, she'd pay Drake and solve one problem. The fact that she had only twelve hours left to do so? Well, she'd manage it, somehow. Once she told Edward about this morning's note from Drake, he would no doubt demand to go with her to the unsavory meeting place Drake required.

When she, Blackbeard, and her cart were on board, the platform jerked into motion. Church bells clanged over the grinding of gears, and she gave a wry smile as the medical school came into view. No students would be waving cadaver parts at the passing incline today. It was too cold for even them. She adjusted the scarf around her mouth tighter to fight the biting wind and shifted her gaze to the cityscape below. Gray and brown snow coated every building, and smoke billowed from blackened chimneys, creating an incredible landscape no one would want to purchase should she paint it. How she longed for the day when money wasn't scarce. Then she could create whatever tugged at her imagination. People snuggled under blankets and enjoying the warmth of a fire. Children playing in snow.

Or Broderick's eyes.

She released a frustrated sigh. That man was impossible to dispel from her mind. What would he say about Drake's threat?

No case is ever worth risking your life.

Broderick's words ricocheted through her heart, wounding it anew. She should have asked someone else to help her. Lydia's detective husband, for instance. Instead, she'd allowed the small thrill of seeing Broderick to cloud her judgment.

Contentment with Edward would be impossible as long as Broderick lingered. The ghost of his caress slid across her knuckles, and she wrapped the reins around her hand until tingles radiated down her fingers.

Edward is my future. I will marry him and be . . . happy, even if I have to force it for a time. He's successful. There will be no concern about debt, and I'll support Grandfather and remain safe.

Shame heated her cheeks. These were hollow reasons for marriage. No excitement stirred her emotions. No real affection for the fiancé who could free her was evident. Yes, she enjoyed Edward's company, the feeling of being wanted and protected, but nothing compared to the passionate love she once held for Broderick. *Edward's is a practical love, and there's nothing wrong with that.* Broderick was a passing fancy, one that would disappear as soon as he did.

"He's back only because Grandfather is—"

What? A suspect? A victim? A criminal? Her chest squeezed at the implication.

The platform attendant glanced at her with a raised eyebrow before turning to make the Elm Street Station connection. Goodness! She'd spoken aloud, and with the platform empty save herself, her lunacy was apparent. As Blackbeard plodded onto the slush-filled street, she ducked her head. It would probably be best to use the Mount Auburn Incline on the way home. A trip to the Longview Lunatic Asylum would only worsen her situation.

With a deep breath, she focused on the route to the row houses of her middle-class clientele, people rich enough to want paintings but poor enough to settle for a no-name artist.

Bells marked each hour, a constant reminder of her mission's urgency. After the third successful delivery, a familiar voice called. "Theresa! Wait!"

She abandoned her climb into the cart and turned toward Lydia. "What are you doing here? Yesterday Dr. Pelton said you'd had premature labor pains and he'd prescribed you bed rest."

Lydia waddled forward at remarkable speed for one with such a large, protruding midsection. Her husband, Detective Abraham Hall, scowled as he exited their carriage.

"Father's overly protective. The pains passed and have yet to return. Besides, I could ask the same of you. You near coughed up a lung just days ago."

Theresa offered an awkward hug. "You are well familiar with deadlines, friend. Ill or not, we work."

Abraham came alongside his wife and folded his arms. "Her book deadlines are hardly the same as delivering paintings in this cold. I'm certain your clients can excuse a day or two of tardiness."

They might. Drake would not.

"Yes, I'll be inconsolable if you relapse and cannot attend my sister's debut ball at our home this evening." Lydia's eyes took on a mischievous glint as she grasped Theresa's arm. "Father's invited a gentleman with whom you *must* dance."

"Lydia, I'm en—"

"Engaged. Not married. Once you meet Mr. Darlington, you'll not give Edward another thought. Mr. Darlington is a detective." She waggled her brows and smiled. "Not as good as Broderick, but you know you can't resist a lawman."

Oh, yes, she could. Especially with Grandfather's dubious activities an issue.

Lydia continued to encourage the match. "Your success as an engraver intrigues him, and he's eager to meet you. In fact, we're heading to Father's to meet him beforehand. You should join us. The carriage will be warmer than your cart."

Lydia and her schemes. "What would I do with Blackbeard and my paintings? I'm sorry, I can't, but I promise to come tonight no matter how I feel. Grandfather will probably want to coerce Dr. Pelton into providing another examination anyway."

"Does Colonel Plane still plan on joining you?" Abraham's tone held a seriousness the inquiry didn't require. Had Lydia broken her oath of secrecy and shared Theresa's concerns?

"As far as I know. He never misses an opportunity to exchange war stories with Dr. Pelton."

"Good. I have a few things to discuss with him." Abraham looped his arm through Lydia's. "We best part ways. I don't want either of you too fatigued for the festivities."

"I suppose he's right." Lydia pouted, and then her eyes brightened. "But you should stop at Father's house for a break from the cold when you're finished."

A break, indeed. Theresa climbed into the cart and urged Blackbeard forward before Lydia could formulate a more substantial ploy to introduce her to the newest marriageable prospect. Edward may not be the most romantic choice, but he was the most practical, and she needed practical more than ever.

For the next three hours, Blackbeard led her from one client to another, until only her most significant project remained. The three-feet by two-feet painting of a train leaving the Plum Street Depot was the most expensive and demanding painting she'd ever been commissioned to create. Bright-colored buildings and patrons contrasted with the iron engine and the grimy smoke, which had taken hours to perfect without ruining the entire image. She'd added details of the engineer's family throughout the painting, making it a game for each member to find themselves during the reveal. Not only would this piece bring joy to share, but it would fulfill half of her promised payment to Drake.

As she secured the masterpiece for the final trip, Edward appeared at her elbow.

"What are you doing, Theresa? I thought you were ill."

He, above everyone, should know why she braved the cold. She tugged the scarf from her mouth. "Mr. Drake requires the rest of the payment tonight. I had to make deliveries."

"Colonel Plane is responsible for his debts, not you."

"If I don't act, I'll lose Grandfather. Mr. Drake's threatened to kill him unless I pay him tonight."

Nostrils flared, and his lips flattened. After brooding for a moment, he yanked the reins from her hand and climbed onto the one-person seat. The cart groaned under his weight.

"Where is this painting going?" Edward's angry tone stiffened her spine.

"Where do you think *you're* going? That cart is made for a woman, not a man."

He snatched the address from the corner where she'd tucked it and thrust a handful of coins toward her. "Hire a hack and go home. Now."

"No." It was the last delivery, and she would see it through.

He ignored her and slapped the reins across Blackbeard's back. The mule flicked his head but remained firmly in place. *Good boy.*

"Get out of my cart before you—"

Edward slapped the reins harder.

This time Blackbeard bucked. His feet crashed into the cart frame, and the whole thing shook. She lunged to keep the painting from falling as it tipped. Edward twisted to aid her, but Blackbeard kicked again, and wood splintered. The cart crashed to the ground. Her fingers grazed the surface of the painting as it toppled to the curb the same instant Edward landed on top of it—cracking the frame and puncturing the facedown canvas.

Frozen, she gaped at her masterpiece. Weeks of work. The investment of materials. Her reputation as a reliable artist. The only way to pay off Drake and remove his threat. All of it. Gone. Lost to the temper tantrum of the man she was supposed to marry.

There were no words.

Edward pushed from the ground, punching another hole through her work.

If she didn't leave, she'd lose her own temper and cause a scene. She turned her back on Edward and yanked Blackbeard free from the wrap straps.

"Theresa, I'm sorry."

"Don't."

He huffed behind her. "This wouldn't have happened if you hadn't promised Drake that money."

"That promise saved both our lives, not just Grandfather's." And now his life was threatened again.

The cart shafts fell and slapped across her toes, freeing Blackbeard from the wreckage.

"He wouldn't have threatened us if you didn't consistently pay Colonel Plane's debts. Your life is better off without him."

"Is that what you believe?" She turned to face him. "Tell me how *your* life improved when your family died."

She immediately regretted the barb. He didn't flinch, but the pain broke through his icy glare. He'd lost his family in a tenement fire. Regardless of her unorthodox upbringing, at least she had Grandfather. Edward had no one.

"I am accountable to no one but myself." His answer rang hollow.

"A freedom you would sacrifice if you could save your family."

Stony silence.

Fine. He could deny it if he wished. "I can and will save my family, no matter what it costs me."

Using the broken cart as a mounting stand, she slid onto Blackbeard's bare back. She needed to apologize to her client and repay the partial advance they'd given her. After that, she'd find a way to come up with more than a hundred dollars.

"You can't ride that way. I'll hire us a hack."

She huffed and gave Blackbeard an encouraging pat. His ears flicked, and she soothed him with strokes along his neck. When Edward touched her elbow, she scowled. "I need space, Edward. You've ruined my way of paying Mr. Drake this evening, and I need to think of another plan."

His fists clenched at his side. "You are not to go near that man. Go home and prepare for the ball. I will pay him."

With no idea how to raise the money on her own, she had no choice but to comply. "Fine." She shoved Drake's note at Edward.

He frowned as she pressed her legs against Blackbeard's sides. Bless the mule's obedience. He trotted forward and removed her from Edward. She didn't dare look over her shoulder but searched for his reflection in a window as they turned a corner. There he was, kicking the side of the broken cart. Well, he deserved it. If he'd let her continue with her business, none of this would have happened.

She rubbed her forehead and allowed Blackbeard to maneuver through traffic at his own pace. Every couple fought. Lord knew she and Broderick had had more than their fair share of arguments. This was no different.

God, please, don't forget Your promise to protect Your children. Help Edward to acquire what's needed and end this madness.

Maybe He'd listen to her this time.

Theresa peered at City Hall's clock as Blackbeard clopped past. Her breath hitched. Five hours until the deadline. Would Edward follow through despite his objections? Perhaps she should ask Broderick to follow him.

What was she thinking? Broderick couldn't be trusted. He'd failed to stay by her side through sickness and health. He was also in town to work a paying case, not give her charity. Grandfather had said he'd consider reaching out to Broderick, but as far as she knew, nothing had come of it. Solving her problem with Drake was her responsibility. She must trust Edward to deliver the payment. Grandfather's life depended on him.

CHAPTER 7

AFTER A COLD, WET MORNING working the ferries, more dock hands than usual swarmed Dirk's to commiserate with friends and warm themselves with drink. Men crowded the illegal gambling tables in the back, leaving no room for Broderick to converse with his criminal network. He sat at the least crowded end of the bar and watched for Fitz's arrival. Not once in the seven days since the cemetery incident had the man made contact or ventured into Dirk's.

As much as Broderick hated to admit it, Darlington's alternative plan might be the saving grace to their unraveling case. While Broderick continued his futile undercover investigation, Darlington worked his connections within the Cincinnati police force and delved into making informants out of competitors. Isaacs alternated between shadowing Colonel Plane's movements and aiding Darlington when his skills of charm were needed. Tonight, he did Darlington's bidding at a tavern called The Exchange.

For now, the divergence of tasks preserved Theresa's anonymity. Unfortunately, that wouldn't last long if Broderick couldn't establish where he stood with the counterfeiting ring. Duty to his country would eventually require he divulge Colonel Plane's involvement. He'd do his best to protect Theresa from the ramifications, but he could do little to save Colonel Plane.

"Any idea when Fitz will be back?"

Broderick's attention snapped to the two men next to him. He knew their faces if not their names. They were among the regulars who gathered at the docks each morning hoping to be hired to load or unload cargo. Broderick spent a couple of mornings each week drift-ing through and picking up jobs. The connections and information gleaned had led him to a dozen of the men on his arrest list.

The bald, squat man shrugged. "I doubt they'll let him back after getting copped."

"Why'd Fitz get copped?" Both men's gazes swung to Broderick.

After a moment, recognition lit Baldy's face. "Gave the dock man-ager a nose-ender. Man had it coming, if you ask me. Accused Fitz of stealing cargo when his accounting came up short."

"Where's Fitz now?"

"Don't know. He spent a couple nights in quod but got let go."

Baldy's twiggy friend spoke up. "I bet he's laying low with his sis-ter. Between walloping the dock manager and the cemetery accusing him of body snatching for the medical school, them coppers won't let him be."

"Body snatching?"

"Yeah. He got caught at the cemetery after hours four nights ago, and a few graves were found empty the next morning."

Broderick wouldn't put it past Fitz to have his hand in that mor-bid business. Medical schools were notorious for paying for cadavers without asking questions. After a few more minutes of conversation, Broderick excused himself. Fitz's sister lived in one of the tenement buildings near the slaughterhouses in Camp Washington, and going unannounced gave him the advantage over a planned meeting. It was time to discover if his cover remained intact.

He stopped at Krohn, Feiss & Co. for some leaf tobacco as a good-will offering and then made his way toward Camp Washington.

At the stockyards, cows lowed and pigs squealed as they were off-loaded from train cars into corrals, where they were sorted and pre-pared for delivery to the slaughterhouses. The recent consolidation of slaughterhouse operations to the Camp Washington area made it a logical place for the factory workers to settle, but Broderick doubted anyone enjoyed living here. Even two squares away, the smell of animal and blood was odious. Summer must elevate the stench to intolerable.

Two- and three-story homes lined either side of Sutter Avenue. Most were only a few years old, but they burgeoned with evidence of large families living together in confined spaces. Even with a cold drizzle falling, children were shooed outside to play.

Broderick stepped down from the hack in front of the brick house where three redheaded boys wrestled in slush-covered grass.

"What you be doing here, Smith?" Fitz emerged from the shadows of the covered porch, smoking the last of his cigarette.

"I heard at Dirk's that you had a run-in with the dock manager and were laying low. We need to talk business."

"Denis, Martin, Peter." The boys on the ground stopped their wrestling and looked up at Fitz. "Wander, wudye?"

With some grumbling they rose to their feet. Not quite finished with their fight, the tallest one dropped a handful of slush down the shortest one's back and took off.

"I'll knock yer pan in." After shaking the wet loose, the boy pursued with threats pouring forth the entire way.

Fitz sat on a brick half wall and tossed the nub of his cigarette over the side. "Now, what be the problem?"

"You didn't show for our meeting."

"Why should I? You were out gallivanting with Miss Plane like a glunterpeck. "

At least Fitz wasn't calling him anything worse than an idiot. "There was no gallivanting. Until I saw you waving a gun at her, I hadn't seen Theresa in years."

"I knew you were letting on about being there together. Why were you in the cemetery if not with her?"

"Following you. I told you, I don't trust anyone I haven't met. If I'm going to part with thousands of dollars, I want to know who I'm working with. You'd do the same thing in my position."

"The cheek of ya!"

"You know it's true." Broderick pulled out the box of tobacco leaf and passed it to Fitz.

He opened the box and took an indulgent sniff. "Aye, I do." After taking time to roll a new cigarette, he tucked the box inside his coat. "Who's Miss Plane to you?"

Broderick leaned against the post and crossed his ankles. Anything he shared must hold truth enough to withstand any information Colonel Plane or Theresa revealed. "We were neighbors and friends until I left years ago. Colonel Plane didn't like my criminal connections." Ironic that the colonel hated Broderick's family because of his brother Nathaniel's connection to counterfeiting when Colonel Plane himself turned to the same crime. "I'll not see her hurt, but there's nothing between us."

Fitz smoked his cigarette in silence until nothing but the nub remained. He tossed it aside and then nodded. "We keep the deal, but you'll be my gopher for anything needs doing. And put a kibosh on playing hero to Miss Plane. She's a job to do herself."

"Since she didn't recognize you, I didn't think she was involved."

"She isn't, but if you control the lass, you control the lad. I aim to make a lot of money, and if that means holding a gun to her blithering head to get the work done, then I'll do it and you'll watch. Are we of a like mind?"

"As long as you don't pull the trigger, we're agreed."

"Good. Now be off with you. I'll deliver instructions in a few days."

Fitz disappeared inside, and Broderick walked toward the stockyards in search of a hack. For now, his position as a potential production firm member remained intact, but Fitz's lack of concern for Theresa's well-being left Broderick unsettled. Most criminals drew a line at harming women and children, but Fitz and Grimm already proved to be the rarer breed. Did Colonel Plane have any idea how much danger he'd put Theresa in by associating with these brutes?

At least Broderick had done whatever necessary to make up for his mistake and protect her. He'd pursued and prosecuted his traitor brother and then left town. Putting her safety above his wants always took priority. Colonel Plane didn't even have the decency to meet her basic needs, but Broderick would force his hand.

He climbed into the hired hack at the corner of the stockyards. "Keppler Hotel."

He needed to review Isaacs's notes on Colonel Plane's movements and the minimal information he'd collected on Edward Greystone. If he had to relinquish Theresa to another man, Broderick would ensure he was worthy of and able to care for her—and keep her safe.

Dusk had shifted to overcast night by the time the hack arrived at the hotel. With Darlington attending some affair with a local connection, there would be no worry of interruption. He passed through the tall entrance and tried to ignore the tantalizing smell of today's special coming from the restaurant. Roast beef. Maybe he'd have a plate brought up to Isaacs's room later.

"Sir!" The front desk clerk waved him closer and then retrieved an envelope from a locked drawer. "A gentleman delivered this for you early this morning. He said it was urgent, but we couldn't find you or Mr. Isaacs."

Broderick accepted the weighty envelope and frowned. His real name was scrolled across the front, not in Theresa's impatient style but with strict precision. Darlington would not be foolish enough to risk exposing Broderick's cover, and Isaacs's writing competed with a chicken for legibility. A glance around the lobby and restaurant entrance revealed no one waited to observe his reading. He took the envelope upstairs and locked the door behind him.

After a quick examination for clues on the outside of the envelope, he broke the seal and opened the trifold letter. Two sets of train tickets to Philadelphia rested in the center fold with Colonel Plane's bold signature beneath them.

> *I have failed to detect my enemy's advances until too late and have no choice but to turn to you for help. Theresa's life is in imminent danger. If she doesn't secretly leave Cincinnati today, I fear what may happen to her. Tonight she is to attend a ball at Lydia's. Get*

*her alone and persuade her to escape with you to Philadelphia. I
don't care if you have to drug her and kidnap her. No one is to know
where she goes. Once you arrive in Philadelphia, send a telegram.
I will respond with where to find everything you need to arrest the
entire counterfeiting ring to which your brother once belonged,
including me.*

*A trunk containing her needs is waiting at the station. Under no
circumstances is she to return to the house. Once my associates realize what I've done, their anger will know no bounds. Against my
better judgment, I'm trusting you with her. Do not fail me again.*

Godspeed,
Colonel N. Plane

Of all the nights for Colonel Plane not to have a shadow. Broderick
shoved the letter and tickets into his coat pocket. Isaacs should still
be charming information out of the serving girls at The Exchange.
Going there would take Broderick in the opposite direction of Lydia's
home on Jefferson Street, but disappearing for days without warning
would infuriate Darlington and worry Isaacs. As much as he wanted
to leave straight for Theresa, she would be safe at Lydia's for the time
being. They'd already missed the 7:25 p.m. express to Cleveland, and
the next one wouldn't leave until 5:25 a.m. He could meet with Isaacs,
apprise him of the situation, and then send him on to watch Colonel
Plane's movements. Soon the case would be finished, arrests made, and
Theresa safe.

CHAPTER 8

WHY COULDN'T THE BALL HAVE fallen on another night? Theresa twisted the cameo at her neck as she watched the quadrille begin. She should be with Edward paying Drake or at home with Grandfather until the danger passed. Not here, feigning enjoyment.

"Why aren't you dancing?" Lydia asked. "Has Edward not arrived?"

"Not yet." But he should have by now.

More than two hours had passed since Edward dropped her off. What if Drake had attacked him and stolen the money? Edward might be lying in a ditch, shot and helpless. The image stole her breath.

No, Edward went prepared. He would be safe. The fear lay in Drake never showing.

Oh, Grandfather, why wouldn't you come with me? Mrs. Hawking isn't even home tonight. Perhaps she should have told him about Drake's threat, but she knew he'd try to interfere with Edward's mission.

"Mr. Darlington has arrived." Lydia's sing-song tone grated on Theresa's nerves. Why couldn't her friend hide from prying eyes in her bedroom and partake in a normal confinement period like most women? She was in no mood to tolerate a matchmaking scheme tonight. "I'm not dancing with him."

"Oh, come now. A single dance is hardly a risk to your undying love for Edward. Unless, of course, that dance were with Broderick."

Theresa snapped her attention to Lydia's face, and the Cheshire Cat grinned. She frowned at Lydia before sweeping her gaze across the room of attendees. No Broderick. Too bad that knowledge didn't slow her racing heart.

"Even now, his name flushes your face. Are you certain Edward is the one you should marry when the mere mention of Broderick's elicits such a strong reaction?"

"Nonsense. The room is over-hot."

Lydia snorted in an unladylike fashion. "And Gettysburg was just a skirmish." She clutched Theresa's arm and pulled her toward the punch table. "Come. You promised Father you would dance with Mr. Darlington, and a Plane never goes back on their word."

Could she be held to a promise she hadn't meant to make? The way Lydia practically dragged her across the room, no excuse would be accepted. Fine. She'd give Mr. Darlington one dance, and then she would leave. Grandfather needed her.

Dr. Pelton conversed with a lean man with bushy sideburns in what must be a borrowed suit. It hung too large on him—not overly so, but enough to know he did not employ a tailor. Not that Theresa could judge him on that. She hadn't had anything but remade or borrowed dresses for years.

"Ah, there you are, girls." Dr. Pelton gave them each a peck on the cheek. "Allow me to introduce Detective Andrew Darlington. Andrew, you remember my eldest daughter, Mrs. Abraham Hall—Lydia."

Mr. Darlington did not offer a kiss to the hand but gave a curt nod. His manners, like his looks, left something to be desired. Still, Theresa offered him what she hoped was a tolerant smile when Dr. Pelton directed his attention toward her.

"And this is the daughter of my heart, Miss Theresa Plane." Dr. Pelton lavished her with his well-known and often teased-about toothy grin.

"It is a pleasure to meet you, sir." She extended her hand to force Mr. Darlington's manners. When he shook it instead of kissing it, Theresa struggled to hide her disapproval. He either lacked the knowledge of social graces or didn't care.

A few piano notes encouraged guests to find a partner for the next song.

Mr. Darlington grimaced. "Would you care to dance?"

He appeared even less eager than she felt. Perhaps he'd been conned into this arrangement as well.

"Do take care of her, Mr. Darlington," Lydia said. "She needs a good man in her life."

Theresa bit her tongue as Lydia gave a little wave and wobbled off to a safe distance. A good thing, too, for she was tempted to strangle her so-called friend. For heaven's sake, she sounded desperate by Lydia's description.

Mr. Darlington took her arm and half yanked her toward the dance floor.

"I am afraid Lydia may have misled you, Mr. Darlington. I have already found a good man and am engaged."

"That is quite all right. I have no interest in courting you."

She flinched at his bluntness. A sharp retort came to mind, but she choked it back. For Dr. Pelton's sake, she would act the part of a lady. A pleasant smile would have to do, though, for no acceptable response came to mind.

Instead of sliding into the circle of dancers, Mr. Darlington halted at the edge of the designated dancing space. His brows knit together as he observed the other dancers already waltzing around the floor. *Oh, no. A non-dancer.* Her toes curled in anticipation of the oncoming onslaught.

Confident of proper positioning, he hovered one hand above her waist and latched onto her waiting hand with the other. After a few bumbling attempts, he moved them onto the floor. Evening shoes offered little protection from his cannonball attacks.

After falling into an irregular rhythm, he looked her in the face. "Dr. Pelton tells me you're a skilled engraver. How long have you been engraving?"

She slid her foot from beneath his and tried not to wince. "Almost six years. My grandfather owns a printshop, so I take on occasional projects."

"And what would those be?"

"Advertisements, mostly. Some illustrations for books or stationery."

They bumped into a couple and disrupted another when he righted them. What an oaf! She mumbled her regrets and took over leading the dance. He probably hadn't had a lesson in his life, and he didn't seem to notice he'd relinquished control. Edward would have fought for it immediately. Broderick, on the other hand, would have viewed her maneuver as a challenge, pulled her close, and made her laugh until she forgot who led. Why couldn't she be dancing with him?

Pain throbbed in her big toe as Mr. Darlington's foot found its mark again and ruined her fantasy.

He continued prattling on without an apology. "Dr. Pelton mentioned you and Mrs. Hall have had some wild moments, including a jail stay."

Did he have no discretion? Such a comment was one thing if you were a friend, but a stranger? She ground her teeth before deciding to skirt the edges of politeness.

"Gossiping is a sin, Mr. Darlington."

"In my line of work, seeking the truth is paramount." He tightened his grip on her hand. "I can search out your record."

Abraham treated convicts better than this. "Allow me to save you the trouble. Lydia and I stole a three-legged goat from the circus." His eyebrows shot to his dark hairline. "What your record will fail to mention is that Tipsy was abused. I cannot abide the ill-treatment of man or beast. I tried to purchase her, but when that failed, Lydia and I rescued her. Only it didn't go as we expected." While ashamed she'd stooped to breaking the law, the actions did have some benefits. Abraham had been their arresting officer. It might not have been a traditional romantic start, but it was an unforgettable one for her friend.

Mr. Darlington fell silent for a moment and then shook his head. "Dr. Pelton fears you might have become entangled in some criminal dealings. Is there a reason he should be concerned?"

Her breath caught and stumbled her step. Did this man know about Fitz and Grimm? She dropped her hands and pushed away. "This dance is over. Enjoy the rest of your evening."

Theresa ignored the turned heads as she stormed from the center of the floor to the open ballroom door. Mr. Darlington hadn't been chosen to usurp Edward. He'd been hired to investigate her. How could Dr. Pelton betray them? Had he confronted Grandfather? Was that why Grandfather refused to come? Nails bit into her palms. She should have stayed home.

Mr. Darlington reached her at the foyer entrance and clasped her shoulder. "I meant no offense. It's my duty to ask."

Duty, indeed. "Your allegation would offend any lady."

"Not an innocent one."

If the volley of rifle fire exploding in her mind could inflict real damage, he might reconsider that answer. "Just because I rescued an animal does not make me prone to criminal activity."

"But you *have* fallen on hard times. Debts totaling thousands of dollars make a person desperate." He leaned in. "Desperate enough to make a little money on the side."

What had Dr. Pelton told him?

His eyes narrowed on her like a fox intent on eating Bleu. Her chest huffed as she threw her shoulders back and chin up. No man would treat her like this. "I will no longer endure your company. Bid the Peltons good evening for me."

Gerard, the butler, met her at the door with her cloak. "I couldn't help but notice your need for a quick exit. The Pelton carriage is free for your use."

Bless his soul. That man deserved sainthood.

As she strode to the carriage, she shrugged on her cloak. How blind had she been to not see this coming? Lydia had a detective husband, for heaven's sake! Given Abraham's quiet unease around her lately, a full investigation must be underway. If not, it would be after tonight. She needed to be prepared. No matter what Grandfather had done, she had to protect him, and to do that she needed answers.

During the twenty-minute ride to Plane Manor, she formulated her plan of attack. For it to work, she'd need to corner Grandfather and bombard him with the facts she knew and direct questions. He might try to lie, but she would not be fooled.

An arctic wind blasted her as she stepped down from the carriage in front of the Gothic stone mansion. Pinnacles and parapets stood a commanding three stories high with wings and bays extending in all directions—a perfect home for a man like Grandfather. Regardless, she would win tonight's battle.

She stepped onto the portico—and her feet slipped in opposite directions. Fiery spasms seared her leg as she crashed onto the icy stone. Why couldn't she have turned her ankle before being forced to dance with Mr. Darlington? With nothing to grab on to, she scooted to the front door on her knees. The handle stabilized her but refused her entry.

With Mrs. Hawking not expected to return before Theresa, the door was locked. She should have known better than to leave without a key. Darkness cloaked the front windows, meaning Grandfather must be closeted in his office on the far side of the house. He'd never hear pounding on the front door or the twist of the doorbell, and she doubted he would hear her at the side yard entrance either. Using the wall for support and lifting her borrowed skirts from the mud, she limped her way along the perimeter of the house toward the back office window. Shivers traveled throughout her body as the dampness soaked through the thin material of her shoes and numbed her feet. From now on, she would take the extra key.

A distorted shout cut through the night air as she rounded the corner. Was that . . . She stopped and strained to hear. Had Drake beaten her to Grandfather? Her heart raced at the notion. Where was Edward? *Boom.*

Though quieter than in the carriage a week ago, there was no mistaking that sound. A second shot shattered the hush, and she launched forward. Each step radiated blinding pain in her ankle, but she dared not slow. Not until she entered the arc of light coming from the office did logic force her to stop. She was unarmed. What could she do without jeopardizing her own life? A sour taste accompanied an ache in the back of her throat.

The front door slammed.

Maybe Drake had left. She bit her lip. What had Broderick taught her about approaching potential danger? *Evaluate a room without being seen. Check corners, doors, floors, and furniture. Don't expose limbs or head until the room is cleared.* Her hands trembled as she shifted to peer through the glass panes of the office window.

No one.

She released her breath. Bolder, she stood in front of the window. No one sat in the chairs by the fireplace, but Grandfather's large oak desk concealed the lower half of the room. A step to the right revealed the bottom of crisply pressed uniform trousers and two attached polished boots on the rug.

Her heart pounded in her ears and muffled the glass rattling in its frame under her fist. "Grandfather!"

His leg twitched but nothing more. He was in trouble, and the well-made window wouldn't let her through.

She scanned the ground for a sturdy branch, grateful their meager funds no longer provided for a groundskeeper. Hefting a fallen limb over her shoulder, she swung like a home run batter for the Red Stockings. The glass exploded. Sharp slivers landed on her face and clothes. She raked glass from the sill before discarding the limb and then climbed through the window. Debris crunched underfoot as she rounded the desk.

God have mercy.

Grandfather lay on his back, his face contorted with pain and a hand clutched over his chest. Darkness spread across his navy coat beneath red-stained fingers. She gripped the desk and tried to breathe. This couldn't be real. It had to be a nightmare. But no matter how many times she blinked, the scene before her did not change.

Sputtering gave fire to her body and focused her mind.

The blood. She had to staunch its flow. Forfeiting her cloak, she dropped to her knees and pushed aside Grandfather's hand. More blood than the cloak could absorb puddled on its surface. Heaven help them. She wadded the material and leveraged her body over the wound.

"Help!" Useless, but what else could she do? She couldn't leave him.

Grandfather sputtered, drawing her gaze. "Forgive . . . me." Each word struggled to escape like a mouse from a trap.

Forgive him? Her mind couldn't wrap around the request. People asked for forgiveness only when they believed they were going to—

She screamed for help again.

His gasp captured her unwilling gaze. The face she loved and chafed under no longer held the proud lines of her regal colonel. Purple lips contrasted with a complexion whiter than paper, and flesh sagged toward the ground as his glassy eyes stared beyond her.

"Help's coming. You can't surrender. You've got more battles to fight."

His head lolled to the side.

"Grandfather! Look at me!"

His eyes fluttered at the command, and a foreign liquid shimmered from the corners.

Tears? But he'd never cried before.

A breath soft as butterfly wings fluttered from his chest but did not return.

No! This couldn't be it. "Breathe."

She pumped his chest as if that action would force air into his lungs. For long minutes she tried but to no avail. Her hands cramped, and she had to stop.

"Come on, *breathe*."

She stared, willing his chest to rise. The command went unanswered. She could deny it no longer. He was gone.

A sob constricted her throat as she released the blood-soaked material and wove her fingers into his still-warm ones. Curling against him, she laid her head on his chest like she had in the days after her parents' deaths. The steady beat of his heart had brought comfort. Now? Nothing.

The mantel clock chimed. How could time still exist? Her gaze lifted to the clock face, but the crucifix above caught her attention.

The one shred of tangible faith left to her, and even that blurred under her scrutiny.

Returning to her curled position, she closed her eyes. Before long, blessed oblivion claimed her.

CHAPTER 9

MUSIC AND CONVERSATION WAFTED FROM an open window of the three-story Hall home. Carriages and their drivers lined the street, biding time until the partygoers finished their merrymaking. As he knocked on the door, Broderick lifted a prayer, asking God to help Theresa cooperate.

"Are you sure about this?" Isaacs said from his place near the porch. He'd adjusted his coat to hide his gun.

Despite Broderick's plan for Isaacs to go straight to Plane Manor to shadow the colonel, Isaacs had insisted his letter reeked of a setup. Until the train pulled out with Broderick and Theresa, he'd stay nearby as extra support.

"The only danger I face inside is a tongue-lashing."

The door opened to a stern-faced butler. "May I help you?"

"I need to speak with Miss Theresa Plane." Broderick stepped forward, but the butler blocked his way.

"Do you have an invitation?"

"No, but it's imperative I speak with Miss Plane immediately."

"This is a private party. I cannot give you admittance."

"Then bring her to me."

"Debt collectors are not welcome here. If you have a problem, Colonel Plane can be found at his home. Now, leave before I summon Detective Hall and the other officers in attendance."

Debt collectors? Did this entire household know of the colonel's debts? And Lydia's husband was a detective?

A husky female voice came from beyond the door. "Is there a problem, Gerard?"

"Nothing to concern yourself with, Mrs. Hall."

Lord, don't let her turn me away. "Lydia, it's Broderick."

Gerard glanced behind him and then opened the door wider. Lydia stood with arms folded over her large girth and cocked an eyebrow as he stepped into the polished foyer. Being seen would further compromise the situation. He stepped behind the hall tree. "I need to see Theresa."

Lydia dropped her arms and gestured to a closed door. "Gerard, see to it that we are not disturbed."

The butler did not move from his station. Neither did he send anyone to retrieve Theresa. Broderick checked his frustration and followed Lydia into a small office lit by a dying fire, then he closed the door behind them and cast Lydia in shadow.

"You cannot barge in here, pretending you didn't break Theresa's heart and demand to see her." Lydia struck a match and lit the desk lamp. "She deserves better than that."

If he had any choice in the matter, he'd agree, but this wasn't about romance. "Her life's in danger. I need to see her."

"You'll have to do better than that lie to convince me."

"There isn't time. I've been sent to protect her and escort her to safety." He stepped forward and barely restrained the urge to shake her. "Where is she, Lydia?"

Her eyes widened. "You're serious, aren't you?"

"Yes." Though he wished he wasn't.

"She left nearly two hours ago. Went home. What's happened? What's wrong?"

His stomach pitched. *Under no circumstances is she to return to the house.* Two hours she'd been gone. Two hours possibly at the mercy of those Colonel Plane feared. He couldn't waste time giving Lydia details. It might already be too late.

Lydia's voice followed his exit. "I'm sending my husband and Father."

Broderick sprinted from the house, and he and Isaacs mounted their waiting horses. If everything were fine, he'd deal with the consequences of the two men's presence later. However, if Theresa were hurt, he'd never be able to live with himself.

Lord, don't let me be too late.

The horses' heaving sides gleamed with sweat by the time he and Isaacs reached the backside of Plane Manor. Though he wanted to charge through the front door, he forced himself to proceed as trained by his father. They dismounted in the woods, leaving the horses ground tied, and sneaked toward the stone mansion.

Wind haunted through the trees and covered any faint sounds that might have been heard by their rushed approach. With silent communication honed by years of partnership, he and Isaacs circled wide and approached with weapons ready. No footprints sullied the snow around the house's boundaries, but that didn't mean ring members weren't inside.

Broderick paused at the maple's base to peer up at Theresa's room, but no light or movement revealed occupancy. She must be in another part of the house. Not a comforting thought. His pace quickened as they continued to the western corner of the mansion. Once there, he sunk low into the bushes and peeked around.

Light fell across a wide expanse of disturbed ground. Grass lay crushed under footprints, the snow swept aside in a wide circle. Though no sound came from inside the room, he crouch-walked to the base of the window and examined the scene.

Jagged edges of glass protruded from the broken window, while wood framing hung from the tangles of a discarded tree limb. Someone with sprite-sized shoes had broken in. Broderick's gut clenched. She'd been here, but why didn't she go through the front door?

He rose and pressed against one side of the window. Keeping his head out of view, he examined the right half of the room. A gas chandelier provided illumination from above. The fire in the grate sputtered and popped as a lone log crumbled into embers. Two empty wingback chairs framed the hearth, a book splayed on the floor between them. He angled to see what hid below the window. Glass littered the floor like a field of thistles, but he saw no shadow of a human form.

"Cosgrove." Isaacs's whisper held a warning from the opposite side. "I'll get inside and clear the rest of the house. You better go in through the window. It doesn't look good." He didn't wait for a response and slipped farther down the wall.

Broderick steeled his nerves and stepped into full view. Beyond the desk, black and burgundy skirts spread from the crumpled form of a woman.

"Theresa!"

She didn't respond. His heart raced as he leaped through the window, crunching the glass under his landing. A quick sweep of the room revealed it devoid of threats. He shoved his Colt back into its holster and rushed to her side.

God, don't let her be . . .

He swept aside stiff hair to find her eyes closed and dried blood caked over most of her face. Trembling, he searched for a pulse on her neck, the thrum of his own making it difficult to detect. With concentrated effort, he closed his eyes and slowed his breathing. There it was—a strong, steady beat. The tightness in his chest released. Now to keep it that way. He opened his eyes to see hers flutter and blink at him through a daze.

"Theresa, do you know who I am?" A head injury could explain all the blood.

Her eyes fixated straight ahead. "He's dead."

The simple statement jolted, and he followed her gaze. Glassy eyes stared from a pale face that deepened to shades of purple toward the floor. Colonel Plane's death in any manner would have devastated her, but this was no natural cause. Had she been present during the attack? He returned his gaze to her. "Can you sit up?"

She stared into her grandfather's face in silence.

Where words lacked, gentleness would have to do. Broderick wrapped his arms around her shoulders and cradled her. She didn't fight his touch or whimper in pain but tucked her head against him. Whether in shock from her injuries or from the emotional trauma, he couldn't determine. Her gaze stayed rooted on Colonel Plane even as Broderick pried her fingers free of the man's stiff ones.

"The house is empty. All doors except the front are locked." Isaacs stepped into the room, holstering his pistol. His eyes fell to Theresa's back. "Is she . . ."

"Alive but hurt, and Colonel Plane's been murdered. Lydia said she was sending Dr. Pelton and her husband, who apparently is a detective with the police. Will you hasten them?"

Isaacs nodded with somber acceptance, then disappeared again, pulling the door to the room nearly shut. The thud of the front door echoed moments later.

A quick check proved no critical injuries, and removing Theresa from the gruesome sight and chilled room would be the first thing Dr. Pelton required. He carried her to the door and pushed it open with his back.

Theresa jerked forward, almost causing him to drop her. "No! I can't leave him."

She may not like being separated from her grandfather, but God had already seen fit to do that. Broderick tightened his grip and held her steady as she fought until her strength waned. Once assured he wouldn't drop her, he entered the hall and kicked the door shut. Theresa's nails scraped deep into his skin, but her whimpers wounded him most. No matter what the police demanded, he would not subject her to that scene again.

"Shh, I've got you." The soft reassurance made her clutch him harder.

Lord, why didn't I come sooner? He might have been able to protect her. Save her from this horror. Now all he could do was nurse her until help came. He hugged her close for a moment and then maneuvered down the hall to the kitchen.

A single stool provided a potential resting spot, but she'd never stay atop it with the way her body trembled. Broderick tested the temperature above a floor vent and frowned. Colonel Plane must have let the coal furnace run out of fuel. Holding her steady, he shrugged from his coat and let it fall to the frigid floor as a barrier. Theresa's arms choked him as he knelt to settle her against the wall.

"Don't leave me." Terror laced her voice as she nearly upended them both.

"I need to start a fire to warm you." He slid his hands along her arms until he reached the clumps of shirt trapped in her grip. "Be brave and rest here. I promise I won't be far."

She gulped but released his shirt and wrapped her arms around her knees.

"Good girl." He resisted the urge to kiss her forehead until he knew where the blood came from and turned to the task at hand.

After lighting the wall sconce, he tackled the cold cast-iron stove. More temperamental than he remembered, he fought with the rusty damper and reluctant matches. Minutes passed before the kindling ignited, and he poured what was in the nearly empty coal bin into the firebox. He lifted the lid on the reservoir and tested the water. Tepid at best. He dunked a small pot into the water and set it on the hottest grate.

When Theresa whimpered, he turned to find her rocking back and forth, her chin tucked to her knees. Lord forgive him when he caught whoever did this to her. If at the wrong moment, he might not act within the confines of the law. A part of him wished for it. To inflict the same pain he saw on Theresa's face. No. Worse. The man would beg for his life.

Vengeance is the Lord's.

The whisper did little to cool his anger, but he checked his thoughts. No matter if his anger was righteous, he could not repay evil for evil. Justice would prevail. He'd ensure it.

Water hissed, and he scowled at the pot. This was taking too long. He rechecked the temperature. Not as warm as he wanted, but it would have to do. The water in the half-full pot sloshed against the sides as he carried it over.

When the warm rag touched her face, she jerked back and lifted her hands in defense.

"Shh, it's me."

She blinked a few times, then released a breath and dropped her hands.

Instead of gathering her into his arms again, like he wanted, he dabbed at the dried blood. What had she endured tonight? Had her attacker assumed her beyond saving and left her for dead? What all had been stolen from her? His stomach roiled as his mind worked through all the possibilities. With her dress ripped and blood tainted, anything could be possible.

Her head bumped against the wall, and he forced himself to gentle his touch. "Sorry, Reese." Sorry for not controlling his temper. Sorry for not being there to protect her. Sorry he'd left her at all.

She made no reply but leaned her head back as he continued his ministrations. Slowly, her face emerged from the dark stains. No visible wound explained the presence of blood, but her matted hair might hide the source.

"Broderick?" Her eyes blinked rapidly, but no tears fell.

Maybe now she could tell him the source of pain. "Where are you hurt?"

She shook her head and reached her arms toward him. "Hold me."

The ache to comply tore at him. "I need to clean your wounds first."

"The blood," she choked. "It's not mine."

He wasn't sure whether to praise God or rail at the fact she'd not been protected from witnessing such a death. Drawing her onto his lap, he rested a cheek on her head as she shook in his arms. Binding sprains and sewing sutures he could do, but these invisible wounds left him fumbling for words. Nothing he could say would bring Colonel Plane back. No action he took would ever erase this night from her mind.

When hiccups replaced sobs, he retrieved the rag. The blood may not be hers, but it had to go. As the evidence of death disappeared, he prayed silently over her and then hummed. Her breathing normalized, and she molded against his body. This was where she belonged.

"Sing the words." Her hoarse whisper barely rose above the hymn meant to soothe.

Maybe he'd been too quick to dismiss a possible head injury. "My voice hasn't improved over the years."

She tilted her head back and ran fingers over his beard. "Please."

Her pleading gaze drew him like a siren. He couldn't deny her anything, even if singing was the least of his skills. The words of his favorite hymn flowed easily, albeit off-key.

"When through deep waters I call thee to go, the rivers of sorrow shall not overflow"—she sniffed and nestled against him—"for I will be with thee, thy troubles to bless, and sanctify to thee thy deepest distress."

Soft hair brushed against his lips as he sighed. How God could sanctify this moment of deepest distress was a mystery. What good could come of tonight?

He continued to sing and abandoned the soiled rag to dip her hands in the water. His thumb scraped something sharp while he massaged her palm, and Theresa yelped. He lifted her hands and tilted them until a dozen glass fragments glinted in the light.

Her head shifted beneath his chin. "It must have happened when I broke in."

The desire to shield her warred with the need for information before more time passed and tainted the facts. "What happened?"

She trembled. "It's all my fault. I didn't get Drake's payment to him in time."

"You're not responsible for the actions of a monster."

Silence rebuffed him.

If it took a lifetime to free her from guilt, he would persist. "Did you see Drake?"

"No, but I heard him . . . I think. The voice was distorted."

Hardly enough to prove Drake as the murderer when a long list of suspects existed.

Theresa shook her head. "You need facts, not my assumptions."

With a deep breath, she stiffened until her body no longer rested against him. Everything about her hardened as though an iron gate had slammed shut on her emotions, caging the vulnerable woman who needed him inside. Broderick tried to ease her against him, but she resisted his comfort. *God, please don't let her do this again.* Restoring her to life after the death of her parents had been a monumental task. Breaking through the barrier this time might prove impossible.

With cold, measured words, she described the evening as if writing a daily report. "I left Lydia's after a detective accused me of being a criminal. A Mr. Darlington."

Broderick tensed. How had Darlington found her already? The wolf was more efficient than he'd feared.

"The front door was locked when I arrived, so I walked around to the side of the house, thinking Grandfather was in his office. Someone yelled. Two gunshots followed. The mur—" She swallowed. "The person escaped through the front door, but I didn't see him. I broke into the office, but it was too late."

Though he again encouraged her to rest against him, she remained rigid. He was a fool to have asked. It would have been better to let the evidence speak than this.

A door banged at the front of the house.

Took them long enough. "We're in the kitchen!"

A single set of footsteps moved their direction. At a minimum, there should be two. Broderick kept one hand to Theresa's back and reached for his Colt with the other. Only a fool would return to the murder scene. Unless he realized there could have been a witness. Before he could shift Theresa off his lap and into the safety of cover, Edward Greystone filled the doorframe, gun at the ready and a snarl twisting his mustache.

Chapter 10

"GET YOUR HANDS OFF MY fiancée." The cold hatred in Greystone's eyes warned Broderick there would be no hesitation to shoot.

Broderick released the grip of his revolver and eased Theresa off his lap and onto the floor. He wasn't as smooth a talker as Isaacs, but it was the safest tactic at his disposal.

With raised hands, he stood and sidestepped to shield Theresa. "Miss Plane is wounded. She needs a doctor."

"What have you done to her?"

A grunt came from behind Broderick. *Please, Theresa, don't.* Despite his inward plea, she used his legs to bolster her attempt to stand.

"Stand down, Edward. It wasn't him." She winced as she took a few unstable steps forward. Broderick reached to steady her, but Edward pulled her beyond reach and then lifted her to the tabletop. Theresa's hands slapped the surface to steady her sway.

"Careful with her." Broderick closed the distance, ready to catch her should she fall.

"I'm fine." New lines of blood stemmed from the shards in her palm as she waved off his concern.

She was not fine. She'd denied any injury and yet two known ones existed—the glass in her hands and something with her foot or ankle. Now this monster tossed her around like a half-empty potato sack? She needed care and treatment. Why hadn't Dr. Pelton and Isaacs returned yet?

Greystone glared at Broderick. "Who are you?"

Spoken with such malice, it was a wonder the words didn't come with a physical punch.

"Broderick, this is my fiancé, Edward Greystone. Edward, Broderick is an old family friend."

How convenient for Theresa to omit his last name. Either she had her wits about her enough to remember he was undercover or she didn't want Greystone knowing how to find him. The reason didn't matter. He would use it to his advantage.

"Then why have I never met him?" Accusation laced Greystone's tone.

The corner of her mouth tugged upward. "Grandfather doesn't like him."

"That makes two of us." Greystone faced Theresa. "What happened? Why didn't you stay at the ball like I told you?"

"A detective started asking questions, making accusations. I needed to talk to Grandfather, but when I came home—" Her words ended in a wince.

The brief moment of color she held drained as if she'd just remembered the ordeal of the night. Her eyes squeezed shut, and she wobbled.

Greystone supported her with a hand. "I saw. I'm sorry. Are you hurt?"

Now the man thought to ask her? What sort of fiancé was he? Enough blood was on her clothes and in her hair for her health to be anyone's first concern.

She lifted her hands and examined her palms. "I guess, but I can't feel it." After a moment, her chin jerked and her eyes flashed. "Was Mr. Drake paid?"

"He never showed."

"Then it's my fault."

Broderick ached to remove those damaging thoughts, but he could only stroke her back in comfort. Greystone's face flared red. Broderick wasn't looking for more enemies, but the lout couldn't be trusted with Theresa's care.

Voices called from the front of the house, interrupting their glaring match. Broderick responded, and soon Dr. Pelton entered. A few steps behind, Lydia waddled in. When she saw Theresa, she sobbed. Much of the blood had been removed from Theresa's face, but no amount of rag water could erase the trauma of tonight.

"Control or remove yourself, Lydia." Dr. Pelton stepped around Greystone.

The doctor looked grayer than he had the last time they'd met, and a cap of baldness revealed itself when he laid his hat aside. His lips, already grim, pressed into a tight line as he examined Theresa.

"She has shards of glass in her hands." Broderick recalled her hobbled walk. "And something's wrong with her foot."

Dr. Pelton spared him a glance and began issuing orders. "Lydia, go start a fire in the parlor, light some lamps, and prepare my instruments. Edward, carry her to the sofa and make sure she's comfortable."

Greystone's gleam of victory pinched, but Broderick released his hold on Theresa.

Dr. Pelton faced Broderick. "And you, sir, heat some fresh water."

As the room's occupants jumped to action, Broderick dumped the pot of water into the sink and watched the red disappear. Colonel Plane's blood, not Theresa's. For that, he lifted a prayer of thanks. He frowned as Greystone carried Theresa from the room. That man didn't have an ounce of the gentleness she needed. Broderick refilled the pot and set it on the stove. Someone should oversee her care, and no one knew Theresa's needs better than he did.

Dr. Pelton closed the door before he could exit and turned toward him. "Lydia suspects you're working a case."

The reminder of his real purpose in Cincinnati jarred. Though he wanted nothing more than to be with Theresa at this moment, he couldn't forget his job. Not when the murderer was likely one of the ring members. The sooner he arrested them, the sooner Theresa would be safe and receive the justice she deserved. For once, his duty to country and duty to Theresa were aligned.

"I am, and for all concerned, I'm Brody Smith. A family friend with a questionable history."

Dr. Pelton nodded. "Stop by the house tomorrow morning. You should know some things about Colonel Plane, and it's best if Theresa doesn't hear."

Broderick tensed. "She won't be staying with you?"

"Lydia will care for her. Separating the two right now would be unwise, for both of them. Her husband is a detective with the Cincinnati police. Theresa will be safe."

"Are you certain you can trust him?" The reputation of the Cincinnati police had been under fire for years. More honorable officers existed than corrupt, but one never knew if a villain hid behind the uniform.

"Do you think I would have let him marry my daughter if I weren't certain I could trust him?" Dr. Pelton gave a half-smile. "Go give your statement to Abraham. I'll be in to see to Colonel Plane shortly." Dread for the task ahead darkened Dr. Pelton's features.

This was a grievous night for everyone.

Broderick opened the door to the hall and forced himself to turn the opposite direction from the parlor. Theresa needed someone who could bring security, safety, and stability to her future. The only way to do that was to find the murderer, close his case, and then exit her life forever. He just hated to leave her to the likes of Greystone.

At the threshold of Colonel Plane's office, he evaluated the scene with fresh eyes. Despite the evidence of a murder, the room was tidy. Nothing appeared to be ransacked. Whoever came in here was purposeful. If something was missing, the perpetrator had known precisely where to look and took it. A shiver passed over him. Thank God for His protection. More than one body could have been felled tonight had the murderer lingered.

Broderick's gaze slid to the handkerchief draped over Colonel Plane's face. Darkness across the coat attested to massive blood loss. The Angel of Death would have whisked him away even if the best doctor had been on hand. A man dressed in formal attire—presumably

Lydia's husband—stooped over Colonel Plane and prodded the tear in the ribbon of Colonel Plane's Medal of Honor. The bronze eagle resting on crossed cannons, and holding the star, dangled by a stubborn piece of thread.

Isaacs joined him at the door and spoke in a low voice. "That's Detective Hall. He knows I'm a Secret Service operative investigating Colonel Plane, but he doesn't know about you. He's sending me to retrieve men from the station." Isaacs gave a grim "Good luck" before exiting.

Hall rose and approached with an extended hand. "I'm Detective Abraham Hall." He glanced down at Broderick's shirt. "I see you've come in contact with the body."

Broderick blinked and regarded his blood-stained clothes. "Miss Plane was draped across her grandfather. Some of the blood must have transferred when I removed her. Other than my closing the door when we left, the room is untouched."

"You were looking for Miss Plane at my home earlier and told my wife she was in danger. Why?"

"Yes, I would like to know that as well." Greystone appeared at the door with crossed arms and wide stance.

The truth would expose Broderick's case. Perhaps Detective Hall could be trusted but certainly not Greystone.

Vague truth served him better than an outright lie. "Colonel Plane had some concerns and asked me to ensure Theresa's safety. When I determined she'd returned home, I came here."

Greystone dropped his arms and stepped forward. "He should have come to me. Theresa is to be my wife soon."

Detective Hall scoffed. "It'll be a good six months before you can wed. No matter how much you disliked the colonel, Theresa loved him. She'll want the full mourning period or longer."

"Who will care for her in those months? Marriage will afford her the care and protection she needs."

"Lydia and I will care for her."

Greystone started to argue, but Detective Hall returned to his line of questioning. "Do you know what concerned Colonel Plane?"

Broderick shrugged. "Theresa believes his death is related to unpaid debt."

The man narrowed his eyes. He hadn't missed the evasive answer. What Broderick knew and Theresa believed were different answers.

Greystone, however, pounced on the information. "Vincent Drake is who you should search for. He threatened Colonel Plane's life if Theresa didn't pay his debt, and he never showed to receive his payment tonight." He removed a crumpled paper from his pocket, then smoothed it. "This is the note he sent Theresa this morning."

Broderick read what he could as the brief note passed by him. *Pay or the colonel will,* then *Dirk's Saloon.*

One did not easily forget the scarred face of Vincent Drake, and not once in Broderick's masquerading as a criminal had the man shown that face in the saloon. Given the hostile nature toward outsiders, Dirk's made an odd choice of location.

"And you took the payment alone?" Detective Hall sounded as skeptical as Broderick felt.

"Drake is dangerous. I left Theresa behind and took my manservant with me."

"I'll need his name and a written statement." Detective Hall turned back to Broderick. "Where might I contact you if I have further questions, Mr.—"

"Brody Smith. I lodge at Catherine's Boarding House off George Street."

The man no doubt already knew Broderick's real identity, courtesy of Lydia, but he hoped he would play along in front of Greystone for now. Hall frowned, a myriad of questions obvious on his face.

"More like Cat's Den of Iniquity." Greystone sneered. "I suppose we know what kind of man you are."

"A cheap room with pleasant entertainment is all any man desires."

"And you say Colonel Plane contacted you?" Detective Hall's brow furrowed.

"When a man is desperate, he will reach out to even his most despised enemy." And enemies they had been, from the first time Broderick confronted Colonel Plane about his lack of care for Theresa until he demanded Broderick rescue her. For the latter, he could find a place of respect for the man.

"Thank you for your time, Mr. Smith. I'll be in contact." Hall gave a firm handshake. "Edward, please escort Mr. Smith out."

"My pleasure." Knuckles cracked before bear paws clawed Broderick's shoulder.

Broderick shook off Greystone's grip and led the way down the hall. He paused at the parlor door and took one last look at Theresa. Dark, wet hair, now completely free of blood, hung straight as Lydia ran a comb through it. Her closed eyes and pinched lips revealed her discomfort as Dr. Pelton hunched over her palms. Each plink of glass into a metal dish drove a shard into his soul. She didn't deserve this.

"I shouldn't have encouraged you to dance with Mr. Darlington." Lydia set the comb aside and began braiding. "I told him to leave the moment I heard he accused you of being a criminal."

Broderick flinched at the reminder the wolf had found his prey. No matter who protected her or how she hid, Darlington would hunt down every detail of Theresa's life—including their connection. Broderick's career and her freedom were both at stake. He had to find that evidence and arrest the production firm before Darlington ruined both their lives.

A hand grabbed his collar and shoved him forward. Broderick could count only a few men he truly disliked, but Edward Greystone ranked at the top of the list. Leaving Theresa to his care was the last thing Broderick wanted, but the Peltons would protect her. For now, he had a murderer to pursue.

The door slammed behind his exit, followed by the resounding click of the lock.

CHAPTER II

FROST GLISTENED OFF GRAVESTONES AND snow crunched underfoot as Theresa trudged with Louis to the plot being prepared for Grandfather. Eight days since she entered this colorless, lonely world. One week of a lifetime to come. How would she endure the knowledge she was the last—the end of a crumbling legacy?

God, why? Why would You let him die?

The bite of bitter wind and the scrape of shovels breaking through the frozen ground spoke in God's place.

Louis stopped at the base of the path that wound its way to where the workers dug. "Are you sure you want to do this now?"

Want? Of course not. No one wants to chisel the final date of a loved one onto their tombstone.

"No, but I need some time alone. The Peltons and Halls are smothering me with their attention, Edward's demanding we marry, and the police have so many questions." The only one who wasn't bothering her was the one man she wished to see more than anyone. She rubbed her temples, but it did little to alleviate her headache.

Louis patted her shoulder and gave a sympathetic grimace. "I'm sorry, love. Go easy on them, though. They want what's best for you, especially that man of yours. The comfort a husband can provide is far different from a fiancé. I'd be doing the same thing were it my Mary." He handed her the necessary tools. "I'll send the boys on a coffee break and give you your privacy."

She gripped the chisel and blinked back tears. Louis may be right about Edward, but that didn't mean she was ready to marry. Not yet. Not now.

The gravediggers abandoned their shovels, and she stiffened. To see their looks of pity would be her undoing, but to avoid their glances would be weak. Grandfather disdained weakness. She raised her chin to look each man in the eye. With a fortifying breath, she managed a smile and polite "Thank you" for their hard work. They mumbled their condolences and shuffled past. Though tears threatened, they did not fall. Grandfather would be proud.

She waited until the group crossed the main path before turning to the task at hand. For the next two hours, she knelt before the tall obelisk surrounded by muddied snow and chiseled away the marble. A replica of Grandfather's Medal of Honor filled the empty space next to Grandma's engraved flowers. Her final gift to the man who'd been difficult to live with but loved her in his own way.

"Forgive my intrusion, but I thought you might need a cup of hot coffee."

Theresa startled at Nathaniel Cosgrove's voice and shifted to face the man who'd once been Broderick's favorite older brother. Nathaniel stood with one hand shoved into his muddied groundskeeper coat pocket. The other extended a ceramic mug, the contents inside steaming. His insecure stance and confident tone were at odds with each other, much like the strange sense of solace and anxiety she felt in his presence.

"Thank you." She accepted the mug but continued to stare at the pariah of the Cosgrove family. Grandfather probably clawed at his coffin knowing the man who'd thrown her into the river and nearly killed her six years ago stood not three feet from her. While she'd managed to extend forgiveness eventually, Grandfather never had.

Nathaniel stepped back to the foot of the grave and examined her work. "What will you do now?"

As she considered his question, the coffee warmed her throat and forged a path to her stomach that expanded to push back the cold.

Tomorrow, she would don her black-dyed uniform and give a farewell salute to the grandfather she loved with all her being. After that? Life would drag on, with or without her participation. Best to gain control before someone else did.

"It's time to move back home. I need to evaluate my current situation and make plans for the future."

Nathaniel said nothing, but his eyebrows drew together. He had the good sense not to argue with her. Too bad the same could not be said for the others in her life. Regardless, the time had come. At home, she would be Commander in Chief. There she could grieve in solitude, wrapped in the physical presence of her memories. A cardinal landed on Grandfather's obelisk as if giving approval to her plan.

Nathaniel cleared his throat. "Stay with my family in Philadelphia. They may not welcome me, but they'll always be there for you. Broderick might show up, and you two could make amends."

"Broderick is here." And he would leave as soon as he concluded his case. Maybe he already had. A pang of disappointment pushed a tear free, and she swiped a loose lock of hair aside to mask its appearance.

"Good. Then you two can marry."

"No." She pushed from the ground, the tenderness of her palms reminding her of the weakness she'd shown in Broderick's arms. "Our chance has passed."

Nathaniel assisted her to her feet. "That's not true. Not if you don't allow my foolishness to continue to drive you apart."

"Broderick made his choice. He could have stayed, but he left."

"He wouldn't have left if I hadn't—"

"The guilt for Broderick's absence is his alone. Yes, you made a terrible mistake by joining those counterfeiters, and yes, I almost died because you needed an escape—"

Nathaniel winced.

Theresa gentled her tone. "But you need to forgive yourself. You said you planned to let me go on the other side, and I believe you. If I hadn't fought back, your partners wouldn't have forced you to choose between shooting me or throwing me in the river. You did what you thought best. Neither of us could know I would nearly drown before Broderick reached me."

"I should never have gotten involved."

"No, you shouldn't have, but we all sin. What matters now is you are not the same man you were. It might have taken four years in prison to become that changed man, but you are forgiven. Forgive yourself, and then go seek forgiveness from your family. Take it from a girl who has no one. Family is a precious gift."

She moved past Nathaniel, then pressed kisses on her parents' headstones before marching down the path despite the twinge in her ankle and foot. Time to go home and cherish what she had left of her family. Death may have robbed the house of their presence, but her family resided there in her memories. She could never live anywhere else.

Nathaniel called to her as she reached the main path, "If ever you need anything, you know where to find me."

There was no point in responding. If she needed something, she would get it for herself.

"Brody, sweetheart." Cat's voice purred from the other side of the door as Broderick climbed through the window of his rented room. "I have a message for you. A note. Let me in so I can deliver it properly."

Not a chance. The day had been long enough without parrying her advances. He closed the window and rubbed his eyes. "Slide it under the door."

"Uh-uh. You want it? You have to retrieve it."

Smoke from the saloon clung to his hand after raking it through his hair. Bed called to him. Twenty-four hours of hunting information without a wink of sleep, and still, he had nothing. Cat's message probably wouldn't add anything new.

After a pause, she added, "Grimm had a bottle of whiskey and revealed a secret."

If she weren't his most reliable informant, he'd have abandoned this place within the first week. All right, he'd play her game. Broderick unlocked the door and cracked it open, but Cat wasn't satisfied. She bumped the door with her ample hips and entered with a seductive sway and a cloud of perfume.

Her fingers wriggled their way into his. "Come now, puppet. Wouldn't you prefer to search for the note?"

Heat radiated up his neck as he yanked free of her grasp. "My message, please."

She kicked the door shut and sauntered over to his bed. "Information ain't free, sweetheart. Why not get a little enjoyment out of your coin?" The bed creaked under her weight as she stretched across it.

"Business is my only pleasure." He folded his arms and leaned against the door. Getting any closer would fuel her schemes.

"Oh, I'm all business." A wicked grin twisted her lips. "You won't get what I know unless you give me what I want. And I want you."

"I'm already taken."

Her eyes narrowed, and her lips pursed. "Whoever she is, she must not know you live with the pleasure of sixteen women. How unfortunate it would be for her to make that discovery."

"Blackmail doesn't suit you, Cat. I'll give you the usual wage for the note. Double if I find it useful to my case. Triple if you stop trying to entice me into bed." He held the bills aloft.

She sat up and frowned. "So you're not worried about me telling your woman?"

"Not even a little bit."

Her gaze flitted between Broderick and the money. "Fine." She plucked the note from her bodice and tossed it halfway between them.

He retrieved the folded paper from the floor and flipped it open.

Coppers getting close. Plans on hold. No contact. —F

Great, after a week of placating Fitz and worming his way back into his good graces, the ring members were spooked. He crumpled the paper.

"Bad news?" Cat's eyes twinkled with knowledge. "What a pity."

He flipped the usual wage toward her and shoved the rest of the wad back into his coat pocket with the note. "Now, what's this about Grimm?"

"Quit standing so far away, and I'll share what he let slip to Nelly." She patted the edge of the bed and smiled.

The viper knew how to play her game well. Broderick flipped his one chair around and scooted it against the bedframe. Using its high back as a barrier to her planned advances, he rested his arms across the top.

Undeterred, she leaned closer. "I do so love a challenge, and you, sir, will be my greatest conquest."

"Your information, Catherine."

"Soon." She wrapped her arms around his neck and nibbled at his ear.

He jerked free of her grasp. "No touching or no money."

She folded her arms. "Then I want all that money you waved in my face."

"It's yours, but I remove a random bill every time you touch me." He withdrew the wad and pinched the largest denomination.

Cat angled against the wall and glared. "Grimm stumbled in a few hours ago. It seems they've lost the fifties plates, and his boss is killing mad. If they aren't found and completed by the end of the month, someone will pay."

This was new information. "Any idea where the plates are?"

"The engraver had them last, but he's dead now." That confirmed Colonel Plane's role in the production firm. "Grimm has his suspicions, but he didn't say where." She reached for the money, and he pulled it away.

"You know more than you're telling me."

When she continued to wait for payment in silence, he handed her half the money and pocketed the rest.

"I told you what you wanted to hear."

"Yes, but not everything you know. Partial information, partial pay."

She folded her arms like a thwarted child. "He also said they will force some girl to make new ones if they don't find them. That's it. The fool passed out. Didn't even have the price he promised Nelly."

Broderick went to the door and tossed the remaining bills into the hall. Cat scrambled from the bed, hissing at him as she passed. Once clear, he secured the door.

Sleep would have to wait. That "some girl" had to be Theresa. The notes Dr. Pelton sent indicated she was still staying with Lydia, but how safe could she be? Though cleared by the Chief of Police as trustworthy, Detective Hall was too busy to protect her. Broderick would have to enlist help. The clock hands blurred under his scrutiny—four in the afternoon. Isaacs should still be in the office. Now to get there undetected.

He opened the window, and a blast of cold air revived his senses. The tail Fitz hired to follow him must be somewhere in the alley. A girl giggled nearby, followed by the deep murmurs of a man. Broderick slipped out the window and peeked around the corner. There he was. Distracted by one of Cat's girls near the side door. For once, Broderick appreciated the diversions a brothel could provide.

It didn't take much stealth to make it to the main roads, but he still kept a watchful eye for a second tail. Nearly twenty minutes later, he made it to the post office without an indication he'd been followed. After the hours he'd been awake already, Fitz would never expect him to be anywhere but bed. Only by the strength of God and the hope of coffee did he still stand.

To Broderick's chagrin, Darlington manned the office.

"It's about time you reported in." Darlington scowled from his place at the desk. "Although you could have spared time for a bath. You smell like horse manure. There's soap by the basin. I suggest you use it."

Broderick ignored the directions and went straight for the coffeepot. The brew smelled strong enough to burn a hole through the floor. Good. Maybe he'd stay awake long enough to ensure Theresa's safety.

"Discover anything of use?" Darlington set his paper aside.

Not much that he wanted to admit to Darlington. Colonel Plane's involvement with the ring ran deep. Once the pride of the Plane name, the printshop had been transformed into a mere front for the ring's activity. How many men on the payroll were involved—and which ones—he couldn't determine. From the moment Grimm let the location of the counterfeit operations slip, Fitz had kept Broderick busy far from the printshop. Until he could get physical evidence to convince the police, they couldn't petition for a warrant. Darlington would relish his failure in obtaining proof. He had to find a legitimate way into that printshop.

Broderick took several drinks before answering. "You'll find it all in my report."

"And where is that?"

"I haven't written it yet." He poured a second cup. "Where's Isaacs?"

"Raiding Vincent Drake's apartment, but you would know that if you'd checked in."

Broderick clamped down on a yawn. "Fitz has me running errands for the ring nonstop. When I'm not, I have a tail."

"Sounds like they don't trust you. I thought you were good."

Broderick took another sip and let the liquid scald the reply from his tongue. "Any progress on your end?"

"We believe a dispute over counterfeiting operations led to Colonel Plane's death. Hall found large quantities of counterfeits hidden in the colonel's office along with the tools necessary for engraving plates."

"Were plates found?"

"No, but I'm confident Drake stole them when he murdered Colonel Plane." Darlington's smug smile needled Broderick's raw nerves.

"Why Drake? He's a creditor."

"With ties to the counterfeiting ring. Evidence suggests he distributes large sums of counterfeits through the loans he gives. It's an obvious connection you overlooked."

Isaacs and Detective Hall entered the office, saving Broderick from a retort about jumping to conclusions. Broderick blew out a relieved breath at Hall's presence. If they had to partner with the police department because of the Secret Service's inability to carry out warrants or make arrests, Detective Hall was the best choice. At the private meeting with Dr. Pelton after Colonel Plane's murder, Hall revealed he was familiar with Colonel Plane's suspicious activities and already investigating them. His vested interest in Theresa's well-being due to his wife's relationship with her made it easy to convince the man to keep Broderick's connection to the Plane family quiet—for now.

"Glad you're here, Cosgrove. Saves me the trouble of tracking you down." Isaacs plunked the torn, maroon-and-brown carpetbag Broderick recognized from the cemetery onto the desk in front of Darlington. "Is this the bag Fitz had?"

Broderick nodded and turned to pour more coffee. "I suppose it was in Drake's apartment?"

"Yes, but he's still missing. No one has seen or heard from him since before the colonel's murder." Hall extracted the bag from Darlington's grip and passed it to Broderick.

Broderick rummaged through the misprinted and half-printed counterfeit notes inside. Corrections filled the margins of an unfinished fifty and identified Colonel Plane as the engraver. It was evidence, but nothing pointed solidly to a connection with Vincent Drake. For all they knew, Drake merely stole the bag from Fitz somewhere along the way.

"We also found this in his apartment." Isaacs fished a ring from his pocket.

Broderick blinked. It couldn't be. He lifted the opal ring and examined it. There was no denying it was the one he designed for Theresa. It took over a year to earn the cost of having it made. How had it landed in Drake's possession?

"We confirmed Drake doesn't have a woman in his life, and"—Isaacs glanced at Broderick—"Detective Hall recognized it as belonging to Theresa Plane."

Darlington jumped from his seat. "I knew she was involved."

No surprise there. He'd told Broderick and Isaacs about his "visit" with her at the ball the next day, when he learned of the murder. Isaacs had no choice but to investigate Theresa as Darlington asked.

"Don't jump to conclusions." Hall folded his arms. "Theresa told Lydia she gave it to Drake to pay toward a debt. It's not evidence of involvement with the counterfeiting ring, merely confirmation of her story."

So that's what she threw at Drake.

"You're sure this ring is hers?" Darlington asked. "Any woman could have one like it."

Hall responded. "It was one of a kind, and she wore it every day until last year."

"Did she specify what that debt was?" Darlington asked.

"No, but Drake wasn't the only creditor."

"I'll bet you he's the only creditor with ties to the counterfeiters. That ring could have been payment for work done."

"Why pay Drake when the corrections clearly identify Colonel Plane as the engraver?" Isaacs voiced the question before Broderick could.

"Engravers aren't the only ones who get paid," Darlington said. "She could be paying Drake for supplies or to double-cross Colonel Plane. As a woman with a criminal record, her word can't be trusted."

Broderick almost dropped the ring. Since when? And for what?

Hall matched Darlington's defensive pose. "The circus dropped those charges and allowed her to purchase the goat."

Tipsy. No wonder she hadn't expounded on the rescue mission.

"She's no counterfeiter." Hall's tone dared anyone to argue with him.

"As Miss Plane is your wife's friend, you cannot be an impartial judge. Thank you for your cooperation, Detective Hall. We will take it from here." Darlington gestured to the door.

"Murder is out of your jurisdiction, and it's not yet clear if Drake was a counterfeiter. I could block access to Theresa as a witness, and it would be within my department's rights."

Broderick tempered the smile that threatened to expose his pleasure at Hall's gumption.

Darlington's nostrils flared. "I can fight it."

"My placing an officer at her door until you win could derail your investigation."

The threat would have been perfect if the circumstances were different. Broderick stepped forward. "It's too late for that. I received word the counterfeiting ring is spooked."

"All the more reason to stop Miss Plane before she destroys the evidence. If she hired Drake, he may have given the plates to her."

"The only thing in danger of being destroyed is her." Broderick tempered his tone lest Darlington detect his personal concern. "Grimm said they'd force her to engrave new plates if the others weren't found." Darlington may be as bullheaded as God made, but he wasn't stupid. Willing participants did not need to be threatened into compliance.

"That doesn't mean she's innocent."

"Innocent or not, the woman bears watching." Isaacs stared at the floor as if piecing together a plan. "For her safety and for the sake of the case."

Hall pivoted toward the door. "I'll take her to my house for safekeeping."

Broderick tensed. "I thought she was already staying with you."

"The stubborn woman is moving back to Plane Manor today."

Of course she was. Someone had to talk some sense into her, and it was apparent Hall had already failed.

Isaacs stilled Broderick as he strode past. "We can't impede her freedom. Living in that house gives her access to the counterfeiting ring."

"And the ring to her." Broderick grit his teeth. Had Isaacs forgotten whose side he was on?

"Which is why we need someone to get close to her. To earn her trust." Isaacs blocked Hall's attempt to open the door. "Miss Plane won't talk to you since she discovered you were investigating her grandfather. Isn't that right?"

"She'll talk to Lydia."

"Will she? I imagine Miss Plane understands a wife's loyalty to her husband is stronger than loyalty to a friend. No, she'll be too guarded to reveal anything of importance. We need someone else."

Isaacs rubbed his chin as if in deep contemplation, but Broderick knew better. The Charmer was working his magic to ensure Broderick was the chosen man.

Isaacs turned to Darlington. "She'll be leery of a stranger like me, and she hates you."

The man grunted but didn't deny the statement.

Isaacs completed his effort. "That leaves Cosgrove."

That irrefutable logic left Darlington silent. Hall was not as easily convinced. He dissected Broderick with his gaze. Broderick had the distinct feeling Hall knew more about him than Broderick knew about Hall. Given that the detective's information likely came from Theresa through Lydia, what he knew couldn't be to Broderick's benefit. Neither would his unfortunate odor of bar and brothel.

Broderick gripped his rock and held Hall's gaze. "I assure you, Miss Plane will be protected and treated with the utmost respect."

"A man is judged by the promises he keeps." Or breaks, the unspoken accusation in Hall's gaze indicted.

"I understand."

His stiff stance eased. "Then I'd hurry. She's likely already there, and Mrs. Hawking is away, visiting her sister. Lydia has sent for her, but we don't know how soon she'll arrive."

Broderick left before further objections could be raised. Theresa was foolish to return home, but he well understood her reasons, flawed as they were. No argument or person could budge her from the sanctuary of her grief. If he wanted to protect her, he needed to convince her to let him in.

Chapter 12

Theresa stood with her valise in the cold, hand hovering over the door handle. The concept of coming home had been easy when she'd fought with Lydia, but now reality stood in stark contrast to the vision she'd created in her head. The black crepe wreath rustled in the breeze as a bleak reminder of what lay beyond. Not that she needed it. The memories haunted her even in the sparing moments of sleep. The iron scent of blood stung her senses no matter how she tried to cover it with perfume. This was the birthplace of her nightmares, yet she would not, could not, turn back. Not even with Mrs. Hawking absent.

She grasped the handle and turned.

What if the murderer returns?

Lydia's voice inside her head sent chills down her back, and she held the door in place. Drake still evaded arrest. What was to stop him from being inside now? She should turn around and leave. Yet where would she go? Dr. Pelton would try to keep her calm through constant laudanum, a drug she'd come to despise. Lydia would suffocate her with kindness, and Abraham would interrogate her. If she turned to Edward, he'd demand marriage.

No, she couldn't go back. Drake likely had fled the area with no intention of returning. And if he did? Well, she had Grandfather's armory at her disposal. Before courage abandoned her, she pushed.

The door swung open on the creaky hinges she'd meant to oil. Darkness cloaked the interior, and the air tasted stale. She swallowed past the rock in her throat and forced her feet forward. Loneliness echoed with every tentative step across the wooden floor. Everything stood where she'd left it. Her mother's favorite painting next to the stairs, askew as it was often wont to do. The vase on the entryway table with the crack down the side hidden by silk flowers and draped green fabric. A knitted blanket from the grandmother she barely remembered folded over the back of the sofa visible through the ajar parlor door. The house remained the same, yet everything had changed.

As she deposited her bag on a chair in the foyer, she heard no hum of voices drifting from the servants' quarters. No banging around in the kitchen. No clipped orders from Grandfather demanding she close the door. Only a silence that made her ears ring like the aftereffects of a fired cannon. Tears built pressure behind her eyes and threatened to break her carefully maintained dam. She closed her eyes and constricted her chest until the urge passed. Crying fixed nothing. It only left her pained and empty. A shattered vessel unable to hold its worth.

The shock of a cold breeze at her back forced her to obey Grandfather's forever silenced command. With a deep breath and squared shoulders, she locked the door, then lit a wall sconce. Light followed the hiss of gas and illuminated the clock purposely stopped at the estimated time of Grandfather's death, as tradition dictated. What would she give to have one more minute with him? To have answers. A chance to hear him say he loved her. But it was not to be.

She turned, but the rest of the foyer stood just as grim. Portraits were covered in crepe or laid facedown—an act of superstition by Mrs. Hawking to protect her soul from Grandfather's haunting, no doubt. Theresa righted one and made it to the base of the stairs before the memories strangled her breath. Silent shots exploded. Blood, though long washed away, slicked her hands. Grandfather's pale and purple-blotched face declared her failure.

Cold from the banister filtered through her glove as she gripped it for support.

He's dead because of you.

You should have delivered those paintings sooner.

You should have been the one to face Drake. To find him wherever he was.

She dropped to her knees. A sharp-edged step bit into her forehead as she leaned forward. How would she live with herself? Live with the knowledge his death was all her fault?

Quit feeling sorry for yourself and get up, soldier.

Grandfather's command at her parents' deaths echoed into the future. He was right, even in death. If memories and nightmares too gruesome for polite company had not cowed the real soldiers in her life, then she must not succumb either. Her arms and legs shook as she rose and stared up the twenty-three steps to the second floor—dark and dismal as her future.

Lord, please don't continue to forget me. Help me.

The cold ache did not fade. No supernatural peace or comfort descended upon her. Wasn't God supposed to be near to the brokenhearted?

Where is my Shepherd? You promised to be here.

Still, no comfort came. Her Shepherd was long gone. He'd realized she wasn't worth His care and culled her from the herd. She would have to face the stairs and every obstacle beyond alone.

Broderick scanned the boundaries of Plane Manor. Securing it would require some ingenuity. Windows graced every room on the ground floor, the exceptions the kitchen and servants' sitting room at the back of the home. Most of the second-floor windows were entirely inaccessible, but the maple tree outside Theresa's window posed more danger than a fall. He was no tree trimmer, but if the carriage house still housed a hacksaw, he would remove all the branches that could give access. Securing the exterior shutters would be his first priority after he checked on Theresa.

Did she already regret her decision? Knowing her, it didn't matter if she did. Stubbornness stronger than a general's steeled her. Once committed, she would not turn back, an admirable quality and a terrible nuisance all at the same time. Given a choice, he would pack her up, escort her to his mother, and promptly leave her in his family's protective care. With his three detective brothers, two sisters trained in self-defense, and parents who could scare off the most courageous villains, Theresa would never have to fear again.

Too bad it was a useless fantasy.

He lifted his hand to knock on the front door but froze before his knuckles made contact. Gouges splintered the frame around the handle and latch. Missing chunks of wood littered the ground. Hairs pricked on the back of his neck as he fingered the crack between door and frame.

Trouble had beat him to Theresa.

With supplies and lantern set aside, Broderick yanked his Colt free and stood at the side of the door. *God, please don't let there be a body.* He flung the door open, and it bounced off the wall. Good. No one lurked there.

His gaze swiveled high and low, searching the dark as he slipped into a safe corner. Nothing moved. No human-shaped shadows loomed. He waited and listened for any hint of another person. Theresa should have responded to the crashing noises in her foyer, but not a floorboard squeaked.

Backstepping to the porch, he retrieved the lit lantern and brought it in. A lump at the base of the stairs flamed orange. He moved forward and grimaced. A body, but not Theresa's. Feathers fluttered with the breeze, giving life to the headless bird. Poor Cordon Bleu. Her clawed foot pinned a paper to the floor, and scraggly letters were written in blood.

You're next.

Chills battled his boiling blood for dominance. No one threatened his Theresa.

A gun cocked near the top of the stairs, and Broderick ducked into the parlor for cover.

"Declare yourself." Theresa's shaky words released a breath he hadn't realized he held. He may be relieved, but he wasn't foolish. Little doubt a gun in Theresa's hand equaled sure-fire injury. The colonel would have taught her well.

"It's Broderick," he called from the safety of the parlor.

Her sigh echoed, followed by the creaking of steps. He chanced a peek around the door. Her hair fell in disheveled waves around her shoulders, and red lines creased her face as if she'd been sleeping. He cringed at the way she carried the rifle. If she jostled her grip, the thing was liable to go off. If she saw the chicken . . .

"Wait there. Let me come to you." He stepped from the protection of the wall.

"Should I uncock the gun first?"

A wise idea. "Do you know how?"

Her scrunched nose matched her brow. "Push the hammer thing back down?"

So Colonel Plane expected his granddaughter to act like a soldier but never taught her how to use a gun.

Maybe the chicken would convince her to leave. Her safety would be easier to ensure at Lydia's home. Until she sneaked out.

Lord, help me protect this woman.

"Just set the rifle on the stair as gently as you handled that hawk with the broken wing."

She nodded and twisted around, causing the barrel to swing to his position. A quick prayer of thanks escaped his lips when it safely moved past. Once set on the stair, she moved away, and he took the steps two at a time. The Spencer carbine lay half-cocked and unusable. She hadn't known how to pull it back all the way. Praise God, she'd not faced an actual intruder. He ejected the round, then reset the hammer and dumped the other six rounds into his hand from the tube in the butt.

"You took ten years off my life, Theresa."

"Good." Though she smiled, her pale face and dark-circled eyes revealed weariness. "Care to explain why you barreled through my door like a bank robber?"

"Not particularly."

She frowned at his response until a yawn forced its release. Thank goodness he'd taken the time to change and quickly wash up before coming. If she'd smelled him beforehand, she'd have asked questions he'd rather not answer.

After uncovering her yawn, she spoke. "They sent you to coerce me back, didn't they?"

"No." But that didn't mean he wouldn't try.

He glanced at the still-open door. That needed to be dealt with, along with the hundred other tasks required to secure the house.

"Come with me." Broderick clasped her elbow. "We need to talk."

He guided her down, blocking her view of Bleu as best he could and then kicking the chicken under the foyer table when he reached the bottom.

Theresa's head tilted to see around him. "What was that?"

He shifted. "Nothing."

"That didn't sound like nothing." She started to step around him.

"Do you have any coffee? I have news about the case."

She spun back. "What news?"

"Coffee first."

Bless her curiosity. After lifting a valise from a nearby chair, she almost ran down the hall to the kitchen, completely missing the dead bird in her haste. Banging pans echoed as he retrieved the poor creature and chucked it into a bush out front. He would bury Bleu later.

After cleaning the mess, he retrieved his pail of tools and slid the foyer table in front of the door. He entered the kitchen, and the rich aroma of fresh coffee beans permeated the air. Theresa bustled about, also throwing together a quick meal. "Lydia insisted I bring a loaf of bread, and we'll use some of Mrs. Hawking's canned preserves."

How often had he come home to a cold, empty apartment and imagined this scene?

Theresa's hair tumbled in waves about her waist and begged to be smoothed beneath his fingers. She peered into the firebox, and then her lips puckered as she tapped the edge of the empty coal bin. How he'd missed that face. If life had been different, if his brother hadn't betrayed them, he would be free to wrap his arms around her waist, pull her close, and tickle the soft place of her neck with his beard until she giggled.

But he could not. Her long-term safety depended on his distance. Moments like this, watching her outwit the reluctant fire, would have to satisfy the emptiness he endured without her.

She shoved in heaps of kindling and blew gently until flames licked the edges. Once satisfied, she added pieces of scrap wood. Her eyes reflected the dancing light as she watched for a moment more and then banged the door shut. Her triumphant smirk brought him back to the days of sneaked kisses. Those were the best—filled with both the danger of being caught and the delight of passion.

"What?" Theresa had caught him staring. "Do I have soot on my face?" She swiped her cheek, putting streaks where none had been.

"A little by your nose." He squeezed the rock in his pocket rather than touch her. As she wiped at it with the corner of her dirty apron, he asked, "How can I help?"

"Tell me what news you've discovered."

"Coffee first."

She harrumphed, then poured from the coffeepot before plunking a mug on the table in front of him. "There, coffee. Now talk."

A glance at the liquid confirmed what he already knew. "But the water is cold, and I can see clear through to the bottom."

She folded her arms and lifted her chin. "You didn't qualify it must be a good cup of coffee. I've held up my end of the bargain, and it's time for you to do the same."

The little minx always loved finding a good loophole. "We have a solid suspect in your Grandfather's murder."

"Vincent Drake. I already know. What else?"

"I gave you news, but you didn't qualify it should be new news." He couldn't help the smirk that followed.

"Bah!" She spun from him and yanked the storage closet door open. Muttering under her breath, she reached on tiptoes.

"Allow me." He came from behind and leaned past her, steadying her with one hand on her back while reaching with his other. "What do you need?"

"I can get the plates myself."

Sure she could, but then he wouldn't have the excuse to be near her. The warmth of her body sent distracting tingles through his arms. How long could he prolong this moment without raising suspicion he was enjoying it? Not nearly long enough.

He stepped back and handed her the plates. "We found the bag Fitz had at the cemetery. It contained evidence your grandfather engraved banknote plates for counterfeiters."

Her back thudded against the still-open door, and she clutched the plates to her chest as if they would shield her. After a long silence, she squared her shoulders. "Tell me everything."

Smoke from the stove rescued him from answering. He left her standing in the closet and removed the iron grate. Green wood hissed and sputtered smoke, but the flames had all but disappeared, much like his ability to speak. A hand came to rest between his shoulders, but he could not look at her. How could he tell her they'd been betrayed again? This time the betrayal entangled her with determined criminals and brought her under the suspicion of a man just as threatening. Maybe more so.

Chapter 13

Whatever Broderick knew, it had to be bad. The tension in his muscles could shatter stone. Theresa massaged his back in little circles, the rigidity of her own growing with each moment of silence. Danger from creditors hadn't ended with Grandfather's murder. She wasn't foolish enough to believe that. However, Broderick's brazen entrance and struggle to share what he'd learned indicated more than debt threatened her future.

"Please, Broderick. I need to hear it from you."

His shoulders slumped in surrender. Her hand followed his turn until it rested over his heart's steady beat. As long as she could feel his heartbeat, she could face whatever lay ahead.

"I'm sorry." His words were husky as he withdrew, leaving her bereft of his touch.

Admittedly, that was proper. They weren't married, and she was engaged to another man. Broderick couldn't be her shelter. She needed the information so she could protect herself and not depend on others.

He poured another mug of barely coffee and then gestured for her to take a seat on a stool. "I work as an undercover operative for the Secret Service. Your grandfather engraved banknote plates for a counterfeiting ring responsible for nearly three hundred thousand dollars' worth of bogus money."

She dropped onto the low stool. Three hundred thousand dollars in counterfeits? Broderick had to be mistaken. With that sort of money, they wouldn't have been struggling to survive these last years. No, she refused to believe it—no matter how much worry niggled at her mind.

Broderick took a deep breath and held her gaze. "With your grandfather dead, there's reason to believe his partners will try to force you to finish the work."

The niggling grew, and she looked away, but that didn't quiet her thoughts. Grandfather encouraged her to engrave, pushed her until her skill nearly matched his own. She'd done it to please him, but in the end it meant nothing to him. No wonder he'd court-martialed her when he discovered she'd taken money from his hidden stash to pay for groceries.

Her stomach twisted until the meager scraps she'd managed to eat that morning rose to her throat. How could he do this to them? To *her*? Hadn't he loved her at all? Or had he merely loved what she could provide in his quest for financial gain? And now that he was gone, his partners planned to use her as well?

Never again would she be a victim. "Teach me how to shoot."

"You're safer with Lydia."

"If you think a few threats will scare me from my home, you're mistaken."

"These are no idle threats, Theresa." Broderick scrubbed a hand over his face. "They broke in while you were sleeping. They killed Bleu and left her on your foyer floor with a note."

Her mind could barely grasp the concept of Bleu's death before Broderick shoved a wrinkled paper into her hand. She stared at the ink. No, not ink. Blood. Only a monster could be so callous.

"You know it must be Fitz or Grimm. Arrest them."

"I can't. Not until we identify the rest of the production firm members. If we arrest them too soon, the others will flee, and you'll still be in danger."

"Grandfather raised me with the heart of a soldier. I will not be cowed." She slid off the stool and moved toward the door. "If you'll excuse me, it appears I need to secure the house."

"Then you won't leave?"

She looked over her shoulder and arched a brow at his grim features. Did he expect her to retreat? "No one, not even skunks like Drake or Grandfather's partners, can chase me off. This is *my* home. My sole connection to family, and I dare anyone to remove me."

Broderick sighed. "I have a few ideas if you're willing to let this skunk help you."

Some of the fire in her veins cooled. He wouldn't fight her. "Given all that's happened, I'll consider you a skunked dog."

He gave one of those dashing smiles that crinkled his eyes and skittered her heart. "At least there is hope the stench will eventually leave."

"Maybe." She gave a saucy grin that quickly faltered.

The stench *would* leave eventually, and him with it.

They quickly ate their bread and preserves, then in the foyer Broderick presented a plan of action along with the tools to complete it, proving he'd known her answer before he arrived. They latched the exterior shutters from the outside and nailed the interior sashes shut. Her maple tree was not the threat he supposed. After all, it had nearly killed her, but she appreciated his attention to detail. Overall, the plan was solid. Everything would be secure once they dealt with the broken door. A shiver coursed down her back. How had she slept through the commotion of someone breaking in?

Broderick knelt by his bucket as he unpacked the tools he'd need. "I'll install a bar across the door, but I'll sleep on the sofa to ensure no one tries again."

Theresa's attention snapped from the gouged frame to Broderick. "What did you say?"

The skunked dog remained kneeling as if he hadn't just suggested they spend the night together. "You heard me."

"You are *not* sleeping in my house!"

"Lydia sent for Mrs. Hawking. When she arrives, she'll ensure all measures of propriety are maintained."

She groaned inwardly. Why hadn't she thought of propriety sooner? Over an hour alone with Broderick, and she hadn't once stopped to consider the consequences. It had been too easy, too natural, to be with him. If Edward discovered this indiscretion, he might drag her off to the preacher. No matter how logical it might be, she could not make such a commitment. Not while grieving, and certainly not while Broderick remained close enough to remind her what she forfeited.

The man could not stay a minute longer. "A servant does not count as a chaperone."

Broderick observed her from his crouched position with a devilish smile. "Mrs. Hawking is an excellent chaperone. It always took incredible ingenuity to escape her watchfulness."

Heat spread from her belly at the reminder of the times they'd sneaked off. Long walks under moonlit skies. Kisses that reached forward to the present to send tingles along her neck. The temptation they barely escaped by the grace of God. How easy it would be to fall back into the comfort of those memories. The comfort of his touch. It was precisely the reason Mrs. Hawking would not be enough.

Theresa twisted her engagement ring instead of thumping reason into his head. "We can't. It isn't right. What will people think? What will Edward think?"

All mirth dropped from his countenance as he rose from the floor and chastely held his hands to his sides. Even so, his smoldering gaze captivated her. If she could breathe, smoke would fill her lungs and suffocate her. Which might be for the best, because right now, she couldn't remember what Edward looked like.

"Hang their thoughts. You're too important to risk losing again. If you stay here, I stay here."

Why on earth could this man not be as ugly as a hairless raccoon and pliable as bread dough? His fierce declaration overpowered her tired resolve, and she drew close enough to feel his breath. She could hand her troubles over to him. Trust him to save and protect her. Allow him to be her hero once again. She tilted her chin, and her gaze fell on his lips. Heaven help her, they were tempting. *Lord, stop my traitorous heart.*

"I'll finish securing the house outside and install the bar when I come back." Broderick turned away, the movement rigid. "Shove the table in front of the door after I leave."

Her muddled brain barely processed the words before he was gone. She closed her eyes and tried to ignore the way her lips burned with forbidden desire. What would she do when Edward arrived to escort her to the funeral tomorrow morning and discovered Broderick had spent the night?

Broderick punched the thick decorative pillow into a more comfortable position and stretched the too-short blanket over his toes. Stupid, stupid, stupid decision. Sleep deprivation must have robbed him of all sensible thought. He would never have demanded to sleep on Theresa's parlor sofa otherwise, even with an armed Mrs. Hawking chaperoning.

Theresa was safer without him there. He saw it reflected in her face at the allusion to what had passed between them so long ago. Felt it as he escaped to the freezing carriage house to cool his thoughts and reestablish his professional frame of mind. This was madness. Cat posed no threat, but Theresa? He should have picked her up, kicking and screaming, and deposited her on Lydia's stoop.

He rolled again, this time losing the blanket to the floor. As he reached to pick it up, Theresa's shrill scream shattered the silence. His hand clasped the familiar grip of his Colt in the same moment he rolled off the couch.

Mrs. Hawking blinked owlishly as he jumped over her bedroll in front of the parlor door. She could hold her own if need be. Theresa couldn't.

Another shriek pierced his heart. He pounded up the steps and threw open the door to Theresa's room, aim directed at the window where an intruder would be.

No one lurked there. Or anywhere else in the room, for that matter.

Theresa shrieked again, sitting straight in her bed. "Breathe! You can't die."

His chest heaved from the exertion as realization dawned. No physical danger elicited such terror. It was worse—a threat from which he couldn't protect her.

Mrs. Hawking bustled past him and guided Theresa to lie back down. "Hush, child. 'Tis nothing but a dream."

Theresa whimpered, drawing him deeper into the room. She needed to be held and comforted.

"It's bad enough you sleep on the sofa. You can't have her bed too. Out! Now!" Mrs. Hawking marched him out the door and slammed it shut once he was clear.

The lock slid into place. He listened a moment longer—Theresa crying out, Mrs. Hawking murmuring. Who would have guessed the jagged woman could speak so gently?

As elusive as sleep had been before Theresa's screams, it would be impossible now. He lit a candlestick from the hall table and plodded downstairs, then toward Colonel Plane's office. No sense in wasting the predawn hours. Mrs. Hawking would likely remain in Theresa's room, freeing him to search the colonel's office. Hall had found counterfeits and engraving tools there, but his men had searched only for evidence pertaining to the murder, and with the Secret Service's inability to get their own warrants, Broderick and Isaacs had been unable to come back for a search. There could be more to find.

Someone had cleaned the office. Blood no longer stained the floor. Boards sealed the window to protect against the weather until replaced. Nothing remained of the crime. Broderick walked the perimeter of the room, opening drawers and rifling through them for anything related to counterfeiting. Most drawers held random supplies or old correspondence from the war. He removed each book from a small bookcase and flipped through the pages, looking for anything hidden. Peering under rugs and behind old portraits revealed no secrets. Other than what had already been found, the room was simply a former colonel's retreat from the responsibilities of his granddaughter and a failing printshop.

He dropped into the colonel's desk chair and tapped his chin with tented fingers. "If I were you, where would I hide such pertinent information?"

Somewhere military-related posed the most potential. Not the office, and he'd already scoured the carriage house where Colonel Plane had kept the retired war horses. Did he hide an armory in the house? Theresa would know and probably insist on target practice.

Broderick shook his head and examined the papers from the desk drawers again. Colonel Plane had been a master at writing in code. Perhaps correspondence held the key. Yellowed with age, most were simple notes from home—prayers for safety, pleas to return, death announcements for the colonel's wife and eldest son.

No wonder the man was stoic. These letters were enough to remind Broderick why he could never marry.

The remaining pages were coded beyond understanding.

Coded or not, Colonel Plane would not hide incriminating papers where they could easily be found. The desk must contain a hidden compartment. Broderick examined every joint, hinge, and drawer bottom to no avail. Frustrated, he collected the scattered papers and tapped them into a pile. A small gouge marred the edge of the cherry inset. Using a letter opener, he pried open the inset and discovered a small moleskin journal tucked into a hollowed-out portion. Colonel Plane knew how to hide information well.

Broderick flipped through the pages. Some contained code words and their meanings, others had lines of numbers and arrows. Given the handful of words he recognized, Broderick held the key to ciphered production firm papers. Now he just needed the papers.

The iron knocker on the front door echoed through the house. Broderick glanced at the mantel clock—7:25 a.m. Far too early for visitors. He returned the inset to its place and stowed the code book in his pocket as he stood. The pounding intensified as he neared the door. A glance at the top of the stairs showed Mrs. Hawking with the Spencer Carbine trained at the opening. Good. He could count on her for backup. He drew his revolver, then shoved the table aside and opened the door to gray morning light.

And Edward Greystone's fist.

Broderick ducked and prepared for another swing as Goliath eyed him from head to toe. Other than his boots, Broderick was fully clothed. Thank the Lord for that. Anything less, and the giant might outright shoot him.

Greystone shoved the door further open and grabbed Broderick by the shirt. "Where is Theresa? What have you done to her?"

Broderick slid his Colt back into its holster. As tempting as it would be to shoot the firebrand, concern for Theresa's safety drove Greystone's actions.

"She's still resting," Mrs. Hawking called, rifle still aimed. "Come back in an hour."

Greystone's eyes narrowed on him. "Why are you here?"

The door creaked behind Mrs. Hawking, and Theresa stepped around, tying her wrapper closed. Broderick's mouth went dry, and he dropped his gaze. It was hard enough keeping his thoughts professional without her making an appearance in her nightclothes. Ducking his head did not erase the memory of a pale, vulnerable Theresa crying out.

Her croaky voice brought him back to Greystone's accusatory question. "I hired him for protection."

"Protection?" His fist tightened on Broderick's shirt. "I'm supposed to be your protection."

"Now is not the time to discuss this." Mrs. Hawking's tone warned against arguing. "Miss Theresa, go to your room and dress properly."

In his mind, Broderick could see Theresa's frown as she released a loud breath. "Take them to the kitchen. I'll be down presently."

The door closed, signaling it was safe to look.

Broderick opened his eyes, and a fist connected with his jaw. He flung his arms up to block a second attack and tried to blink Greystone into focus. Another jab, but this time he dodged. He slid too close to allow another punch and jabbed his elbow into the space between neck and shoulder. Greystone dropped to one knee and roared.

"That is enough!"

Though Mrs. Hawking's words echoed throughout the foyer, her rifle encouraged obedience. Broderick retreated several steps with hands raised. Greystone launched toward Broderick but froze when the rifle's barrel pressed into his abdomen.

"I said enough! Now, lead us to the kitchen and behave yourself."

Broderick grinned as Greystone obeyed the order, gun to his back and hands raised in surrender. On many occasions, Mrs. Hawking had been his adversary. What a change to have her an ally.

Once in his shoes, Broderick joined the others in the kitchen. Greystone planted himself against the far wall of the kitchen, arms crossed, and stayed there while Broderick aided Mrs. Hawking in making a simple breakfast with the fresh supplies she'd brought. Silence strained the room until Theresa walked in with the bearing of a soldier, dressed in a black-dyed uniform. Even in the colonel's absence, she tried to fulfill his orders. Too bad the curmudgeon's command hadn't been to live the cared-for life she deserved.

Greystone stomped toward her. "He shouldn't be here."

Theresa winced. "I'm sorry. I know this is upsetting—"

"Upsetting doesn't begin to cover it."

"I had no choice. Someone broke in and killed Cordon Bleu while I slept."

"You should have sent for me." Greystone's voice ricocheted off the walls. "It's my job to protect you, not his." He took a deep breath and rolled his shoulders before continuing in a calmer voice. "This is foolishness. You can't stay here. The pastor will be at the funeral. He'll marry us today."

Broderick bit his tongue to keep from objecting. He couldn't fault Greystone. He'd demand near the same if it were within his right. The conversation wouldn't be happening if he hadn't put Theresa in this position. Nevertheless, he couldn't allow her to feel pressured into a decision. "The mourning period exists for a reason. She shouldn't make life-altering decisions during deep grief."

Greystone lunged at him, but Mrs. Hawking stopped him with the rifle. "None of that."

Theresa's weary voice drew all their attention. "Edward, I've already agreed to marry you. Just not today, nor any day before I feel ready." She rubbed her temple as if a headache pulsed there. "This has nothing to do with Broderick. I just can't. I need time."

"You can't afford to wait." Greystone folded his arms.

That was the wrong thing to say if he wanted to win her over. Broderick watched her face harden as her hand dropped and chin lifted.

"I can and will wait."

He stepped forward undeterred. "You need me. Colonel Plane left you with nothing but debt and no real way to pay it. All that mattered to him was status and his soldiers. He didn't care what happened to you. I'm the only one who can provide what you need."

Greystone's words were worse than a shot in the back and served no purpose but to wound and control her. Broderick clenched his fist and prayed for restraint. He might be able to surrender Theresa to a better man, but Greystone would never qualify.

"My decision is final." Cold steel edged Theresa's tone. "Mrs. Hawking, I will eat breakfast upstairs. Broderick, please see to my animals. Edward, you need to begin your walk to the cemetery if you're to make it on time. After breakfast, I'll hire a hack for the rest of us."

Broderick released a slow breath. It was good to know she could hold her own against the boor's tactics, even though Greystone would likely hire a hack for himself.

Theresa strode from the room like a regal queen, and Mrs. Hawking hit Edward over the head with a broom. "You speak to her like that again, and it will be the rifle you feel. Both of you best find somewhere else to spend your nights. I will protect her." Mrs. Hawking marched out, leaving Greystone and Broderick together.

"Get out, Smith. Theresa is mine."

"She asked for my protection, and I'll not step aside because you say so." If push came to shove, Greystone could overpower him, but Broderick had won more fights with brains than brute strength.

Greystone stepped forward. "I'm not leaving her alone with you. You're manipulating her."

"Yet you're the one using the situation to push marriage when she's not ready." Broderick gestured to the doorway with his Colt. "Now, I believe the lady told you to take a long walk."

Greystone's nostrils flared, and his neck grew red. After a moment, a slow, withering smile curled his blond mustache. "Better watch your step, Smith. I'll fight for her, and I won't fight fair."

Theresa deserved better. Engaging in battle with a jealous fiancé wouldn't help his case, but if it kept her from making the biggest mistake of her life, Broderick would go to war.

CHAPTER 14

THERESA CLUTCHED HER CLOAK AGAINST the rising pain in her chest, eyes fixated on the flag held taut over Grandfather's coffin. It shouldn't be this way. His betrayal should have made saying goodbye easier and freed her from grief's burden. Instead, her body sagged with an invisible weight, and her knees trembled. Two soldiers who once served under Grandfather sidestepped with the flag in hand and snapped to action. Each fold and tuck of the flag squeezed her throat tighter until swallowing became impossible. One soldier approached her with the tri-corner flag, his face stoic, his eyes refusing to meet hers.

Please take it to someone else. Anyone but me.

He didn't hear her silent pleas. Instead, he transferred the heavy triangle into her arms and saluted as she absorbed it into the depths of her cloak, adding its weight to her burden. The pastor's final words mumbled on, incomprehensible, and before she was ready the mourners dispersed. Flanked by Edward and Broderick, she wobbled to the mound of dirt next to the pine casket. How could she miss a man who loved her so little? But she did miss him. She even missed that obnoxious bugle.

Plunging her hand into the frozen clumps of dirt, she tossed a handful into the hole. It fell like the patter of rain on the wood.

"Come, my dear. It's time." Edward's hand lifted her elbow and led her away.

As she turned her back on the mound of dirt, pain radiated from her chest. It was as if the cords that bound her to Grandfather pried her heart from its place. They stretched tight and thin, slicing the tender surface. Slow, shaky breaths were all she could manage as she clutched the flag. Tears hung in the crease of her eyes, unable to fall, but there all the same. Voicing the word *goodbye* would shatter her, so she remained silent and tried not to think of the cords, let alone dwell on them.

But when her feet hit gravel, the final cord snapped. She stumbled as it released her mangled heart. Someone steadied her, but the world blurred beyond recognition. Her family was gone, and she was left to face the wickedness on this earth alone. Her eyes burned with the need to cry, but she had no privacy to do so, and a Plane did not show weakness. She pressed her lips together to keep the sob at bay and the tears in place.

"Excuse me, Miss Plane. I require a moment of your time."

Theresa blinked away the fog to focus on the wiry man with the shrill tone.

Before she could summon her voice, Edward intervened. "Can you not see this is a funeral? Certainly, anything you have to say can wait."

The man pushed a pair of glasses up the bridge of his nose. "I assure you, it cannot."

Edward's attempt to control his temper would have been admirable if it hadn't resulted in a vice grip around her arm. Tingling snakes formed within seconds. She pulled her arm free and passed the flag to his empty hands. A distraction had to be better than this grief.

It took a couple of swallows and a clearing of her throat, but her voice reached an audible volume. "How may I help you, sir?"

"I request a private audience with you." His eyes flickered from Broderick to Edward. They both stood with fierce frowns and wide stances.

"And you are . . ."

He straightened and lifted his nose in the air. "Frederick Townsend, executor of Colonel Plane's will."

"I believe we have an appointment set for next week. We can meet at that time." She stepped around him.

"Not if you wish to save your home."

Could he not wait a single day? The mortgage didn't mature for another year. Perhaps he was concerned about her ability to take over the payments. No easy task but feasible as long as Edward didn't ruin more paintings.

"I believe a bench near the lake will suit our needs, provided my fiancé and friend are within sight." Theresa gestured to a location far enough away to prevent Broderick and Edward from hearing yet allowed them to intervene should the man prove a scoundrel.

He cast another wary glance at her protectors. "Very well."

She led the way, purpose giving her strength. Dexter Mausoleum cast a shadow over her path and her confidence. Would she be able to make the payments on her own? Shaking off the momentary doubt, she took a seat on the iron bench and gestured for Mr. Townsend to join her. Best not to leave him doubting her ability even if she did have concerns. Edward and Broderick hovered a respectful distance, but it wouldn't be long before they inched closer. "Whatever your fears, I assure you, I am capable of taking over the payments."

Mr. Townsend wrung his hands. "It's too late. The bank denied your grandfather's request for an extension on eviction."

Her throat closed off all but a single word. "Eviction?"

"After four months of extensions, they're convinced money for the back taxes and missed payments will never be produced."

What had Grandfather done with the payments they'd scraped together? They shouldn't be behind. The mortgage had always been a priority in their budget.

"They've found a buyer and want you out by the first of the month."

Out by February first? Sixteen days until God succeeded in taking everything from her? There had to be a way to fight this. "But the house is in my name. Can't new terms be agreed upon?"

"I'm afraid not. You must fulfill the loan obligation before the eviction date."

"What is the outstanding balance?"

He shifted uncomfortably. "The amount is $3,967 and a few cents."

Heaven's sake! Had Grandfather made any payments in the last two years? She rubbed her temples, trying to think. She had two minor painting commissions that might pay for her dinner, but she had no savings. Edward and Broderick inched into her peripheral, but she did not want them to know the full extent of her problems.

She lowered her voice and asked, "Is anything of value left to my name?"

"You are the majority owner of the printshop." His meek reply grated her nerves.

Of course Grandfather used everything except that wretched shop as collateral. It was the one thing that rivaled his obsession with his military career. Well, his obsession would have to be her salvation. That shop would provide her with the funds to save her home—even if she had to sell the very building.

"Thank you for this information, Mr. Townsend. I suppose there is no need to meet next week?" He shook his head. "Good. Please inform the bank their buyer will need to find another property. I will have their funds by the first."

His eyes widened, and his hands stilled. "The full amount?"

"The full amount. I give my word."

And a Plane never went back on their word. One way or another, she would have that money.

Chapter 15

Theresa ran a gloved finger across the sill as dawn's glow peeked through the broken shutter slats outside her window. Perfect. No one required the inspection, but a small piece of her found comfort in the routine. After several minutes of intense examination, the room appeared pristine, but just to be sure, she tugged at an imaginary crease in her covers and fluffed the pillow.

Only perfecting her appearance remained. Her boots already shined with fresh blacking, and her wool overskirt lay over her extra petticoats without a wrinkle. Every detail, down to a rogue curl, submitted to her commands. Convincing Mr. Whist to obey would not be as easy. Today would be the greatest test of her upbringing. She opened the door as Mrs. Hawking topped the stairs.

"You're up early." The housekeeper did nothing to hide her surprise.

"It is a quarter past six. Grandfather would have put me in solitary confinement for such tardiness."

Mrs. Hawking gave a curt nod. "Breakfast will be at the table shortly."

Before the woman could pivot, Theresa mimicked Grandfather's authoritative tone. "I'll not be eating breakfast today. I have business that needs my immediate attention. When Edward and Broderick arrive, inform them their presence is not required."

"Where are you going?"

Nowhere that concerned her. The traitor would try to dissuade her or reveal her location to Edward and Broderick. Neither man would support her decision. "I told you, I have business. Once the men leave, see if you can sell the animals, minus Tipsy, to one of the farmers at Findlay Market. Those that can't be sold will need to be given away or released. Then you may have the rest of the day off." Mrs. Hawking opened her mouth to object. "You are dismissed."

Mrs. Hawking schooled her features into stoic compliance. "Yes, little soldier."

The stab of Theresa's nickname strengthened her resolve. She would need to hold on to that persona today. Few men would dare go toe-to-toe with Grandfather, but Mr. Whist was one of them. No doubt, he would see her as nothing more than an annoyance to be bullied into submission. If this plan were going to work, she must prove herself stronger-willed than Grandfather.

Once Mrs. Hawking disappeared downstairs, Theresa pulled a hatbox from under the bed and retrieved the only gun Broderick hadn't managed to confiscate. She rotated the spinney part until the hammer rested on an empty chamber, as Broderick had called it, and then slipped it into a hidden pocket at her waist. It didn't matter what law she broke. She would never go anywhere unarmed again.

By the time she and Blackbeard reached the warehouse district near the river, the sun peeked over buildings, vendors bustled about trying to keep warm, and trains whistled past. Except for a few rare occasions, she'd not worked at the printshop—not since her curves formed and Grandfather declared her a distraction to his men. Distraction or not, she'd make her appearance today. The tall brick building stood between two sets of tracks with filmy windows carefully arranged to capture the most light throughout the day. A swathe of discoloration wrapped around the building's second floor, evidence of its survival from the spring flood.

She guided Blackbeard to the hitching post, and a band tightened around her chest as she dismounted. She could do this. She could march into a man's world and demand her place. No, demands were what toddlers and villains made. She would command it, just like

Grandfather always had. With shoulders back and chest out, she lifted her chin into Grandfather's regal position and stepped through the door with peeling paint.

A grim-faced man slouched over the service counter and sent spittle flying into the corner next to her. "Whatcha want?"

No wonder the printshop struggled. Mr. Whist had less business sense than she imagined if he'd made such a rude oaf the first person a customer met. "That is no way to speak to your new employer. Or to anyone, for that matter. Straighten your posture, and greet me and all customers with a smile, a kind word, *and* correct grammar."

He cracked his neck from side to side and sent another stream past her. "Last I heard, Mr. Whist is the boss, not some chit. You gotta problem? Take it up with him."

"By the end of this day, you will be looking for new employment, sir."

"Not likely, sweetheart."

It was a good thing she couldn't kill him with merely her eyes or she'd be heading to jail. "That is Miss Plane to you."

"Plane, huh?" He gave a twisted smile and gestured for her to pass between him and the counter.

She "accidentally" elbowed him in the gut as she squeezed through the narrow gap. The ogre didn't even have the decency to *oomph*. Firing him would be a pleasure. Too bad not all tasks would be as delightful.

Her to-do list grew as long as the narrow order room where she stood. The place resembled a stable, not a business. Examples of work dangled from insecure clips or were stuck to the floor. Boxes were stacked in haphazard towers that threatened to topple. Reaching the pressroom entrance without stumbling was a feat of skill. She needed an entire day to make it presentable to customers.

Thankfully, the pressroom must have been Grandfather's domain. Organized and clean, it wouldn't take much to make it presentable to potential buyers. A loud steam press occupied nearly the entire back wall, while eight handpresses lined the ground floor's windowed edges. Each station matched the instructions in the handpress manual she'd read last night, but she'd need to do a thorough inspection. With a few minor adjustments and staff reassignments, she might pull off a profitable sale of the business—as long as the financials weren't as bad as Grandfather lamented.

She climbed stairs to the second floor, and all optimism fled. Half-empty drying racks and paper-bearing lines were scattered across the open room. Two gopher boys—instead of the usual six—scrambled around, carrying half tokens of paper ready to be dried. Like her home, the printshop had become a mere shadow of itself.

Male voices carried from the back corner and drew her deeper. A tall man juxtaposed the short man next to him as they leaned over a table. "We'll make more of the old plates." The shorter man raked a hand over a balding spot at the back of his head.

The taller man shook his head. "No one will buy them."

"They will at a discount, and that's better than making no money."

"Practical," Theresa said, interrupting them, "but you won't acquire new or enough business using such methods."

Both men spun around. The tall one hid what must have been a proof behind his back and acknowledged her presence with a respectful nod.

The short one narrowed his eyes and crossed his arms, then spoke to the other man. "You got your orders. Get to it."

This had to be Mr. Whist. Grandfather had been merciless in his snarky references to Mr. Whist's height. He couldn't be more than two inches taller than her, which was quite disadvantageous for a man given her short stature. The taller man rushed past as if the fires of Hades nipped at his heels. Given how Mr. Whist narrowed his hard eyes until they were crinkled slits, he wasn't far from wrong.

"Customers are not allowed up here. I suggest you leave."

Direct and unwelcoming. Not wholly unexpected. She clasped her hands in front of her and offered him a controlled smile. "I assure you I am no customer, Mr. Whist. I'm Theresa Plane and the new majority owner of this shop."

"You have no ownership. The business reverted to me upon Plane's death." Mr. Whist scooped a stack of rolled papers from the table and marched toward the stairs.

He thought to dismiss her so easily? Arrogant man. She followed half a step behind him. "I'm afraid that is not what the will or your contract says."

Mr. Whist ignored her and continued down the crudely repaired stairs.

She followed behind him. "My attorney has reviewed all the paperwork."

When they turned into the pressroom, his pace hastened.

"Ignoring me, Mr. Whist, will not change the fact that I am the legal majority owner of this printshop and have the power to do with it as I please."

Mr. Whist pivoted to face her, and half a dozen pairs of eyes turned their direction. An approaching gopher boy glanced from the crushed papers in his fist to her and then back to Mr. Whist again before scurrying off. *The man's temper is as short as he is.* Grandfather's lamentation rose to mind. It would not do to provoke him. No man wanted to be put in his place by a woman, especially not in front of his peers. Protecting Mr. Whist's pride would go a long way to starting amicably. "Let's discuss our partnership in the office, away from prying ears."

"Fine. This way, *Miss Plane.*"

The way he said it gave no illusion of good manners. Mr. Whist twisted the paper the entire way to the small office, muttering incomprehensibly. This was not likely to go well, but what choice did she have? She would not lose her home for the sake of a failing business she despised.

Surprisingly, he allowed Theresa to precede him through the office door. She froze at the sight of Grandfather's molded leather chair behind the massive desk. Never again would he fill that space. She alone would sit there to make decisions that determined the printshop's future.

Mr. Whist slammed the door and almost knocked her over when he whirled about. "You'll sign the business over to me and then leave."

The blazing fury in his eyes warned she engaged in battle with an enemy, not a partner. He weighed a good eighty pounds more than her and appeared capable of making her regret much. She'd just have to be proactive about her defense and adapt as the situation demanded. It was too late to change strategy now.

She held Mr. Whist's gaze as she maneuvered around the desk and stood with her hands on the back of the chair. "If you wish to buy me out, I'll gladly accept. The price is four thousand dollars." That would be enough to save her home with a cushion to hold her over until she gained more commissions.

"The entire shop isn't worth that much."

A lie. The bank had valued it at three times that a few years ago. With a little work, the printshop could sell for at least double what she asked.

"Then it appears we are to be business partners." She slid into the chair and positioned herself with easy access to her gun.

He leaned over the desk, his hot, vile breath violating her senses. "The only kind of partner you'll be is a silent one."

A chill skidded down her back, but she would not cower. "You do not scare me."

"I can smell the fear on you like that of a cornered rabbit."

The poor man must have never cornered a rabbit. They kicked and bit like crazy. "That's strange, because all I can smell is your breath. Grandfather kept a stash of peppermint candy over there. Please, take a whole stick." She waved a hand toward a bookcase.

"You'll regret that." His steel grip encased her wrist and yanked her forward.

The edge of the desk cut her breath short and sealed off access to her gun. With another jerk, he tried to pull her across the surface. Pain seared her shoulder, and she gripped the desk as her heels lifted from the floor. She couldn't hold on like this forever. Intimidation was the only language Mr. Whist spoke, but what could she say?

"Drop her!" Edward's command exploded throughout the room.

Mr. Whist released her, and the chair skidded backward with the force of her descent. She stared over the edge of the desk, unsure if she should stand or hide. Never had Edward's voice been so cold and threatening.

Mr. Whist faced Edward. "Then you had better take your wench home."

Brave, stupid little man.

But Edward didn't punch Mr. Whist as she expected. Instead, he circled the desk and aided her to her feet. "We're leaving. Now."

Though reason yelled at her to comply, Mr. Whist's smug smile sparked an explosion of defiance. "No. This is my business, and I won't be bullied out of it."

Edward stared at her as if she'd taken leave of her senses. Perhaps she had, but she would not admit defeat and leave. She would not lose Plane Manor, even if it meant dealing with this brute.

"You're overwrought, Theresa." Edward's tone softened as he placed a gentle but firm arm around her waist. "This has all been too much. You need help, not a business to run."

"I do have help." Not altogether true—yet. "My friend Nathaniel Cosgrove will be working with me." He'd said if she ever needed anything to turn to him. Well, need had become an understatement.

"You what?" Both Mr. Whist and Edward bore down on her with corded necks.

"He's a known criminal, and you would bring him here?" Mr. Whist sputtered.

She should have expected they would have heard of Nathaniel. His trial had been big news in Cincinnati. "He is a *reformed* criminal with substantial knowledge in running a printing business." Even if his experience fell into the illegal realm.

"I'd like a word alone with my bride." Edward spoke to Mr. Whist though his glare never left her face.

Mr. Whist shut the door behind him without argument.

"Theresa, what have you done?"

Technically, she hadn't done anything yet, but Nathaniel owed her, and she couldn't back down. "I need Nathaniel. I'll lose Plane Manor if I don't squeeze nearly four thousand dollars from this business by the first."

Edward released her and folded his arms. "I can provide us with a house. You don't need to work here."

"I don't want another house, Edward. Plane Manor is my home. Everything dear to me is there. The memories. The feel of Momma and Father with me. No other home will provide that. I need Plane Manor as much as I need your support."

"That man almost ripped off your arm." Edward gestured to the closed door. "You can't stay here. It isn't wise or safe."

"Then pay off the debt on my house."

His stiff stance deflated. "I love you, Theresa, but you know I cannot do that. We'd have nothing with which to start our lives."

"We'd have a house."

"With nothing left for necessities. If you're so determined to work, come be my secretary at the shipping office. We'd be together, and you'd earn what you need."

"I can't earn four thousand dollars in a lifetime as your secretary, let alone in fifteen days." Theresa nibbled her lip. Manipulation tactics left her feeling dirty, but some battles couldn't be fought fair. "Agree to my working here, and I could be persuaded to marry sooner." She fingered his sleeve, unwilling to look him in the eye. "Nathaniel owes me. Between him and a few words from you to Mr. Whist, I'll be safe."

Edward's hand blocked his face as he rubbed his forehead.

Though her legs shook and pain stretched from the red on her wrist to her shoulder and neck, she remained standing. If she didn't get Edward on her side, he would do everything possible to keep her from disobeying him.

After countless ticks on the clock, he took a weighted breath. "I'll try to make a deal with Mr. Whist *if* you promise to have Mrs. Hawking with you at all times."

That was a simple enough request. The woman would no doubt demand it once informed of the situation anyway. "Thank you,

Edward." She rose on tiptoes to kiss his cheek, but he rejected her touch. A first, and it wounded more than she expected.

"You have until the first, Theresa, and then you'll abandon this foolish notion. Do you understand me?"

After the first, it wouldn't matter. She'd have either saved the last piece of her family or lost everything. She stared at the floor and nodded.

"Good. Stay here while I go speak to him."

Once he left the office, her legs gave way, and she collapsed into the chair. She'd done it. Now to convince Nathaniel to lend her his criminal expertise and pray Broderick didn't learn of her plans.

CHAPTER 16

"HAVE YOU LOST YOUR MIND?" Broderick curbed the urge to shake Theresa by the shoulders. Walking into the printshop alone was foolish enough, but to trust his brother, who'd tried to kill her? The woman was attracted to trouble like a mouse to a trap.

Theresa rose from the wingback chair in Lydia's parlor and stepped to the tea service, the tea no doubt cold by now. "Are you quite finished? You've berated me for the last half hour. I'm aware that my methods are not of your choosing, but I'm not answerable to you."

"We're all concerned." Lydia spoke from her propped position on the couch. "Nathaniel may have repented and asked for your forgiveness, but that doesn't mean you should trust him."

"He's a changed man. Ask Abraham." Theresa poured tea as though this were a party and not a battle of reason. "In the two years since his release, Nathaniel has done nothing illegal."

Broderick gripped the back of a chair. "He just hasn't been caught."

Theresa shot him a glare. "He's trying to live a Christlike life, and I see no evidence indicating I shouldn't trust him."

"He's dangerous!" How could she not see that? "Do you not remember how he took you hostage, dragged you into a boat knowing you couldn't swim, and then shoved you into the river to drown?"

His breath came in gasps as the memory played like a nightmare before his eyes.

The skiff stopped moving halfway across the river. Nathaniel stood,

Theresa pinned in his grasp. He glanced toward the shore and Broderick, then callously shoved her overboard. Her scream pierced Broderick like a sword. She thrashed for a moment, then soul-crushing silence accompanied her descent into the abyss.

Each desperate stroke brought Broderick closer, but not fast enough. He dove for her. His lungs pinched, and air from his mouth created bubbles before he grabbed her hand. He pulled her to the surface and toward land. Her dead weight bobbed against him. He dragged her body ashore and pumped water from her lungs. Begged God to breathe life into them. All because of Nathaniel.

"He knew you would rescue me. He told me as much before he pushed me in."

Theresa's voice cleared the image of her lifeless body from his mind. He squeezed the rock in his pocket to stop his hand from trembling. Nathaniel could not be trusted. Ever.

She took a sip from the teacup and her nose wrinkled. Setting the cup back on the saucer in her hand, she sighed. "I'm not making this decision lightly. I've considered all my options, and Nathaniel is my best hope for working at the printshop."

"Then either you're a fool or you're not remembering what happened clearly enough."

Her eyes sparked, and the cup and saucer clattered onto the table. "I'm no fool, and I remember every detail with painful clarity. Including waking up to find the one man who promised never to leave me gone." She marched toward him and jabbed a finger to his chest. "I remember every single day I waited for an explanation that never came. At least Nathaniel had the decency to apologize."

This argument had nothing to do with his decision and everything to do with Nathaniel. "Nathaniel is the villain." Why could she not see that?

She clenched her fists. "He's a God-forgiven saint. He came to me with remorse and a turned heart. You're not here because you want forgiveness. You're here because of your case."

"I'm here to help—"

"I don't need your help. I've taken care of myself for the last six years, and I will continue to do so. The printshop provides me a way to save my home. Even Edward has agreed to my plan."

"No man who cares would agree to such lunacy."

Her face dropped into the stony facade she used whenever hurt. "Thank you for reminding me why I'm marrying him. I'd almost forgotten." She stormed out of the parlor, slamming the door in her wake.

"I'll go talk to her," Lydia grunted as she rose to her feet. "We both want to protect her, but that was as foolish as your leaving in the first place. There will be no changing her mind now."

Lydia called after Theresa as she waddled into the foyer, passing Hall. He came in with a file and settled into a chair. "What has Theresa ruffled this time?"

"She's determined to hire my brother Nathaniel as protection while she works at the printshop." Broderick rammed a hand through his hair. "The man almost killed her six years ago, yet she thinks him a saint." And Fitz and Nathaniel working at the same cemetery didn't sit right with him. Coincidences didn't exist. Somehow, Nathaniel had to be involved.

"Her heart's bigger than her head sometimes, but I've watched him for more than a year. He appears to live an honest life now, and his interactions with Theresa are respectful. I don't fear a second attempt to harm her. Not from him." Hall leaned forward and handed Broderick the file. "I took another look at all Drake's correspondence with the Planes. These are the two notes Theresa received from Drake and the two retrieved from Colonel Plane's belongings. I want to know what you think."

Broderick accepted the four notes and examined them. The pair addressed to the colonel indicated loan amounts and terms. Poor spelling and word choice, plus distinct lettering, filled the pages. However, Theresa's note threatening her grandfather if she didn't make payment contained crisp penmanship and no spelling errors. Though written in Cordon Bleu's blood, the second note matched.

"These aren't from the same source." Broderick shook his head. How many enemies did she have?

Seriousness creased the corners of Hall's mouth. "Who else would have threatened her before the colonel's death?"

"Any of his partners could have targeted her to control him." Fitz said as much himself, but the crisp penmanship did not match his impatient scroll. "And tomorrow Theresa's walking into the den of thieves."

Detective Hall leaned forward again, elbows on his knees. "You need to tell her the full truth. It might change her mind."

"If I tell her the men who work at the printshop are counterfeiters and potential murderers, she's more likely to confront them and end up hurt. If by some mercy she isn't, then her revelation could scatter the ring before we can arrest them."

"Are you really willing to risk her safety in order to preserve your case?"

Hall didn't know Theresa like Broderick did. Reason and logic rarely guided her actions. "I'm protecting her by not telling her."

Hall shook his head. "You're lying to yourself. Withholding information will only get her hurt. You need to go tell her now, before she has a chance to speak to Nathaniel. Once she has him on her side, you'll never convince her to stay home."

On that last point, they agreed. Theresa did need to know the truth, but not about the printshop. Broderick rose and gave Hall a curt nod before walking out. Whether or not Theresa believed it, Nathaniel was no ally. If he could get her to understand that, she'd abandon her foolish plan.

Why couldn't Broderick focus on his case and leave her alone? Theresa huddled deeper into her coat as she marched down the narrow path of shoveled snow toward Spring Grove Cemetery. Her safety shouldn't matter to him. He would soon leave. She stumbled but caught herself. Kicking the invisible obstacle from her path, she harrumphed. If she wanted to trust Nathaniel, that was her choice.

Granted, Broderick wouldn't have known her plan if she hadn't opened her big mouth to Lydia. All she'd wanted to do was borrow the Hall carriage so she didn't have to walk while the farrier repaired Blackbeard's shoe. Yet here she was, marching through the cold anyway. Halfway to meet Nathaniel at his cemetery job, and her chest burned with each breath. The idea of warmth beckoned her to turn around and follow the line of smoke to a cozy chair and a blazing fire.

Homelessness is worse than an hour or two in the cold. I need Nathaniel.

She covered her mouth with gloved hands to heat the air and trudged along. Hooves clip-clopped behind her and gave rise to hope. The coin for a hack would be well spent tonight. When she turned, a horse from Lydia's carriage house—not a hack—approached.

Broderick dismounted with the resolute face of a man on a mission. Too bad he would fail.

"You're not changing my mind." She wouldn't allow him the chance to start lecturing again.

"I recognize a fruitless task when I see one."

Obviously not. "Then why are you here?"

"It's getting dark and cold enough to freeze the most stalwart man." He extended a coverlet he must have brought from Lydia's. His consideration both warmed and infuriated her.

She ignored the offering. "I'm not going back home until I talk to Nathaniel."

"Please, Theresa. Your nose is dripping."

She sniffed, horrified to discover he was right.

"And you're shivering." He wrapped the blanket around her shoulders and then passed her a handkerchief. "If you're going to hire Nathaniel, you need to know everything—the full extent of his betrayal and why I left and then stayed away."

His words rose against her opposition and threatened to defeat her resolve. Grandfather and everyone else she knew had shielded her from gossip and flatly refused to answer questions. What conspired in the hours, days, and weeks after she hit the water and was then confined to her bed remained a mystery. One Broderick offered to solve. She glanced toward the cemetery. Nathaniel's shift didn't end for hours, but did she really want to know the full truth? Sometimes ignorance made forgiveness easier.

"I purchased chocolate and milk this morning. It's at Plane Manor."

Give a woman chocolate, and she can face anything. "Are you trying to bribe me?"

"Hot chocolate never failed me before."

Broderick made a handsome rake when he gave that cocky grin. She should refuse and prove hot chocolate had no sway over her, but the thought of a cup coating her sore throat and easing the tightness in her chest was too tempting. Besides, Spring Grove was a long way by foot, and it had been a trying day.

"Fine, but just one cup, and then I'm going to see Nathaniel."

His teeth shone.

Let him think he had won. She was getting chocolate *and* her way. "I'll ride, you walk."

Mrs. Hawking laid a tray with two mugs of hot chocolate on the parlor's serving table and then took up residence in a corner seat. She gave Broderick a challenging glare before settling in to mend clothes. He should know better than to expect privacy. Maybe the truth would improve the woman's opinion of him. It certainly couldn't make it worse.

Theresa reached for a mug and then snuggled into the folds of a worn quilt. She closed her eyes and inhaled the scent, a contented smile lighting her face. No matter how upset she became with him, a cup of hot chocolate always signaled the beginning of reconciliation. He prayed that remained true tonight.

After a long drink, she wrapped her hands around the mug and rested it on her lap. "All right, Broderick, I have my chocolate. You may proceed with your explanation."

Taking a seat, he massaged the back of his neck. What to say without making her defensive? "How much do you know about what happened?"

"Only the few pieces I've put together on my own. No one would speak to me about it, and Grandfather forbade me to communicate with your family."

"And you obeyed?" That was a first.

Her gaze dropped to the steaming chocolate. "By the time I recovered enough to try, your family had moved, and I didn't know to where."

A purposeful move on his father's part. With Colonel Plane's threat of legal action and the scandal in Cincinnati tarnishing the family name, they'd moved quickly. Communication about Theresa's health came through a single missive from Lydia. She'd live but would likely remain fragile the rest of her days—a burden he'd carried ever since.

"I suspected Nathaniel of illegal activity long before the river, but I had no evidence."

"And you didn't tell me?"

"Pop taught us evidence must come before accusation. I didn't want to tarnish my brother's reputation if I were proved wrong. Then you and I saw him at the river loading counterfeiting equipment into the boat with his partners."

She nodded. "I remember his panic when I attempted to steal a few notes for you to take to the police."

Broderick bit his tongue against saying *I told you not to do it*. He needed to win her to his side, not alienate her.

Theresa continued. "Nathaniel had no choice but to take me hostage when his partners saw me. His idea prevented them from shooting me."

"He did it to save himself, not you." Clenching the rock did little to mollify his desire to punch the turncoat.

"You weren't close enough to hear their threats. He saved me."

"A trick of the mind. He didn't care what happened to you"—his throat thickened—"or to me." The older brother he admired betrayed them then—and again in the weeks following.

"That's not true."

"It is. He almost killed me during the manhunt."

She blinked at him, her head shaking. "An accident, surely."

"No, Theresa. When the police and I tracked his partners weeks later, Nathaniel broke off from their group, and I pursued." The wrestling match that followed had been a fight for his life. "Nathaniel pinned me to the ground and then aimed his pistol at my head. I looked him in the eye as he cocked it. There was no hesitation."

Even now, he could see the anger in Nathaniel's gaze as the barrel pressed against Broderick's chin. If the threat had been hollow, he wouldn't have pulled the hammer.

"Oh, Broderick." Theresa came to him, hesitating only a moment before embracing him as he stood.

He dropped his head until it rested atop hers, surprised to hear no objection from Mrs. Hawking. How he'd missed this. Missed her. "He blamed me for making him the villain, said I'd forced him to throw you into the river. A good detective would've kept you safe."

She leaned back. Compassion creased her face as she rubbed his jaw with her thumb. "You are a good detective. Telling me your suspicions beforehand might have changed my decision to snatch the evidence, but probably not. We both know I'm impossible."

"Propriety, Miss Theresa." Mrs. Hawking's warning had Theresa rolling her eyes and stepping back.

She continued. "What happened isn't your fault. As for Nathaniel, he was running scared. I can't believe he would hurt you now."

How could she still defend him? "He would have killed me if Pop and the other officers hadn't come on us. Instead, he used me as a shield and then pushed me over a ridge when he was finished. I was lucky I didn't die from the fall. Nathaniel knew what he was doing, and his betrayal destroyed our entire family."

A war of emotions flickered across her face as she stared at him. Now she would understand the full monstrosity of Nathaniel's character.

After a long time, she gave a heavy sigh. "Nathaniel wronged you, but God convicted him, and he's a different man now."

Was she blind to the truth? "Can't you see his betrayal has ruined both our lives?"

"It didn't have to. You could have stayed. Or come back."

"I was protecting you." He gripped her arms, willing her to understand.

"I think we both know how well that went."

There was no denying he'd failed her, but who could have known leaving her with her guardian would be as dangerous as a life with him?

Mrs. Hawking coughed and sent him a death glare as she nodded to his grip on Theresa. With a frustrated sigh, he dropped his hands.

Theresa's gaze bore into his. "Tell me, now that you're back, will you stay?"

The question kicked the air from his lungs. He couldn't answer that. Not in the way they both wanted. "You're engaged."

Her defiance melted. "And if I weren't?"

As much as he didn't want to see her with Greystone, breaking her promise to the man wouldn't change his answer. "I'm one of only twenty Secret Service operatives, Reese. I'm sent all over the country with no time lines or guarantees of safety. I couldn't take you with me, and I can't protect you from enemies when I'm gone. There's no future for us."

She whirled around and snatched the second mug from the tray.

Chocolate wouldn't fix things this time. He ran a hand over his face. They needed to get this conversation back on track. Nathaniel was the bigger issue, not a battle they'd already lost. "I want you safe, and Nathaniel still has criminal connections. Having him near you is dangerous."

She drained the mug before turning to face him. "People change, Broderick. You may not be willing to give him a chance to prove himself, but I am. I'm hiring him."

Did her persistence never flag? He gripped the rock as frustration mounted. He couldn't tell her John Whist and others were members of the counterfeiting ring without compromising his case. Moreover,

Darlington's suspicions would only grow if he discovered she knew who the other members were. "I'll work at the printshop instead." It would provide a legitimate cover for discovering who played what roles in the production firm and allow him to protect her at the same time.

She shook her head. "You've made it clear. You have your case and can't follow me around. I need Nathaniel."

"It's the perfect solution. Working there will help my case, and I can protect you."

"You'll never be able to do both. Come to the printshop if you'd like, but I'm still hiring Nathaniel." She retrieved her cloak from the back of the sofa. "Tell Lydia I'm borrowing her horse." Theresa exited the room with Mrs. Hawking on her heels.

Broderick pounded his fist on the wall. This case would be the death of him. Never had he felt so divided. So out of control. How was he to balance his duty to country with his duty to Theresa?

CHAPTER 17

THERESA ROLLED OVER AND YANKED the covers to her chin. Would morning never come? She closed her eyes, but sleep continued to evade her. Last night's argument with Broderick pounded in her head. *There's no future for us.* What had she expected? That a few days together would reignite the passionate love they once shared? That he would battle the obstacles they faced so they could be together? She rolled over again.

You're engaged.

A truth too easily forgotten with him around.

God, what is wrong with me? Why can't Edward be the one my heart cries for? When I envision my future, why is all I see Broderick and the life we planned?

She peeked at the laudanum sitting on the nightstand. If she'd taken it instead of discarding the dose Mrs. Hawking gave her into the dying plant by her window, she would be sleeping. Dr. Pelton was right. She should take it and quiet her mind. Oblivion had to be better than facing the mess of her life—even if the respite was temporary.

The cold glass fit perfectly into the palm of her hand as she worked the cork free, but bitter scent stung her nose, and she shoved the cork back in place. No, medicine couldn't be the answer to her problems.

She flung back the covers and opened the nightstand drawer to hide the bottle. Father's Bible filled the small space. When was the last time she'd nestled in her favorite chair and cherished quiet time with God?

Two years ago? Right around the time Grandfather's debts caught up with them and survival consumed her every thought.

Why did You abandon me, God? What did I do wrong?

She set aside the laudanum and fingered the gold-leafed edges of the tome. Momma said the answers to all life's problems lay inside, but she hadn't dealt with counterfeiters, death threats, potential homelessness, family betrayal, or a former fiancé who didn't want to marry her but wouldn't leave her alone.

Theresa lit the kerosene lamp and flipped open the cover. Momma's note to Father after the war filled the page. She might not have written it for Theresa, but a dose of Momma's wisdom would do a world of good.

My dearest Henry,

I give you this Bible so that you will have hope again. When death haunts you, the nightmares become real, and you feel there is no escape, God is with you. Even if you reject Him for a time. Don't be angry with Him because of the trials you've faced. He spared you for a reason. Let's be like the Israelites in 2 Chronicles 20. Stand still with me, and set your eyes on our Lord. He is with you. With us. Together with Him, we can overcome the nightmares of war. Healing lies within these pages, Henry. Don't abandon hope. Even if our lives aren't like we planned.

With all my love and prayers,
Cassandra

"Ye shall not need to fight in this battle: set yourselves, stand ye still, and see the salvation of the Lord with you."—2 Chronicles 20:17

Theresa rested her hand over the loopy script. Momma's love and desire to fight for her husband shone through those words. Words that reached forward into the future to Theresa. Death did haunt her. The nights were dark. Her nightmares real. And like Father, she was angry.

She reread the letter, allowing the words to sink deep into her aching soul.

God is with you. Even if you reject Him for a time.

Had He been there over the last six years? Painting commissions had come from unexpected places, always giving her just enough to pay the creditors—even Drake. Edward had been the one to ruin that opportunity. Even so, God had brought him into her life and provided hope for a secure future. Surely God would help her love Edward as passionately as she'd loved Broderick.

She bristled at the underlined portion of the verse. *Ye shall not need to fight in this battle . . .*

It was one thing to accept God was with her, but to not fight for her home, her future? That was unacceptable. Momma must have left out the word *alone*. She would not need to fight this battle *alone*. That made perfect sense. After all, God had sent Edward, Broderick, and Nathaniel to help.

Don't abandon hope. Even if our lives aren't like we planned.

Her breath whooshed. *Even if.* She'd lost so much already. Her family, a future with Broderick, her dreams. How could this life be better than what she planned?

The hall clock announced the seventh hour, and she set aside the Bible. No sleep and getting a late start. This was bound to be a difficult day. She rushed through her morning routine, taking care to ensure her revolver remained unnoticeable beneath her skirts. Broderick would try to confiscate it if he knew.

A crash echoed in the foyer.

Great. More trouble. Undoing her careful work, she cracked the door with her gun ready.

"You have no business helping her." Broderick's voice carried from below.

She slipped to the top of the stairs and peered down.

Nathaniel rubbed his jaw but didn't engage in the battle Broderick seemed intent on fighting. "For your information, I tried to talk Theresa out of it."

Evidently both men had come to escort her to the printshop. She shook her head. They were brothers forever, no matter how Broderick denied it.

He spared you for a reason. Momma's words to Father reverberated through her. Her reason for being spared must be to facilitate their reconciliation. After all, if she weren't in this mess, Broderick and Nathaniel wouldn't be forced to face each other.

Nathaniel dropped his hand. "Whether you like it or not, I'm going to the printshop. No one knows better than I what men like Whist are capable of. You stay near Theresa, and I'll deal with him."

"So you can betray us again? No. I'm not letting you out of my sight."

She pocketed the gun and descended the stairs. "Good morning. Ready for breakfast?" No doubt Mrs. Hawking was already including them in her preparations.

Nathaniel nodded, and Broderick glowered. She stepped between them and slipped an arm through each man's crook. Being framed by the two rigid brothers felt right, like being part of a family again, even if they were at odds worse than Generals Grant and Lee. But God willing, that would change. If she had to endure this mess, she might as well make something good come of it.

"Coffee is ready." Mrs. Hawking appeared in the hall, carrying a tray of food to the dining room.

"It's so nice to be together again. Isn't it?" Theresa squeezed their arms.

Broderick's nostrils flared, but he made no remark.

Nathaniel, however, took the opportunity. "About as nice as an outhouse in summer."

Theresa smiled. "Then I suppose it's a good thing I have plumbing."

Once through the dining room door, Nathaniel broke off and held a chair for her. Before she could act, Broderick released her and bumped Nathaniel out of the way. Perhaps Mrs. Hawking could switch the coffee for chocolate.

She ignored the proffered chair and selected one at the head of the table. The chairs on either side of hers scraped as they claimed their spots. Boys and their tiffs. They glared at each other as they fought for the top piece of ham. Then they clashed over the eggs, toast, and coffee. By the time they finished, more food had landed on the table than on their plates.

Mrs. Hawking poured a cup of chocolate for Theresa, then glanced at the table and set the whole pot down. "There's more if you need it."

Bless her. Theresa turned her attention to the warring brothers. "Shall we pray?"

Nathaniel and Broderick began at the same time, then stopped.

"Go ahead, baby brother. I imagine you could use a good talk with our Maker." Nathaniel waved Broderick on.

"I believe it is you who needs to pray. You must have some recent sins you'd like to confess." Broderick leaned forward.

Mrs. Hawking commanded bowed heads and silent mouths. "Lord, bless this food. May it not be poisoned by such bitterness. Guard these men's stomachs against the pain they deserve and protect Miss Theresa from fools. Those present included. Amen."

Theresa added, "Mend fences where they are broken and prepare us for the day ahead. Thank You for family. In Jesus's name, amen."

At least the men had the presence of mind to keep silent for the rest of breakfast and pretend to be sheepish. With these two, returning to daily conversation with God might come easier than she anticipated. *Lord, help these brothers to reconcile and grant me a miracle. I don't want to lose this house.* Food no longer appealing, she reached for her cup of chocolate. She better ask Mrs. Hawking for an ample supply to take with her if she was going to survive the day.

Nathaniel pushed from the table. "I'll wait for you outside, Theresa."

Once he was gone, she turned to Broderick. A hand with white knuckles gripped his fork, and a frown chiseled his face. She squeezed his wrist to draw his attention, and the scowl lessened.

"Give him a chance, please." She rubbed her thumb over his knuckles. "For me."

"I don't trust him."

"Trust me instead. I've seen his heart. He means us no harm."

That scowl hardened back into place. Oh, to be free to kiss away his puckered frown. Too bad she wasn't and never would be. The mission now was to save her house and the brothers' relationship, not lose her heart to someone who would leave again. She patted his shoulder before stepping over scrambled eggs. Today would be a long day.

Broderick had to wait only a minute or two until Mrs. Hawking distracted Theresa so he could finish with Nathaniel. Five years had passed since he'd testified against the man and attended his sentencing. The time had reduced their stature difference, and Broderick planned to use every inch and pound to his advantage.

He finally found him at the carriage house, and grabbing Nathaniel's collar, he rammed his brother against the door. "If you even look at Theresa wrong, I'll use every tool at my disposal to send you back to jail."

Nathaniel grinned. "Good to know you still love her."

"Love has nothing to do with this. I know what you're capable of." The monster should have hung for attempted murder, not been given a second chance.

"I'm more capable of protecting Theresa than you. I'm not the one working a case."

Broderick speared him with a glare. "I quit the detective business after you ruined our family."

"You may no longer work for Pop, but I know an undercover detective when I see one. Mr. *Smith*." He shoved Broderick and crossed his arms. "I'm willing to bet whoever you're after does too."

An all too possible truth, and with Nathaniel's presence, his cover was almost certainly ruined. Moving forward without acknowledging that reality was as deadly as walking into Dirk's Saloon in a police uniform. "I accepted this case for Theresa's sake alone."

Nathaniel snorted. "You never did master the art of lying."

"Truth is what sets men like you and me apart."

"Then you better stop lying to yourself, little brother. If you were really here for Theresa's sake, you'd haul her to Mom and Pop for safekeeping."

Broderick released him. "You know she wouldn't go."

"Excuses." Nathaniel brushed off his coat and pulled the carriage house door open. "It's a good thing you two didn't marry. She deserves someone who cares more about her than a case."

"You can't give advice about something you don't understand. You never put others above yourself."

Nathaniel abruptly stopped, and Broderick narrowly missed colliding with him. "I came out here to prepare the carriage for Theresa. Where is it? Where are the horses?"

Maybe he wasn't as close as Theresa indicated. "Long gone to pay debts."

Nathaniel's gaze flitted around the room. "How bad?"

Theresa appeared and then slid past them to scratch the bleating goat's head. "Bad enough to warrant working with Mr. Whist despite physical opposition."

Physical? Theresa had made no mention of being touched.

"Don't look so horrified, Broderick. After all the bruises I've received in the last month, the ones from him are merely a trifle." Her attempt at a lighthearted laugh fell flat as she rubbed her wrist.

"Whist is more than a trifle dangerous," Nathaniel said. "His reputation precedes him."

"Then it's a good thing I hired you." She opened the stall door, and Tipsy ambled into the aisle with a hopping gait.

"Being guilted into it isn't the same as being hired."

"You were the one who said to come to you if ever I needed anything."

Broderick stopped her from grabbing the feed box scoop and turned her toward him. "You don't need Nathaniel. I'm perfectly capable of protecting you."

"Until your case needs your attention."

Nathaniel coughed behind him, no doubt a victorious smile on his arrogant face. Why couldn't Theresa see the truth? A single word from him to Whist or Fitz, and it could all be over, including their lives. Maybe he *should* haul her to Philadelphia kicking and screaming. It would benefit both her and his case. Except Darlington suspected her and would accuse Broderick of aiding and abetting.

He opened his mouth to argue, but her calloused fingers covered his lips. "This is my choice, Broderick. You can either choose to go with us to the printshop or stay behind, but you can't stop me from doing what's necessary to save my home. We're not engaged anymore."

The woman knew exactly how to hit her mark. He may no longer have the right to guide her to better decisions, but he'd learned from his past mistakes. Theresa was safer with him than without. Working at the printshop and marrying Greystone were both mistakes she'd regret. Lord forgive him, but he couldn't allow her to face those consequences. Somehow he'd figure out how to balance this case with protecting her.

"I'm sure you both will find your way. Would you please saddle Blackbeard for me while I take Tipsy into the house? Be sure to keep your hands from his face and watch your feet. He's always extra ornery after getting a new shoe." She gave a wry grin before patting her skirt. "Come, Tipsy. You're staying in the house from now on."

The bleating goat followed Theresa in playful bounds.

Nathaniel hoisted a saddle and frowned. "I hope you're close to an arrest, because this arrangement won't last long."

Close? Not near enough, and at the rate he was progressing, an arrest might be too late.

CHAPTER 18

BLACKBEARD STOMPED ON BRODERICK'S FOOT, protesting the intrusion into his area of the printshop delivery bay. Broderick grunted but remained crouched by the rope barrier meant to keep the ornery beast from the horses. Less than a day at the printshop, and already Nathaniel had wormed his way back into the counterfeiting ring. Broderick wasn't one for cursing, but Nathaniel sorely tempted him. The traitor wasn't fooling anyone—except Theresa.

The moment Nathaniel thought Broderick distracted, he'd sneaked off, and Theresa hadn't questioned his flimsy excuse to step away. Instead, she'd banished the other workers to the pressroom and shifted her organizing efforts to the front counter. For the moment, she would be safe.

Whist spat on the ground near where Nathaniel unloaded supplies from the back of a wagon. "You shouldn't have agreed to come."

"Better me than someone else." Nathaniel hefted a box to his shoulder and carried it to a stack against the wall opposite Broderick. "With her connections, she could have hired an off-duty officer."

Blackbeard nipped at Broderick's arm, nearly knocking him off balance. The pesky mule would give him away. He removed one of the carrots Theresa gave him for bribery and tossed it to the side.

"The police have already been here asking questions and snooping. Plane's death created more problems than it solved."

"Murder usually does, and she was close to the old man. If she finds evidence of counterfeiting or foul play, she'll report it."

The muzzle of a neighboring horse butted Broderick's pocket. Carrots were the demand of the hour. Broderick pulled out another and tossed it to the horse.

"She'll regret the consequences if she does."

Nathaniel set down another box and then crossed his arms. "Theresa's an old friend, Whist. I'll not allow harm to come to her."

"Then see to it she stays ignorant until we need her."

At least the traitor had some interest in protecting Theresa, an interest that would disappear the moment he had to choose between her and himself. The sooner Broderick could arrange an arrest, the better.

Whist popped his neck. "What do you know about Smith?"

Broderick tensed. Nathaniel could not be allowed to answer. Yanking the remaining carrots from his pocket, he extended one to Blackbeard and one to the horse. The treat immediately drew their attention. He dropped the carrots together in a pile.

"Smith's no—"

Blackbeard brayed and charged the horse leaning in for a bite. Broderick scrambled out of the way and dashed for the pressroom under the cover of crates. Behind him, the horse neighed and hooves pounded against the stone floor. By the sound of things, the two were declaring war. Nathaniel's and Whist's voices mingled with the bedlam.

The commotion drew a crowd, and Broderick slipped into the edges unnoticed. A couple of the men joined Nathaniel and Whist as they tried to snag the leads. The circling equines reared and clashed against each other, nipping and biting. When the horse broke free, Blackbeard chased it, scattering the men trying to stop the fight.

Theresa burst through the group. "What's going on here?" She stopped short and balled her hands into fists. "I told you to keep Blackbeard away from the other horses."

Her head followed the swing of the rope, eyes focused with a calculating intensity.

Broderick broke from the group and grabbed her wrist as she sprinted toward the ruckus. "No. It's too dangerous."

She stumbled to a stop and shot him a disapproving scowl. Before she could argue, Nathaniel and another man snagged Blackbeard's lead, and the other horse escaped to freedom through the bay doors.

"I'll go after it," another man called as he dashed outside.

Blackbeard pranced and tossed his head, but the men didn't lose their grip. After several minutes, the mule stood in one place, sides heaving and a sweaty sheen to his coat. Blood matted a few spots, but nothing appeared too serious.

Theresa clawed his grip until he let go and then marched toward Whist. "I warned you to keep him separate. Now he's injured."

"No one's fault but his." Whist sneered. "Just like you, the beast is too stupid to know when he's lost."

Fury clouded her face and likely her judgment. Broderick pinned her against him before she did something foolish, like punch the man. Too bad he couldn't stop her mouth.

"It looks to me like Blackbeard won." Her nostrils flared as she leaned forward. "I wouldn't underestimate your foes, Mr. Whist."

"I'd take your own advice, Miss Plane." Whist marched past her. "Everyone, back to work."

Broderick released his hold on Theresa. She closed her eyes and took several breaths, no doubt trying to calm herself. After a moment, she faced Blackbeard as Nathaniel led him to a stall far from the horses.

"He's limping." Her face crumpled. "And I can't afford to help him."

Broderick denied the desire to pull her into a comforting embrace and rubbed her back instead. "I'll take care of it."

He owed Blackbeard that much. The mule had done his job and saved Broderick's cover. Although how long could it remain intact with Nathaniel around?

Heaven help her. She was weary. Theresa allowed her body to sag for a moment in the quiet of her front porch before knocking. Her fourth full day at the printshop, and she wanted to collapse into bed and never crawl out. As if business troubles weren't enough, managing Broderick, Nathaniel, and Mr. Whist was worse than wrestling with Grimm at the cemetery. Thank goodness growing concerns of flooding at the shipping docks prevented Edward from adding to her headache. His little notes and gifts of apology for his absence were nice, but she didn't have the energy to do more than return a few lines of thanks.

Wood scraped against metal before the door opened to reveal the end of a shotgun. It lowered, and Mrs. Hawking stepped back. God bless her for listening to Broderick's reasoning and staying behind to protect the house.

Before Theresa could drop the bar back into place, the woman launched into a list of grievances. "We've no coal left, the groceries won't last another day, the gas company cut off supply, and your goat has destroyed the parlor furniture."

Tipsy bleated from the other side of the closed parlor door as if denying the claim.

Why couldn't an hour pass without added trouble? "Use the fallen branches from the yard to build fires, and reduce our meals to one a day."

Mrs. Hawking stored the shotgun in the umbrella stand. "The branches are green. They'll not produce anything but smoke."

"Then I suggest we wear all our layers. Gather the kerosene lamps and candles to use until I can pay the gas company."

"I have, and we're almost out of both." Mrs. Hawking crossed her arms. "We need to ask for help."

"No." The word escaped before she could temper her tone. "We'll search the house. Grandfather couldn't have spent everything. Start in the office"—she could never walk into that room again—"and I'll search his bedroom."

Mrs. Hawking opened her mouth, but Theresa held up her hand. "Please, Mrs. Hawking."

Thankfully, the woman complied. Theresa was too tired to argue much more. She forced her feet to mount the stairs. Money had to be somewhere in the house. She wouldn't ask Lydia for help, and she certainly couldn't turn to Broderick. The man continued to inundate every thought, overthrowing the fiancé who should be king of her heart and mind. Allowing him any more heroics in her life would be her undoing. Edward, undoubtedly, would give her an ultimatum of immediate marriage or no help, and she wasn't ready for that. Try as she might, she couldn't set a date without feeling sick. No, scraping together every penny they could find was the best recourse.

Please, God, help us find enough.

After taking a fortifying breath, she entered Grandfather's room. Other than a thin layer of dust, it was as meticulous as the man himself. With the scant amount of furniture, she had few places to search. Still, he'd been good at hiding things. She just had to be thorough.

An hour later, she'd emptied every drawer, checked for false bottoms, unfolded every piece of clothing, searched among socks, flipped through books, and pried up loose floorboards. Nothing. She'd even stripped the bed and put a slit in the mattress to search the contents.

"I found the bugle case at the top of the linen closet." Theresa jumped at Mrs. Hawking's voice. "It might have what we need." She set the black wooden case on the bed in front of Theresa and stepped back.

After all those mornings of cursing the rotten thing and wishing to destroy it, the bugle finally lay within her grasp. She flipped the latches and lifted the lid. The brass instrument lay snug in its cloth bed, waiting for a day that would never come again. Theresa laid aside the bugle and then plucked free a corner of loose material inside the box. A neat roll of banknotes lay tucked in the padding.

Thank You, God.

Their needs might be provided yet. She separated the bills into piles. Fifteen ones and four tens. Enough to pay Mrs. Hawking's salary and stretch their fuel and food supplies until she repaid the bank. But could she trust them to be real? Grandfather was a counterfeiter.

She inspected the tens. They appeared genuine, but what would she know? It wasn't as if she spent her time studying banknotes. Best not to use them until she had Broderick check. That left the ones. Broderick hadn't mentioned anything beyond counterfeited tens, so these should be safe, right? Mrs. Hawking wouldn't abandon her for lack of pay, but she might go around Theresa's orders and alert someone if Theresa didn't provide for their basic needs. Theresa chewed on her bottom lip. The ones had to be genuine, but just to be safe, she'd use as few as possible.

After stuffing the tens and instrument back into the case, she closed the lid. "We'll have to make this stretch until the bank is satisfied. One meal a day, and we'll heat only the kitchen."

"You'll be sick by the end of the week."

"I'll be fine." She had to be.

Chapter 19

Three hundred dollars—hardly enough to cover payroll, let alone pay the bank. Theresa leaned back against the leather chair and stared at the ceiling grayed by years of printing dust. Her first full week at the shop had been a disaster. Projects, far from the quality Grandfather once demanded, barely met their deadlines. She'd lost a crucial client this week and had to offer a discount on two late projects. Mr. Whist had also purchased more ink even though the supply closet held plenty of colors she could blend to meet their needs.

Numbers swirled in her mind until her ears hummed. Their shrinking client list and poor sales numbers scared off investors. The sole interested party wanted to buy the presses at a quarter of their value but not the building or the partnership. Without the presses, the business would fold and bear the cost of a useless building. Even she recognized the offer as terrible and had declined.

But with one week left until eviction, she couldn't give up. A dozen letters to their competitors offered an opportunity for a buyout. Only one needed to agree, but with businesses still struggling from last year's flood and the chances of another quickly developing, she didn't hold much hope.

"What am I to do, Lord?" she asked.

"Pack up and go home for the weekend. Or better yet, visit my family in Philadelphia," Broderick answered from the doorway.

How could she have forgotten he hung closer than a thorn on a bush? Although—and she wouldn't dare admit it aloud—his presence did comfort her. "You know very well I can't leave."

"You'd be safe." He set a crate on the floor, then leaned against the doorframe.

"I'm not some brittle piece of china that needs to be packed away and forgotten."

"No, you're not. You're a beautiful, independent woman who drives a man to distraction. You can't fault me for wanting to protect such a precious gift."

Heat spread across her cheeks, and her heart pounded. He must have abandoned arguing with logic and decided to charm her out of her senses, for he certainly hadn't changed his mind about renewing his promises.

He rested his hands on either side of her ledgers and leaned over the desk. "I spend more time worrying about you than I do thinking about my job, and given the circumstances, that's dangerous for both of us."

"So you're saying you want to send me away so you can forget me and protect your career."

His smile fell as he straightened.

Ha! She'd ousted his enchanting manners ploy, and he knew it. She smiled at the brief flicker of frustration on his face. Oh, how she'd missed arguing with him. The game of wits had always brought her joy. Too bad winning against him didn't pay her debts. Her gaze fell on the ledgers littering the surface of her desk. Other than setting a wedding date, what would it take to convince Edward to pay off the mortgage on the house?

Broderick skirted around the desk and turned her chair toward him. "I know you think money will solve your problems, but it isn't what you need."

"You have no idea what I need."

He clasped her hand and knelt on one knee.

Past overpowered present, sweeping her back to their hidden spot beneath the willow and the last time he'd knelt like this before her. He'd worn that ugly striped coat he loved with the worn-out elbow.

Maintaining her composure while he stumbled over the question he already knew the answer to had been a challenge. Maybe he did know what she needed—him.

"I know you need God to heal you. Family to surround you and protect you." His hand caressed her cheek, and her breath caught. Charming her with touches should be against the rules. He knew how much she craved it. "You need someone to lean into, to share this weight with. Let me help you bear it."

Wait. Was Broderick charming her? Or was he proposing? All week they'd played an awkward game of pretending their attraction didn't exist, but she'd seen him sneaking glances at her. Noticed the excuses to stay close and brush against her to reach something. Had he realized his mistake and wanted a second chance?

"You don't have to make this printshop work, Reese. You'll never be homeless. You have a home with"—her breath hitched—"Lydia."

The world that smelled of winter and ink instead of summer and love slammed back into place. This wasn't a proposal. It was merely a game. Those eyes that had once carried love and hope now held mere friendship and concern. He didn't want to renew their love. Leftover residue from her pot of chocolate thickened her throat with a grit she couldn't swallow past.

The creak of floorboards drew her gaze to the door.

"Edward." Her chair bumped against the wall as she pushed from Broderick and stood. "What a surprise. I didn't realize you were coming."

"Evidently." Red mottled his face, and cold hatred poured from the gaze directed at Broderick.

She best lead a hasty retreat and save them all from terrible consequences. She collected the paperwork for the engraving projects she'd determined most profitable to complete and shoved them into her satchel. "Broderick, please help Mr. Whist distribute payroll tonight, and be sure the Milton project gets finished on time tomorrow. Edward and I have plans, so I won't be in."

"I'll meet you first thing Monday morning."

Something thudded, and she whipped her head toward the sound. Edward had pinned Broderick against the wall with an arm and icy glower. Her stomach twisted. If she spoke to Broderick's defense, Edward might descend into violence. Broderick didn't break eye contact.

"Smith, get out here," Mr. Whist called from the front room.

Edward shoved Broderick before releasing his grip. Once Broderick exited, Edward slammed the door. "Where is Mrs. Hawking?"

Her hands shook as she took her cloak from a hook on the wall and slipped it on. "Broderick offered to work here, allowing Mrs. Hawking to protect the house."

"That is not what we agreed."

"I know, but—"

"Fire him."

Not an option. Broderick claimed working at the printshop helped his investigation, and she'd not keep him from doing his job.

"What do you say we redecorate the house?" She forced a smile. "I have a few pieces I'd like to get rid of."

"Don't change the subject." He took her satchel and guided her from the printshop with a firm hand to her back. He waited until they were outside to add, "Smith is playing games with you, Theresa, and I won't let some brothel-loving criminal steal you."

Brothel-loving criminal? "How absurd! You don't even know him."

"I know him better than you think, and what I know is too vile for your delicate ears." He helped her into the waiting hack. "He's overstayed his welcome. Send him packing, or I will. Do you hear me?"

"Yes." But that didn't mean she agreed.

She straightened her engagement ring, and its sharp contours pricked her conscience. How would she feel if she discovered Edward consorted with another woman? Betrayed. Hurt. Angry. She looked at his grim face cast with light and shadow from a nearby streetlamp. Flowers shoved against the carriage wall indicated he'd come excited to surprise her. Instead of finding a fiancée delighted to see him, he found her alone with another man. The fault belonged to her.

Broderick's serious face appeared in the printshop window, and she toyed with her sleeve for a moment before averting her gaze. Continued fantasies were unfaithful to Edward. Her future with Broderick died long ago, and nurturing the idea of a renewed relationship with him was unhealthy. Hope for security and love sat right here in the carriage, and she couldn't risk losing that. She wouldn't dismiss Broderick, but she could placate Edward.

"How does a wedding on February first sound?" By that time, she'd have settled her affairs with the house, good or bad.

Edward's stiff stance relaxed, and he drew her close. "Perfect."

The kiss that followed should have tingled down to her toes. Instead, a cold ache spread through her. Why did marriage to Edward seem more like the death of love than the beginning of it?

Allowing Theresa to go with Greystone didn't sit well with Broderick. The man would find a way to make her feel guilty—only nothing had happened except Broderick had nearly promised Theresa forever with him.

"Careful," Nathaniel whispered as he stacked a set of completed prints. "Whist is taking note of your interest. He might think Mr. Smith is more than a family friend."

Broderick moved from the window and collected the payroll ledger. His duty to the Secret Service and to protecting Theresa had warred from the moment he'd walked through the printshop door. So far, nothing indicated Nathaniel had exposed his cover, but playing Theresa's protector curried no favor with Whist. Every task assigned to him fell under legitimate duties. Other than the conversation between Whist and Nathaniel, and one other about the missing fifties plates, he'd gathered no evidence to redirect Darlington's concentrated attention on Theresa.

Nathaniel laughed with a fellow printer in the corner of the room as they waited for payroll distribution. That man had no trouble melding with the tight-knit group. They'd accepted him as if he were a long-time friend. The scoundrel likely was. If any counterfeiting activity occurred, Nathaniel knew about it and kept the information to himself. Broderick needed to change tactics.

As everyone left to spend their pay, he hid in the alley and waited. Plane Manor held nothing left valuable to the case, leaving the printshop as Broderick's final place to search. After checking the area for stragglers, Broderick knelt in the snow to pick the delivery bay lock.

"You're so predictable." Nathaniel chucked him on the shoulder. "What did I teach you about preparing ahead? I unlocked the third-floor window days ago."

Broderick shoved his tools into his coat. Predictability killed in his line of work. Knowing his brother had thought ahead of him sickened him like a bad case of food poisoning.

"Come on. We'll use one of the poles around back." Nathaniel disappeared around the corner.

Broderick hesitated and flicked his rock's tip. The risk of following would be worth it if he could get Nathaniel to blunder and provide information. It helped to know he wasn't blindly walking into betrayal this time either.

He joined Nathaniel at the base of a metal pole extending to the roof. After a fire in the early '70s, Colonel Plane had vowed lives would never again be lost because they were trapped in his printshop. While convenient to slide down, climbing up posed a challenge. "You first."

Nathaniel didn't argue, instead jumping to hug the pole with his hands and legs. Alternating between thrusts and pulls, he made quick work of the first floor. Broderick waited until Nathaniel couldn't cause a fatal fall before following. After shinnying up three stories, they climbed through the window into a room filled with broken and rusted equipment. As they caught their breath, Broderick surveyed the room. Thick dust coated every surface except for the recently swept main aisle and a single side path. The layer there couldn't be more than a few weeks old.

After too short a rest break, Nathaniel headed straight to the stairs.

"Whist said Colonel Plane hid the new set of plates before he died, and he believes they're somewhere in this building. He's already checked the main floor, so I suggest we search the drying room."

No mention of the swept aisle? Nathaniel never missed a detail that obvious when he worked as a detective. Broderick walked the cleared path to the side aisle. A broom leaned against a rickety supply shelf halfway down the swept portion. Had Colonel Plane meant it as a marker? Or had he simply set it down before finishing the chore?

"Are you coming? We don't have time to waste," Nathaniel called from below.

Broderick glanced around for any obvious signs of shifted equipment, but nothing stood out. If he were Colonel Plane, he'd hide the plates on this floor. With all the clutter and chaos, searching the area would require a concentrated effort that would take hours. Knowing Colonel Plane's penchant for puzzles and codes, he'd left the broom as a clue. He'd have to return later without Nathaniel.

Downstairs, Nathaniel tilted an empty drying rack. "There you are. Why don't you start in the far corner, and we'll meet in the middle."

Nathaniel must have revealed Broderick's identity and convinced the ring they could use him to find the plates for them. Not an ideal situation, but Broderick could use that to his advantage. Subverting the ring's leaders worked like dancing with Theresa. He'd allow them to think they controlled the situation. Then at the right moment, he'd cause a distraction and take the lead—waltzing them right into prison.

They searched the room for a couple of hours, and every drawer, cabinet, and loose board revealed the same thing. Nothing. No surprise there. Broderick knew Colonel Plane wouldn't hide the plates in such obvious places.

Metal grated on the floor above, and Broderick looked up from the last box of discarded projects. He should have known better than to take his eyes off Nathaniel. By the time Broderick reached the third floor, his brother had swept the entire room clean.

Nathaniel leaned the broom against one wall. "We better head out.

I noticed a cop taking an interest in this building. We can't have him finding us here and asking questions."

Theresa said to trust Nathaniel, but his gut twisted. "Why did you sweep the floor?" *Prove me wrong. Tell the truth.*

"It wouldn't take Whist a minute to figure out what we did if he saw the footprints. Sweeping away the evidence is a safeguard."

He'd swept away the evidence all right—and proved that traitors never change. What had Nathaniel found?

CHAPTER 20

THERESA BLINKED THE GRIT FROM her eyes as she looked up from her engraving project to the parlor's mantel clock. Edward should arrive soon. After canceling their Saturday plans at the Bellevue House due to a work emergency, he'd promised to return in time to escort her to Lydia's for dinner. Not that they should go. If Lydia wasn't trying to convince Theresa to move back in with her, she was comparing Edward's undesirable qualities to Broderick's much-desired ones. It was hard enough for Theresa to keep her own fantasies at bay without curbing Lydia's.

At least Lydia hadn't slipped and expounded on Broderick's merits in front of Edward. He had reason enough to hate Broderick without Lydia's help.

Someone knocked at the front door, and Mrs. Hawking hurried by with shotgun in hand. Must every knock be considered a threat? It wasn't as if thieves and murderers announced themselves.

"Miss Plane is needed urgently." The panicked voice of a boy came in with the blast of cold air. "The baby's coming."

Baby?

Lydia! But it was too early. The engraving plate clattered to the floor as Theresa lurched from her makeshift desk. Surely God wouldn't do this to her again. She grabbed her coat as she passed the hall tree and yanked the door wider. "Where's Detective Hall?"

The boy twisted his cap. "Called in to work. Not home yet. Mrs. Hall begs you to come."

"Mrs. Hawking, see to this boy's needs and then send him back on Blackbeard. I'm taking his horse."

She didn't wait for confirmation and mounted astride the skittish animal. Cold pierced her stockings to her knees. Mrs. Hawking barked about the impropriety, but what did propriety matter during circumstances such as this? Like a blessed angel, the horse responded to her prompting and flew down the street, avoiding obstacles and disgruntled observers who called out her reckless run. Mud from the thawing snow splattered across her skirts and exposed limbs. Pins loosened as the wind raked through her hair. She would look a mess when she arrived, but that didn't matter.

You say You're in control, but why do You keep allowing people around me to suffer? Don't let Lydia have the baby today. It's too soon.

Without waiting for the poor beast to come to a full stop, she flung herself from the saddle and barged through the front door. A single maid rushed down the stairs.

"Where is she?" Theresa skidded across the clean floor.

"In her room."

"Dr. Pelton?"

"Gerard has gone to find him."

"Detective Hall?"

"We sent another boy—"

Theresa took the steps two at a time and opened the door with barely maintained restraint. Her gaze flew to the bed, where Lydia leaned forward, face contorted, grasping the covers with whitened fists. Theresa rushed to her side and froze. What could she do? After a minute, Lydia leaned back, breathing hard with a sheen of sweat over her brow.

"How long has this been going on?" Theresa dampened a rag to pat it around Lydia's neck.

"It started as a backache yesterday, and I couldn't sleep last night because of the pain. Then about an hour ago"—red flamed her cheeks, and she lowered her voice—"I thought I'd had an accident, but the wetness wouldn't stop. Since then, the pain has been coming in waves."

"Is that normal?"

Lydia took a shaky breath. "I don't know."

"But it's too soon." Try as she might, she couldn't keep the panic from her voice.

"The Lord is my strength and salvation." Lydia said it as if trying to convince herself of its veracity. "I have to trust Him."

"But He might take everything from you." Theresa clapped her hand over her mouth. Those words belonged in her head, not out where they could shred her best friend's faith when needed most. "I'm sorry, I shouldn't have . . ."

Lydia took another shaky breath before patting the bed. Theresa climbed next to her dearest friend and wrapped her arms around her shoulders.

"I'm scared, Theresa. I've been praying and begging, but I keep wondering why I should escape suffering when Jesus, God's own Son, did not."

Theresa squeezed her eyes shut. *Please, don't let it be so.* God couldn't take the child's life. It wasn't right. The baby had done nothing to deserve death. It hadn't even breathed its first.

Jesus did nothing to deserve death either. The reminder came as a gentle whisper to her heart, but she couldn't contemplate it. Not right now. Maybe not ever.

This isn't the same, God. Please, don't do this to us.

The silence stretched as she held Lydia and rocked. Soon another bout of pain overtook Lydia, again contorting her face and curling her body. Theresa clenched her teeth as Lydia squeezed her hand and moaned. Bits and pieces of prayer flew from Theresa's mouth on frantic breaths, but nothing changed. Once again God had abandoned her during a great time of need.

Lydia released a quivering breath and fell back against the pillows panting. "I have . . . to trust Him . . . even if . . ." Her hand cradled her abdomen as she fell silent.

Trust was beyond Theresa's reach, but she would not allow her friend's trust to falter. In the face of death, hope lay in believing the best could still happen. Theresa pushed down her misery and reached into whatever reserves of humor she could find.

"You'll need that trust when this baby learns to walk and takes after you. I can see her now." She wiped Lydia's brow with a damp rag and allowed the image of a miniature Lydia to form. "She'll climb the dresser, run full force across the top, and leap off the edge with arms wide, ready to fly."

Lydia chuckled and swiped at a tear. "I suppose I should begin investing in thick rugs and floor pillows."

"I don't know. You might be better off selling all your furniture and sleeping on the floor."

"I can see Abraham's face." Lydia made a poor attempt at mocking it and then released a full belly laugh. Once she settled, she squeezed Theresa's hand. "Thank you, friend. I needed that."

Theresa allowed a brief smile, but the darkness of fear pushed back against the light of hope and laughter. Exhaustion already marred Lydia's features, giving her a deathlike pallor. Would she have the strength to do what needed to be done? Childbirth was dangerous. Theresa could hope for the best all she wanted, but hope didn't mean freedom from suffering.

The door opened, and a thin woman with a black bag stepped through. "Good evening, Mrs. Hall. I hear there is to be great rejoicing soon. Let's see how things are progressing." She flipped the covers from the foot of the bed, bent Lydia's legs, and leaned in.

Theresa scrambled off the bed and turned her back to the scene. For heaven's sake! Heat flared up her neck and radiated to every inch of her body. She didn't know what she expected, but this was not it.

A tap to her shoulder forced her to look back. "Would you be a dear and hold back her shift?"

"Her shift?" Beyond the midwife, Lydia's bare knees pointed to the ceiling, the cotton material between them draped like a tent.

"Yes, dear. After I'm finished checking her, you can escape downstairs. The screams should be less distinct there."

"Screams?" The word squeaked out.

"Maybe if Adam and Eve hadn't sinned, she would sing. Come, dear. Take a few steps back, and I will hand you the material. You don't have to look."

There was no chance of that happening.

Lydia's face scrunched, and a groan gave voice to discomfort.

Another one, so soon? If this was what it took to have a family, God could forget that little request. Plenty of orphans like her were running around. She could adopt some. No pain. No groans. No—

"Ahhhh!" Lydia's scream left Theresa cold and ready to retreat.

"Breathe, darling. Like this." The midwife demonstrated some breathing strategy that added to the dizzying sensation in Theresa's head. She loved Lydia, but if this went on much longer, the midwife would have to peel Theresa off the floor. Nope, no children. Not a one.

When a maid appeared, Theresa caught Lydia's eye. "Go . . . find . . . Abra—" Lydia leaned into another groan.

Theresa didn't need any more encouragement. She retreated, pausing at the door long enough to throw out a promise to pray.

Abraham rushed through the front door just as she reached the landing. "How is she?"

Before Theresa could answer, a groan-turned-scream came from behind her. Abraham almost knocked her over in his rush up the stairs. She should warn him. The door thudded off the wall. Too late. He'd discover soon enough what terrors awaited him, but maybe being an officer of the law would provide him with the courage she lacked.

Theresa made her way to the parlor and found a seat. Each scream punctuated the silence and sent a shiver down her back. Begging and making promises with God had never worked before, but she wasn't above trying again. Chin to knees, the words poured out of her with growing speed. *Please, let everything go well. Let Lydia be okay. Let the baby live.*

Dr. and Mrs. Pelton bustled into the parlor with the joy of attending a party. Didn't they know their daughter was dying upstairs?

Another scream rent the air, but Dr. Pelton merely set his medical bag in a corner and claimed a nearby seat. Surely he wouldn't leave his daughter to face this alone.

"Aren't you going to go help?"

He waved off her concern. "If the midwife needs me, she'll send someone down."

"But it's too soon!"

"Sooner than I like, but not dangerously so." The man was infuriatingly calm.

"What if Lydia or the baby dies?" The words choked on a sob.

Mrs. Pelton sat next to Theresa and patted her back. "I have every confidence they both will be fine, but"—she lifted Theresa's chin until their gazes met—"even if things don't go as planned, our hope is in Christ. He's the one who promises death is not eternal. That even in the suffering, He is with us, bearing us up and holding us close." Strength and peace beyond understanding resided in her tone and demeanor.

If Theresa didn't know about the losses Mrs. Pelton had suffered herself, she would dismiss the woman's words as flippant and inexperienced. But the war had dealt a heavy hand to all, and the Pelton family was no exception.

Still, her words did not ease the soul-deep ache. "But I don't feel Him."

"Oh, honey." Mrs. Pelton's arms wrapped around her shoulders and pulled her close. "Feelings change, and they can lie, but God's presence is constant and true. Whether we feel Him or not." Another, more prolonged scream echoed down, and she gave a wry smile. "Even in the throes of childbearing, He is here."

Dr. Pelton lowered his pipe. "I assure you, child, Lydia is in good hands. If things were amiss, I'd be there. Childbirth isn't pleasant, but in the end, Lydia will be beaming with happiness."

"Every fear and moment of pain will come together in a glorious way that only a God who loves and cares can design. It seems like the end, but it's just the beginning." Mrs. Pelton smoothed Theresa's hair. "When it's your and Broderick's turn, you'll understand."

Truth pierced the intended comfort like shrapnel to the heart. "You mean Edward."

Mrs. Pelton exchanged glances with her husband. "Certainly, dear. If that's whom you love."

They all fell silent, and Theresa stood and paced the floor. She didn't want Edward. She wanted Broderick. Oh, how she wanted him, but she couldn't alter the truth. Wedding bells would never ring for them. Tears pricked but remained dammed. How could life be so unfair? Could she have none of her dreams? Even Lydia might be stolen from her.

Theresa gripped the back of a chair as the loudest, longest yell yet rent the air. A different cry—a sort of mewling sound—followed.

"Did you hear that?" Mrs. Pelton jumped from the seat and scurried to the parlor door. "We're grandparents!" She twirled with a wide grin splitting her face. "How long do you think they'll make us wait?"

Dr. Pelton rose and joined his wife. "I believe we made your parents wait over an hour."

"How cruel of us."

The easy banter between husband and wife eased the knots in Theresa's muscles. If they weren't panicked, and Dr. Pelton hadn't been summoned, then everything must be fine. Except they'd heard only the baby, not Lydia. Something could still go wrong. Time dragged. She paced in front of the fire, sat when Mrs. Pelton commented on the motion making her dizzy, and then returned to pacing out of the woman's view.

A door above creaked, followed by footfalls. Each step fell like petals from a flower, only they predicted life and death. *Lydia is alive. Lydia is dead. Lydia is alive. Lydia is—*

A blood-stained apron preceded the midwife into the room. "Mother, father, and son are doing well." She removed the apron quickly, as though she'd forgotten she still wore it, then folded the stains from view.

Theresa's breath whooshed.

"Did you hear that? I got my boy!" Dr. Pelton tossed his hat into the air.

"May we see them?" Mrs. Pelton's face shone with the hopefulness of a child awaiting permission to open a gift.

"They requested I invite the family on my way out." The midwife squeezed Theresa's shoulder before she exited the room.

Theresa hung back as the Peltons moved toward the stairs. Until she saw Lydia, she wouldn't rest, but she couldn't intrude when Lydia had invited only family. If the boy hadn't yet returned with Black-beard, she would walk home and come back in the morning.

"Where are you going, dear?" Mrs. Pelton asked from the base of the stairs.

"I'll allow you your family time. Tell Lydia I'll check on her later."

"Pshaw! You are family. I may not have had the privilege of birthing you, but you are as much my daughter as Lydia and Madeline. Love, not blood, makes a family. Now, come, dearest. I am most eager to meet my grandson." Dr. and Mrs. Pelton each took an arm and pro-pelled her upstairs.

Family. The word stuck in her throat like a lozenge, melting to soothe an ache she'd long accepted as permanent. Her blood relatives were gone, but the love flanking either side of her pulsed with life and healing. They may not always see eye to eye, but they cared. More than that, they wanted her.

When they stepped through the bedroom door, her artist's heart beat with renewed life. Darkness softened the edges of light like a vignette, focusing all attention on the most poignant portrait Theresa had ever seen. It was as if all the light in the world emanated from Lydia's and Abraham's smiles as they peered down at the small bundle. Oh, to catch the way Abraham caressed Lydia's arm as their heads joined together in sweet admiration. No amount of artistic ability would ever display such pure, shimmering love. Its warmth wrapped around Theresa and drew her in.

Lydia looked up, little crystals glittering in the corner of her eyes. "Oh, Momma, Papa, Theresa, he's perfect."

Mrs. Pelton pushed Theresa closer until all three squeezed shoulder to shoulder next to the bed.

Abraham gazed at his son with the glowing smile only a new father could carry. "We've named him Gabriel Michael Hall."

A perfect name for a little angel. The temptation to touch Gabriel's ruddy skin was too much. She traced the contours of his round jaw. How could skin be so soft and smooth? Better than the finest silk ever made.

"We want you to be the first to hold him." Lydia held Gabriel out like a sacred offering.

Theresa's breath hitched. "But your parents—"

"We agree wholeheartedly, dear." Mrs. Pelton pushed her forward. "But don't hesitate. We're anxiously awaiting our turn."

The mattress curved under her weight as she accepted the light, little bundle. The terror of moments ago vanished and left her in awe of such a perfect being. Gabriel melted into the crook of her arm as though he'd been designed to fit there. His fuzzy head couldn't be larger than a bread plate. Tiny, pink lips suckled as his dark lashes fluttered against splotchy cheeks.

More precious than gold. How could Lydia bear to let her hold him? If she were his mother, she would never want to release him.

"He *is* perfect," she whispered.

Dr. Pelton coughed behind her, and her cheeks warmed. It would be unkind to deny the new grandparents any longer. What a blessing to have been the first to hold the little man aside from his parents. After a tender kiss to his wrinkled brow, she passed Gabriel to his grandmother.

"I never dreamed it would be like this." Lydia's hand wrapped around hers and squeezed. "Thank you for being with me. For not letting me lose hope. For trusting God with me."

Heaviness dampened the tender moment. Theresa hadn't trusted.

Not really. Like her faith, the encouragement had been a sham, but she didn't want it to be. She wanted to believe God was for her and not against her, that she could trust Him with her future.

Gabriel whimpered. His face grew ruddier and scrunched, and then the strangest, angry sound she'd ever heard came from his opened mouth. Lydia reached for him, and the little family became whole again.

God answered Theresa's prayers this time, but that didn't mean He would in the future. Could she trust Him with what little she had left? But trust didn't mean she'd get what she wanted. So what did it mean?

Chapter 21

ANGRY SHOUTS AND CRASHING TABLES erupted in Dirk's Saloon as men fought over a card game. Nothing like a bar fight to distract Grimm from tailing him. Broderick ducked under a flying mug and edged his way to the exit. No good. Grimm spotted him. Escaping to answer Isaacs's summons proved more difficult than he anticipated. He'd have to drag Grimm into the fray before Dirk successfully put an end to it.

Broderick worked his way into the fight, evading flying fists while throwing a feigned one. Beefy hands gripped his shoulders and spun him around. Perfect. The clod staggered as he swung. Broderick dodged and then gave a shove to his backside. The man upended Grimm's table and catapulted ale into the riled group. Heads turned, and those directly hit by the drinks converged on Grimm.

"It weren't my fault. He's so drunk he can't see a hole in a ladder."

"Oh yeah?" The oaf rose and punched Grimm's bruised-green nose.

Renewed shouts of encouragement erupted from those watching, and a thick circle formed around the two wrestling men.

Broderick slipped out the back into another rainy evening. Between the late January thaw and constant precipitation, the river swelled and heightened tensions. Tempers flared with little provocation—perfect for distracting tails, but the weather made for miserable escapes. A quick glance around the alley revealed no one waited for him. Though a direct path to the Keppler Hotel would save him from a thorough soaking, he needed to be certain a second shadow didn't follow. He splashed through connected alleyways and private gardens with a constant eye to his surroundings.

For Isaacs to risk an appearance at Dirk's, the news must be crucial and time sensitive. He'd been investigating Nathaniel's activities. Maybe he'd come across information that would allow them to arrest everyone, especially that traitor. Broderick circumvented the crowded restaurant and took the service stairs to their shared room.

Isaacs opened the door at his knock. "About time you arrived. We've got a problem." He let Broderick pass through before locking the door behind him. "Vincent Drake is dead."

Problem? More like a relief with one less threat to Theresa prowling the streets. The problem must be in the details. "How and when?"

"Murdered almost four weeks ago."

But that put his death before Colonel Plane's. "Are you certain of the time line?"

"No doubts. Drake had tickets to a boxing match on January fifth in his pocket. He blackmailed one of the competitors into dropping but never arrived to collect his winnings."

Broderick threw his gloves on the table and wished they made more than a dull thud. He'd suspected Drake wasn't Plane's murderer, but someone had gone to a lot of trouble to frame the man. Considering the threatening note was delivered after Drake's murder but before Colonel Plane's, the colonel's murder had been premeditated. They were dealing with a calculating criminal.

"We need to take another look at that carpetbag," Broderick said.

"Already did. I found this." He passed over a scrap of newspaper with a description of the imperfect counterfeits for the public to identify. "I checked. The first time the papers printed it was the eleventh."

The bag may have once contained useful evidence, but whoever murdered Drake had left behind only what he wanted them to find. Someone had carefully and meticulously orchestrated every detail. Fitz was smart, but he wasn't a long-range planner. He wouldn't have thought to write the notes supposedly from Drake, then murder Colonel Plane, and then plant evidence. Whist was disorganized, but he managed to produce counterfeits for years without getting caught. Could there be more to Whist than he suspected?

Or was there another, more dangerous player?

Broderick grabbed the rock from his pocket and began flipping it through his fingers. "Whoever killed the colonel could have known about Drake's death and used it to his advantage, but my instinct tells me the same person who killed Colonel Plane killed Drake."

Isaacs leaned against the wall and rubbed his chin. "I agree. The bullet that killed Drake was the same type that killed Colonel Plane. Likely the leader."

"But why kill your engraver before the plates are completed?"

"Maybe they were finished, but Colonel Plane upped his fee? The leader killed him and then stole the plates."

"Plausible, but then why are the plates still missing?"

Isaacs frowned at the floor as if it might hold the answers.

They were missing something or someone. For the production firm to be successful, each member must provide a specific contribution—capital, supplies, potential customers, or skill. Whist had unscrutinized access to the supplies and the skill to run the press, Fitz provided access to potential customers, and Colonel Plane had the engraving skills. Yet none of them had the finances to fund the several-thousand-dollar operation. If Colonel Plane refused to release the plates, the financier would be the one to lose the most.

"I don't think Whist is smart enough to pull off this scheme or run the counterfeiting ring on his own." Logic left him with one other suspect. "Part of Nathaniel's plea bargain was to reveal where the unused counterfeits were hidden. What if he didn't reveal all the locations? The first reported counterfeit appeared one month after his release from prison. Louis confirmed that Nathaniel and Fitz have worked together at Spring Grove Cemetery several times, and Nathaniel had no problem renewing relationships with other ring members. I know he's involved."

"It makes sense, but we have to consider another viable leader."

By the look on Isaacs's face, Broderick suspected what was coming.

"We have no evidence that Theresa is a member of the ring, let alone a leader."

"Miss Plane has clouded your judgment, Cosgrove, and Darlington sees it. He's recommended you be removed from the case."

Of course he had. Without Broderick and Detective Hall's effective barrier around her, he'd have free access to go after Theresa in whatever manner he deemed necessary. "That would be unwise."

"For now, Chief Brooks agrees, but that won't last long if you continue to ignore the truth." Isaacs pushed from the wall, then took a stack of papers from his nightstand and extended them. "This is my full report with all the details of her involvement."

Broderick ignored the report. If he held it in his hands, he might destroy it. "What evidence is there beyond Darlington's pure determination that she's guilty?"

"She has connections to the ring all over the place and the skills necessary to complete the job. What woman perfects engraving skills as a hobby?"

Broderick paced to the window and back. "Colonel Plane had her do it for the sake of the business."

"A business she wasn't even allowed to visit? Such a flimsy claim would never hold up for anyone else you suspected. Then there's the matter of her passing counterfeit notes before Colonel Plane's death and several times since. She's careful about it, never using more than one bill at a time. The only reason we haven't brought her in for questioning is we don't want to tip her off."

She wouldn't knowingly use counterfeits. "There has to be an explanation."

"Probably the usual one. She's desperate." Isaacs returned the report to his nightstand, then crossed his arms. "The executor of Colonel Plane's will informed us she has three days until eviction from that house."

Broderick stilled. Everything Theresa did was tied to staying at Plane Manor. Losing it would be a devastating blow, one she would do almost anything to avoid. Except this. She'd never stoop to counterfeiting. He knew her too well.

Isaacs continued. "She's the one who chose to go to the printshop after Colonel Plane's murder. Then she was adamant about bringing Nathaniel into it. No amount of denial on your part will stop her arrest once we have hard proof. I know you like her, Cosgrove, but is she worth your career?"

He cared about both. That's why he concealed case details from her—to preserve the integrity of his investigation and to protect her from knowing too much. In the end, all it had done was work against them both and place her in more danger. Revealing Whist's involvement to her now would only further prove his lack of judgment to Darlington and Isaacs, but her safety had to take precedence. Tomorrow he'd tell her and convince her to leave the printshop. Truth would prevail in the end. It had to.

Theresa hugged her coat tight against her body as she escaped to the empty rail yard next to the printshop. Forty-two degrees might be a veritable heat wave, but the unexpected visitor to her office had left her chilled to the bone.

How had Fitz slipped past Broderick and Nathaniel?

The sunset flamed red as that bully's hair. He'd materialized behind her while she shelved a ledger and pressed his gun to her waist, leaving her no room to maneuver between his body and the bookcase.

"Not a sound, lass. I've brung a message. Turn over the fifties printing plates by tomorrow or you and the house burn."

"But I don't have any plates."

"Then you better be finding where Colonel Plane hid 'em." He jabbed the gun harder into her side. "You go telling anyone, and you'll be asking him in person."

He'd disappeared as quickly as he'd come, undetected by anyone who would care, and she hadn't stopped shaking since. *God, I'm trying to trust, but why do more problems keep coming?*

"What are you doing here alone? You know it isn't safe." Broderick approached from behind.

It wasn't safe anywhere anymore. Not at home, not at the shop, and certainly not near the river.

She watched the muddied waters churn and nip the shore well above their natural boundaries. Already the flood predictions called for a repetition of last spring. A shiver coursed down her back though ten yards stood between her and the swollen river. Was there anywhere she could feel safe again? "I needed to evaluate the water levels."

"Thinking of going for a swim?" Broderick said, teasing.

"Not funny. Drowning once was enough."

Broderick's arm brushed hers as he lifted a hand to squint against the setting sun. Though material separated their touch, tingles enticed the always loitering desire to lean into him. She sidestepped lest she give in.

"It doesn't look too bad," he said. "Another ten feet until it reaches the tracks. Plenty of room for the river to swell without affecting the shop."

His confidence soothed her nerves, but nothing made her more anxious than being near water. Except maybe being in it.

Her mind returned to Fitz. She should tell Broderick about the threat, but he'd likely lock her up at Lydia's for safekeeping. All hope of saving her home would be ruined. However, if Fitz were in jail, he couldn't set fire to her home. "Are you close to making arrests?"

Broderick's heavy sigh did not encourage hope. "We could make some, but not the whole ring." He paused. "Theresa, Whist is involved. I'm doing my best to protect you here, but you need to stay away from the shop until we're able to make all the arrests necessary."

She should have guessed Whist was involved in all this. He must have been the one to send Fitz in undetected. Threats, debt, floods—it was enough to bury a person alive. Heaven help her, she couldn't bear this alone. *Please, God. Show me I'm not as alone as I feel.*

Like an immediate answer, Broderick's concerned face shifted in front of hers. He knew her need, could see past the strong facade to the depths of her soul—her broken, aching, terrified soul. She twisted the engagement ring on her finger and swallowed past the lump in her throat. God forgive her adulterous heart. She didn't want anyone but Broderick to comfort her. Even if Edward held her close, it wouldn't compare to the relief just seeing Broderick brought.

"Something more than the case and water levels has you upset." When she stayed silent, he stroked her cheek with his thumb. "Talk to me, please."

Peace and strength seeped into her through his touch and concerned gaze. Denial was no longer possible, and she understood it to the core of her soul. She still loved this man, with no room left in her heart for another. He was her better half, the one who tempered her follies, guided but did not crush her spirit. Edward was a good man—loyal, protective, and hardworking—but he wasn't enough for her. Would never be enough. Love, passionate or practical, belonged to Broderick. She'd known it all along.

Grandfather might have been a counterfeiter of money, but she'd committed a far worse crime. She'd counterfeited love, all in the name of obtaining a secure future. Edward deserved better. Continuing to pretend this farce was genuine would be an unforgivable offense.

"I can't do this." She retreated.

"Do what?"

Fear pulsed through her. Either she was sentencing herself to a life of spinsterhood—and a short one at that if Fitz had his way—or hope would blaze to life. "I can't love you and marry Edward."

He blinked and then gathered her into a tight embrace. "Oh, Reese." The nickname came out soft and agonized.

She took a ragged breath and allowed his finger to lift her chin until their faces were a mere breath apart. Before he could say anything she didn't want to hear, she bounced to her toes. The world receded as her lips found his. His gentle response fell like spring rain, washing away the grime and death of a long, harsh winter. For the briefest of moments, she felt whole again.

He released her. "Theresa, we can't."

She dropped her gaze to the muddied ground. *Rejected. Again.*

"Not yet." His words jerked her gaze back to his. "This case has complications I can't explain, but please don't marry him. When this is over, we'll go to Philadelphia and see where God leads us."

Where God leads us? She swallowed back the fear. Could she risk hoping God would give her the desire of her heart? Endure if He didn't? Trust wasn't easy, but she had to try. After all, look where carving her own path had led her.

"Miss Plane!" Theresa stepped back from Broderick's hold and turned toward the errand boy running toward her. "Mr. Greystone's here for you, and Mr. Whist is closing for the night."

She shook her head as she processed what the young boy said. He must be wrong. The shop wasn't due to close for several more hours. "But the projects due tomorrow won't get finished."

The boy shrugged and ran back toward the building.

Whist, the spiteful man! This was punishment for trying to sell the steam press to a competitor. Had the buyer contacted her instead, the man would never have known. If she didn't lose her house to arson, she'd lose it to debt. Two days wasn't enough time.

Broderick touched the small of her back and drew her attention. "I'll finish the projects. You go home."

"I'll stay and help."

"No, you need to keep as much distance from the shop as possible. Go home and paint. A break from all this would do you good."

"I don't know what to paint anymore." A sad truth. The image of her home burning consumed her mind and allowed for nothing else.

"I can think of several things. Gabriel, Tipsy, Blackbeard . . ." The corner of his mouth curled. "Us."

She smiled despite the ache in her chest.

"Come." He took her arm. "I'll escort you home."

"No." As much as she would prefer his company, she owed Edward an explanation. "Edward will take me."

Broderick frowned. "I don't trust him."

"He's a good man, and I've done wrong by leading him on. I need to do this, please." A war between the options played across his face. "Trust God to protect me. He's done it thus far." Sort of.

He frowned but gave a curt nod.

She watched Broderick stalk back to the delivery bay, then turned toward the front of the building. Edward stood at the corner, arms folded and stance spread. He'd witnessed their nearness, maybe their kiss. Her stomach flipped as she walked toward him. What would he say or do? Would he save her from breaking the engagement by doing it himself?

Lord, let this go as well as possible.

"Edward, I—"

"I don't want to hear it. Just get into the hack."

Theresa bit her lip and struggled to step into the carriage unaided. He wouldn't even look at her, just glowered at the open door. After he spoke to the driver in a muffled but controlled voice, he squeezed into the narrow spot beside her without a word. She tried to give him more space, but no matter how she shifted, their legs and arms touched. Fists clenched in his lap, he stared straight ahead while his jaw sawed side to side and his mustache twitched.

She deserved his fury, and so much more.

The silence stretched until she could no longer stand it. "Edward, we need to talk."

"About your infidelity?" The words hurt, but she could not deny the truth of them. "There's nothing to say. He's turned you against me."

"He's done nothing to turn me against you. It's my own traitorous heart. I never stopped loving him." His fist pounded the carriage wall, and she flinched. "We were engaged years before you and I met. I never thought I'd see him again."

"And you never thought to share this with me?" A curse slipped. "We are to be married in two days."

Had he not noticed she'd made no plans for a wedding? Not even the simple one she'd offered originally?

"I can't marry you, Edward. I don't love you, and I will never love you. You don't deserve that kind of marriage." The rock in her throat almost choked her. This wasn't going how she planned. Not that she'd had a plan, but ending their engagement while stuck in this conveyance had not been wise.

"We *will* marry. I'll not allow any other choice."

He'd not allow it? She blinked. Maybe he'd not understood. "Edward, it's over."

His red face deepened to an almost purple. "You . . . cannot . . . end this."

He couldn't force a marriage. The man just needed time to cool off and accept the truth. Something better done alone. She leaned forward to tap on the glass and signal the driver but then paused. When had they crossed over to this part of town? Her heart raced. Nothing good happened on George Street. "Where are you taking me?"

"To teach you a lesson." He crushed her right hand in his and held it firmly in his lap.

She tried to yank free, but it was no use. She was trapped.

CHAPTER 22

BRODERICK FLIPPED BLINDLY THROUGH THE stack of unfinished projects. What had he been thinking, hinting at a possible future with Theresa? His heart had kicked his mind aside and insisted a way could be found to make marriage work for them. Only it couldn't. Not if he stayed in the Secret Service. Most field operatives didn't have families for a reason, and Theresa wasn't the type of woman contented to be left behind. He loved his career in the Secret Service, but could he balance his duties as an operative and a husband without Theresa getting hurt again?

He released a slow breath. *God, guide me to what's best.*

"There you are, now." Fitz entered the shop through the door Broderick had propped open, a cigarette hanging from the corner of his mouth.

What was he doing here? Broderick had observed Nathaniel with the man, but Fitz hadn't contacted him since the ring got spooked.

"We be done foostering about." Fitz clapped Broderick on the shoulder and blew a victory smoke circle. "Tomorrow we print."

With information like that, he, Isaacs, and Darlington could catch the ring dead to rights, and none would be able to escape jail. "You found fifties plates, then?"

Fitz didn't bother to lower his voice. "We didn't, but that fiery lass don't be having much choice than to hand them over. That house'll burn with herself in it if she don't."

Broderick's gaze shot to where Theresa had entered a hack with Greystone ten minutes ago. He should have known the moment she'd scurried from the office pale and arms wrapped around herself that she'd received another threat. At the very least, the question about his case should have tipped him off. How was he supposed to protect her if she hid information from him?

"Don't be looking so glum, lad. I know you fancy her skirts, but you best be finding yourself another lass. The big gun'll do whatever he pleases with her, and there be no stopping him. Come now, a tall mug and a game o' cards be calling our names." Fitz turned toward the door.

"Thanks, but I have things I need to do." Namely, get Theresa out of that house.

"Don't be thick as a plank. The big gun be paying for everything, he is."

Broderick clenched his rock. Theresa wouldn't abandon the house on her own, but he couldn't ignore the chance to identify the big gun. That missing piece of information could be all he needed to prove Theresa's innocence and bring the case to closure.

"Will Nathaniel be there?" Broderick set the projects aside and grabbed his coat. Either answer meant leaving.

"He won't. He prefers women to cards. We won't be seeing him 'til morning. Cat promised to introduce him to all the strumpets." Fitz elbowed him. "There you go, now. That's what you be needing to get your mind off the lass's skirts. The big gun would understand. Cat's one of his favorites."

"Thanks, but I prefer cards."

"Then why we be wasting time?" Fitz opened the door and gestured outside with his head.

As the door closed behind them and the lock clicked into place, realization hit him like a boulder to the head. He'd been duped. The only reason for Whist to close early and coerce Broderick from the building would be the assurance of not being discovered printing money tonight. The ring didn't trust him and had assigned Fitz to distract him while they finished the job. If he could catch them in the act, Theresa would be safe. But first, he had to escape Fitz's vigil.

Theresa shifted uneasily as the hack worked its way farther down the unkempt road of George Street—a place most officers despaired of reforming. During daylight, it passed as merely a dirty part of town. After dark, it became the devil's playground. One research trip for a dime novel with Lydia provided more than enough material for a dozen stories, both fact and fiction.

The stench of unwashed bodies, rotten food, and something she'd rather not identify overpowered Edward's heavy-handed use of bay rum cologne. Men wandered into and staggered out of drinking establishments. Women hocked their bodies with no more deference than selling an apple in Findlay Market. She shuddered to think what circumstance forced them into such a soul-breaking means of survival.

"Where are you taking me?"

"It's time you know the truth about Smith." Edward knocked on the roof, and the hack stopped outside a three-story building with the words Catherine's Boarding House painted in bright colors. Music filtered into the street, and red light glowed from the upper floors.

A boarding house, indeed.

Edward handed her down and then led her to the front door. "I'm sorry to expose you to this, but I cannot allow Smith to continue this charade with you."

When he opened the door, soft piano music and hushed chatter drifted out of the large parlor papered in deep red. Paintings, flower-filled vases, and tasteful parlor furniture decorated the space like any other boarding house, but that was where the similarity stopped. A woman in a white, lacy dress with less material than Theresa's chemise flirted with a man on her way upstairs. Others similarly clad paired off with potential clients throughout the room—some standing in the man's arms and some seated on laps.

A robust woman in an emerald dress rose from a nearby settee and primped her raven ringlets. Crimson lips curled as she drew near. Theresa stepped back, but Edward stayed her with a hand.

"Well, what have we here, handsome? Bringing me a new girl?" The woman ran a hand down Edward's chest as she examined Theresa as though she were a horse at auction.

"Are you the madame here?" Edward asked.

The green paint around her eyes crinkled for a moment and then smoothed. "I'm Catherine,"—she winked at him, completely ignoring Theresa—"but you can call me Cat."

"We're in search of information. My fiancée's friend resides here, a Mr. Broderick Smith."

A wicked and dirty smile spread across the seductress's face. "Oh, yes. Brody's a particular favorite of mine. He rents a room in the back, so he's never far from a bit of entertainment."

Broderick rented a room here? But he'd told her to contact him at the Keppler Hotel. She glanced around the parlor. Surely he wouldn't stay here even as an undercover operative.

"I don't believe you. It goes against his morals. He would never stay here."

"My, aren't you an innocent one?" Cat shook her head as if disappointed by the knowledge, making her long curls bounce around her bosom. "If you'll allow me a few minutes alone with her, I'll open her eyes to Brody."

The woman was mad. No man would leave his supposed fiancée alone with this feline. Yet Edward nodded and moved off to an empty area by the door, arms crossed and face stoic. Theresa clenched her teeth. If he expected his actions would endear her to him, he was sorely mistaken. Broderick would never bring her here, and he certainly would not leave her alone.

Cat looped her arm through Theresa's and guided her across the room. Images of being turned into one of Cat's girls sent shivers down her spine as she checked for the bump where her gun remained hidden.

Edward might have abandoned her to the wiles of this woman, but she would not fall prey.

Once in a quieter hallway, Cat spoke. "You must be Theresa. Brody's spoken of you often."

Theresa faltered. Edward hadn't introduced her nor spoken her name.

"Although *I* wouldn't describe you as homely. You're much prettier than that, but he does prefer his girls curvy." She ran a hand down her waist, emphasizing the voluptuous shape.

Heat flushed Theresa's neck. Maybe she did resemble more of a post than an hourglass, but Broderick never cared. He looked beyond a woman's appearance to what lay in her heart. This woman spoke with honey-coated poison, and she would not be weakened by it. However she knew Theresa's name, it came through a game of deceit.

Cat stopped in front of a door and lifted a key from the chain around her neck.

Theresa's chest tightened. No one would hear her scream from here, not with all the music and chattering voices. She slipped her hand into her pocket and clutched the warm grip. If working with Whist had taught her anything, it was to be proactive. "Where are we?"

"This"—Cat unlocked the door with a flourish—"is Brody's room."

Whoever stayed here kept it meticulously clean. A trunk stood at the end of a bed made with lines as crisp as her own. No women's clothing or rumpled sheets littered the room. On the desk, a pocket Bible lay at odds with the unholy acts occurring beyond the walls. "I see nothing that suggests this is his room. Or that he does anything more than sleep here."

Cat grabbed the Bible and then exclaimed, "Oh dear, that's where I left this." She bent and retrieved something from under the bed. No, not something—a chemise. "I'm forever losing my clothes."

Theresa's stomach burned, and an unfamiliar desire to hurl herself at the woman spread through her. Lies. That was all they could be.

Cat placed the Bible in Theresa's free hand, and Theresa swallowed.

Opening the cover required her to release her only protection, but leaving it closed meant the truth would evade her. She studied Cat, who watched with folded arms. The woman couldn't hide a weapon with so little fabric to conceal it. Theresa released the gun.

Please, don't be his.

She held her breath and curled back the cover. A scrap of paper lay tucked in the crease, and Ecclesiastes 4:12 was written in a familiar hand across the white space. *And if one prevail against him, two shall withstand him; and a threefold cord is not quickly broken.* It was the verse she and Broderick had chosen on which to base their marriage years ago. Not a good sign. She lifted the scrap and flipped it over.

"No." The single word escaped before she could stop it.

The doodle of her and Broderick embracing that she'd completed last week stared back at her. He must have taken it from her desk at the printshop. No one else would want it, and even if they had, only he would know what verse to scribble on the back. This Bible belonged to him and no other.

She closed her eyes, and images of Cat in his arms bombarded her.

"Since you're an innocent and I have a soft spot for the naïve, let me shed some light on your friend." The woman patted a spot on the bed, but Theresa wasn't about to sit where who knew what had occurred.

"I'll stand, thank you." Theresa clutched the Bible to her chest. Maybe it would shield her from whatever Cat had to say.

"I exploit men for a profit, but Brody is using you to gain access to your connections. He's a detective, and all he cares about is solving his case."

"Not true." Well, the detective part was, but not the rest. He cared for her.

"What have I to gain by lying? You want proof?" Cat knelt by the trunk, then picked the lock and rummaged until she found the desired item. "Brody's been keeping this from you. He's had it for weeks."

Cat extended a small moleskin journal toward her. It couldn't be. Yet there was no denying Grandfather's code book. She had a matching copy in her desk from the days when he'd taught her how to cipher. Why would Broderick take it? She accepted it along with the heaviness of doubt. What else did Broderick hide from her?

The door opened, and Cat rushed past her. "Ah, Brody, sweetheart."

Theresa spun to see Cat's barely contained chest smash against Broderick. A second girl hung on his arm, and his eyes widened as they spotted Theresa. His escort deserted him and shut the door behind her. Before anything could be said, Cat kissed Broderick with vulgar familiarity. Theresa pivoted toward the wall and gulped for air. No. It wasn't possible.

The sickening smack of lips preceded Broderick's bewildered question. "What are you doing here?"

She couldn't face him. Couldn't manage a breath to answer. The world swam, and she clutched the wall for support.

"It's only fair that she knows the truth about us," Cat purred.

The truth? God help her. This couldn't be the truth.

CHAPTER 23

THE TRUTH? CATHERINE'S SMIRK EXPLAINED everything. That woman and the devil were in league with each other. Broderick pushed Cat aside and scraped the stickiness of her lip paint off his cheek. What lies had the woman spoken to get Theresa here? How did she even know Theresa? "Get out, Cat."

"I can't leave this poor girl alone with you. I must protect her innocence." Cat's weak attempt at nobility slapped the faces of all honorable people.

Theresa whirled around, eyes narrowed and posture stiff. "I can protect myself, thank you."

Broderick stepped toward her, but she made a wide arc around him with the crisp steps of a soldier. The dark depths of hurt and anger doused the earlier glimmer of hope in her eyes.

Cat sidled up to him and leaned in despite his attempt to yank free. "I think it's time you take your leave, dear. Brody and I have some things to . . . discuss. You understand, don't you?"

"Oh, I understand perfectly." The Bible in Theresa's hand—his Bible—smacked the side of his face, and fiery tingles chased momentary numbness. Theresa's nostrils flared. "That's the right hook I owe you."

Cat chuckled. "I like her."

"Reese, I—"

Theresa turned a stony face toward Cat. "Thank you for the talk and returning my grandfather's journal."

The colonel's journal? His gaze dropped to the moleskin code book in Theresa's other hand. He knew better than to keep it here. Cat must have broken into his trunk.

Broderick glanced at the calculating seductress, and Cat's lips collided with his. Theresa gasped and then followed up her Bible-bashing with a shove to his back. Before he could steady himself, Cat wrapped her arms around his neck and moaned as if delighting in a passionate kiss. He thrust her from him, but the door slammed before he could fully escape.

Cat reattached herself to him and smiled like a feline after a successful hunt. "I think she's jealous."

More like furious. Whatever lies Cat spoke would take hours to illuminate, but first he had to get Theresa to safety. Cat's clients wouldn't need any encouragement to assume Theresa was the newest girl.

"Why don't you stay and work my information about Colonel Plane's book out of me. I might even tell you who his murderer is"— her finger traced down the front of his coat—"if you give me what I want."

He shoved her back and opened the door. The murderer was likely a counterfeiter. Once he had Darlington and Isaacs raid the shop tonight, Cat's information wouldn't matter.

Cat jumped in front of him. "Leave, and I'll never tell you anything again."

A gruff voice echoed down the hall, asking about the new girl. Better lost information than Theresa's harm, and based on tonight's performance, Cat played him the fool. He shoved her aside and slammed the door in her face.

"You've made dangerous enemies, Brody! I was your last ally."

If Cat were an ally, he'd rather face his enemies.

He stalked into the main room, where Greystone leaned over a burly man whimpering like a beat dog. Broderick should have known the oaf would risk Theresa's safety to make a point. He gripped the rock in his pocket instead of Greystone's neck and searched the faces of observers for Theresa. Beyond the crowd, her black hat bobbed near the front door, and a man with clear intent in his gait followed her outside.

Broderick drew his revolver, and the clump of Cat's girls scattered. As he reached the door, Theresa screamed. He flung the door open, and at the base of the steps, Nathaniel wrestled the man who'd followed Theresa. Theresa stared in horror at the display as she pressed against the side of a hack.

"Hurry, miss," the cabby hollered.

Theresa jerked to action, and then the cabby set off at a hair-raising pace.

Broderick would never be able to catch up on foot, but at least Theresa was safe. She'd either go home or to Lydia's, and he wouldn't be far behind. He turned, intending to cut through the alleys to the nearest livery, but he stopped when Greystone burst through the front door.

"Where is she?"

Broderick gestured to the retreating hack. "Safe for now. What were you thinking, bringing her to this part of town?"

"I wanted to protect her. She needed to know what kind of man you are."

Nathaniel huffed as he released the pinned man to stagger off and wheeled toward them. "Neither of you protected her. If I hadn't been here, that man would have treated her no better than one of them." He gestured to a gaggle of women peeking out the door.

"If she left you, Eddy, we're still available. We've missed you this week." The girls blew kisses and giggled.

Broderick scoffed. "And I'm the scoundrel?"

Greystone threw a punch, but Broderick dodged. He didn't have time for this two-faced liar. He cocked his gun and turned it on Greystone. "Go back to your women. I'll ensure Theresa is safe."

"You're finished, Smith. She'll never have you again."

"As long as it means she doesn't have you either."

Red mottled Greystone's face, and he stalked down the street, leaving behind a chorus of disappointed sighs.

Broderick released the hammer and holstered his weapon. Nathaniel came alongside him smelling of perfume. Neither Greystone nor Nathaniel were the moral pillars Theresa believed them to be, and her trust in them proved increasingly dangerous. He needed to get a message to Isaacs and Darlington to raid the shop before it was too late, but Theresa had likely chosen to go home instead of to Lydia's. Both problems needed immediate attention but required going in opposite directions.

Getting Theresa to listen to reason might take hours, risking the chance to catch the ring in the act of printing money. Then again, going to Isaacs and Darlington first would leave Theresa and Mrs. Hawking trapped in the house alone for hours with the threat of arson.

He chafed under the decision but forced himself to think it through. If the ring were already printing money, they'd be too busy to burn down her house. Mrs. Hawking could manage Theresa's protection for a couple of hours. The raid would have to take priority.

"We can't let Theresa go home." Nathaniel cut to the alley with long strides and spoke over his shoulder. "Grimm boasted in there about how he planned to force her to give him the plates tonight. I tried to intercept him, but he escaped."

Filthy liar. He'd say anything to distract Broderick from the case—just like when they searched the upper floors of the printshop. "Give it up, Nathaniel." Broderick caught up and shoved him against the wall. "I know you're one of them."

Nathaniel grimaced but didn't attempt to break free. "I swear I'm not. I've been trying to help your case. They suspect you but not me. I used that to my advantage so I could finally do the right thing by you and Theresa."

"Lies. You've not given me a single bit of information I didn't already know. I'm familiar with your tactics."

"It's not my fault that's all I've been able to discover."

He didn't have time to stand here arguing with the traitor. Broderick pressed his Colt into Nathaniel's gut. "You're under citizen's arrest for producing and dealing counterfeits."

He'd drop him off at Hall's police station and then connect with Isaacs and Darlington.

Nathaniel raised his hands in surrender, but his face showed everything but submission. "I swear on my life I'm telling the truth. We need to ensure she's safe first. If I'm lying, Grimm won't be there, and all you've lost is time. But if I'm right, Grimm's been begging for a chance to make her suffer for breaking his nose."

Broderick bit back the desire to swear. He didn't have time, but Grimm posed a genuine risk. Darlington and Isaacs would use tonight against him, but he couldn't ignore the potential threat to Theresa.

Abraham crossed his arms and stood over Theresa like an overbearing brother. "What do you mean Edward took you to George Street?"

Theresa accepted the teacup from a stricken Lydia and set it down before it revealed her trembling. "I didn't have a choice. He forced me and then left me with the madame to learn the truth about Broderick. The woman not only enlightened me to his rooming situation but pulled Grandfather's code book from his trunk."

Abraham ran a hand over his face. "Give it to me. You know it's evidence."

She retrieved the journal from her pocket, warm from her body, and examined it. The emblem stamped on front, representing gallantry and bravery at the risk of life, mocked her. Her heroes lay shattered at the base of their pedestals. The red ribbon could have been dyed by her blood for all the stabbing pain she felt.

"Here. You'll want to interview Broderick. Cat said he's had it for weeks."

"And you believe her?" Abraham cocked an eyebrow as he slipped the book into a coat pocket.

"I don't know. She and Broderick have some sort of . . . agreement." The kiss—no, kisses—between the two seemed indicative of a lusty relationship. Her stomach cramped as their embrace materialized with every wretched detail. She tried to focus on Broderick's face. Was he pleased, surprised, or disgusted by the act? Cat's black curls and groping hands cut off a clear view. Had that moan of pleasure been his or hers? It didn't matter. What mattered was Broderick hadn't rejected the woman's advance.

A hand rubbed her back and freed her from the moment. When had her own hands become the sole support of her head? And why was her face wet? She shouldn't be crying. Not for Broderick. He wasn't even hers. The thought brought forth a sob.

"Oh, sweetheart, he doesn't deserve you." Lydia's soothing tone did nothing to ease the pain.

"Don't pass judgment yet. We don't know all the facts." Abraham's voice echoed reason, but she wasn't convinced. He hadn't seen what she'd seen.

Theresa wiped her face with his offered handkerchief. "I should go home. Mrs. Hawking will be distraught that I haven't arrived."

"You're staying here. No objections, or I'll arrest you for shoving."

"The only person I shoved was Broderick, and I don't think you can arrest me for that."

Lydia mumbled, "You should have shot him."

Perhaps, but a part of her still hoped Cat was a good actress and Broderick the fool.

"You misunderstand me. By *shoving*, I mean you've been paying for goods with counterfeit money." Abraham's declaration should have shocked her, but she couldn't muster even surprise. The banknotes from the bugle case had been a gamble, and she'd lost.

"I should've known Grandfather's stash was as fake as our wealth. I will replace every note with the profits from the shop. You can check the bills first for authenticity."

"No need. The merchants have been recompensed, but I'll need to examine what money remains."

No doubt Abraham funded the compensation himself. She didn't deserve this family, but how grateful she was not to face this alone. "Mrs. Hawking knows where I keep everything." Her head beat a steady tempo and accelerated when the latest threat came to mind. If she was under pseudo-arrest, no hope remained for saving her home. "You should know Fitz threatened to burn down Plane Manor if I don't hand over some missing press plates by tomorrow. But I don't have them. I've never even seen them."

Abraham was silent for a moment, the gears in his mind working visibly through his far-off gaze. After a short nod, he dispensed orders. "Theresa, you're not to leave this house for any reason. Lydia, I'm arming Gerard and posting him at the door until I can get an officer to stay. Don't answer the door for anyone." He exited the room with long, purposeful strides.

"We'll be safe here." Lydia leaned into her and gave an encouraging squeeze. "Now, tell me everything."

Though it was as painful as living it the first time, Theresa spared no detail. Their tea went cold and pastries untouched.

"I don't believe I've ever been so jealous." Theresa picked pieces off a biscuit and rolled them between her fingers. "What am I going to do, Lydia? I have no way to raise the funds to save my home, and even if I could, Fitz might burn it to the ground. I can't marry Edward, and now Broderick . . ." She shook her head. "I have nothing left."

"You have God." Lydia's soft words hit a tender spot.

How easy it was to forget. Even so, the reminder didn't change her situation, her pain. Theresa discarded the crumbs into the basket and shook her head. "We're barely speaking."

"I'm pretty sure that's your fault, not God's." Lydia gentled her tone as she took both of Theresa's hands in hers. "I know you've been struggling, but no matter what happens or what you think you've lost, you cannot lose God. He pursues you with an unstoppable passion. He wants to be with you, and sometimes it takes stripping everything away for us to realize how much we need Him. If you have nothing left, then turn to the One you do have. He's there waiting."

"I love your unfettered faith, Lydia, but my relationship with God isn't like yours."

Gabriel whined from his place in the bassinet near them, and Lydia swept the baby into her arms. "I don't mean to be brutal, but it's time for you to accept your part in the relationship and feed it. You can't love or trust someone you don't spend time with. Now I need to go feed Gabe. Please, think on what I've said."

Theresa slowly rose to her feet as Lydia disappeared into another room. She hated it when Lydia was right, especially when it meant she was in the wrong. It had been a long time since she'd invested in her relationship with God. A spattering of prayers and reading Momma's letter didn't replace dwelling in His Word. With nowhere else to go, she might as well spend time in the Bible—and on her knees.

She retrieved Broderick's pocket Bible from the table—her only remaining physical tie to the man—and retreated to the guest bedroom. Once settled in the window seat, she took a deep breath and reread the verse on the back of her drawing. How she needed that cord to survive. By herself, she couldn't prevail against the circumstances. But with God, anything was possible. Could a cord be made with two instead of three if one of them was God?

God, You have to be enough. Teach me Your plans are enough.

CHAPTER 24

BRODERICK AND NATHANIEL RODE THEIR horses onto Plane Manor's drive to the chorus of gunshots from inside the house. The front door flew open, and Grimm ran out, ducked down with arms protecting his head. Mrs. Hawking barreled out the door, loading another shot and hollering at the fleeing man's back.

Grimm stumbled past. "Run, ya fools!" He kept going until Broderick no longer saw him.

"I always said that woman was meaner than a badger caught by surprise." Nathaniel shook his head.

Precisely why Broderick liked her for Theresa's protection when he was gone. They went inside, and he barred the door behind them as he glanced around the foyer.

"She's not here," Mrs. Hawking said.

Then she *had* gone to Lydia's. "Good. Pack everything in the house, beginning with what Theresa would find most important to keep. She'll not be back."

Mrs. Hawking nodded and marched toward the stairs. No need to worry about her dawdling.

He turned to Nathaniel. The man had been right about Grimm, but that didn't mean he spoke the truth about the rest. Once a traitor, always a traitor. "You're coming with me."

By the time he'd sent a message to Hall to keep Theresa at the house, placed Nathaniel under the watchful eye of an officer, and orchestrated

212

a raid with Darlington and Isaacs, it was too late. The ring had dispersed and left the printshop empty of any evidence. Nothing about this night had gone right. Midnight tolled as he reached Lydia's house. An unreasonable hour to call, but he couldn't let another minute pass without attempting to talk to Theresa. If she were asleep, he'd stay in the parlor until she woke.

After Broderick identified himself, an officer with a raised revolver opened the door.

"Let him in," Hall said.

Broderick made it through the door but no farther. Lydia blocked his path with crimsoned cheeks and folded arms. "How dare you come here."

Not a good sign. "I need to speak with Theresa."

"Absolutely not! How could you live and consort with the madame of a brothel?"

Is that what Theresa really believed? "I've never consorted with *any* woman."

"You deny the kiss, then?" Lydia's brow rose in a dare.

Hall gently tugged Lydia out of the way, saving Broderick from a response. "This is between Theresa and him. Let the man pass."

"No. And if you let him see her, you can sleep in the carriage house tonight."

Her baby cried, saving them from further lectures.

Hall shook his head as he watched his wife march upstairs. Once she'd disappeared into what Broderick assumed was the nursery, he faced Broderick. "Don't take my allowing you to see her as approval. God called us to be heads of our households, and it takes a mature man in Christ to put the needs of his wife above his career. You've been lying to yourself about what choice you made. You have one chance to make things right." His mouth twitched. "If you don't, you're paying for my hotel room. Theresa's still awake in the guest room. Upstairs, last door on the left." Broderick turned but stopped when he spoke again. "The door stays open, Cosgrove. I trust you, but I'll not risk a private reconciliation. Lydia and I will be across the way."

The warning almost tempted a smile. Reconciliation hung by a thin thread of hope, but even so, he'd never compromise Theresa's honor. He nodded his thanks and jogged up the stairs to where Lydia blocked his way, patting the baby's back as though it were a war drum. With protective friends like her, Theresa would be safe here. Even Whist would cow under such a glare.

Hall passed Broderick and guided Lydia back into the nursery across from the guest room.

At the threshold, Broderick hesitated. Theresa sat curled in the window seat, reading and oblivious to his presence. She appeared to be in one piece despite the cabby's dangerous escape down George Street. Bits of hair fell around her face, and the lantern gave a halo effect as she tilted her head to continue reading the turned page.

Lord, lend me Your words. I can't lose her over Cat.

The creak of the floorboards announced his approach, and red-rimmed eyes snapped to meet his. Pink suffused her cheeks before she laid the book aside, then stood with the regal poise of a queen and nodded toward one wall. "If you're looking for entertainment, you're in the wrong place. George Street is that direction."

He stepped forward, ready to catch her fist should she decide another shot necessary. "It's not what it appeared. I promise."

"So you weren't staying at Cat's when you told me to send messages to the Keppler Hotel?"

He hadn't lied. Just omitted a detail. Except Theresa would never see it that way. "At the time, we had no possible future together, so I had no reason for you to know. I sleep at Cat's and use her girls to collect information, but that's it."

"Oh, I saw how you collect information."

"That's not what happened."

"Are you suggesting I imagined that kiss?" Her entire stance bunched like a wolf prepared to pounce. At least if she attacked he could pin and hold her until she listened to reason.

"Cat kissed me, not the other way around."

"But you enjoyed it too much to stop her."

The accusation bruised worse than if she'd actually thrown a punch. Did she really think so little of him? "I tried to stop her."

"Obviously not hard enough, and you didn't deny enjoying it."

He rammed a hand through his hair and tugged. Her ability to twist words frustrated him in the best of circumstances. "By all that is good and holy, Theresa, I swear there is and never has been anything between me and Cat or any of the other girls. I've never kissed a woman but you."

"Until tonight."

Broderick growled. "Yes, but not by choice, and it was neither desired nor enjoyed."

"What about the other woman you brought into the room? That wasn't unplanned."

He'd almost forgotten about his attempt to convince Fitz he didn't need a shadow. Cat had skillfully dug his grave, and he'd stepped right into it with Lizzy on his arm. "I paid her to give the appearance of doing her job so I could sneak out the window to meet my partners."

Her gaze bore into his, merciless in her pursuit to evaluate his answer. Broderick met and held it. Let her see the truth. He loved her and would never betray her. Tonight's fiasco resulted from his failure to recognize the ring's carefully crafted trap.

"Your job doesn't excuse you. You should have told me."

Though her posture remained stiff, the words indicated progress. She at least believed him innocent of willing participation. "I can't share everything about my job."

"I don't need to know everything, but I do need to know I can trust you." Her stiffness melted, leaving behind a melancholy that saturated her expression. "How can I do that when you compromise your convictions by staying at a brothel just to have access to information?" Her arms wrapped around her middle. "What if next time the information requires something more . . . intimate?"

The truth behind her fear pierced like a double-edged sword and cut to the marrow. He *had* compromised his convictions. Never before this case had he entered a brothel during active hours. Whenever he'd made use of a madame as an informant, they met in civilized clothes in public parlors. Yet fear of failure had driven him to reason his way into accepting things that contradicted his beliefs. Staying at the brothel had been only the beginning. Lying and withholding information had taken root as the only solution to protecting Theresa, and he'd done it without a second thought.

Hall was right. He'd been lying to himself. All his decisions pointed to choosing his career over God's leading and Theresa's needs. Even his decision to abandon her after the river.

Lord, forgive me and help me be a better man.

Theresa cradled herself in the soft glow of the lamplight. Vulnerable. Afraid. Aching. Alone. Again, his choices injured her, but this time he would do right by her. With God's help, he would be the man he should have been all along.

"I've made many mistakes regarding you, but dallying with other women will never be one—not even for information. You are the dearest, most precious woman on this earth, and it grieves me to know I'm the cause of so much suffering." He took a tentative step forward. When she did not retreat, he took her hands in his and stroked the soft knuckles. "I'm sorry for leaving you when you needed me most, for putting this case above your needs, and for straying from the man I should be. I don't deserve your forgiveness, but I ask for it all the same. Will you forgive me? Allow me another chance to prove worthy of your trust?"

Tears slid down her cheeks as her coffee gaze searched his. Years of failure stood like a canyon between them. She had every right to deny him and turn him away forever.

After an eternity of waiting, she exhaled. "I want your solemn oath. No other women."

"You have it. Forever and always."

They melded together like two halves to a whole, as they should have from the beginning. One problem resolved, but others remained out of his control.

He breathed in the honey scent of her hair and released a slow breath. How would he protect her after tonight? Isaacs knew the reason for his delay in organizing the raid, and Broderick could no longer deny Theresa's influence over his decisions. Tomorrow he would face Darlington, confess he withheld information, and face the consequences. By God's mercy, Darlington would understand and allow him to remain on the case, but Broderick didn't hold out hope.

"I know that sigh." Theresa lifted her head and cupped his cheek. "What's wrong?"

"This case is a mess. My partners believe you're a member of the counterfeiting ring. Once they successfully remove me from the case, I don't know how to protect you."

"Maybe you're not supposed to."

She pulled away and retrieved the pocket Bible from the window seat. Head bent, she tilted the book toward the light and flipped through the pages. "Momma wrote a letter to Father in his Bible to encourage him, and she referenced a story. I've been reading and rereading it all evening." She stopped flipping somewhere in the Old Testament. "When the Israelites were surrounded on all sides and unable to win, God told them, 'Be not afraid nor dismayed by reason of this great multitude; for the battle is not yours, but God's.'" When she looked up, moisture glimmered in her eyes. "We have to trust Him, even if things don't go as planned."

"I can't chance losing you again. If I do nothing, you'll either end up in jail or hurt."

"Does that make God any less in control?"

Broderick dropped onto the window seat and took a deep breath. They'd always been good at pushing each other to see hard truths. "Of course not, but that doesn't make it easy."

She gave a mirthless chuckle as she nestled into the spot next to him. "No, it doesn't, but"—she tugged her sketch from inside the Bible and flipped it so the words faced him—"we are a threefold cord. We don't face this alone. You and I have been trying to overcome our problems on our own, but that's not how God wants it. Sometimes He has to strip us of everything—even the illusion of control—for us to see our need for Him."

He found her hand and entwined their fingers. "You better be careful. Spout too much more wisdom and I'll have to make sure you're not hiding gray hair under a wig."

She smiled. "Better gray hair than a bald head. I've seen your father. I know what you're heading toward."

"You'll have to learn to like it. I refuse to wear a toupee."

"I suppose I could always paint hair on you." Her laugh soothed his anxiety.

"First, we have to get past this case. The ring's scattered, but if I can arrest them, I can prove your innocence."

"They can't have gone far. Fitz demanded I find some missing plates by tomorrow." She dropped her gaze to their hands. "I'm sorry. I should have told you."

"We've both made some missteps, but we'll blame it on learning to trust again. Mrs. Hawking is already packing the house. I'm borrowing a wagon so she can bring your things back here. I'll stay and wait for the ring members to show."

"You know about the threat, then." Her whole body sagged. "I didn't want to tell you because I knew you'd never let me go back, but God saw fit to make that happen anyway. Abraham's promised to arrest me if I leave here."

He'd have to thank Hall for sacrificing the household's sanity. A caged Theresa could make everyone miserable, but she'd be safe. "Memories live in your heart, not your home. They can never be stolen from you."

She rested her head against his shoulder and sighed. "I know, but it hurts to think I've lost it."

He kissed her temple and held her. He could do nothing to change the outcome. The house was beyond redemption. The best he could hope for was to catch the ring in the act of searching for the plates or burning the house. If he failed in that, they'd be in hiding before the Secret Service could reorganize, and Theresa would be left to the mercies of a jury while he watched helplessly from the courtroom gallery.

"I take it you forgive him?" Lydia stood like a bailiff at the door, ready to haul him out if Theresa gave the word.

Theresa lifted her head, and her eyes focused on Broderick, picking up the reflection of the lamp in their depths. Her silence unnerved him. She hadn't explicitly said she forgave him. He held his breath, hopeful but well aware of Theresa's unpredictable nature.

At last her hand caressed his face. "I do. I forgive everything."

Those last three words reached beyond Cat's brothel and covered years of regret with peace and healing. He didn't deserve this woman, yet she wanted him. If only he could be as certain of their future as he was of his love for her.

Chapter 25

A FLUTTERING MOURNING DOVE STARTLED Broderick awake as the soft rays of early morning filtered through the carriage house loft window. He ran a hand over his face and blinked gritty eyes. How long had he dozed? Smoke tinged the air and hay stuck to the blanket as he shifted to better observe Plane Manor. A thin line of woodsmoke puffed from the farthest chimney, indicating someone had broken inside.

How could he be so foolish as to fall asleep? Broderick checked his Colt and spare derringer before peering down to the ground floor. Though dawn's light barely filtered through the high windows, it allowed a cursory evaluation of the room. Quiet and empty. Good. Dust puffed around him as he jumped from midway on the ladder to the floor.

He stretched out a few knots and then snuck toward the house. Everything remained shuttered and locked tight—no sign of life but the smoking chimney. Unease twisted in his gut. No one lit a fire while they ransacked a house. Could the laudanum Lydia slipped Theresa have worn off already? She'd turned near-hysterical once her belongings arrived in the middle of the night and the reality of losing her home became real. He wouldn't put it past her to slip away to try to see the house one last time.

The front door bore no fresh markings of a break-in, and he used the key Theresa gave him to unlock it. He eased the door open and cringed when it creaked.

No movement sounded anywhere else in the house.

Light poured from the wide-open parlor door, but no one investigated the creak. Broderick crept inside. The contrast of light and dark played tricks on his eyes. If someone lurked in the deep shadows, he couldn't discern it. A haze of cigarette smoke drifted from the parlor. Fitz. And likely not alone. Broderick was no coward, but he knew a trap when he saw one. He needed Darlington and Isaacs before proceeding further.

A board creaked behind him.

Broderick spun, and the barrel of a pistol brushed his nose.

"Been waiting for ya." Grimm yanked Broderick's revolver from his grip.

Whist stepped out of the parlor with a cigar hanging from his mouth. "Bring him in for the family reunion."

Grimm shoved him forward until he stood in the center of the ransacked room. Nathaniel leaned against the wall, tied and gagged. Swollen face and blackened eyes lifted to meet Broderick's gaze. How had they gotten Nathaniel out of police custody? Whist must have a corrupt officer in his pocket. Though Broderick wanted Nathaniel to suffer for his past transgressions, seeing his brother in such a state coiled his muscles.

"Have a seat, Smith." Whist gestured to a single chair in front of the fireplace. "Or is that Cosgrove? It's fascinating the details Cat will share for the right price."

Broderick glanced around the room for escape ideas, but Grimm shoved him into the chair, and Fitz wrenched his arms behind his back.

"Tie him up, good an' tight." Whist dropped onto the couch and stretched his arms across the back, a savage glint to his gaze.

Grimm found the derringer, then lashed Broderick's feet to the chair legs while Fitz bound his wrists. Once satisfied, Fitz tipped the chair back until it balanced on two legs. Heat seared Broderick's backside. If he fell, it would be right into the flames.

"I've waited a long time to do this." Whist rose from the couch and used Broderick's thigh to extinguish his cigar. The material singed, and Broderick grit his teeth against the sear of burning flesh. "You shouldn't have upset Cat. She told me everything, starting off with your ties to that meater."

Broderick caught Nathaniel's eye—the one not swollen shut—and grimaced.

"So tell me, Cosgrove, what agency do you work for? The police department? Pinkerton? Secret Service? Something private?" Whist nodded to Fitz, who tilted the chair closer to the flames.

Sweat beaded at Broderick's neck, and the smell of singed hair filled the air around him. As long as they didn't know, he'd continue the ruse. "Being a lawman doesn't pay. I work for myself."

"Ah, but we know all about the Cosgrove Detective Agency. After all, Nathaniel was the best they had. Pretty pathetic if you can't tell your own detectives are corrupt."

For once, having a scoundrel brother might work to his advantage. "One tends to turn a blind eye toward family, but Nathaniel ruined it for the rest of us. Increased scrutiny forced me out. Father does not abide padding our pockets."

"Claiming corruption, are you? Interesting." Whist jerked his chin. "What do you think, Fitz?"

The chair leaned further—its legs slipping. Broderick tensed as heat scorched the base of his head. He jerked. The chair toppled to its side, leaving him a hair's breadth from the embers scattered around the fire grate.

"Put 'em through. Leave no seam unexplored." Whist stepped back and smirked as Fitz and Grimm set to work freeing Broderick's arms from the chair.

They ripped off his coat, and then Grimm ran a blade along every seam until the thing matched a tailor's template. His only warm jacket for the winter was fit to join the rag bin. At least Hall held his credentials. Nothing on him would identify him as Secret Service. Fitz searched his pockets.

"Have a look at it. Matches Nathaniel's, even." Fitz displayed the gold watches Pop had given his sons when they'd officially joined the

Cosgrove Detective Agency. High quality and intricately engraved, the watches were meant to remind them why they rubbed shoulders with the wicked.

Fitz flipped open the cover. "'Defend the poor and fatherless: do justice to the afflicted and needy.' Sounds like the creed of a copper sure."

Or the command given in Psalm 82. "You don't reject a gift of that value, no matter the words written in it." Not that a logical explanation would deflect suspicion.

The watches disappeared into Fitz's pocket. "Guess I won't be hitting your scruffy face since I be getting a nice sum for 'em."

How generous.

After a thorough search of Broderick's clothes, Grimm stepped back. "He ain't got nothing else but some rock."

Broderick rubbed his wrist, grateful his treasure survived and keenly aware his freedom lasted only as long as Grimm's trigger finger didn't start to itch. "I told you. I'm no copper."

"That is yet to be seen. You don't have to be a copper to be a traitor. Ask Nathaniel here." Whist yanked on a wad of Nathaniel's hair. "He testified against us in a plea deal, and then the fool came back, begging to return to the ring. Good thing Fitz kept an eye on him at the cemetery, or we'd have killed him. Turned out we had a use for him after all."

This could be a manipulation tactic to throw suspicion off Nathaniel. Although, his brother had never been one to take a beating, even for a cover. Broderick glanced at him. He looked worse than a tenderized steak. As much as he wanted to believe Nathaniel was in on this, he couldn't. They were both in more trouble than Andersonville prisoners.

Whist released Nathaniel and yanked the gag free. "Lucky for you, I require disposable men. A shipment of government paper got shifted to storage after a mistake at the station. A despicable lot of upstanding officers are guarding it. You have two options. Retrieve the paper or forfeit your lives." He planted a foot on the couch and leaned forward with one forearm resting on his knee as if he fancied it made him appear more intimidating.

The double click of Grimm's and Fitz's weapons did a far better job of instilling fear than Whist's ridiculous pose. Broderick turned toward Nathaniel. The same knowledge lurked behind his gaze. Either way, they died. However, agreeing to steal the paper bought time. He could get a message to Isaacs and Darlington. They'd catch Whist in the hock and arrest everyone.

"I can see your mind working, Cosgrove, but I've accounted for everything. I know Miss Plane takes laudanum every night to combat nightmares. It would be a shame if somebody switched her bottle with something more poisonous."

Ice cracked through Broderick's veins and stopped his heart. As far as he knew, only Dr. Pelton, Lydia, and Mrs. Hawking knew of the nightly doses. Neither Dr. Pelton nor Lydia would harm Theresa, but Mrs. Hawking had faithfully served Colonel Plane for years. Had he corrupted her? The possibility raised his hackles.

Nathaniel responded to Whist's statement before Broderick could form a response. "You wouldn't kill her. You need her engraving skills."

"She never came up with the missing plates, and since we didn't find them here either, I'm not convinced she's as necessary as others believe. Even so, let's consider it a hollow threat for now. What's not a hollow threat"—Whist flicked his wrist toward Grimm, whose smirk turned filthy—"is that a woman can be made to suffer without affecting her engraving ability."

The gleam in Grimm's eyes revealed the eager hope they would refuse to steal the paper.

Broderick's stomach churned. "She's well protected."

"Until she decides to go off on her own." Whist wandered to the mantel. "It won't take long. She's independent with a false sense of invincibility."

A truth that drained the life from him. No matter what Hall did, Theresa would find a way to do what she wanted. Eventually, she'd leave Lydia's house.

"So what do you say? Die now and ensure Miss Plane's fate? Or attempt to retrieve our paper and prolong her independence?"

Stealing the paper violated his oath to his country. It contradicted everything he stood for, but so did sentencing Theresa—or any innocent person, for that matter—to the wiles of such vile men.

He closed his eyes against the choice, for no choice existed.

CHAPTER 26

"I SAID I DON'T NEED it." Theresa knocked over the laudanum bottle, disappointed the cork didn't give way to spill the contents.

"I'll bring you a plate of breakfast, then." Mrs. Hawking picked up the bottle and slid it into her pocket.

Did the woman think her such a fool that she wouldn't see through another attempt to dupe her into compliance? Unless Theresa prepared it herself, she'd take no food or drink. The door shut, and she stared out the window toward her home. No, not her home. Not anymore. She'd failed and lost it all. What little remained to her name was stored in Lydia's carriage house.

Lord, help me trust Your plan, even if it isn't what I want.

She squinted at the roof-lined horizon, where a dark column of smoke rose to mingle with clear skies of midmorning. Something wasn't right about the color. Chimney smoke from the other homes came out gray or white. Her breath caught. The fire at the printshop eight years ago produced billowing black clouds like those now hovering above Plane Manor. A cold chill swept down her back though she'd been more than warm enough a moment ago.

Theresa tossed her wrap aside and dressed in a hurry. By the time she'd tied her boots, the line of smoke had turned into rolling billows. She raced from her room and down the stairs.

"Fire!" She called as she hit the foyer. "My house is on fire!"

Abraham rushed from the dining room and stared at her. "Are you sure it wasn't a nightmare?"

"I'll get the laudanum." Mrs. Hawking swerved from her path to the dining room back to the kitchen.

"I don't need laudanum. I'm not hysterical."

Abraham folded his arms and looked to be chewing on his response as though it were an overcooked piece of meat.

"I'm not! Black smoke is billowing from the direction of Plane Manor."

"Gerard, look out the guest room window and tell me what you see." Abraham turned to face her. "Theresa, I understand this is a challenging time for you, but even if your house is on fire, you cannot go to it."

"I don't care about the house." And for the first time, she realized she didn't. "Broderick's there, trying to catch the counterfeiters. If there's a fire, it could mean he's hurt."

Gerard came down the stairs. "Could be a fire, sir, but it's not close enough to concern this house." The sympathetic glance he shot her revealed he believed her a simpleton.

"Thank you, Gerard. Theresa, I'll go check with a colleague. Officer Stevens will stay in the foyer. Do not leave this house. Do you understand me? This may be nothing, but it could also be a trick to lure you out. I'll be back with information as soon as I have it."

He was a good man. She would comply with his demand unless they discovered Broderick was hurt. *Please, Lord, let Broderick be safe.*

Abraham took Lydia aside for a few moments and then left the house. When she joined Theresa at the parlor window, the reason for the discussion became clear. "I've been meaning to ask if you would paint some miniatures of Gabe. We'd like to hang one in the nursery and send some to Abraham's parents."

A poor attempt at providing a distraction. Theresa wrapped her arms around her middle as she watched smoke spread across the sky. Had Broderick been in the house when they started the fire? Securing it had been a fine idea, but they'd missed the fatal flaw of leaving only one exit. *Please, let him have escaped.*

"Here, hold Gabe." Lydia shoved the baby into her arms, then grabbed Theresa's shoulders and directed her upstairs to the nursery—opposite any view of the smoke. "I know you're concerned, but worrying will put you into hysterics again. Please, allow me to distract you."

Giving in to her friend's plea, Theresa settled into the rocking chair with Gabe. She tried her best to follow along with the conversations Lydia led, but as the time stretched and turned from minutes to hours, worry turned to panic.

The lunch tray brought to them went untouched as she paced the room. "Something's wrong, Lydia. Abraham has been gone for four hours. It takes twenty minutes to get to Plane Manor."

"We need to wait—"

Theresa pivoted, then marched downstairs while Lydia sputtered behind her. Waiting drove her mad. She needed answers. The officer blocked her way at the base of the stairs. As she debated the merits and consequences of knocking a police officer unconscious, the front door opened, and Edward rushed in.

"You're alive." He crushed her in a hug she couldn't escape. "When I saw the house burning, I feared the worst."

She pushed back from him as her stomach flipped and roiled.

Abraham passed his soot-covered coat to Gerard and spoke with a grim tone. "By the time we got there, it was too late."

"Too late for what?" Her heart clenched at the implication.

Edward leaned in and gripped her hand. "The house isn't salvageable. The roof fell in, and the stone walls are crumbling. There's no house to return to."

A collapsed roof? Crumbling walls? If Broderick were inside . . . Darkness clouded her vision.

Abraham spoke in low tones to Lydia, but his words carried to Theresa. "Be prepared. We had to rescue Broderick's horse from the carriage house when we arrived. He's still missing, and it doesn't look good."

God, please, no! Her legs gave out, and she slumped against Edward. *God, please let them be wrong. Protect Broderick, wherever he is, and bring him back to me.*

Broderick rubbed on the heart-shaped rock until his thumb grew raw. Each hour locked in Dirk's upper room frayed his nerves worse than a wire brush taken to a wool coat. Theresa promised to stay with the Halls without a fuss, but he wouldn't put it past Whist to contrive some urgency that would entice her to sneak out. Even if she stayed put, the threat of poisoning loomed large in his mind.

Nathaniel stared out the window, where long shadows darkened the brick alleyway. "Have you devised a suitable plan yet?"

"Not one that would work." Whist proved more thorough than Broderick expected, Fitz was no bumbling idiot, and Grimm thirsted for any opportunity to harm them. Making a move while they traveled to the train station was unlikely to end well and would only place Theresa in more danger. Their best hope would be encountering the police at the train station, but even that posed a risk.

The door opened, and Fitz grinned. "Let's go, lads."

Grimm followed through the door and cocked his pistol. "Any more escape attempts and we get to shoot." A wicked grin spread across his face. "Then Miss Plane'll be all mine."

Broderick breathed a silent prayer for inspiration as he caught the ragged coat Nathaniel tossed him. By the determined set to his brother's jaw, they both understood tonight would end in blood no matter how they cooperated. Grimm led the way out of the tiny room while Fitz brought up the rear, brandishing both his and Broderick's guns.

Rain threatened as they cut through alleys toward Plum Street Depot under the cover of night. Broderick's mind raced with possible tactics that could preserve his commitment to both serve his country and keep Theresa safe, but each idea would leave him for dead and Theresa at Grimm's mercy.

If he could somehow get word to Isaacs and Darlington, they wouldn't question his vow to the Secret Service, and Theresa would be protected. But no opportunity presented itself. Once they stepped onto the main road, Fitz and Grimm dropped behind, their crunching footfalls a constant reminder they observed every move. Vendors shuttered and locked windows, eager to rush home to family and a warm meal.

"Got a plan now?" Nathaniel's whisper barely rose to audible.

"Play along until a better opportunity presents itself."

They walked a little farther before Nathaniel spoke again. "If we get through this alive, we'll both be criminals." Anguish weighted his whisper.

"I'll convince Isaacs of the truth." Darlington would be another matter.

Nathaniel shook his head. "When we get to the station, focus on escaping and getting to Theresa. I'll keep them distracted as long as possible."

He'd already contemplated that plan, but one if not both of them would die in the process. "Dying a hero's death won't erase your past."

"No, but you deserve life, and only one of us has a chance at it." Nathaniel paused and rested a hand on Broderick's shoulder. "Let me do this."

The words encouraged faith in the man and weighed on his conscience. They may have chosen different paths, but he couldn't willingly allow his brother to die. "We do this together or not at all."

"Spread out," Grimm barked from behind.

They complied and walked in silence. Somehow, he had to concoct a plan that at least kept them alive—doubtful as that was. A train whistle blew, and the squeal of braking announced an arrival.

"Don't be getting no fancy ideas, now. Talk to anyone, deviate from the plan at all, and you'll be dead." Fitz handed Broderick his useless, emptied revolver.

Fitz broke off to confiscate a horse and buggy from a livery down the street, and Grimm followed them to the short hedge bordering the rail yard. So much for his observing from a safe distance. With Grimm present, Broderick would never be able to alert the guards to their situation.

Using the hedge as cover, Broderick scanned the area. Whist claimed the paper was stored in the engine house until transported out of town. The tall, brick building stood about one hundred and fifty yards away with a small outhouse a few yards closer. Though the cloudy night hid any details, the land was flat and potential cover was sparse. Most rail cars sat farther up the track, but a handful remained near the brick building. A stack of lumber lay twenty yards ahead of him, leaving an empty expanse of over seventy yards to the rail cars. Transporting a crate that distance without being caught would be nearly impossible. No wonder Whist wanted them for the job. He'd risk anyone's freedom but his own to get what he wanted.

Nathaniel grabbed his shoulder and pointed to an unnatural shadow leaning against the back wall of the building. The shadow shifted and then returned to stillness. A hidden guard. Light flickered from the front corner where another huddled near a bonfire. A third emerged from the outhouse and joined the first shadow. Broderick crouched lower. It was unlikely those were the only guards present.

A crate of rolled paper required at least two people to carry, leaving one person to defend against attack—Grimm, most likely. The situation held potential. If he waited until the right moment, he could catch Grimm off guard, out of sight from Fitz, and alert the police. Without credentials, it would take some work to convince the authorities of his identity, but someone could warn the Halls and Theresa against the threat of poisoned laudanum. By God's grace, the plan would work.

The brakes of another approaching train squealed, and he tugged Grimm lower as the freight cars passed at a slowing pace. This was their chance. He nudged Nathaniel to move parallel to the train's progress. The train switched to a holding track, and as they approached, switchmen uncoupled the cars from the engine.

The engineer leaned out the cab window. "The old girl's in bad order."

"Take her to the barn," a yardmaster called back.

No one would question a train returning to the engine house. After a nod in the direction of the engine, Nathaniel led the way farther down the line. Grimm followed behind Broderick. After a man uncoupled the brakeman's car from the boxcars, the yardmaster waved the engineer on. The workers turned to deal with the abandoned cars, leaving the engine to rumble off unobserved.

Nathaniel cut through the bushes ahead of Broderick and grabbed hold of the tender car's back coupling. He fumbled for a moment but managed to swing up to the ladder. Not elegant, but they weren't going for style. Broderick did slightly better, and Grimm followed with ease, evidence of life as a vagabond.

No one noticed the engine's extra passengers, but they kept low as they walked across the water jacket to the coal bunker. Broderick peered down into the nearly empty bin. With the fireman and engineer facing forward and the tender door to the engine shut, their descent into the tender should go unseen. He gestured to Nathaniel and Grimm. While they maneuvered down the slope, Broderick watched the engineer and fireman tinker with valves and levers. With all other noises overpowered by the hiss and chug of the engine, they remained distracted by their tasks.

Once Grimm and Nathaniel crouched low on either side of the tender door, Broderick slid over the edge. Coal dust coated his hands and clothes as he skidded down to where his feet met coal. He swiped at sweat dripping down his temples and immediately regretted it. Grit scraped his face and worked into the corner of his eye, making it sting and water. Nathaniel and Grimm appeared no better off. At least the black coating camouflaged their presence. The scent and taste of metal, oil, and smoke coated Broderick's nostrils and tongue as the train bumped its way across the tracks. If this worked, and they lived, he'd need more than a bath to rid himself of the filth.

Steam hissed, and the train slowed. Rail yard lingo bounced around them as the engineer and yard workers maneuvered it into the engine house. The roundabout turned, and workers shouted as the engine chugged in reverse. The darkness of night shifted to a lamp-lit bay. After a few minutes, the steam engine hissed. As the fireman and engineer walked around the cab conducting final checks, Broderick held his breath. Being discovered now would be disastrous.

Eventually, boots sounded on the platform and then down the ladder.

"Fresh coffee is ready in the office. Come and tell me what's wrong with the old girl." Footsteps crunched along the gravel and out into the night.

The engine creaked as it cooled in the cold night air. An occasional cough from the officer standing guard somewhere near the entrance punctuated the moments of silence. When no one returned to the engine house some minutes later, Grimm gave the signal.

Broderick gripped the edge of the bunker and scanned their surroundings. No obviously hidden guards, but the spot in the corner could harbor someone, and another could be concealed in one of the other engines. He hung and examined the darkness for any movement until his muscles trembled from holding his weight. Nothing indicated a person hid among the housed engines. The police may not have deemed it necessary to keep a guard inside, but he wouldn't take any chances. Alerting them too soon could end with Grimm shooting an innocent.

Broderick opened the tender door and used the steps on the darkest side of the tender car to reach the graveled ground.

Once they were together, Nathaniel pointed to two rectangular crates stacked near the back wall. They looked the correct size and shape to hold a roll of paper, but the stamped markings were indistinguishable from this distance. Each careless clump from Grimm wound Broderick's muscles tighter. Broderick needed to catch the guard in private, not have Grimm sound the alarm.

At the crates, Nathaniel kept watch while Broderick and Grimm examined them. Each crate bore the emblem of the government licensed paper manufacturer, Crane Currency. Not sufficient evidence for Grimm, he pried off the top, and his coal-dusted hands stained the sheet as he tested the texture.

"We got what we need." Grimm slid the lid back on. "Take the top one."

Nathaniel hefted one end while Broderick gripped the other. It would be a miracle to carry the heavy, awkward crate without being noticed. They maneuvered the box to the farthest engine from the officer. At the entrance, Broderick peered at the guard. Though huddling near the fire, the officer kept vigilant watch. There would be no sneaking past him.

Perfect.

Grimm grabbed a large rock. "On my mark."

The rock sailed across the engine house and banged against the farthest tender car. The guard's head snapped in that direction, his hand going immediately to his gun. As he disappeared down the aisle, Broderick, Nathaniel, and Grimm slipped around the corner toward the line of boxcars. Broderick slowed their pace, using the crate's awkward shape as an excuse. If he could delay them enough to be caught . . .

The guard called the alarm as they reached the back corner of the engine house. Fast-paced crunching indicated the two hidden guards split ways, one coming directly toward them. Grimm aimed and waited. Broderick dropped his end of the crate on Grimm's toes and snagged a rock. Better to risk getting shot himself than allow a fellow officer to take a bullet. He didn't want to hurt the officer, but a bump on the head beat a bullet wound.

When the officer slowed at the corner and Broderick lifted the rock high, Grimm shuffled behind him, but Broderick's body sufficiently protected the officer from a clear shot. As the barrel peeked around the corner, Broderick brought the rock down on the weapon. It discharged but missed. He yanked the officer around by his weaponless hand, and the man swung his weapon wildly. Broderick dodged and then tackled his midsection.

Wrestling while avoiding the butt of the officer's weapon left Broderick breathless, but he had to explain. "I'm working—"

The officer abandoned his gun and slammed Broderick's chin. Broderick's head jerked back, and his vision flashed. The world spun, and his body smacked against the ground. Somehow, the officer pinned Broderick's body beneath his own.

"I'm on your side—"

A shot fired, and the weight on Broderick's chest slid off. The officer's body thudded next to him, unmoving. Broderick twisted to check his injuries, but he needn't look beyond the slacked jaw and glassy eyes. No one would believe Broderick's innocence now. He'd firmly crossed the line of criminal activity.

"Get movin'!" Grimm said. "Or I'll take care of you too."

Broderick's stomach roiled as he claimed his end of the crate. Grimm would hang. He would see to it.

They ran with Grimm pressing from behind. Bullets whizzed by from the other alerted officers. As they rounded the stack of lumber, a fist landed square across Broderick's face. He staggered and dropped the crate. Before he could gain solid footing, his assailant pounced. They crashed and rolled across the ground. Gravel abraded Broderick's clothes and scraped his face. He managed to grab the officer's collar and twist. As the man's face grew red, recognition slammed into him.

"Darlington!" He immediately shoved him off and jumped to his feet.

"Cosgrove, I knew you were in on this." Darlington intensified his attack.

"Whist forced"—he dodged Darlington's fist—"me."

When Darlington's other fist came, Broderick grabbed his wrist and twisted until he'd trapped the arm. "They threatened to kill Theresa and us."

"Then you're a fool." Darlington hooked his foot behind Broderick's leg and jerked.

Broderick stumbled against the logs, and Darlington twisted free to pin him in place.

"That woman is the head of this." Darlington reached behind him.

"Let us escape, and I'll prove you're wrong." Cold metal slid around Broderick's wrist, and he tensed.

"Not a chance."

Curse the man's bullheadedness. His arrest would encourage Whist's plan for Theresa. He leveraged his foot on the logs and pushed. Darlington stumbled, and the fetters fell to the ground. Broderick delivered a solid punch that knocked Darlington flat, then snagged the fetters.

As he locked the restraints in place, he looked Darlington in the eyes. "They're taking the paper to the printshop. Catch them in the act tonight, and don't let Theresa have any laudanum." Grabbing Darlington's gun, he stood. "And I'm borrowing this."

Darlington called warnings to the other guards as Broderick darted to the cover of the boxcars. Nathaniel and Grimm were almost to the road, where Fitz waited with the wagon.

"Halt! Or I'll shoot," echoed as he reached the first boxcar.

A bullet ricocheted off metal. More followed, pinging like a rainstorm. Fitz and Grimm returned fire and scattered the officers who pursued. Broderick reached the wagon as it jerked into motion. Fitz and Grimm continued to fire at armed train agents, and Nathaniel urged the horses forward. Broderick drew his weapon and made distant shots at the ground. He'd continue the ruse for Theresa's sake, but not at the expense of another man. His heart raced long after they'd left the firefight behind and disappeared into the downtown alleyways. He slumped in the wagon's back, lightheaded and breathing hard.

Fitz holstered his weapon and turned toward Broderick. "You best take care o' that or we be discarding your body with the rubbish."

Broderick looked to where Fitz indicated on his left arm. Blood—and lots of it.

CHAPTER 27

THERESA FUMED AS SHE PACED her bedroom. It would be better to be confined to prison than stuck in Lydia's home. At least in jail no one would pretend she was free to do whatever she wanted. In fact, she'd probably have more liberties. She tried the knob again and resisted the urge to pound on the door when it remained locked. Why was everyone's solution to distress to lie about and rest? She was not hysterical. In this entire house, she was the only one with a sensible head on her shoulders.

"Deep breaths, Theresa. Attack this like a soldier. Make a plan." Talking to herself helped, and she stopped pacing.

Four long, heart-wrenching days had passed since the house burned and Broderick went missing. A search through the ashes revealed no human remains, so he must be held hostage by the counterfeiting ring. If they found Whist, they'd find Broderick, and maybe Nathaniel, who was missing as well. Except that outside of the printshop, she knew nothing of Whist's behavior. Did he have a favorite drinking establishment? Gambling house? Relatives? Had she not been so shielded, she might be able to direct the investigation. Someone had to know Whist's habits.

She walked to the window and peered down at the carriage house where everything left to her name remained. A few precious items that once belonged to her parents. Art supplies. Almost two crates of nothing but Grandfather's notes and belongings. She snapped her fingers.

That's it! Grandfather kept a close eye on Whist's activities once they became partners. There had to be something useful in his notes.

Metal scraped inside the keyhole, and then the door opened slowly on well-oiled hinges. Lydia poked her head in. "Oh good. You're awake."

"Good? Don't pretend you didn't try to lace my tea with laudanum again. I thought the goal was for me to pass the day in oblivion."

Pink tinged Lydia's cheeks. "You scream off and on throughout the night and pace all day. Quite frankly, between you and Gabe, I'm exhausted. Perhaps I shouldn't try to drug you to ensure I get some rest, but you, my dear friend, are more impossible than a colicky baby."

Theresa nibbled her lip as she took in the dark circles under Lydia's bloodshot eyes. Maybe she had been a little difficult to deal with the last few days. "I'm sorry, but you should tell me these things, not drug me."

"Then consider yourself informed. Abraham needs you downstairs. You have a visitor."

Edward. Again. When would that man get her answer through that thick skull of his? No matter how he argued his point, losing the house changed nothing. Maybe throwing the ring he insisted she keep out the door would convince him. She rummaged through the desk drawer for the offending jewelry and then followed Lydia to the stairs.

"I'm going to sleep for as long as possible. Be a good friend and behave yourself for a few hours." Lydia slipped into her room and shut the door, leaving Theresa to go downstairs and past the front door unsupervised.

That would be too easy. Still, the idea of sneaking out held merit. She could retrieve Grandfather's notes in the carriage house and begin a well-planned search. Theresa made it to the coatrack before Abraham stepped into the foyer.

"No need for a coat. We're meeting in here." Abraham gestured to the office door behind him.

It had been worth the try, even if only for the momentary thrill of hoping she could do something productive. She led the way through the door, surprised to find not Edward but a black-eyed Mr. Darlington and another man standing near the desk. She slipped the ring into her pocket.

"Have a seat, Miss Plane." The order from Mr. Darlington could not be confused with politeness.

"I'd rather stand, thank you." It was easier to make a quick exit that way. If he attacked her character again, she might resort to a fisticuff.

"Theresa." Abraham's warning tone prompted her to sit in the proffered chair. She obeyed—not because Mr. Darlington demanded it but because she owed it to Lydia to behave. Abraham took a seat behind the desk and leaned back with crossed arms.

"Miss Plane, it's a pleasure to finally make your acquaintance." The new man had considerably better manners.

Blond hair curled despite a generous amount of pomade, giving him a boyish appeal. A genuine—if not sad—smile lit his face, and tortoise-colored eyes regarded her with kindness. Since he was about the same height as Broderick, she didn't have to crane her neck to see him. He was the type of man whose mere presence made one relax. Mr. Darlington could take a few lessons from him.

"I'm afraid I didn't catch your name." She folded her hands like a proper lady and tried her best to return the favor of good manners.

"Josiah Isaacs. Mr. Darlington and I are Cosgrove's partners."

No wonder Broderick never mentioned his partners' names. She'd be ashamed of working with Mr. Darlington too. She shook her head to rid the thought. "Where is Broderick? Is he all right?"

Mr. Isaacs shifted uncomfortably. "We don't know. We're here to ask you a few questions."

"Why are you here if you don't know? He could be in trouble. He wouldn't go anywhere without letting his partners know." That was the creed they'd worked by years ago. Even if she didn't know where he was when working a case, she could trust his father did.

"Perhaps he would have, had not a certain woman corrupted him." Mr. Darlington stepped closer.

"Cat was an informant. He would never be corrupted by—"

"Not her." Utter disdain filled Mr. Darlington's stare. "You."

"But I—"

"Is this ring yours?"

He extended his hand and revealed the opal ring she'd given Drake. Her chest constricted at seeing the beloved piece, especially now that Broderick was missing. Would holding it bring peace to her soul? She reached for it, but Mr. Darlington shoved it into his pocket.

"Is it yours?" He emphasized each word.

She dropped her hand. "It was until I gave it to Vincent Drake as payment toward my debt."

"Ha!" Mr. Darlington sent a triumphant smile toward Mr. Isaacs, who frowned in response. "She admits it. Proof of her connection."

"It's proof that I paid a man a debt I owed. Nothing more." The cur was bound and determined to make her a criminal.

"It proves your connection with the counterfeiters. We know you're an engraver and that you shove counterfeit money."

Theresa bit down on her tongue and closed her eyes to combat the urge to pummel him. How had this man become a detective? Had he done any investigation beyond the surface, he would have found the truth of her situation. Once she felt she had control of her words, she spoke. "I told you before, I engrave only advertisements and illustrations for books or stationery. As to the counterfeit money, I didn't know it was counterfeit until Abraham brought it to my attention a few days ago."

Mr. Darlington looked ready to launch into more accusations, but Mr. Isaacs stepped forward. "Where did the money you used come from?"

She glanced at Abraham, who gave a brief nod. Dragging her grandfather's name into this mess would not help her case, but neither would evading the truth. Besides, if they were Broderick's partners, they already knew of Grandfather's involvement.

"Grandfather hid the money in his bugle case. I didn't know anything was wrong with it. I'd rather scrape together coins from the gutters than swindle anyone." She held Mr. Isaacs's gaze, praying he could see the truth and not a biased version of it.

"Do you know how your grandfather came to acquire the counterfeit banknotes?" Despite the implication, he maintained a gentle and comforting tone.

"After his death, I learned he engraved banknote plates for a counterfeiting ring. The notes must have been his cut. Either that or he stole them from the others." None of this could be new information for them. "Why don't you stop asking questions you already know the answers to and get to the point?"

Mr. Isaacs gave a half-smile. "Cosgrove said you were sharp. Where are they printing the money?"

Broderick must be the only one left who believed her innocent. "Despite your opinion that I'm a criminal, I have no idea. Again, you should be searching for Broderick instead of wasting everyone's time."

Mr. Isaacs opened his mouth, but Mr. Darlington beat him. "You better hope we don't find him."

That was not the answer she'd expected, even from someone as heartless as him. "I beg your pardon?" She glanced at Abraham for an explanation, but he avoided her gaze.

"If you give us the location, we can negotiate probation instead of jail time," Mr. Isaacs said.

"I told you I am no criminal." She rose from her seat and skirted around Mr. Isaacs. "I demand an explanation for your statement, Mr. Darlington. What do you mean, I shouldn't hope you find your partner?"

"A good man died because Cosgrove chose to do your dirty work."

A man dead because of Broderick? How preposterous. She turned toward Abraham, but he didn't deny the accusation. "No, you're wrong. He'd never kill a man, not willingly." They could think what they wished about her, but not Broderick. "Abraham, tell them what an upstanding man he is."

Abraham took a deep breath, then stood and approached her. All hope of his support disappeared. "Broderick, Nathaniel, Grimm, and Fitz escaped Plum Street Depot after stealing government printing paper."

Broderick and Nathaniel? "The ring must have forced them. They would never break the law otherwise." Nathaniel had made a clean start to his life. He wouldn't go back to his criminal ways and risk all he'd gained.

Mr. Darlington scoffed. "Broderick claimed they threatened to kill you if he didn't. A lie to justify his treachery."

"Wait, you didn't tell me you spoke to him." Mr. Isaacs turned on his partner. "Given the threats they already leveled at her, he'd take that one seriously."

"Yet here she stands, unscathed, like with every other threat." Mr. Darlington turned toward her again. "Tell me, Miss Plane, how long did it take to plan your overthrow of the counterfeiting ring? Did you feel any remorse as you murdered your grandfather?"

Shock kept a coherent response from forming as she stepped back.

"That is enough." Abraham clasped her shoulder and directed her toward the door. "Go upstairs, Theresa. This has devolved to the ridiculous."

Abraham would not remove her from this conversation. If these men were Broderick's partners, they were sorry excuses for detectives. Someone had to straighten them out before this case deteriorated any further and Broderick hung for a crime he didn't commit.

She planted her body against the still-closed door. "What kind of officers are you? You hold back information and make accusations that have no factual grounding. Have you given any real consideration to the case?" All three men opened their mouths to speak, but she barreled on. "My grandfather was a fallible man who chose to get involved with a counterfeiting ring, but that doesn't mean I am involved."

Mr. Darlington tried to cut in but had no chance.

"He was all I had, and no matter what trouble he dragged me into, nothing would have induced me to murder him." Too angry to stand still, she pushed off the door and marched toward Mr. Darlington. "And Broderick is an upstanding man who values truth and justice above his own opinions. He would never commit a crime for anyone. Me or otherwise. If he did something, it was to protect a life other than his own." The pounding in her chest continued as her words died.

Mr. Darlington glowered as if nothing she'd said had penetrated that thick head of his, but Mr. Isaacs nodded. "She's right. Cosgrove would risk his life to protect an innocent."

"The dead officer at the station would disagree."

Abraham stepped forward. "Did you see him shoot Officer Crumb? Or could the fire have come from Grimm or Nathaniel?"

A flicker of hesitancy crossed Mr. Darlington's face. He hadn't seen. "That doesn't make her an innocent." The man couldn't concede a single point.

"You believe me to be unscathed, but everything I have left to my name is contained within the five crates and one trunk stored in Abraham's carriage house. I've lost my family, my home, and all freedom to move about as I choose because those men who threatened me are serious. Don't take my word for it. Abraham has all the threats, knows the details. Search through all my belongings. You'll find I'm guilty of nothing but being the granddaughter of a foolish man. I'm no criminal, and neither is Broderick."

"I want everything—your diaries, paperwork, every scrap left." Mr. Darlington folded his arms.

If exposing every personal thought and belonging to his scrutiny helped, she would do it for Broderick.

She nodded, and Abraham walked toward the door. "I'll have everything brought in."

"No, we'll go to the carriage house. I'll not have evidence hidden because you want to protect her." Mr. Darlington passed Abraham, then opened the door and gestured for Theresa to go through. "Lead the way, Miss Plane."

For hours she watched as they emptied her crates onto the dirty floor and rifled through the contents. Mr. Isaacs took great care to keep her belongings clean and intact, but Mr. Darlington rummaged like a pig through refuse. Only by bouncing between cuddling Tipsy and grooming Blackbeard did she keep her emotions intact. If she'd learned anything through this ordeal, it was that objects were not as valuable as she'd once believed. Memories were held in the heart.

"What are you trying to hide in these notes?" Mr. Darlington lifted a stack of papers.

She left Tipsy behind and examined what he held. "Those are Grandfather's. He communicated via route cipher in the war. The South never broke it, so he figured it was safe to continue to use. Anytime he had important information he wanted communicated but not shared, he used the technique. Those are from the war." And in case he couldn't figure it out for himself, "You can tell by the dates and the color of the paper. Anything newer would have the letterhead I created for him with a Medal of Honor at the top."

"Letterhead like this?" Mr. Isaacs held a letter with the custom design.

She accepted the sheet from his hand and examined it. After appraising the first two coded lines, she handed it back. Well did she remember the cruelty of the message hidden in those words. "Yes. This is the note he wrote to notify me my engagement was over and Broderick was never returning."

"Returning? Engagement?" Mr. Darlington dropped the papers he held and snatched the note from Mr. Isaacs's hand.

Her stomach flipped. Had Broderick not told them? Such information would have been pertinent to their case. His hiding it did not bode well. "It was more than six years ago." She turned to Mr. Isaacs. A turn of discussion seemed prudent. "Do you know how to break a route cipher?"

When he shook his head, she walked him through the process. Each cipher required the creation of a grid. The note's first word was a key to let the receiver know how many columns to create. Grandfather kept a code book where he recorded the keywords and the number of columns each required. Once they identified the number of columns needed, the decipherer put one word into each column until they completed a row. The process continued in a new row until no words remained. Grandfather always filled one column with null words to be removed later. To finish decoding, a series of numbers and arrows directed the decoder which route to take. The genius idea had endless possibilities. Given the time-consuming process, Grandfather reserved it for matters of great importance—or detriment.

"Grandfather always used the same route with me. Down 6, down 1, up 8, up 7, down 3, up 4, up 2, down 5, down 9. My parents died June eighteenth during the cholera outbreak of '73, and the rest of the numbers make up my birthday, April 2, 1859."

Mr. Isaacs crouched to collect the stacks of paper spread across the floor. "I'll need you to write that down. We'll decipher any coded correspondence to verify your information."

With no choice but to comply, she headed toward the trunk. Mrs. Hawking said Grandfather had packed it with plans of sending her away the night he'd died, and she hadn't brought herself to unpack it yet. The one time she'd tried, she'd seen the paint box he'd purchased and engraved for her. Grief forced her to shut the lid and not return.

Grief, however, could not win this time. The paint box was the only place in the carriage house with clean paper and a sharp pencil. She took a fortifying breath and opened the trunk. Finding the box right on top, she pulled its handle and grunted at its weight. Either her paints had dried and turned into bricks, or she'd become a weakling over the last month. Neither sounded plausible.

Hunching over, she released the box latches and lifted the lid. Two sets of engraved steel plates lay on top of a pile of coded papers.

How could Grandfather do this to her? There would be no convincing Broderick's partners of her innocence now. She snapped the lid closed. Whatever she chose to do would condemn her—and Broderick too. The longer she stared at the closed latches, the tighter her stomach churned. Why did doing the right thing have to be so hard?

I'm trusting You, God. Show them the truth.

She stood and hefted the box. "I just found something you should see."

CHAPTER 28

THERESA TOYED WITH THE CURTAIN in the kitchen under Mrs. Hawking's supervision while Abraham, Mr. Isaacs, and Mr. Darlington debated what to do with her. Even if she had an ally in Abraham and Mr. Isaacs, Mr. Darlington demanded her immediate arrest. If it removed Broderick from all suspicion, she would gladly wait behind iron bars until justice released her, but justice felt as likely as ice-skating in July.

She whipped the curtain closed, and the rod crashed down. Flour, milk, and half-prepared bread dough exploded across the counter and onto the floor. Lydia's cook jumped out of the way and jammed her hip against the counter. The poor woman yelped and wobbled.

"Go get a broom to clean this up." Mrs. Hawking shook her head as she rushed to the injured woman's side.

Turning her back on the mess, Theresa walked around the corner to where a broom hung on a peg by the back door. Too bad escaping would hurt Abraham's arguments for her innocence.

She reached for the broom the same moment a light tap sounded on the windowpane next to the door.

Nathaniel? She scrutinized the bruised face before her to be assured it was indeed him. He placed a finger over his lips, then gestured for her to come out. After a glance to ensure no one noticed, she joined him in the cold. He grasped her arm and practically dragged her as he raced toward the hedge. "What happened? Where's Broderick?"

"Not now." His terse reply caught her off guard as they stopped at the street.

He gave a brief wave, and a two-person carriage bounced out of a drive toward them. The conveyance paused long enough for her to squeeze between the driver and Nathaniel before it bolted down the street.

She gripped the splatter guard as each rut in the road threatened to propel her forward. "Answer me, Nathaniel. What's going on?"

They bumped and skidded down the steep incline as he continuously scanned their surroundings. "The ring trapped us."

Her stomach twisted. "Broderick?"

"Not good. I've tried for four days to get to you, but we're wanted men. Even Abraham can't save us."

"Exactly how bad is not good?"

He spared her a grim look as he returned to his vigilant watch. "I hope you've acquired some doctoring skills over the years."

Unless Broderick suffered a splinter or headache, she'd be useless.

The cold numbed her cheeks and fingers as she clutched her collar and prayed through the rest of the wild ride. Tall, well-kept row houses gave way to the slums of Cincinnati after they crossed over Mill Creek. Sewage and factory smoke each fought to outdo the other in stench. A pig paused in its rifling through abandoned refuse to squeal at them. The carriage stopped in front of a long row of tenement buildings, each one sagged against the other for support with the fear of crumbling a genuine concern.

"Broderick's in the first room on the left." Nathaniel turned to talk to the driver. "I owe you one."

"You owe me more than that, Nate . . ."

She approached the uninhabitable building. Dark splinters spiked from the warped door, and a grimy line of baked-on mud ended above the frame. Unlike the printshop, this building couldn't claim to have survived last year's flood. The knob refused to turn in her hand, but a hard shove with her shoulder opened the door. The smell of mold assaulted her senses, and her chest immediately hurt and begged to be given access to the sewage air instead. This wasn't a healthy place for Broderick to recover.

Covering her mouth and nose with a handkerchief, she moved further inside. A stairwell with wavy and sometimes missing steps led to the darkness above, while the long, decrepit hall faded into shadows at the end. This place could be the setting of one of Lydia's dime novels.

Shaking her head, Theresa stepped forward, right into a soft lump that audibly squished. She froze and clenched her eyes. *Don't look.* She held her breath for a few beats, then capitulated to curiosity. A dead rat, bloated and fly-infested. Her stomach flipped as she stepped back. No one should hide here.

Swallowing, she jumped over the offending rodent and followed the dark-splotched wall to the first door on the left. At least this one appeared sturdier than the entrance. The knob didn't resist her application and swung open on hinges loud enough to be heard from Spring Grove Cemetery. She peered in. The swath of light from the foyer provided nothing more than a dim outline of her shadow.

"Broderick?" Her voice squeaked, but no response came.

After stepping inside, she shut the door and allowed her eyes to adjust to the darkness. Slowly, a room smaller than the butler's pantry at Plane Manor came into view. Broderick leaned against the wall on a narrow bed with closed eyes and a gun lying next to him.

"Broderick, it's me. Nathaniel said you're hurt."

He groaned.

In three steps, she sat at his side and evaluated every inch of him. No easy task with the darkness. A makeshift bandage peeked from beneath a tear in his left sleeve around the bicep. Was that blood or mud spattered across it? She lifted her hand to investigate, but he caught it in his right one, a sure sign it was the former.

"I'm . . . fine."

The heat burning her hand indicated otherwise. "You're not fine. I can see it even in the dark."

Whether he liked it or not, she'd add light to the situation. Flinging the dusty curtains open proved useless. Why, she could touch the other

building! She knocked against a rough table and a kerosene lamp teetered. After steadying and then lighting it, she turned back to Broderick.
No wonder he preferred the dark. The filth of the room crawled when lit.

"Happy now?"

She ignored the grime that no amount of cleaning could remove
and examined her ill-tempered patient. A line between the dirt and his
pale skin revealed where he'd washed his face and arm, but the bandage
remained as dirty as the rest of his clothes. If he didn't already have an
infection, he would soon.

"We have to get this off."

He stopped her fingers from working the knot. "I just need a little
rest."

A little rest her foot. Without treatment, his nap could turn into
the long sleep. Broderick could whine and argue all he wanted, but
she would tend that wound. The first step, heat some water. Then that
bandage would come off if she had to clobber him over the head to
do it. The potbelly stove with a crooked pipe in the corner looked
suspect, but it would have to do. She fiddled with the damper and then
knelt before the opening where a door should have been.

"Don't. It'll burn the place down."

Agreed, but that left one choice. "Then I'm taking you to the
hospital."

"I'm wanted. We can't."

The fever must have relieved him of all sense. A woman has
instincts, and hers told her Broderick needed more help than she could
provide. He wouldn't like her plan, but when had he ever? "Stay here.
I'll be back in a few minutes."

He stiffened. "You can't. It isn't safe."

Quicker than he could respond, she grabbed his gun and wheeled
around. "I'll be fine. Besides, Nathaniel is outside."

He called after her, and the creaking bed indicated he struggled to
follow.

Nathaniel met her at the splintered door to the building and
frowned. "I don't like the determination in your step."

"You don't have to. Tell your friend we need his carriage again. Broderick needs a real doctor." How four people would fit into that two-person contraption, she hadn't determined yet, but she would.

"He'll go to jail, Theresa." He blocked her exit.

"Better jail than the cemetery. Either get your friend to take us, or get out of my way."

He stepped back, revealing the carriage long gone. "He won't be back. I've used the last of my favors to escape Whist and retrieve you."

There had to be a way. She scanned the dank road and spotted a peddler hawking wares to anyone within yelling range. For the right price, she might be able to persuade him to help. She approached him with Nathaniel trailing behind. The man must have scavenged his merchandise from a trash heap. Not good for business, but good for her. "Sir, my friend needs a doctor. Would you please transport us?"

He gave a hole-filled grin as he swept a hungry gaze over her, his eyes pausing at the gun in her hand. "Gonna shoot me if I don't?"

"No, but I might shoot you if you keep looking at me that way."

"I like 'em pert." He chuckled. "But I don't give rides fer free. Not even fer a pretty 'un like you."

She reached into her pocket. Edward probably never envisioned his ring exchanged for a ride in a trash heap.

"Do you see this ring? It's a real emerald in a gold band. If you pawn it at Harney's, he'll give you a good price."

He eyed the jewel. "How do I know it ain't glass?"

"It's a risk, but real or not, you'll make a lot more hawking it than you will these wares. Take my two friends and me to Orchard Street, and you can have it."

He rubbed his chin as if he considered rejecting the offer. She'd played this game far too many times with Harney to not recognize the bargaining tactic. Placing the ring back in her pocket, she shrugged. "That's all right. I believe I saw a hack down the way."

"Richard will give us a ride if you have that to offer," Nathaniel said.

The peddler spat on the ground. "That two-bit cheat? Get your friend, and let's be off."

She smiled. "Good. Make space for him in the back, please."

Once he began moving the junk around, she turned toward the building. Her breath caught as her gaze landed on Broderick leaning against the doorframe. How he'd finally managed to stand, she couldn't fathom. He looked worse than the dead rat in the hall—all the more reason to move with haste.

"Did you extinguish the lamp? We'll not be back."

"We're not leaving." He folded his arms but lost his balance, and Nathaniel had to swoop in to steady him.

"No one is safe here, and you promised to protect me. Are you going back on your promise?"

He narrowed his gaze but didn't respond. Good. Maybe he retained some sense after all.

"Wait here." The less he moved, the better.

In the room, she extinguished the lamp, grabbed what she could find of use, and shut the door on the hovel. When she returned, she helped Nathaniel support Broderick. Heat from his body warmed her even before she slid under his arm. His fever had to be unreasonably high. *Please let Dr. Pelton be home.*

The toothless hawker didn't bother to help them struggle over his mountain of rubbish. Apparently, an emerald ring didn't buy sympathy or an extra set of hands. Despite the uncomfortable ride, Broderick slept, waking once when a rut threatened to toss them. Each square they traveled brought a new prayer for his restored health.

When they stopped in front of the row house, Broderick balked at their location. "Not here."

She scooped the shifted wares aside and hopped to the ground. "Would you prefer a hospital where the police will find you?"

"This might as well be the police station."

Broderick could be worse than a stubborn toddler. "Dr. Pelton may have a son-in-law who's a detective, but he's also a physician and a friend. Quit arguing and help us get you out."

She turned to their driver, who extended his grubby hand. The ring disappeared as quickly as the hawker himself. By the time they'd struggled to the top of the stoop, a new rut was the only indication he'd transported them at all. With both hands needed to support Broderick, she kicked at the door.

The housekeeper opened it, and her eyes grew wide with horror. "Good heavens! What happened?"

Not a question Theresa wanted to answer, so she went with the obvious. "We need help." Theresa tensed as Broderick swayed and nearly toppled them.

"This way, miss." The woman rushed to open the door to Dr. Pelton's examining room.

The housekeeper watched as Theresa and Nathaniel struggled to get Broderick settled on the table in the middle of the room. "Is Dr. Pelton home?"

"No. The Peltons are both out searching for you, miss."

Great. Just what she needed. "Get me clean water and then try to find them, please."

The woman nodded and dashed away.

Nathaniel turned to her. "Can you help me remove his shirt? We'll never get him clean otherwise."

Theresa's cheeks competed with Broderick's fever. Not even when they were engaged had she seen him without a shirt. A wet shirt plastered against his chest and taunting her? Yes. Bare flesh exposed for perusal? Never. But this was different. He needed her, and the man was certainly in no condition to do it himself as he lay half-conscious on the table.

Her mouth went dry as she fiddled clumsily with the buttons. She didn't dare look Broderick in the eyes as she did it. The material stuck like a label on a bottle. In spots, it refused to give way and required her to pry it free. Filthy residue remained behind.

"You need to see this, Theresa." Nathaniel's grim tone scared her.

She followed Nathaniel to where he'd exposed the injured arm for cleaning. Red, inflamed skin peeked through the dirt and extended beyond the bandage. She closed her eyes and fought against the desire to cry. An infection didn't necessarily mean he had blood poisoning.

Infections could be fought. People recovered from them all the time. She just needed to get Broderick cleaned and ready for Dr. Pelton.

"Here's the water. I'll be back with help." The housekeeper walked in and out of the room like a breath.

Nathaniel settled into a chair across the way and seemed lost in thought as she cleaned around the bandaged area. Broderick's face tightened with pain though his eyes remained closed and her touches were as light as possible. Soot smeared across his skin and required several passes before it disappeared.

"What did you do? Roll in a coal bin?" Her attempt at levity fell flat.

"Close enough," Broderick grumbled.

Silence reigned as she dipped the rag into water, wiped away the soot, and repeated. If only the infection disappeared as easily. An almost purple color appeared around the edge of the bandage. Soot and debris must be stuck in his wound.

"Careful. Keep nibbling, and you won't have any lip left."

She lifted her gaze to where Broderick watched her. Beads of perspiration lined his brow and dripped down his face. Discomfort dampened his smile, but oh, those eyes! If they could still be that vibrant, he couldn't be too sick, could he?

"I'll be fine. Don't fret." Despite his words, his voice sounded weak and hoarse. When this was over, she'd never again take its strong timbre for granted. She kissed his hand and returned to removing the soot.

The front door banged. Dr. Pelton rushed in, his wife close behind. "Do you know what kind of trouble you three are in?"

Nathaniel stood with hanging head, but Theresa met the doctor's gaze with all the courage she could muster. "Not as much trouble as Broderick was in before I pulled him from the trash heap he was in." No matter what happened to her, she had to keep that in mind. Bringing him here meant life instead of death. Her life spent in a prison cell was better than a world without Broderick in it.

Dr. Pelton frowned as he shrugged out of his coat. "Henrietta, escort Theresa and Nathaniel to Abraham before this situation grows any worse. I'll tend to Broderick."

"No. I'm not leaving his side. Nathaniel can meet with Abraham and explain." Broderick gave a soft objection, but he was in no position to win an argument with her.

"Have you forgotten I'm a fugitive?"

She turned to face Nathaniel while still clutching Broderick's hand. "So am I, but hiding will not improve our situation. Broderick needs attention, and I won't lose him again by leaving. It has to be you."

All color drained from his face as he shook his head. "I can't go to jail. Not again."

"We don't know what will happen, but we know turning ourselves in is the right thing to do. You promised me you changed, and that you're a new man in Christ. Don't let fear keep you from doing what He called you to do. We have to trust Him to work out this mess."

He continued to shake his head. "I can't."

Heaviness weighed her down as she glanced at Broderick's face. Of all the things she wished him to be wrong about, never had she wanted it more than now. "Nathaniel, please be the man I hope you are and not the coward you're proving to be."

"I'm sorry." He fled the room.

"So much for facing this together." Broderick's mumble broke her heart.

Mrs. Pelton worried her hands. "What should I do?"

"Let him go. And send Madeline with a maid to inform Abraham of the situation. I realize now I'm going to need your help." He turned to Theresa with a furrowed brow. "If I find what I think I will under this bandage, I'll have to cut away infection. There will be lots of blood. Can you be in here and handle that? I can't allow hysterics or tend you if you faint."

Memories of Grandfather's injury played before her eyes, and she took a steeling breath. Nightmares already plagued her life. What did it matter if she added a few more? At least her nights would have variety.

"Theresa." Her name on Broderick's lips drew her back to his pain-marred face. "Don't stay."

Dr. Pelton coughed and swiveled to rummage through his bag, giving them a moment of privacy.

How she loved this man, faults and all. "I'm not leaving until death do us part."

His frown deepened. "We never said that vow."

"Well, I'm vowing it now. I'm not leaving you."

She leaned forward and kissed his brow, catching Dr. Pelton's mumbled words as she drew back—"I pray that's not soon."

Broderick must have heard them too, for he took a deep breath and let the words out on a long breath. "Until death do us part, then."

CHAPTER 29

SOMEONE SHOOK THERESA'S SHOULDER. HER eyes gritty and dry, it took a few blinks before her vision cleared enough to see Broderick's still form. Wetness pooled under her cheek on the blue counterpane. She must have enjoyed more than a short doze. As she wiped the drool from her face, she did a visual check of Broderick. Deathly pale except for his flushed cheeks, he barely resembled the strong man who'd carried her weeks ago. Even his breaths were too shallow to do him much good. She reached for his head to test his fever but paused when Mr. Isaacs spoke from behind her.

"You should go rest."

She winced at the crick in her neck when she twisted to face him. "I was until you woke me."

The corner of his mouth tilted but faltered as he walked up and his gaze shifted to Broderick. "How is he?"

An ever-present weight dragged her shoulders down, forcing her hand to drop onto Broderick's heated one. Though the surgery removed the worst and repaired some of the damage to his muscle, Dr. Pelton didn't guarantee recovery. "The exercises Dr. Pelton prescribed make him writhe, his temperature can fry chicken, and he's still never become fully conscious."

Hope toed the edge of despair. After two long, agonizing days, the battle to manage his fever continued to rage. Until death do us part felt dangerously close to being the shortest commitment ever made. She'd meant what she said, but doubt shadowed the memory of Broderick's vow. Had he said it to appease her in a moment of weakness? Or had he truly meant it as a promise of marriage? Oh, how she needed the latter. Life without him in any form would leave her unable to function. Even now, half her soul felt ripped away and cold while the other half festered and burned with the gangrenous infection of despair. How would she ever recover if he left her, whether in death or life?

"I have something that might interest you." Mr. Isaacs pulled her from the spiraling thoughts and turned his back on Broderick.

"Is it wise to share? I *am* a prisoner, after all." She shouldn't be cross with the man. He'd been the one to convince Mr. Darlington to allow her to stay at Broderick's bedside, provided a guard remained in the room. Still, it irked to know everyone believed her a criminal.

He extended a letter toward her. "I'll need this back, but I think you deserve to read it."

Foreign handwriting covered the page, but the bottom indicated Grandfather was its author. "You decoded the papers found with the plates?" Took him long enough, considering she'd provided him with the keyword and path days ago.

"Just this note to you from Colonel Plane. The other papers used a different route we haven't identified." Mr. Isaacs settled onto the settee Mrs. Pelton had brought in and claimed yesterday's newspaper. At least he had the decency to provide her some semblance of privacy. With emotions raw and sleep stolen in snatches, she couldn't begin to guess what havoc Grandfather's words might wreak upon her. She squeezed Broderick's hot hand for strength and began the dismal task of reading Grandfather's final missive.

Theresa,

I cannot excuse my choice to counterfeit, but I will no longer risk your life. The enclosed plates and notes are the evidence promised in exchange for your safety. Give them to Broderick after you settle in Philadelphia. Once he turns them in, there will be nothing for you here. If not dead, I will be in federal prison, and all our belongings will be confiscated. Broderick isn't good enough for you, but marry him anyway so I might have comfort in knowing you are cared for. I wish you the best in life, my little soldier.

You are thus released from my command,
Colonel Nicolas W. Plane

The last words blurred together, and her throat clogged. How like him to be formal and cold. Though she welcomed the directive to marry Broderick, it was merely a way of assuaging his guilt for leaving her to survive on her own. He hadn't cared what she wanted. Even the use of her military moniker felt hollow. He'd released her from his responsibility and tossed her aside without the slightest bit of remorse. His dying plea for forgiveness might have once formed shallow roots, but they'd shriveled with these last words. *Lord, I know it's wrong, but I can't forgive him.*

Her gaze dropped to Broderick's hand, hot and limp. He lay half-dead because of a promise to protect her from Grandfather's selfish ambitions. Everything she held dear, gone because one man decided himself too proud to admit he needed help.

"You can burn this for all I care." She flung the note away, but it wafted on the air, then landed on the bed inches from where her other hand gripped Broderick's.

Mr. Isaacs filled a cup with water from a pitcher and carried it to her. "I'm sorry."

Cool water coursed down her throat but did little to relieve the ache in her heart. How many ways could a heart break before it no longer beat? "His callousness is not your fault any more than his choice to engrave those plates is mine."

"Right. About that . . ."

He shifted uncomfortably and motioned for the guard who'd played chaperone for the last two days to leave. What new evidence showed her supposed guilt now? A counterfeit note used as a bookmark? Or perhaps an account book documenting all her wealth from the money printed? She'd like to see that one. What irony to be presumed guilty of printing hundreds of thousands of dollars when she could barely scrape together two pennies. The one good thing about jail was she wouldn't have to be concerned about where her next meal or dress came from. They'd be provided to her by the good people of the state who'd failed their job in doling out justice.

"As I said, the route you gave us worked only for that note. I can ensure a lesser sentence if you cooperate and provide the other route."

His brain must have absorbed too much of that pomade. "I cannot provide it because I know nothing beyond that which I've already shared. Look me in the eyes, Mr. Isaacs, and discern the truth."

Those tortoise-colored eyes might turn some women into a puddle but not her. Not when freedom hung in the balance. Determination drove her to match his unblinking gaze, the intensity of his search for truth boring to the depths of her soul.

The moment she caught the softening of doubt, he flinched and shifted to the settee. "Do you have any idea what other route Colonel Plane might have used? That code book Abraham gave us contains more than three dozen ciphers. It will take weeks to work our way through them all."

"With the ring scattered, does it really matter how long it takes you?"

"The sooner we can decipher it, the sooner we prove your innocence. Do you want to be separated from Cosgrove? If you don't cooperate, Darlington will insist on your arrest."

Dates had been of great importance to her grandfather, but she couldn't help if most were related to battles or military maneuvers. "I can give you a list of birthdays and anniversaries, but beyond that, I don't know. Is it possible Broderick might know something we don't? He did have the code book, after all."

"I'll look through his case notes, assuming he didn't hold anything back from us there." The weight of disappointment sagged Mr. Isaacs's shoulders as he rested his elbows on his knees—the same weight she'd carried in those early days of waking to find Broderick had left her.

"Whatever Broderick held back, I know he felt it was for the best." She may not always agree with his choices, but they came from a desire to do the right thing.

"Maybe, but at a minimum, he's lost his job. At worst, you both may spend time in prison."

Appointments to the Secret Service were considered one of the highest achievements a man could attain. To be stripped of that honor and dismissed because they believed Broderick a criminal would devastate him. His whole life revolved around pursuing justice for others. Had she not been involved with his case, he would have had no reason to hold back information. Her chest squeezed. Would he come to resent her for the loss of his beloved job? He'd walked away when he thought his career endangered her, but could he stay knowing she'd cost him everything?

No, the fear of *what if* could not win. She had to trust God to work all things to His glory and their good. "The truth will be revealed, and justice will prevail." And if not? *I'm trying to trust, Lord. Help me.*

Mr. Isaacs stood and looked down at her with the soberness of a man at a funeral. "I hope you're correct. Despite what the circumstances might indicate, Cosgrove is my friend. He's a good man, and in the depths of my soul I know he could not have committed those crimes without the worst circumstances forcing his hand. Don't give up on us yet, Miss Plane. We'll uncover the truth."

He exited the room with nothing but the tap of his shoes to fill the silence. Though the door remained open, the guard did not return. Escape crossed her mind, but she laughed it off. Her whole world remained in this room. She dunked a clean rag into the basin and began the process of exchanging the hot ones across Broderick's forehead with cool ones. With the first ones growing hot before she replaced the last, the job stayed never-ending.

When she tired of changing rags, she coaxed broth into his mouth. More than half of it dribbled down his chin as though he were an infant with his first taste of porridge. How long did it take for blood to replenish? She'd gladly give him hers, but Dr. Pelton had refused the offer.

"We're heading to evening services, dear." Mrs. Pelton stood in the doorway, gloves in hand. "Are you sure you don't wish to join us? It would be good for you."

Even if she were willing to leave Broderick's side, she doubted she'd get beyond the front door before Mr. Darlington appeared from the shadows and accused her of trying to escape. "I'll read my Bible."

Mrs. Pelton gave a sympathetic smile before she departed.

Theresa retrieved her tome from underneath the stacks of half-completed sketches and grinned. With no guard or overly concerned chaperones to prevent her, she sat on the bed nestled as close to Broderick as she could and rested a hand on his chest. Each breath lifted it and brought comfort despite the heat he radiated.

Did she need to open her Bible to read 2 Chronicles 20? After all the times she'd read it over the last few days, she could practically recite it from memory. The repeated phrases "ye shall not need to fight in this battle" and "stand ye still" drove her mad. All she'd done was stand still. She could do nothing but watch and pray. She'd tried to read something different, but those verses kept drawing her back.

You tell me to stand still, and that I don't need to fight this battle. But please, God, give me something to do while I wait on You. Doing nothing is pure torment.

When no other prompting came, she sighed. Maybe reading the passage aloud to Broderick would give him the fighting spirit he needed. Resting against the headboard, she tugged the ribbon and found the verses without searching. Words bled together, but she recited them by rote—first Jehoshaphat's plea for his country under attack and then God's reply. It wasn't until she reached the actual battle that the words required her full attention.

"And when they began to sing and to praise, the Lord set ambushments against the children of Ammon . . ."

When they began to sing and to praise . . .

She blinked and read that again. Well, it was something. Maybe God waited to break the fever until she focused on Him. It couldn't hurt to try. She started with Broderick's favorite hymn, then continued with every hymn she could recall, making up the words when her memory failed. Still, the fever persisted. The Bible hadn't said how long the people praised, so she sang again. And again. And again. By the end of the fourth round of countless songs, her voice was strained and cracked.

Lord, I've sung and sung. What more do You want? I can't heal him. Only You can.

Then God seemed to say, *If I don't, will you still love Me?*

The question startled and scared her. Statements like that resulted in extreme circumstances, like Abraham being asked to sacrifice his son. Isaac's salvation came in the last second, but there had been salvation. Job had not been so blessed. He'd lost all his children, his wealth, and his health. Granted, God had restored his wealth and given him a new family, but what about the children he lost? They were never risen from the dead and returned to him. Yet Job still loved God. Could she?

God had asked an honest question, and she wanted to give an honest answer. Would she love Him? Could she still serve Him even if? *Even if*—the two words Lydia had proclaimed when Gabe might have died from an early birth. The words her mother had used in the letter to Father. The same words of faith she'd admired and hoped to have herself. Well, God was giving her the opportunity. She closed her eyes and breathed deeply. Terror fled in the face of the truth. She didn't want to live without Broderick, couldn't fathom how she would survive without him, but loving God extended beyond any fear or trial.

"Yes, God. I will love You even if."

When she opened her eyes, she half expected Broderick to be awake and smiling. Instead, he moaned and then thrashed, yelling warnings to an invisible foe. Alarm shot through her as she dived across his chest to restrain him before he tumbled from the bed. The heat of his fever hit her like a blast of fire before she made contact. He wasn't getting better. He was worse. Much worse.

She screamed for help. Tears blurred her vision as she fought against Broderick. God would do it. He would take Broderick from her. Her words were not enough.

CHAPTER 30

TINGLES SHARPENED INTO KNIFE-LIKE PRICKS along Broderick's arm as he attempted to shift away from the weight at his side. Dots crossed his vision, and he stilled. Where was he? He blinked against the bright spots, but darkness hid any identifying characteristics of the room.

Vague memories nipped at the edge of recollection, but with his head thicker than a tub of lard, they stayed beyond reach.

Wherever he was, he had to be in bad shape. A headache hammered in his temples, and every inch of him ached though the worst pain came from the searing pulse in his left arm.

Sandpaper scraped across his lips as he tried to moisten them. Given a chance, he could probably drink a good portion of Lake Erie. As uncomfortable as he felt, at least he lived.

Quiet, feminine chatter came from somewhere beyond the room. Had Fitz dragged him back to Cat's? But this place didn't harbor the gaudy scent of Cat's perfume, and the air smelled too sterile to be the slum he last remembered. A hospital? He strained to turn his head. No, the room was too small—a doctor's office, perhaps.

Whatever pressed against his side shifted, and a kitten-soft sigh accompanied the movement. Was that . . . He wiggled feeling back into his right hand and then traced the form next to him. A woman? His gut clenched. Had he been mistaken about his location? Had Cat pulled another stunt? He endured the pain to twist his body. Whoever it was had their back to him.

The door opened, and two shadows tiptoed in.

"We should wake her." The gruff whisper sounded familiar, but he couldn't place it.

"I'll take care of her." Lydia's voice. "Go ahead and refill the lamp."

He released a breath. Theresa would be the only woman bold enough to lie next to him. Not exactly proper, but a relief all the same.

A tray rattled on the other side of him, but he didn't bother twisting again. Theresa lay within reach, and he could observe her without notice.

"It's about time she gave up on that chair." Lydia sighed. "Theresa, sweetheart. Wake up. It's time for you to move into your own room." Theresa wiggled closer to him, and he couldn't deny he liked it. "You can't share a bed with him even if he's unconscious."

Theresa rolled over with a grumble and pinned his arm again. It wouldn't be a bad thing if he could adjust to where his arm wrapped around her instead.

"Fine, let's try this. Theresa, you're hurting Broderick!"

Before he could announce the truth, Theresa bolted upright. With eyes fully adjusted to the dark, he could make out the wild strays of hair poking from her braid and her wide but still groggy eyes as she blinked down at him.

"Good heavens!" In her scramble to make space, she tumbled off the bed.

Lydia's yelp overpowered his poor, muffled attempt to call out.

Theresa popped to her feet. "I didn't mean to fall asleep. I just needed a moment to stretch."

She shook her head as if dispelling the cobwebs of sleep and then turned toward him. Her cold hand pressed against his chest, then jerked back before flitting to his forehead. "Lydia, get your father. I think the fever's broken."

Steps faded, and she dropped back onto the bed next to him, a string of prayer-like words escaping until her gaze connected with his.

"Hello." His single word sounded garbled, but she squealed in response.

"Thank You, God."

Her lips found his, and the pain and discomfort dulled. Salt mixed with her kiss that ended far too soon. Whatever had transpired while he slept must have been terrible. He tried to ask, but the room simultaneously burst into light and chaos. Voices clamored as the room filled with people.

Isaacs appeared behind Theresa's head and grinned like a fool. "Welcome back from the land of the dead."

Darlington interjected from the edge of Broderick's vision. "He might wish he were back there soon enough."

Before he could comment, Theresa's face darkened, and she turned on the man. "Someone get that man out of here before I commit a real crime."

"It is ill-advised to threaten an officer." Darlington stepped closer, but to Broderick's relief, Isaacs intervened.

"We'll be on our way," Isaacs said to Dr. Pelton, "but do contact us the moment you feel he's ready for conversation." Then Isaacs nodded at him. "You're in good hands with that woman." His chuckle accompanied their exit.

Dr. Pelton shooed the room of its remaining occupants. "Everyone out. I need to examine my patient."

As Theresa shifted to the edge of the bed, Broderick found her hand and held it. He wanted, no needed, her to stay close. "Not everyone." His words emerged as little more than a hoarse whisper, but they were enough.

Theresa's teeth shone despite the wet glimmer to her cheeks. She scooted a safe distance from Dr. Pelton but stayed within reach.

"You gave us quite the fright, young man." Dr. Pelton gave him a broad smile before plunking a bag on the table. "Theresa, get him a drink, please."

He didn't ask if Broderick could sit on his own but lifted him and plunked a few pillows behind his back. A wave of dizziness overtook Broderick. Closing his eyes, he waited for it to pass. When a cold glass pressed into his hand, he opened them again to find Theresa nibbling on her lip.

"Drink only half at first—and slowly," Dr. Pelton said. "I'll have a good look at this wound while you're sitting up."

Broderick lifted the glass a couple of inches but then lowered it. What was it made out of? Lead?

"Here, let me help you."

Theresa reached for the glass, but he shifted. "I can do it."

"Weakness is normal, son. You lost a lot of blood. It takes time for the body to replace that. Add the infection and four days of fever—"

"Four days?" No wonder Theresa looked done in. More than a single night of poor sleep darkened the circles under her eyes.

"Five or six days, depending on how long you had a fever before I found you." She mustered a smile, but a tremor ran through her hand. He had a feeling she would never share the full extent of how she'd suffered during that time, just as he never would about the aftermath of her near-drowning.

Dr. Pelton removed the bandage, and Broderick tried to ignore the sharp pangs. Theresa distracted him with the glass. Water never tasted so good. What little didn't get soaked by his mouth absorbed in his throat. His stomach probably didn't see a drop. The glass emptied before it quenched his thirst, and Theresa filled it again from a pitcher.

"Give it a minute before drinking more. I'll make some movements with your arm that will be painful, but I need you to respond to a few questions."

The pain was enough to bring any man to his knees, but he managed curt answers and a few movements on his own. Theresa held his hand without a word, squeezing it in response to his hiss of pain. He breathed a sigh of relief when Dr. Pelton finally ended the examination and rewrapped his arm. Dizziness warred with nausea as he rested his head against the headboard.

"You're a fortunate man, Broderick. The bullet missed your artery and humerus. God protected you." He collected instruments from the edge of the bed and deposited them back in his bag. "If you continue the exercises I taught Theresa, I think there's a good possibility the permanent damage can be limited."

Permanent damage? His gaze snapped to Theresa, but she only stared at their linked hands. "How bad?"

Dr. Pelton closed his bag and considered his answer for eternity. "I imagine that arm will have limited mobility for several weeks if not longer and will probably always give you some pain. With hard work and a good diet, you might regain a decent amount of strength, but I don't expect it will ever be the same. I did my best, but you have muscle and blood vessel damage. I might have been able to do more if you'd come to me immediately, but what's done is done."

Theresa stroked his face as if placating a child. "What's important is you will recover."

Though the words were earnest, sadness—and fear?—laced her tone. She concealed something from him. It could be related to his arm function, but instinct told him it was something more. "What about the case?"

Her gaze flicked to Dr. Pelton's, taut with unspoken communication. He'd hit his mark.

"You should rest. There will be enough discussion about the case later." Dr. Pelton pulled the pillows from behind Broderick and eased him back to flat. "Theresa, come. The danger has passed. You need to rest as well."

She again nibbled her lip, her gaze bouncing between Dr. Pelton and him. "Are you sure?"

He didn't wish to be separated any more than she did. "Sir, I would sleep better if she were with me."

Dr. Pelton coughed and gave a stern look that didn't quite mask his grin. "I'm sure you would, and her too, but I cannot allow it. While you were unconscious, I allowed Mrs. Hawking and even officers to act as chaperones. However, it is a completely different matter now that you're back in the land of the living."

Theresa appeared as disappointed as he was but put on a brave face. "Rest well. I'll be back as soon as I'm able." She kissed his cheek, then trudged toward the door.

Dr. Pelton doused the light and ushered her out. As much as Broderick wanted to stay awake and contemplate her avoidance of the case, exhaustion won.

When he woke later that evening, he found Isaacs with his feet propped on the edge of the bed while he sat in a chair and worked from a lap desk. He paused writing and glanced Broderick's direction.

"Well, if it isn't Perrault's Sleeping Beauty, finally awake. I was beginning to wonder if I needed Miss Plane to come in and kiss you." Isaacs winked as he closed the lap desk.

"Where is she?" The dryness in his throat started a coughing fit, and Isaacs helped him with a glass of water.

"I believe Mrs. Hawking was successful in getting her to sleep in a bed."

A warning bell went off in Broderick's head, and he struggled to recall why. Something about Mrs. Hawking and sleep.

"Between the laudanum and her exhaustion—"

Laudanum! His body shook as he struggled to sit and swing his legs off the bed. He had to get to Theresa. He tried to stand, but the room spun.

Isaacs lunged from his chair and stopped him from crashing to the floor. "What's got into your head, Cosgrove? You can barely lift a glass." He aided Broderick back onto the bed.

"Whist poisoned the laudanum. Mrs. Hawking knew she took it regularly, and—"

Isaacs frowned. "Don't get up again. I'll check on her."

As much as he wanted to disobey the order, all he managed to do was sit taller in the bed. Even that effort left a sheen of sweat across his brow and beaded at his neck. Theresa was in danger, and he didn't have the strength to go to her. *Lord, please don't let Isaacs be too late.* Knots formed across his shoulders and neck as he strained to hear.

Footfalls ascended the stairs to the second floor, and creaking boards allowed him to follow Isaacs's progress. He knew the moment he entered Theresa's room, for Mrs. Hawking's squallers filled the whole house. Others responded to her objections, and more footfalls pounded above him. Voices mingled, growing louder until they reached the point of a cacophony. Bedding crumpled under his grip. Broderick dragged himself forward, straining to decipher the words.

Someone shouted Dr. Pelton's name.

That's it. He couldn't remain here any longer. If he had to crawl across the floor and up the stairs, he would make it to her. He tossed the covers aside and pushed until his feet met cold wood. With some rocking, he made it off the bed and staggered to the wall. His progress was slow, but he made it almost to the door before his legs gave out. Arms shaking, he pushed to his hands and knees.

"What are you doing?" Theresa's sweet voice drained what little strength remained, and he slumped against the wall.

"Trying to get to you."

She kneeled at his side, the edges of her housecoat flaring out. "I'm here, but Mr. Isaacs came barreling into my room and is questioning Mrs. Hawking like she's a murderer."

He swallowed back the lump in his throat and lifted a hand to her face, assuring himself she indeed knelt next to him, breathing and well. "The laudanum. It could be laced with poison."

"Laudanum?" A hand flitted to his forehead, and her forehead scrunched.

"Whist knows you take it every night. Only Mrs. Hawking could have told him. He said he'd poison you." Unable to stop himself, he drew her close and breathed in the scent of her, the warmth of her breath on his chest proof she lived unharmed.

"As you can see, I'm well. I refuse to take it. In fact, since everyone started sneaking laudanum into my drink or food to *calm* me, I've avoided anything I haven't prepared myself." Her glower could have made Colonel Planc shrink.

"Thank You, God."

"Yes, we have much to thank Him for, but are you certain Mrs. Hawking is involved? She's been in my life since Father came home from the war."

Certain? Not entirely, but who else would have access to that knowledge, to the laudanum? "Who else knew?"

She shrugged. "It wasn't a secret. Dr. Pelton, Lydia, Edward . . . Even the maids at Lydia's knew. I'm not willing to believe Mrs. Hawking would betray me like that."

"Good. Because I would never betray you."

Speak of the devil. Broderick shielded Theresa, though Isaacs stood behind Mrs. Hawking.

"But the laudanum was poisoned." Dr. Pelton shouldered his way in, causing the small room to grow crowded. "Cyanide, if my sniffer is correct."

"Miss Plane, given the circumstances, I think it might be best if you came with me." Isaacs folded his arms, the familiar determination of a decision clear on his face.

Theresa gripped Broderick's hand. "No, I'm not leaving him again. We've discovered and removed the threat. I'll be fine."

As much as he wanted to keep her close, Broderick was in no condition to protect her. Isaacs would never hurt a woman, and despite Darlington's determination to prove her a criminal, he would never cause her actual harm.

Pushing a stray hair from her face, he prayed she'd understand. "Theresa, you need to go with him."

She reeled back. "No."

Isaacs helped Broderick to the settee, then said, "I'll give you a few minutes to say goodbye while a maid gathers her things. Mrs. Hawking, you still need to answer a few questions." He followed Dr. Pelton and Mrs. Hawking out to the hall, closing the door behind him.

Theresa glared at him as she sat beside him. "You can't ask me to leave you. I just watched you almost die."

"I know, and if there were any other way, I'd take it. But I trust Isaacs with your life"—he clasped her retreating hand and rubbed the bare ring finger—"and our future."

Her face creased as if the battle within were capable of physical pain. "But he says we could still go to prison, and your job . . ." She shook her head, failing to stop the tears before one fell to his hand.

"Is not as important as seeing to your safety. We have to trust God in this."

He tugged, and she moved into his embrace, clinging to him like a cat avoiding a bath. Bruised ribs and a throbbing arm were a small price to pay to hold her close. The truth was they might never share another moment such as this again, but he meant what he said. God never faltered in His promises. They could trust Him.

Theresa heaved a sigh as she looked up, lips close enough to kiss. "Can't we trust Him while I stay here?"

Childlike hope begged him to say yes. How he wished he could, but a strength stronger than his own held him firm. He'd promised to be the man Theresa deserved, and that required putting her needs above their desires. He fished in his pocket for the rock he always carried, but the clean pair of pants were not his own. "Do you know where my clothes are?"

She quirked a brow. "What does that have to do with me staying?"

"Everything."

Shaking her head, she crossed the room to where his clothes hung from the edges of a trash bin. Her nose wrinkled as she retrieved the trousers and turned toward him. "You are not wearing these ever again."

"Bring me what's in the pocket."

When she pulled out the rock, her eyes widened and lips parted. He couldn't help smiling as she tossed the pants aside and caressed the rock like a long-lost friend. "You kept it." Her voice came as an awe-struck whisper.

Had he the energy to move, he'd meet her where she stood. Instead, he settled for beckoning her to return to him. "I couldn't bear to be separated from it, for it would mean giving up a piece of you."

"I spent hours scouring the creek beds to find the perfect stone, all so I could propose to you." She settled against him and chuckled. "What was I? Eleven?" Long before they had any idea true love would form.

"The days ahead will be trying, but I want you to keep it while we're apart, as a reminder that I love you and a promise that I will replace it with a real rock. One that goes on your finger."

The smile that bloomed across her face would have to carry him through the days ahead. She squealed and threw her arms around him. "You mean it? You still want me?"

Her words encased him with the heat of her breath and sent a shiver of pleasure through his body. What had ever induced him to leave her the first time? This woman who went toe-to-toe with criminals without a flinch yet gazed at him with pure vulnerability. No other helpmate existed for him. The energy he thought exhausted thrummed to life.

He leaned in so she could not only hear the words but feel them too. "I've never stopped wanting you."

Their mouths connected, and he couldn't stop. His hand slid behind her head and drew her closer as if the act of kissing could communicate all he could not say, all he could not yet do. Her arms enveloped him, and he drank in the feel of her, matching passion for passion. Hunger to be together fueled his fervor and overshadowed the pain in his bad arm as he pulled her onto his lap. Oh Lord, how he loved this woman. Needed her. Even breaks for breath were too long apart.

"Perhaps I shouldn't have shut the door."

Broderick broke away, and Theresa fell against him, breathing heavily. Isaacs couldn't have worse or better timing. Given how much Broderick had lost himself in her, he might never have found a way out. He rested his forehead against Theresa's and released a long breath. Healing couldn't come quick enough. "You better go."

Theresa nodded, her face pink and her lips full. She scurried from the room, avoiding Isaacs's amused gaze as she passed.

"Don't worry. We'll keep her safe, and when this is over, I expect an invitation to the wedding."

Broderick leaned his head back against the wall, still dizzy from the effect kissing Theresa had on him. "You'll be the first one to know the date. How close are we to getting Whist?"

Isaacs helped Broderick to his feet. "I can't share the details until you're cleared of guilt. However, I will say, if things continue as they are, you'll be fully recovered before we can make arrests."

Broderick staggered toward the bed. "Anything I can do?"

"Rest, pray, and if you happen to know the route Colonel Plane planned to give you to decode the evidence, that will go a long way toward helping your case."

He collapsed onto the bed. The effort of moving drained what energy kissing Theresa had produced. A route? Coded evidence? "I don't know what you're talking about. Tell me all, Isaacs. You know I'm not the enemy here, and I can't help if I don't know."

"All right, but you won't like it."

CHAPTER 31

THERESA DIDN'T LIKE IT, NOT one bit. She clutched her shawl tighter and peered past the streams of rain rushing down the windowpane. When they'd entered this suite of rooms at the Madison House Hotel a week ago—two bedrooms with a common room between—the flood skimmed the edges of the street, well below the steps of the front door. Now water lapped midway to the second floor and continued to rise. Already four feet above last year's devastating flood, some called for it to stand, but the rains defied opinion. How much longer until the waters weakened the building's structure?

Turning to face her less-than-favorite warden, she asked, "Shouldn't we move to another location?"

Mr. Darlington didn't bother to look at her as he continued the arduous task of transcribing the pages of Grandfather's notes into columns for decoding. "This suite is on the third floor. The manager assured me we're quite safe."

Safe from the threats of man, perhaps. "You do realize I can't swim."

"Yes, Miss Plane." He dropped the pen and leaned back in his desk chair. "You've told me twenty times."

Then the man should get it through his head. When she opened her mouth to counter, he raised his hand. "That is precisely the reason we're staying. Here, I have no concern about you running off—whether it be to meet with Cosgrove or the ring members."

Insufferable man.

"Now, would you like to go back to being locked in your room?" he continued. "Or will you remain quiet while I work?"

"If you're unconcerned about me leaving the building, why bother locking me in here at night?" Broderick would probably rebuke her again when she wrote him, but the pleasure from Mr. Darlington's look of annoyance could not be denied. "If you wish me to remain quiet, I could work on decoding those papers. It isn't hard now that you discovered which route Grandfather used from his book. If you would allow me to show you—"

The door opened, and Mr. Darlington popped to his feet with a "Praise God" on his lips.

Mr. Isaacs stepped through and sent her a wide grin as he lifted an envelope. "I'm told you're allowed to read this only if you haven't been annoying Darlington again."

How unfair. In his last note, Broderick had suggested she be nicer, not required it. She folded her arms and returned to the window. No point in asking Mr. Darlington to lie for her. Neither one was inclined to do the other a favor.

"Give her the accursed thing, and maybe I'll have a few minutes of silence." Mr. Darlington snatched the letter and thrust it at her. "Read it in silence, woman." He emphasized each word and then stalked back to the desk.

Mr. Isaacs waggled his brows before joining Mr. Darlington to talk in hushed tones. They'd probably lock her in her bedroom if they realized how clearly she heard their words from her place by the window. Some secrets were best not shared. She flipped open the flap of the envelope, knowing full well Mr. Isaacs probably read the note first, as any good detective should when carrying a communication between suspects. The longer she'd remained trapped in this hotel—and without Mrs. Hawking or another female as a chaperone, no less—the more she'd taken advantage of that knowledge. Each note detailed enough romantic tidbits to make any observer embarrassed. If she suspected it was Mr. Darlington's turn to read, however, she pushed the boundaries of even her own comfort just to make the man suffer. She chuckled as she pulled out two full sheets, front and back. It should be Mr. Darlington's turn next.

Reese,

Don't think I'm ignorant of what you're doing. Please, don't give Darlington any reason to keep you away longer than necessary. I know the temptation to drive the man mad is fierce, but think of my health. Mrs. Pelton has managed to serve me liver, kidney, or bone broth at every turn. She swears it works wonders in regaining one's strength. It might be helping, but I'm to the point the thought of it turns my stomach. I'd much rather eat your cooking—even if it is burned half the time.

Considering Broderick hadn't eaten a meal prepared by her since before she nearly drowned, she could let the insult slide. Cooking wasn't her specialty, but necessity had forced her to develop the skill to passable.

She heard the name Nathaniel Cosgrove and snapped her gaze from the letter to Mr. Isaacs. What about Nathaniel? They hadn't heard from him since he'd left Dr. Pelton's. Mr. Darlington caught her look and turned Isaacs until he faced the wall. She couldn't see their expressions with their backs to her, but the conversation carried clear enough. She feigned reading Broderick's missive, ears intent on the news they wished to keep from her.

"—found where the ring is holed up. He's turning himself in but holding the information ransom," Mr. Isaacs said.

"What's his price?"

"We reevaluate the government paper heist and admit his brother's innocence."

Mr. Darlington harrumphed.

Had Nathaniel done the right thing? After almost two weeks, she'd despaired of it.

"I believe Broderick's innocent. Threats to the woman you love are a powerful tool. Have you never been in love?" Mr. Isaacs asked.

"Love is for soft-hearted fools."

Mr. Darlington probably believed that lie because he was incapable of turning a woman's head. Theresa pitied the woman who would be desperate enough to connect herself with that arrogant man.

"Soft-hearted fool or not, we need to look into this. I've taken the liberty of securing an officer to stay with Miss Plane while we both go question him."

Visions of drowning in floodwaters destroyed all pretense of reading. "You can't leave me here."

Mr. Darlington turned narrowed eyes upon her. "I knew you were listening."

Ever the kinder one, Mr. Isaacs approached, a consolatory frown in place. "You need to let us do this if you want Broderick's name cleared of charges. We won't be any longer than necessary, but I can't guarantee we'll be back tonight."

A night of rain and rising waters spent alone? Familiar panic rose, squeezing until breathing became a struggle. She thudded into a chair without knowing how she got there, and a glass of water was pressed into her hand. Drinking from it did nothing to slow her racing heart.

"Breathe, Miss Plane." Mr. Isaacs's face hovered in front of hers, and once she'd begun taking slower breaths, he spoke again. "I swore to Broderick I would protect you. I would not leave you here if I suspected it unsafe. Even if the waters rose another sixteen feet, you'd still be a floor above. Fear not."

She almost laughed at his words, so close to the ones she'd repeatedly read as Broderick teetered on the edge of death. *God, I hear You. I fear not, for You are with me.*

With a shuddered breath, she nodded. "All right."

He patted her hand and stood. "Good. The officer will stand guard in the hall and give you your privacy."

"What? Afraid I'll try to escape?"

He chuckled. "No, but Broderick would have my head if I left you unprotected."

"We're not leaving these here for her to tamper with." Mr.

Darlington collected all the papers he'd been working on and shoved them into a leather bag.

The men made a few more preparations as she stared out the window, caressing Broderick's rock and repeating "Fear not for I am with thee" in a whisper until the words came as reliably as her heartbeat. God knew how to test her faith, but trust came easier now. By the time the door shut, she maintained a firm grip on her emotions.

Reading Broderick's letter of random tidbits meant to put her at ease and persuade her to behave herself passed some of the time, but the morning dragged. Switching to the pile of discarded newspapers did little to help her discomfort as headlines about the flood filled nearly every space. Food and coal shortages. Pleas for curious onlookers to stay home. Reminders of telegraphs and postal delivery being unavailable. Images of hastily constructed boats carrying refugees and their meager belongings reinforced the devastating effect on those living in the Mill Creek area. One story focused on a train swept off the tracks while another told of the drowning of a group of friends foolish enough to take a pleasure ride. At that story, she abandoned the papers. She needed no reminder of how dangerous water could be.

The door opened, and her guard peeked in. "Excuse me, ma'am. You have a visitor."

"A visitor?"

Edward pushed his way past the man, leaving behind a trail of water. "You are a challenging woman to track down."

She shouldn't be tracked down at all, even by her former fiancé. If he could do it, so could Mr. Whist, Fitz, or Grimm. "Why did you find it necessary to go through the effort? We're not engaged anymore."

He huffed as he stalked forward. Despite the urge to flee, she remained planted where she stood. Edward might be hurting, but he meant her no harm. His giant hand caressed her face.

"Don't." She yanked back and then stiffened into her most commanding posture. "I don't know why you've come, but you need to leave."

"You promised me a wedding." A possessive gleam filled his eyes.

Cold fear snaked down her spine. This was not the same man who'd courted her these last eighteen months. "Officer!"

Edward's hands fisted. "He's not coming. I greased his hands with enough money to buy his family a new home after the flood recedes."

Theresa retreated until the window pressed against her back.

"I've worked too hard for this plan to fail." He clutched her hand. "Come, we're leaving."

Theresa grabbed the curtain as he tried to drag her to the door by the hand. "Edward, stop. This is madness. I'm not marrying you." She twisted and yanked harder on the fabric, gaining a few steps from him. Though where she could go to escape had yet to materialize.

His arms wrapped around her waist and lifted her from the floor. He jerked backward, and the fabric tore from her hands, leaving the rod half pulled from the wall. She kicked at Edward and anything near enough to knock over.

"Stop fighting me. I *will* be your husband."

They passed a lamp, and she thrust herself forward with enough power to grasp it. Swinging it behind her, it made contact with the wall and shattered. Edward dropped her, and the familiar sting of glass in her palms urged her to stumble out of reach.

"I suspected you might be unreasonable. Very well. I came prepared." He reached into his vest.

She scrambled to the other side of the desk and skimmed the surface for something, anything to use. A dull letter opener teetered on the corner. She lunged for the handle, but Edward knocked it to the floor. He came around the narrow desk and captured her waist. Writhing and screaming did nothing against his strength.

With little effort, he pinned her against him with one arm and pressed a damp handkerchief over her nose and mouth. She took a deep breath to scream, and a sickeningly sweet smell filled her senses. Her muffled attempt to call for help died with a gasp for air. What was he doing to her? His grip didn't smother, but she couldn't free herself of the material. No matter how she jerked her head, he held it in place. She grew lightheaded and her limbs heavy. Each frenzied swing or kick forced another breath. Dizziness warred with consciousness. Her head thrummed, and her attempts felt akin to a child trying to kick down a brick wall.

Darkness hemmed her vision. Though the will to fight still beat within her, her body gave out. All hope of escaping floated away with Edward's satisfied words.

"I always get what I want."

CHAPTER 32

BRODERICK LEANED BACK IN DR. Pelton's office chair, hearing the words but not believing them.

"After intense questioning, and revisiting the train depot incident, all charges against you have been dropped. There's no guarantee you will be allowed to return to the Secret Service, but I will admit you did the best you could under the circumstances."

Had those words come from Isaacs, Broderick wouldn't be shocked, but to hear them come from Darlington? He shook his head, words beyond formation.

"Isaacs is gathering officers to raid the printshop. They must be fools to think hiding in a building with the first floor already flooded would keep them from detection."

Considering they hid for two weeks without detection, they weren't fools. Nathaniel, not Darlington, had exposed the hideout. Nathaniel proved a complex man beyond comprehension. Scoundrel, coward, and now sacrificial hero. Which defined his true character? Broderick shoved the question aside. Answering it required more time than he could give right now.

"I want to join the raid." Broderick stood, glad he'd rested most of the day instead of walking laps around the house until exhaustion stopped him.

"You're no use with that arm in a sling, nor are you reinstated."

"Dr. Pelton indicated I can return to normal activities without the sling." Provided they weren't beyond the commonplace. With his job, that included raiding criminals. "Besides, I shoot with my right hand."

Darlington gave a rare grin. "You and Miss Plane deserve each other."

"Gotten under your skin, has she?"

Anxiety probably made her worse than usual with the floodwaters surrounding her. He'd balked at the idea of his partners leaving her at the hotel initially, but Darlington had a point. She wouldn't go anywhere with her greatest fear hemming her in. Sometimes safety superseded comfort.

The door opened, and Isaacs walked in, lifting a set of papers. "Gentlemen, we have a problem."

Darlington twisted in his seat. "Besides wrestling boats in flooded waters to the printshop undetected?"

"An officer finished deciphering the papers Colonel Plane hid in Miss Plane's paint box. Whist is a scapegoat. Edward Greystone is the real leader."

Greystone? Broderick snatched the papers before Darlington could and scanned the notes.

Whist introduced Colonel Plane to counterfeiting as a means of escaping debt, and in a moment of weakness, he'd agreed. The capital for the venture came from a source who wished to remain anonymous. As long as Colonel Plane received his portion, he didn't care—not until the ring used Theresa as a weapon against him when he wanted out.

Greystone confronted Colonel Plane after Drake threatened Theresa, and in his anger revealed his position as financier. No longer would Greystone stand by and watch Theresa be dragged into danger. Either Colonel Plane must tell her he gave his blessing to marry him or Greystone would convince Theresa to elope. A letter from Whist meant to undermine Greystone confirmed Colonel Plane's suspicions about the arrangement. Once they were married, Colonel Plane would have an unfortunate accident, and Greystone would gain control of the printshop. With Theresa's engraving skill, there would be no interruption to production, even if Greystone had to force her participation for a time.

"Where's Greystone now?" Broderick passed the papers to Darlington and stepped into the foyer for his coat.

"Hall is looking into it, but he hasn't visited since Hall banned him from his home once Miss Plane was in our custody."

No man half as intelligent as Greystone relinquished Theresa that easily, especially not with his engraver murdered. "I'll stay with Theresa until you have him."

"The girl's still more important than the case, eh?" Darlington arched a brow. "She's safe in that hotel. No one is going in or out of that building without a boat, and I can guarantee you no one will manage to wrangle her onto the water. She's stuck until the flood recedes."

"If Whist is the scapegoat, Greystone will escape while we arrest the others in a raid. With his shipping warehouse, he has access to steamboats and enough money to start over anywhere. All he needs is the skilled worker, and I guarantee you a little water won't stop him from getting to her."

Darlington considered his argument, then nodded. "All right. You wouldn't be much help at the raid anyway."

Broderick let the comment go unanswered. It didn't matter as long as he stayed with Theresa and ensured Greystone didn't find her.

Theresa's head spun, and her stomach churned. Urgency tugged at her conscious, but the struggle against fog and heaviness kept the reason out of reach. Heat pressed against one side of her body, and chilling cold blasted the other. A deep rumble of words beyond comprehension vibrated against her ear.

Focus, Theresa. Think. Where are you?

No mistaking the rocking motion. Someone carried her. But who? Where? And why? She strained against the weight of her eyelids and managed a slivered peek. A towering giant ducked through a doorway.

Memory slammed through the fog. Edward. She pushed against him with no success.

"About time. I can't have you sleeping through our wedding."

Wedding? "I'm not marrying you."

Even if her words were too garbled to understand, he had to understand the fist to his chest. He dumped her onto a couch and then locked the door. The key disappeared into his pocket. She'd never be able to wrest it from him with her weakened body. Any escape attempt required mental tactics, not physical.

Rich green wallpaper and wall-sized bookshelves established the boundaries of the small office. Behind the massive walnut desk hung a gilded portrait of Edward painted by her hand. At least she knew where he held her captive—his home on Ninth Street. She had no idea how he got her there undetected let alone found her at the hotel, but they weren't far from City Hall and a police station. If she could escape, help would be within reach.

"I've worked too hard to arrange this. I won't let some Nancy-boy copper steal my wife and greatest business asset."

A business asset? Nancy-boy copper? The information didn't make sense. She sat up, and the world spun until she didn't know if she remained straight or half-spilled over. Edward settled next to her, and his leg crushed against hers. She had nowhere to escape—except the floor, which would be a considerably better option if she could control the fall.

His arm steadied her and then traced the curve of her waist. "Not many men can claim to have a skilled engraver as his beautiful wife. Imagine everything we'll have. Your life will rival queens', far better than the scruff and scrabble Colonel Plane gave you. We deserve to have the riches others stole from us, and together we can."

Edward had lost his mind.

"I don't need riches."

"You're too naïve to realize what you need." He fished something from his pocket and held it up. "I discovered you pawned this." Taking her hand, he shoved the emerald ring onto her bare finger. "Had you married me sooner, I would have met all your needs, and you would have been able to keep it."

She leaned back, creating as much space as the couch allowed. "I can't and won't marry you. I don't love you, Edward."

"Ah, but I love you, and soon you'll see things my way." His finger traced her jawline toward her neck and then collarbone.

How dare he take such liberties. She slapped him with all the strength she could muster. "Don't touch me."

He clasped her offending hand in his and squeezed until pain radiated from her knuckles. "You're my wife, and you *will* do what I say. After you engrave the fifties we need, our wealth will be restored, and we can live the life we deserve."

Engrave the fifties? Revulsion churned her stomach and bile burned her throat. All this time, he'd been aware, a part of the very group who'd ruined her life. And now he wanted a life together? "Never."

"You owe it to me to help. I saved you from a life with Colonel Plane." His fist clenched. "Had the fool not ransomed those plates, I might have let him live long enough to walk you down the aisle."

She blinked. Surely he wasn't admitting what she thought. "Let him live?"

"I told you, you're better off without him. I pinned his death on Drake, so there's no concern about the police discovering I shot him. I only wish I hadn't believed Colonel Plane's dying lie that he'd sent you and the plates with Mrs. Hawking to Newport that night. Instead of searching for you, I could have saved you from finding his body."

Edward's confession of murder barreled into her like a train. Derailing every coherent thought, save one. "You're a monster."

"No, just a man who will do anything to protect you." Someone knocked on the door, and Edward's grin spread. "Just the man we've been waiting for."

He abandoned her side to unlock the door. "Good evening, Your Honor."

Your Honor? Praise the Lord! A lawman would never abide what Edward confessed.

"You better make this worth my while." The judge resembled a bent tree as he hobbled into the room. "I had to leave my wife to prepare the house for the rising waters. She was quite angry."

A rock settled in her stomach. Worth his while could not be good.

"She'll change her tune when you buy her that new china set she wants."

The judge flipped through the large wad of money Edward produced from his pocket. "This better be genuine. If any of it's counterfeit, I'll have the law on your tail."

The judge besmirched the respectability of an honorable position with his greed. He deserved to rot in jail with the crooks who padded his pockets.

His knees popped as he turned her way. "This must be your intended."

"I am not marrying him." The ice in her voice should give any man pause, but he blinked with indifference to her objection.

"She'll cost you extra. The unwilling ones are more likely to cause trouble for me later."

Edward reached into his pocket and retrieved a few more bills. "So long as you make it legal and binding."

"Of course."

No! She would not remain complacent. Sliding to the edge of the couch, she tested putting pressure on her feet. They tingled but were manageable. Waiting for the right moment would be as crucial as her legs not giving out. The judge settled into the chair behind the desk and withdrew papers from his valise. When Edward leaned over to examine them, she sprinted for the door.

"Not so fast, my angel."

Her foot crossed the threshold to the foyer and then flew into the air. Edward swung her back into the room and shut the door. No matter how she kicked, his grip remained firm. Surely if she screamed, the neighbors on the other side of the shared wall would hear. She sucked in a breath, and Edward jammed material into her mouth. Though faint, the sweet smell added to the pounding in her head.

"It isn't polite to run from the magistrate."

Magistrate, indeed. A deserter had more honor than this crooked judge.

The man scratched information across the paper and then looked up. "Names."

"Edward Phillip Greystone and Theresa Marie Plane." She lunged forward, but Edward held firm as he spelled both names.

The judge recorded the information and then gave a half-memorized marriage spiel, ending with the dreaded vows. "Do you, Edward Greystone, take Theresa Plane as your wife?"

"I do."

"Do you, Theresa Plane, take Edward Greystone as your husband?"

"No! I do not!"

Waving aside her garbled screams, he said, "Then I pronounce you husband and wife. Please sign here."

Edward dragged her forward and scribbled his name across the marriage certificate. Though she squirmed and fought against him, he wrapped his hand around hers and forced a poor replica of her signature on the paper.

No! God, please. The marriage can't be real in Your eyes. Tell me You do not bless this. Tell me there is escape.

Edward yanked the material from her mouth and forced a kiss. Nausea rolled over her, and as soon as he withdrew, she butted his forehead.

He laughed at her attempt to harm him. "You, my love, are finally mine."

"I'll escape and tell the police everything."

"Tsk-tsk. That's no way to treat your husband. Do you really believe they'll listen to you over me? A bout of female hysteria is easily dismissed. Isn't that so?" Edward gave a devilish grin as he spoke to the judge.

"Aye, and cause for admittance to the asylum."

A useless threat. Time at a lunatic asylum would be preferable to anything Edward might force her to do. Besides, Dr. Pelton had friends at the Longview Asylum. She wouldn't have to suffer long before someone came to her rescue.

"No need for such dramatics," Edward said. "There are other ways to teach a wife her place."

The judge stood, leaving documents on the desk. "I'll file the paperwork in the morning. Enjoy your honeymoon in St. Louis."

She struggled against Edward's one-armed hold to no avail. If they left Cincinnati, she'd be lost forever. A cork popped above her head, and the sweet smell from before reached her nostrils. Not again. She writhed and kicked, knocking the bottle from Edward's hand. His grip on her tightened as he used the handkerchief to absorb the liquid on the desk.

"Come, my darling. We have a long ride."

The refreshed handkerchief covered her face. Try as she might, she could not escape the fumes. Her head throbbed, and her vision blackened. *God, where are You? Where is Broderick?* A single sob escaped as the dark truth ushered her into unconsciousness. Broderick wouldn't be able to save her. Her life was tied to a beast's.

CHAPTER 33

As the sun began its descent into the horizon behind the clouds, Broderick forced himself to walk a sedate pace down Ninth Street. He gripped the heart-shaped rock until it bit into flesh. After discovering the abandoned stone amid the upturned hotel suite, he'd returned to dry ground, then hired a hack and headed straight to Greystone's street to meet Detective Hall. He didn't need to talk to more than one neighbor who'd ignored Theresa's screams to confirm Greystone had kidnapped her.

Hall motioned to him from the steps of Robinson's Opera House and then disappeared inside. Empty of attendees, the dark building allowed for observation of the street without detection. Broderick joined him at a corner window and scrutinized the line of houses opposite. A mixture of three- and four-story brick buildings with stone-carved arches spread the length of the square. Light in many of the windows indicated families obeyed the city orders to stay indoors, but which one held Theresa?

"Edward lives in that stone one, two houses to the left. Just the first floor is lit with lamps." Hall pointed to a three-story Romanesque townhouse. The massive arch above intricately carved pillars and matching details on each floor declared its owner opulent and formidable. If the inside were a decaying, rat-infested hole, the home would fit Greystone perfectly.

"A judge we suspect of corruption left ten minutes after I arrived,"

Hall continued. "No one else has entered or quitted the place since, and we can see Greystone through those front windows."

"Any sign of Theresa?" Broderick tracked the giant's silhouette through the curtained panes. Greystone seemed to be collecting items, but no one else moved.

"Nothing I can confirm."

Theresa must be locked in another room. "Do we have any support?"

"Just another officer who's watching the rear."

As much as Broderick wanted to barge in to face Goliath and free Theresa, reason tempered the impulse. Greystone was too smart not to use Theresa's presence to his advantage. This situation needed a level head. "We need to get in there without alerting Greystone. What's the perimeter look like?"

"A fence and locked gate prevent access to the cellar under the stoop in the front. You can hop the fence, but it requires about a five-foot drop. Crates covered in bells barricade the other doors. There's no way to remove them without bringing attention to the attempt."

If Broderick avoided putting weight on his left arm, the fence hop should be no problem. "Can you provide a distraction?"

"I'll be ready. What about Isaacs and Darlington?"

"They're tracking Whist and Fitz. Bringing down the counterfeiting ring is still priority."

Hall nodded and took position by the opera house doors.

Broderick waited until Greystone's shadow disappeared from view, then sprinted across the street. Slowing enough to ensure his hands grasped only the flat bar across the top of the gate, he vaulted over. The brief moment his left arm bore the brunt of his weight sent crippling pain through him and almost caused him to miss his landing. He stumbled into the stoop wall and swallowed hard.

Lord, please don't let me have ripped open my wound.

Another few weeks of healing and strength exercises and the jump wouldn't have been a problem. Dr. Pelton said he was healing better than expected. A quick check revealed the puckered scar intact. Good. Now to compose himself and focus. He moved to the cellar doors and frowned. Greystone hadn't taken any chances. An iron padlock held the bar in place. With a few tools, he could remove the door hinges, but he'd come woefully unprepared to face a challenge of this sort.

Feet rushed the steps above, followed by pounding on the door. "Quit acting the maggot and get out here, Greystone."

Fitz. Broderick moved deeper into the shadows.

The door thudded open, and a pair of guns cocked.

"Drop it, and maybe I'll let you live." Metal clattered against the stone. "You thought you'd be blowing us to smithereens, did you now?"

Broderick slid across the wall low to the ground until he could see the heads of Fitz, Greystone, and Whist. Either they'd escaped detection from Isaacs and Darlington or the two men hid somewhere nearby. *Please, God, let it be the latter.* Fitz set a large box on the stoop wall, and black powder fell from the busted corner and coated Broderick with the smell of sulfur. He rubbed the residue, and black smeared across his fingers.

"We heard the clock ticking." Whist knocked on the box, and more fell like a black haze.

Gunpowder and a clock in a box? Broderick had heard tales of timed explosions contrived during the Civil War, but he'd never seen a contraption capable of such. He squinted at the unassuming box. If that's what he stared at, Greystone proved more dangerous than Broderick imagined.

"You sap-gags!" Greystone grasped the box and pried off the lid. More powder than reasonable for a cannon rained down on Broderick. "Do you want us all to die?"

Clanking noises followed before a destroyed clock with an odd assortment of parts crashed at Broderick's feet.

"Where are the plates?" Whist didn't seem to care that one spark would ignite them like a firework.

"At the printshop on the third floor, like I told you." Unless other unknown plates existed, Greystone told a brazen lie. "Not that it matters now. You'll never make it back before the others blow."

"You son of a banshee!" Fitz lunged forward and pounded Greystone against the wall. "Me brother's in there."

Evenly matched, Greystone wasn't likely to escape Fitz's wrath. Fitz valued family above all else. Mess with them and Fitz would beat the Angel of Death to his job.

"More importantly, the plates and presses we saved are there." Whist peered down the street. "We need to get back."

"No evidence can remain if we're going to escape," Greystone said.

"We, is it?" Whist snorted. "Grimm, get over here."

The clop of horses' feet and the creak of wagon wheels grew louder and then stopped near the stoop. "I thought we were gonna kill him."

"Change of plans. Fitz, go in and find Miss Plane. I'd bet your life she's in there."

Broderick clenched his hands into fists. Pinned below, he stood at a tactical disadvantage. Any attempt to intervene would fail.

Greystone grabbed Fitz's arm. "Leave her be. She's incapacitated. Lugging her around will be a hindrance."

Incapacitated. Broderick's chest tightened. That word could cover a multitude of problems. None of them good.

"And lose my greatest power over you? Not a chance." Whist spat. "Get in the wagon. We're going for a ride."

Greystone descended the stairs but stopped at the bottom and turned on Whist. Broderick heard more than saw the struggle. Curses punctuated the air. Then, a gunshot. Greystone reeled back, clutching his shoulder. After a moment, he released it. Evidently a surface wound. It might hurt, but it wouldn't interfere with much.

Whist wiped a fist across his mouth, then prodded Greystone with his pistol. "Let that be a warning. Next time it'll be a killing shot." He stepped closer to the doorway. "Find her yet, Fitz?"

"I did, and a bag of money. Enough to sail back to Éire or bring my entire family here with me."

"That bag of money is still nothing compared to what we can make if we save the plates. Come on."

At Whist's prodding, Greystone climbed into the back of the wagon.

Fitz strode down the steps, valise in one hand and Theresa slung over his opposite shoulder. If she were even minutely conscious, she'd be fighting. Instead, she hung silent and limp without a cloak to protect her. Her head hit the side of the wagon as Fitz dumped her into the bed. She gave no reaction. What had Greystone done to her?

Whist knocked on the back of Grimm's seat. "Head to the printshop. Greystone here is going to remove those bombs."

"I told you they'll go off before we arrive, you fool."

Fitz wrapped a hand around Greystone's neck. "You better be wrong about that."

The wagon rolled off, and Broderick grabbed the clock. He didn't know much about explosives, but evidence like this could prove Greystone deserved a hanging.

Hall jogged across the street and met Broderick at the locked gate. Broderick passed the broken clock over, and then with a grunt and foot to the cement fence base, he jumped over. Sweat beaded across his upper lip as he leaned forward and panted. "They're headed for the printshop."

Hall frowned at him with folded arms. "You should go back to the Peltons'. You're in no condition to follow."

"Would you abandon pursuit if you were me and Theresa were Lydia?"

"All right. I'll gather what men I can free from flood duty and meet you at the public landing." Hall strode toward the alley by the opera house as Isaacs emerged from it astride one horse and leading another.

"Sorry, Hall," Isaacs said. "You'll need to find another ride."

Hall didn't argue but changed direction toward the livery.

Isaacs passed Broderick the reins. "Do you know where they're going?"

"The printshop. Greystone planted bombs there, and they're determined to save everything."

"Bombs?" Isaacs shook his head after a moment of shocked silence. "Darlington's already following. Think we can beat them?"

Without a doubt. Even with the floods cutting off the routes he preferred, they could make far better time than five people in a wagon. Instead of following behind Whist, Broderick cut down Elm Street and turned onto Weaver Alley to run parallel. Several points existed where Whist could launch a boat, but the public landing made the most sense. Fewer buildings would block his path, and the current would carry them down to the printshop without much of a fight.

But that didn't mean Whist would choose the logical approach. At each street, Broderick paused to check Whist's progress. The wagon never varied from his Ninth Street path toward Broadway, the direct route to the public landing.

At Main Street, they joined Darlington. "We'll cut them off before they get any farther." As usual, Darlington didn't take into consideration the complexities of the situation. Three against four and Theresa unconscious would not end well, even with one of those men injured. "We follow until we have Hall's support."

Darlington nudged his horse ahead of Broderick's. "I'm lead on this case."

The man couldn't see past his self-importance. How had he become the Secret Service's best strategy? Broderick yanked on Darlington's reins and stopped both their horses. He'd delay only once, so the man better listen.

"We're partners. We all work together and succeed, or we all go toes up together. This isn't about who leads who. I know Cincinnati and those men better than either you or Isaacs. We meet Hall's men at the public landing, and then we pounce. Anything sooner and we risk Theresa's life and our own. I don't care if you take the credit for this when it's over, but we do it together with no man trying to outdo the other. It's teamwork or nothing."

Broderick held Darlington's stare until he nodded in agreement.

"Cosgrove, they're cutting down Sycamore." Isaacs wheeled his horse down a narrow walking path between buildings.

Sycamore didn't make sense. Broderick released Darlington's reins. Whist must have realized they followed.

CHAPTER 34

WHIST SLOWED HIS PROGRESS AND changed his path to unpredictable and impractical. Sometimes he took the wagon at a reckless speed, other times slowing so that Broderick almost passed it and revealed their location. Following Whist became a test of his memory of alleyways and private garden paths. More than once, he lost track of the wagon and prayed for wisdom as he chose a new direction in hopes of intercepting it.

Lord, help us and protect Theresa. Too much is out of my control.

He snorted as he turned back down the alley behind the Masonic Temple. Control. The greatest lie of the devil. He had no more control of this situation than he did of the rising flood levels. Leaving Theresa hadn't protected her. Holding back information hadn't changed anything. She was alive not because of anything he'd done but because of God's grace and mercy. He wouldn't foolishly believe he had any control in the outcome. Everything was in God's hands alone.

Your will be done, Lord, but please let it match my desires. Selfish, maybe, but he couldn't help it. He and Theresa were finally together with plans for a future, and he didn't want to lose that ever again.

The sound of horse hooves and wagon wheels stopped him short. Whist must have made another unexpected turn. Without side paths in the alley to hide in, Whist would spot them. A back door to the Masonic Temple opened in front of Broderick, and a boy discarded the contents of a wastebasket. Broderick had never been one to condone animals indoors, but some situations warranted breaking the rules.

The boy yelped and dodged as Broderick guided the well-trained horse through the oversized door. Leaning low and pulling his legs behind him, the horse managed to squeeze through without doing more than grazing the doorframe. On the other side of a small kitchen area, the rest of the building opened into an expansive tiled room with grand chairs lining the perimeter. Food and clothing were stacked all around, prepared for distribution to the needy.

A man in a black suit and decorative apron approached. "What the devil is going on here?"

Isaacs beat him to an answer. "An emergency forced us to cut through your building. Our apologies. If you point us to the front door, we'll be on our way."

"I say you will." He huffed across the room, then opened a door before rushing to open another.

By the time they exited to Walnut Street, Whist had stopped the wagon near the waterline one building down.

"They're going to launch from Walnut," Broderick said. Two blocks west of the public landing, and far from the police who should be waiting.

Isaacs turned east. "I'll alert Hall. Keep watch, but don't do anything stupid."

Broderick couldn't make any promises. If it came down to a foolish choice or losing Theresa, he'd choose foolishness. Darlington dismounted at a nearby livery and passed his horse off to a stable hand. Broderick followed his lead. They slipped down the street and blended in with the sightseers examining the flood damage for themselves. Though the crowd wasn't as populous as during the day, the dozen people commenting on the water and testing its edges made it easier to go undetected.

Broderick tugged his hat low as they neared the wagon and pretended to examine the water. Grimm paid the crowd no mind other than to hide his pistol from sight. Greystone cradled Theresa in his lap like a wolf possessive of its kill and glared at Grimm with murderous intent. What would be the repercussions if Broderick knocked the back of Grimm's head with his pistol grip? The man would likely drop his gun within easy reach of Greystone. But with Theresa hampering Greystone's movements, Broderick might be able to snag it before Greystone could.

"Don't do it." Darlington's warning pulled his attention. "Teamwork. We need to wait."

What a time to have his own words thrown back at him. Broderick walked past Grimm and forced himself not to look over his shoulder. As much as he hated to admit it, Darlington was right. His rash plan would have ended with one or more people dead.

"I be taking your boat."

Broderick jerked his attention to where Fitz held up a ferryman on the makeshift dock. He wasn't nearly as tall or broad as Fitz, but years of physical labor defined the man's features as he crossed his arms and continued to block access to the boats. "These belong to the bridge company. You wanna ride, you come back in the mornin'."

Fitz crashed a fist into the unprepared man's face. He stumbled off the dock between two boats, then clung to the edge. His friend knelt to aid him but kept as far from Fitz as possible.

"Anyone else want to be testing your mettle?"

No one accepted Fitz's challenge, instead choosing to either escape down Pearl Street or silently retreat a safe distance. Darlington elbowed Broderick's arm and gestured to a spot farther down the waterline. Two against four, and they still had Theresa. Broderick grit his teeth. Choosing to stay wouldn't save her. If he was recognized, Whist would have the upper hand.

Once a good fifteen feet away, they turned to watch as Whist gave orders. "Greystone, carry your woman over here. Grimm, make sure he doesn't try something."

Broderick turned the rock over and over in his hand as he watched

Greystone lumber over with Theresa. Her arm lifted, but the brief hope of revival died when it dropped to dangle at her side.

Whist tugged the boat flush with the dock. "Lay her in the middle and then get in the front of the other boat."

"I'm not leaving her." Greystone held Theresa tighter to his chest.

Grimm pressed his gun against Greystone's back. "I shoot, and the bullet travels right through you to her."

A double kill with a single shot. Broderick reached for his Colt. Just as he grasped it, Greystone laid her down and kissed her head—as if the giant actually cared about her well-being. He stepped back, and Grimm shifted his aim to Theresa.

Whist trained his weapon on Greystone. "Grimm, follow behind. If he tries anything, dump her into the water."

Whist clambered in behind Greystone, keeping a barrel pressed into his back. Fitz released the boat and pushed them into deeper waters, leaving Grimm to fall behind.

This was their chance. The moment Grimm shoved his pistol back into his belt to fumble with the rope, Broderick sprinted. His feet hit the dock, and Grimm twisted toward him. Broderick aimed. Just as he found his mark, Grimm slammed an oar into his left arm. Flashes blinded his vision, and sharp pain sucked the air from his lungs. Another blow came faster than he could recover, and his knees buckled. He grabbed the edge of the boat as he tumbled off the dock. Water gushed over him, threatening to suck him under the hull with the force of its current. The oar cracked against his hand. He lost his grip, and the current dragged him under.

Broderick clawed at the cobblestone of the submerged street. If he could stand, he could walk out. A shot came from above, pinging off the stone near his face. More shots followed in rapid succession but did not enter the water. Darlington must have drawn Grimm's fire. Broderick bumped into a gaslight and managed to get his arms around it before the current yanked him out of reach. His arms strained and screamed in pain as he struggled to get his feet underneath him.

Two people splashed to him from the shore and hooked him through the arms. They hauled him to shallower water, where the current had no strength. And neither did he. He watched with labored breath as Grimm paddled around a building. They'd never catch up now.

Darlington splashed to him. "Cosgrove, you fool! We've lost the element of surprise."

"That was our best chance to avoid a fight on flooded waters." Broderick accepted aid to stand from the man who'd endured Fitz's punch.

"Somethin' tells me you're the law. Name's Reuben." He shook Broderick's hand. "Me and Ira wanna help."

Ira, darker and broader than his friend, gestured to the remaining boat attached to the dock. "We'll row, you shoot."

Darlington reloaded his revolver. "Thank you for the use of your boat, but you can't come. It's too dangerous for civilians."

"Ain't no stranger to danger, sir. Served in the 5th Colored Infantry."

Broderick looked from the two men to the flooded expanse before him. "We need them. I can't row." It chafed to admit, but he'd be lucky to use his arm at all given the beating Grimm gave him.

"This isn't some heroic story to tell your friends. This is life or death." Darlington held each man's gaze as he spoke.

Reuben and Ira nodded. "Understood."

Darlington didn't argue further as they loaded and then urged the boat toward Front Street. Broderick scanned the inky water for any sign of Whist or Grimm, but although the rain had stopped hours ago, the moon had yet to break through the clouds.

Once they moved beyond the buildings, the undertow strengthened and hurtled them downstream. Debris banged against the boat's sides, and Reuben and Ira tossed their weight to keep from capsizing. The duo worked in practiced unison to maneuver through the treacherous water, but none of their skill mattered if they couldn't close the distance.

Broderick leaned forward and squinted at the darkness as they passed under the wooden and wrought iron underbelly of Suspension Bridge. On the other side, two dark shapes emerged downstream with an unnatural path toward the printshop. Without being told, Ira and

Reuben paddled faster. Broderick massaged the throb in his arm as he watched Whist's boat approach the printshop, Grimm's not far behind. They'd be outnumbered in the building, but it would be easier than a fight on the—

Blinding light flashed with a deafening boom, and debris flew like cannonballs through the air, exploding water as it landed. Waves crashed against their boat with such force it took all four of them to keep from capsizing. Once certain they wouldn't fall into the water, Broderick faced the printshop, its third floor gone and most of its second. Water rushed through and around it. If anyone survived the blast, the current had swept them away.

If anyone survived . . .

Broderick sucked in a breath and searched the upset and churning waters. No boats. Whist, Fitz, Greystone, Grimm, and Theresa were gone.

Chapter 35

A SHOCK OF FRIGID COLD made Theresa gasp, but water, not air, filled her lungs. *Water.* She was in water. Panic welled as coughs invited more liquid to invade her mouth and nose. Something rough scraped her face before she slammed against some stationary force. For a moment, the current pushed her to the surface and air.

A cough to expel water and a gasp were all she managed before the current dragged her under again. Her body twisted over and sideways until she no longer knew which direction led to the surface. When she opened her eyes, the murky darkness provided no guidance. No matter how she clawed or kicked, escape evaded her.

Drowning this time wasn't like the last time, when a slow descent pulled her under as light teased from above. No, that river had been sweet, tame, and beautiful compared to the raging demon that thrashed her now.

Something large thwacked her back and tangled in her skirts. Bound to it, she dipped and rolled. It burst through the surface, and for one blessed moment, air was hers. Then it plunged back below, bobbing again to the surface seconds later. Short, cruel breaks at the surface. A gulp of air and then back down. Enough air to sustain but never enough to satisfy. Again and again she bobbed. Kicking. Fighting. Swallowing more water than air.

Then whatever held her bumped against something bigger. The

current snatched her from its grip and thrust her back into the topsy-turvy spin. Down and up. Over and back. Her miserable attempts meant nothing.

Kick! Don't give up.

Her fingers broke through the surface. She stretched to meet it with her head, but her legs failed. Heartbeats pounded in her ears. A deep, familiar pain burned in her lungs.

Please, God, no. Not again.

Something sturdy slammed against her body and stalled her progress downstream. Water rushed around her, squeezing her against the object like paper in a printing press. The rough bumps against her hands and face were familiar and natural. Bark? She spread her arms and legs, and the current pressed them around the cylinder. Praise God! A tree, old and wide enough to bear up under the pressure of these waters. If she could make it higher, she might survive.

Her arms rallied to the battle call, tracing the trunk holding her until she found a limb farther up. Maybe, just maybe.

Give me strength, God. Jesus, please.

Fumbling, she reached for one branch. Then another. Pressure mounted around her, as for a lone soldier fighting against an enemy who took no prisoners. Each inch she gained was possibly her last.

The top of her head broke through to air. Though her face still battled debris and current, a surge of hope strengthened her. She clasped another branch. Her arms shook, threatening to give out, but she would not stop fighting. Her eyes cleared the surface, and she searched for her next handhold. The next branch grazed her fingertips.

Please, just a bit more.

With a final push from legs too numb to feel, she grasped the branch and pulled until her chin cleared the surface. Water cascaded over her shoulders and wrapped around her neck like a too-big scarf. Gasping breaths intermingled with water. She should reach for another branch. Give another kick.

One more.

Her body trembled as she put all her energy into it.

Nothing. Her legs refused to comply. Her arm did nothing but bob with the current.

This was it. She would drown after all, not by sinking but by the taunting breaths of water-drenched air. Face pressed into the trunk, she closed her eyes. At least she wasn't cold anymore. Just exhausted. Ethereal tingles bade her to release this world and drift into eternity.

Broderick's loving gaze filled her vision, and his tender caresses reached beyond the numbness. Her name rolled off his lips, desperate and aching. How she wished she could touch and comfort him. She gave him a bittersweet smile. At least their final goodbye would be serene and private. Arms wrapped around her and gathered her close— the feeling so warm and real that she almost believed the dream real. His *I love you* rolled over her and lavished her with peace.

Yes, she could rest now. Those words would go with her into eternity.

"Theresa!"

Her body shook as someone yelled her name over and over. The Angel of Death was not a gentle being. Maybe she was supposed to look into his eyes before he carried her to heaven. The angel bent her forward and whacked her back, expelling the water with coughs. When she leaned back again, she mustered a peek. Remarkable how much the Angel of Death resembled Edward.

"I've got you."

"Just take me to Jesus."

Coughs interrupted her words, but he got her meaning. "Not today, my love. We've got a future to live."

Love? Future? Those belonged to Broderick. She blinked until she could determine who held her. Frost-blue eyes peered at her in moonlight. She must be alive, for how could God allow this fiend into heaven?

Edward brushed back her wet hair and smiled with the gleam of greed. "Even God ordained us to be together. All we have to do is get off this tree."

She blinked and tried to make her brain work. They had two ways out of this tree: in the water or in a boat. Only one was likely. What was God's point in having her hang between life and death with a monster? The way her body shook, she'd never last until morning even if the branch held. She closed her eyes.

God, I don't understand, but I trust You. Even if.

Though the rest of her was too cold to feel anything, her heart ached. *Give Broderick another chance at love and the life I wanted to give him.*

Edward shifted, and the branches creaked louder than the roar of water. She sucked in a breath and held it. Morning would not come for either of them. *Be with Broderick in the coming days, and don't allow him to blame himself. This isn't his fault.*

The tree groaned. The branch snapped. And then the world fell away.

This is all my fault. I should have gone to Theresa sooner. God, please let me find her. Give me Your eyes.

Broderick scanned the water for any hint of her location, taking advantage of the nearly full moon's brief appearance. Every piece of debris, every chunk of ice, required a second glance. Twigs took on the form of wet hair. Splashes a possibility of her attempts to swim. After all they'd been through, all they'd survived, he couldn't have lost Theresa.

Reuben and Ira paddled around the printshop's ruins where the water rushed over crumbled walls and across the second-floor rubble. A weight pressed around him as they moved past with no sign of either of Whist's boats.

"Looks like Isaacs is arriving with the others," Darlington said from behind.

Broderick turned, and a handful of lights bobbed beneath the bridge, too late for a rescue. This was a recovery mission now.

Collecting corpses was all they were likely to succeed in. No doubt, many of those would appear washed up on the shore downriver when the water receded.

He turned back to the bleakness in front of him. "Ira, see any hope?"

"There's always hope until the Good Lord takes us home."

Home. Heaven. Broderick's heart thrummed so hard his chest hurt, but nothing compared to the pain of losing Theresa. Not again. Not like this. "That's what I'm afraid of."

"Don't give up yet, Cosgrove. That woman would annoy the devil. I'm sure even God isn't ready to have her full-time in His courts."

Darlington's attempt at comfort produced a reluctant smile. Theresa *was* a fighter. If she had any say in the matter, she'd be fighting to survive, and for him to be resigned so soon showed a distinct lack of faith. *Lord, You've protected her thus far. I have to trust that You haven't stopped now.* They traveled past two more buildings, and the landscape opened to the vast expanse that should have been railroad. A tall tree that defied the current with its strength created the only break in the water. A tree that had a deep voice and screamed for help?

"Ira, head straight for—"

"The tree. I see 'em. Give her all you got, Reuben." Ira's paddle cut through the water.

"Darlington, fire a couple off." They'd need another boat to fit any survivors. Hopefully, Isaacs would understand the message.

As they drew closer, details became clear. Greystone clung to a broken branch with one hand and to Theresa's hand with his other. Water swarmed around them like a high-collared coat, and though Greystone appeared to be trying to hold Theresa above it, her head dipped under with such frequency that breathing had to be nearly impossible.

"Careful. The boat could crush them."

Reuben and Ira corrected the path, narrowly missing Greystone, and then skidded the boat into branches on the far side of the tree's trunk—far enough to keep from knocking Greystone loose but too far to easily reach them. Broderick gathered the rope at his feet and eyed the best way to pull Greystone and Theresa to safety. Tossing it would be useless. Greystone couldn't grab it, and Theresa wouldn't be able to keep hold of it even if she could. The only way to get the rope to them was to climb it over.

"Tie one end to the boat." Broderick passed the rope to Darlington and then shed his coat. The less interference he had, the better.

"What's the plan?" Darlington asked.

"I'll climb over to them, and then toss me the rope."

"Can you do it?"

He flexed his arm. It throbbed, but the break since the dock had helped. "I'll manage."

Darlington nodded, and Broderick tested a sturdy branch before lifting himself. Working his way carefully across, he avoided the broken section to which Greystone clung. Once secure in his footing on the trunk, he called for the rope. Darlington tossed it, nearly knocking Greystone in the head before it tangled in the branch above.

"Don't you let go of her or the branch, Greystone." Broderick leaned forward and yanked the rope free. "I'm going to thread this around your body."

"Theresa first," Greystone grunted.

No arguments there. Broderick would take advantage of any glimpse of nobility from the man, especially if it meant Theresa reached safety. He wrapped his legs around the split in the trunk and leaned toward Theresa. Plunging the rope into the frigid water, he threaded it around her waist, then yanked it tight before tying it off with a bowline knot. She wouldn't enjoy the bruised ribs after this, but it was better than the alternative. He tested the strength with a tug before taking a deep breath.

Hold on to her, Lord. "All right, let her go, Greystone."

"I'll murder you if she dies." The threat came at the same instant he released her.

Theresa drifted for a moment before the rope snapped taut.

"Pull her in."

Reuben and Darlington pulled the rope, and Broderick held his breath until they managed to pull her over the side of the boat.

Darlington unhitched the knot while Reuben leaned over her. "Is she—"

A sputtering cough erupted.

Broderick released a breath when Reuben called out, "She's breathing."

The sooner they took care of Greystone, the sooner they could get her help. Darlington tossed him the rope again, but the same method wouldn't work for Greystone. Hauling a man his size through the water and into the boat would capsize it. He couldn't risk it, not with civilians and Theresa inside.

"Pass me the rope and then get to shore." Isaacs and a couple of officers paddled alongside Darlington. "We'll get Cosgrove and Greystone."

The man couldn't have better timing.

"Do you think you can pull him up into the tree and then step over from there?"

It was worth a try. Broderick looped the rope around the tree and secured it before coiling it around his arm for extra support. He leaned to reach Greystone's extended hand.

A snarl twisted his mustache. "I'm not going to jail, and you can't have her."

In a tug that both snapped the branch and propelled Greystone forward, he grasped Broderick's foot and yanked.

Broderick plunged into the icy water. Greystone's weight dragged him down into the raging current faster than any anchor. The rope ran out of slack with a jerk, and Broderick's shoulder popped. The sharp pain made him gasp and inhale water. The joint strained under the pressure of the rope and Greystone's weight like a wishbone. Any moment, Broderick's arm would be ripped asunder. Debris knocked into them, and the weight around his foot disappeared. Whatever hit them had taken Greystone with it.

Arms hooked his shoulders and hauled him into the boat. Pain blackened his vision. Someone rolled him to the side, and the water violently expelled from his lungs and didn't stop until the contents of his stomach took their turn. Eventually, nothing remained, and he lay on his back.

Isaacs slowly uncoiled the rope around Broderick's arm. "Didn't I tell you not to do anything stupid?"

Broderick set his jaw. If his left arm ever worked again, it would be a miracle. "Don't think I had much choice. Where's Theresa?"

"Heading toward the hospital, same as you. Greystone's a lost cause."

Greystone had robbed them all of justice by choosing his death and ensuring no member of the ring faced a court hearing. However, Greystone had saved Theresa. Maybe in some twisted way, he had cared about her. Broderick watched the dim outline of Theresa's boat and swallowed. The case may be over, but the future remained uncertain.

Chapter 36

Theresa groaned. What had she done to herself this time? Being this stiff and sore usually indicated she faced the consequence of some misadventure. A yawn forced air deep into her lungs and prompted a painful bout of coughing.

Ugh. Grandfather would be furious. Maybe if she snuggled deeper into the covers and rested a little longer, the discomfort would settle to tolerable when the bugle finally announced morning. Another, shallower yawn followed, and she winced. She better see what she could handle before deciding whether to admit her ailment to the man.

She opened her eyes and blinked. White walls and ceiling instead of dark blue encompassed her view. This was not home. It wasn't even Lydia's guest room. Her heart thrummed. Not again. Not here. The scratchy blankets tangled as she fought to sit up. Sterile bedclothes and three other beds with sleeping occupants confirmed her fears. Good Samaritan Hospital. Again. She looked out the one window. Dim light filtered through. Whether dawn or dusk, she couldn't be sure.

Theresa swiped at her hair, and gold and glittering green caught her eye. She stilled. There shouldn't be a ring on her finger. Dread pitted her stomach as she held out her shaking hand. An emerald glittered back at her.

"No." The single word failed to stop the crushing wave of memory. Grandfather was dead, and she was married to Edward—the man who killed him. She closed her eyes against the tears that formed. How could she have been so deceived by his character? Yet Edward had saved her from drowning. Spoken like he loved her and truly wanted a future with her beyond counterfeiting. It didn't make sense. He was a criminal and willing to force her to submit to his will. His character was twisted beyond comprehension. She needed to send for help before he could succeed in escaping with her again.

"You're awake."

Theresa opened her eyes to see a Sister of Charity standing at her bedside in a white coif and aproned habit.

The Sister smiled at her before continuing in a hushed tone. "How are you feeling this morning, Miss Plane?"

The words *nauseated*, *horrified*, *distraught*, and *terrified* all ran through her mind, but she doubted that's what the kind Sister meant.

"Is . . . is Edward here?" No one would know he's dangerous.

"Who is that?"

"My husband." The word tasted vile in her mouth.

The Sister's brow knit as she touched Theresa's forehead. "Perhaps they missed a head injury in your examination." Her hand dropped. "You're registered as Theresa Plane, an unmarried woman."

"He kidnapped me and forced me to marry him. Please, I need to speak to the police immediately. He's a dangerous man."

The Sister looked at her oddly, but then said, "Very well, but then we need to get you some nourishment." She exited with a purpose-driven stride, and Theresa rolled to her stomach. How would she tell Broderick everything they dreamed and hoped for had once again been thwarted? She screamed into her pillow. *Why, God? Why would You want me tied to a wicked man?*

Fear not and *trust* pounded in her head as if God Himself were determined to carve the words into her brain so she'd stop forgetting them. Would she ever learn to trust the One with all the answers?

Deep breaths hurt, so she settled for shallow sips and focused on finding pictures in the floorboard grains—anything to take her mind off the pain that encompassed body, mind, and soul. The cluster of curvy lines near the chair leg swirled to make a square face, complete with a crooked nose, cocky smile, and an angular jawline. A perfect match to Broderick's. So much for a distraction.

She rolled onto her back and let out a frustrated breath. Maybe planning what she would say to the police was a better strategy. A few minutes later, Sister's shoes clicked on the tile floor, followed by a second but quieter and faster-paced set.

Theresa turned her head, then blinked. Broderick passed the woman, his features tight, eyes riveted on her. Hair mussed and feet bare, he moved with more purpose than Mrs. Hawking ever managed. His half-tucked shirt flapped at his thighs and appeared to have as many buttons undone as done. His disheveled appearance was at odds with his typical well-maintained attire, but it appealed—far more than it should. How could she have ever compared that wooden image to the breath-taking, heart-fluttering, heat-inducing man padding toward her.

"Thank God." His voice held thick emotion.

Despite one arm secured in a sling, in two more steps he drew her off the bed, covers and all. They dropped onto the wooden chair with a thud, and he pressed his head alongside hers as he squeezed her tight.

"Mr. Cosgrove, this is highly inappropriate, and I demand you release her. Or I'll have the officer arrest *you* when he arrives."

Officer or not, Theresa wasn't about to surrender her position—though she was glad the ward's other occupants still slept. Arms wrapped around his neck, the two of them pressed together as tightly as two bodies could be, she reveled in Broderick's strength and protection.

"I almost lost the woman I love for the second time in my life. I will hold her as long as she'll allow me."

His words traveled with the heat of his breath, down her neck and straight into the broken places of her heart. They'd find a way to be together. They had to.

"But she claims to be a married woman."

Broderick jerked back and gaped at her in confusion.

A knife pierced her heart. "Edward forced me and paid a judge to make it legal."

As much as she wanted to stay with him, stepping away was the God-honoring thing to do. Wrapping the covers tightly around her, she slipped off his lap and back onto the edge of the bed.

Broderick shook his head. "You're not married."

"But I am." Her chest rebelled at her shaky breath as she extended the hand with Edward's ring on it. "He forced me to sign the certificate. The judge has it."

Broderick grasped her hand and lowered it as he scooted the chair nearer. "Hall arrested Judge Harris this morning for his part in the scheme. He found the certificate, without a witness signature, making it invalid. Besides, even if it were valid, Greystone's dead."

Dead? Strange how the news hit with both a wave of joy and deep grief. Yes, she wanted to be free of Edward and for him to face the courts and be served justice for all he'd done. But to die? Despite what he turned out to be, for a time he'd been her friend. "How?"

Sister slipped between them. "I think you should leave, Mr. Cosgrove. You've upset her enough."

"No, please. I need to know." Theresa leaned around the white frock and swallowed. "How did he die?"

The Sister stepped away, and Broderick released a breath before answering. "He drowned."

She swallowed back an unexpected lump of emotion. "What happens now?"

"We recover and look to the future." He tugged the emerald ring from her finger and set it aside. "Our future, if you'll still have me."

His fingers entwined with hers. The hesitancy in his gaze melted her heart. How could he think she'd say anything other than yes? She cupped his face. "Broderick Cosgrove, I will marry you at your earliest convenience."

A wide grin broke across his face, and then it was hard to tell who started the kiss. But it didn't matter. She was free to be his, wholly his. They leaned into each other, two broken halves bound together and healed by God's plan. Six years of missed moments couldn't be satisfied in a single kiss, but this one was a masterful attempt. He held her gently but unwilling to let go, as if she were his greatest treasure, gentle yet unwilling to let go. Their lips danced an intimate waltz and sparked a fire in her body.

Strong arms pried them apart. "That is quite enough." The devil would have run from the look Sister gave them.

Broderick leaned his forehead against hers and closed his eyes. "Sister, is there a priest in the hospital? One who can marry us?"

She harrumphed. "There had better be after a display like that."

Right now? But he looked a wreck, and she couldn't look much better. Not to mention Lydia would be furious to miss her wedding. No, it simply wouldn't do. She didn't need a big affair, but a woman simply did not get married in her nightgown. "We will do no such thing. I will not be denied a proper wedding three times, Broderick."

"But you said at my earliest convenience. We're together, there's a priest, and Sister can be the witness. How much more convenient do you need?"

Men. "A hospital wedding is not what I have in mind."

He frowned as he faced Sister. "How long until she's released?"

"Neither of you is in any condition to be released for several days, especially if you continue breaking doctor's orders. I think it's time you return to your ward, Mr. Cosgrove." The look Sister gave Broderick could wither grass.

He nodded, then looked at Theresa. "You do everything she tells you. I won't be far."

"You may not be far, but you certainly won't be here." Sister began pushing him toward the exit. "If you'll kiss her like that while I'm standing here, then I can't trust you to be here when I'm not. Now, shoo! I've got other patients to tend to."

He broke free of Sister's grasp before giving Theresa one more sound kiss. Then he stepped back with a whispered promise and a wink. "I'll return soon."

She bit her lip to hold back a laugh as Sister ushered him out of the room with a lashing of threats.

God, I don't understand why we had to endure all this, but thank You. Thank You for bringing us back together, for giving us a future.

Finally, the long-awaited promise of her dreams would come to fruition. Leaning back against the pillows, she closed her eyes and relived Broderick's kiss. To think, they would have a whole lifetime of those. A smile tugged at the edges of her yawn. May theirs be a long life, indeed.

CHAPTER 37

May 13, 1884

BRODERICK PACED THE DECORATED BALLROOM in the Hall home as family and friends mingled, waiting for the wedding ceremony to begin. How long did it take a woman to get dressed? He'd already suffered through three months of delay.

Granted, Theresa couldn't be blamed for the whole delay. Dr. Pelton had demanded they allow time for recovery. While Broderick objected, Theresa did not. Some battles were worth fighting, but Isaacs convinced him they'd both enjoy the start of marriage more without the hindrance of illness and weakness. So he'd waited.

The time might have passed more quickly if he'd spent it with Theresa, but duty required his presence in Washington. With the aftermath of the flood hampering travel and communications throughout the entire Ohio Valley, the trip had taken twice as long as usual. He'd expected an immediate dismissal from the Secret Service, but he'd spent two weeks going over the case with Chief Brooks—detail by detail, from his reluctance to reveal his relationship with Theresa to the drowning of the mastermind leader.

He'd waited another week before Chief Brooks decided to reinstate him with only a dress down, and then he reassigned him to Cincinnati. The unexpected location change must have resulted from the political influence of Isaacs's family—a wedding gift he'd forever be grateful for. At least when he traveled, he knew Theresa would be protected and cared for by the Halls and Peltons.

Even Mrs. Hawking had agreed to stay on once she'd been cleared of guilt with the poisoned laudanum, though she'd not likely let him forget his mistake in suspecting her anytime soon. The culprit had been Fitz's sister, who'd switched bottles during her weekly laundry pickup at the Pelton home. Maybe all this waiting was part of Mrs. Hawking's plan to punish him. He wouldn't put it past her.

"Enjoying your last moments of freedom, Cosgrove?" Darlington twirled the stem of a glass between his fingers.

Broderick glared at the doors. "Not in the least."

"I'd get used to it. That woman will test the patience of any saint, and you're no saint."

Isaacs slapped him on the back. "Relax. Women dream of this day their whole lives. Every detail must be perfect. She probably had a wilted flower in her bouquet. It'll be replaced in short order."

Darlington elbowed him in the ribs. "Or she could have come to her senses and sneaked off."

"Don't listen to them. Theresa's so eager to have her own house again that she'll stoop to marrying you." Nathaniel smiled behind his glass of lemonade.

Using his influence within the justice system, Dr. Pelton had Nathaniel released to his supervision for probation. Life as a detective no longer existed in Nathaniel's future, but with the guidance of the Peltons, a new career in the medical field looked possible.

"Apparently she's not eager enough." Broderick rolled his shoulders and watched the closed doors again. If she didn't signal the start of the wedding in five minutes, he'd go looking for her.

The door cracked open, and Lydia's head poked through. Instead of a smile and nod to settle the room, she frowned and crooked a finger at him. Broderick shoved his empty glass into Darlington's hand as he brushed past.

"What's wrong? Is Theresa all right?" A glance around the foyer as he shut the door behind him revealed no imminent danger, but Lydia's strained face spoke of something far worse than a wilted flower.

"I don't know. She won't let me in the room."

Broderick stepped around Lydia, then hurriedly mounted the stairs. He knocked on the guest room door.

"I need a few more minutes." Theresa's voice quavered as if she were trying to disguise tears.

He tried the knob, but it didn't give. "Reese, it's me."

A chair scraped, and her feet plodded across the floor. When she opened the door, she lifted her chin and thrust a piece of paper at him. "I'm sorry. I shouldn't have read this. It was meant for you."

She sniffed and swiped at a renegade tear. Dressed in a light-blue gown and hair swept up into a fancy design, she should be smiling, not sniffling. What the devil did a letter addressed to him contain that would make her cry?

He stepped into the privacy of the room and shut the door before claiming the letter. A glance at the signature revealed it was from Colonel Plane. "Where did you get this?"

"Mrs. Hawking gave it to me. She told me she was sworn to keep it until our wedding day."

Broderick scanned the contents, a little bewildered by the words.

If you are reading this, then you are marrying my granddaughter today. You once told me I was a curmudgeon who didn't know how to love and protect the most valuable person in my life. You were both right and wrong. I didn't protect her as I should, but I do love her, and now I assign to you the greatest mission I ever failed. Love her without reserve, sacrifice to protect her, and if you can find a way to help her forgive me, I will be eternally grateful.

Take care of my little soldier, Broderick. She's worth every headache.

Colonel Plane

"His last letter to me was so cold and hard that I started to hate him." The brokenness in her voice tore at him.

Broderick set the letter aside and gathered her into his arms. "I don't believe you're capable of hate. He was a hard man, but you loved him like no other, and"—he tilted her chin until their eyes met—"he loved you."

"What he did wasn't right, and forgiveness isn't deserved." Peace stole over her countenance. "But I forgive him. I forgive, Grandfather."

The woman's mercy had no end. His lips brushed her forehead. "I fall a little more in love with you every day."

"And I with you."

"Do you think we can say our vows now?"

She blinked as if only now realizing a room full of people waited for that very moment. "I'll be ready in five minutes." She swiveled toward the vanity, but he caught her and brought her back into his arms.

Her head tilted to the perfect angle to capture her lips. What he'd meant to be a quick kiss to hint at the future lingered and deepened. Six years and three months he'd waited for today. His arms encircled her waist, and he pressed closer. Passionate and frenzied, she matched him kiss for kiss.

A knock at the door brought him to his senses. "Is Theresa all right?"

They pulled inches apart.

He grinned at her disheveled appearance. "Still need five minutes?"

"No." A deep flush spread across her cheeks and accentuated her swollen lips.

The knock came again. "Theresa? Broderick?"

He consoled himself with the knowledge this was the last time he required restraint and left a smiling Theresa to go open the door. "She's ready. I'll let everyone know they can take their seats."

Lydia took one sweeping look from him to Theresa and opened her mouth. Whatever reprimand lay on the tip of her tongue remained there as she shook her head. "I'll have her appearance repaired in five minutes or less."

"Less would be preferable." He shut the door and returned to the ballroom.

As he entered, guests regarded him with expectation. His simple nod was all the signal they needed. As Nathaniel brushed past him to take a seat near the back, Broderick stopped him. While they'd reached a point of tentative acceptance, he'd failed to do what God required of him. If Theresa needed to voice her forgiveness to find healing, maybe he could do the same, forgiving a brother who had done his best to make amends for his betrayal.

"You should sit in the front with the family."

Nathaniel shook his head. "I'm content enough to be invited to the wedding. The back is fine."

"No, Nathaniel. It's not." Broderick took a deep breath. "This is the last time we'll ever speak of this, but I have something that must be said." Nathaniel's wide smile smoothed into the resigned frown of a man approaching the hangman's noose. "Nathaniel, I forgive you, and I want you with the family, where you belong."

Nathaniel blinked, and his Adam's apple bobbed. With a slow nod, he smiled and turned toward the front. When he sat in the first row next to Pop, Mother turned and shot Broderick a wet-eyed smile. Healing would take time, but God had taken the mess of this case and turned it into good beyond all imagination. Following His plans wouldn't always be easy, but Broderick would never doubt them again.

As he took his place next to Pastor William, Lydia opened the doors. Theresa stepped forward on the arm of Dr. Pelton and beamed. Yes, God had turned his foolish blunder around and richly blessed him indeed.

Theresa couldn't take her eyes off Broderick. Many men could be considered handsome, but he completely redefined the word in his black tailored suit. How had she not been knocked senseless by his appearance minutes ago? A grin split his face and drew her gaze to his lips.

Ah, yes. He'd knocked her senseless in a much more pleasurable way. Heat flushed her face as the tingling in her lips returned full force.

Broderick winked, and before she realized what she was doing, she'd slipped from Dr. Pelton's arm and passed Lydia in the walk down the aisle. Gentle laughter subsided as she stopped before the altar, and Broderick kissed her hand. Eyes as green and fresh as new spring grass held hers like a cherished prize. Immeasurable love resided there. Real love. How had she ever believed Edward's counterfeit version? Thank God for His intervention.

The last-minute addition of Grandfather's restored Medal of Honor to her bouquet bounced against her hand as Pastor William asked who gave away the bride. Dr. Pelton may be stepping in, but Grandfather's written blessing spoke louder than any declaration. Her heart swelled as she passed the bouquet to Lydia, then took her place next to Broderick. For six years she'd strived for a future of her own making, but only by surrendering her future to God had her heart's desires come about. The life of a Secret Service operative's wife was sure to be filled with danger, stress, and challenges, but no matter where Broderick's job led them, she would trust God with their future.

The ceremony passed in a whir and ended with a kiss that resulted in a few coughs of embarrassment from the guests. When Broderick broke away, the words she'd longed to hear for so long came on a husky whisper. "I love you, Mrs. Cosgrove."

"And I love you, Mr. Cosgrove."

Acknowledgments

No book makes it beyond the author's computer without a huge support network. First and foremost to me is God. I never imagined taking this writing path, but He pushed me on it and used it to teach me who He really is. May His name be glorified always.

Thank you to my family, without whom I would never have started and survived this journey. Holy cow, Travis! You blow me away. I could spend pages gushing over you and your support, but I'll leave it at *thank you* here. Malaki, Nehemiah, Linda, Noah, Mom, Dad, Matt, and Ramey, you guys are my biggest cheerleaders, and I'm so incredibly thankful for you.

I want to personally thank so many people who have walked this journey with me: Amanda Cox, Angela K. Couch, Casey Kohlman, Emily Lowe, Joanna Davidson Politano, Kelly Goshorn, Kimberly Gilbert, KyLee Woodley, Martha Hutchens, Patti Stockdale, and Tammy Kirby. A special shout-out goes to my amazing trio of besties: Angela Carlisle, Lucette Nel, and Voni Harris. You gals have been my sounding board, my sanity, and my support for more than just writing. Thank you for putting up with my insanity and daily messages. Love you gals so much!

I'm so grateful to my agent, Tamela Hancock Murray, and the entire Kregel team for taking a chance on this wannabe author. Your support and suggestions have pushed me to continually grow. Thank you specifically to my Kregel editor, Janyre Tromp, and editor Jean

Kavich Bloom. This book would not be what it is without your poking and prodding. Thank you.

Finally, thank you to my street team and all those helping to get the word out about Theresa and Broderick. You guys rock!

DISCUSSION QUESTIONS

1. How did you see the theme of counterfeit love played out in the story? How can one tell the difference between counterfeit and genuine love?
2. Colonel Plane was a difficult man, and few people understood Theresa's fierce loyalty to him. Do you feel the loyalty was justified? Why or why not? Would you have been as loyal if you had been in her position?
3. Both Broderick and Theresa made compromises to their convictions in order to find security and success in their lives. How did those compromises affect their relationships with others and with God? What consequences did they face by making those compromises?
4. While Theresa's past love for Broderick had been passionate, her feelings for Edward were practical. Given her circumstances and Broderick's insistence they had no future, how would you have felt in her position? What would you have done?
5. Broderick decided the best way to protect Theresa and his career was to lie and withhold information. How do you think the story might have gone differently if he had chosen to speak the truth from the beginning?
6. Theresa was willing to give Nathaniel a second chance. What evidence of being a changed man would you have had to see in Nathaniel's life in order to give him a second chance? What is

the difference between giving someone a second chance and trusting them? Is there a difference?

7. "Even if" is a phrase repeated throughout the story—often in reference to God's presence and the need to surrender to and trust Him even when our plans don't match His. How do you see God's hand in Theresa's and Broderick's lives as He teaches them He can be trusted even if . . . ?

8. As Theresa wrestled with trusting and loving God "even if," she turned to prayer, the story of 2 Chronicles 20, and worship. What strategies do you use when struggling through tough situations? What areas are the hardest for you to surrender to and trust God with?

9. Was Edward's love for Theresa genuine? What leads you to believe this?

10. Both Broderick and Theresa had to learn to forgive someone who hurt them deeply. Were Nathaniel and Colonel Plane worthy of forgiveness? Why or why not?

Author's Note

Dear Beloved Reader,

Thank you for choosing to read my debut novel. I pray it blessed you in some way, whether with a moment of escape or something much deeper. Just like for Theresa, *even if* became a powerful statement for me as I wrote this story. I never dreamed I'd face the complete stripping of everything I knew and have to answer this question for myself: Will I trust God, *even if*? The testimony of that journey can be found on the bonus content section of my website, but I want you to know you're not alone on this journey through life. If you'd like me to pray for you, I'd consider it a great honor. Or you might just want to drop me a line. You can email me at crystal@crystalcaudill.com. I reply to every message I receive, even if it takes me a few days.

As extra fun for you, other bonus content for this story is on my website, www.crystalcaudill.com/books. See my inspiration board, take a tour of Cincinnati, download a book club kit, or learn about the Bible printing ministry this book supports. While there, you can sign up for my newsletter and become the first to hear book news, get family tidbits, and have access to opportunities no other group of my followers will have.

It has been an honor to connect with you, and I look forward to doing so again soon.

—Crystal Caudill

HISTORICAL NOTES

The Secret Service

The history of the Secret Service is fascinating and complex. Today, it's most well-known for protecting the president of the United States. Their origins, however, were born out of the Civil War for the sole purpose of combating widespread counterfeiting. The first president to receive part-time protection from the Secret Service was Grover Cleveland, in 1894, thirty-one years after they were officially established. The complexities of an operative's job, especially within the first thirty years, were so incredible that I had to write about them.

For instance, operatives could not conduct searches or arrests without the support of the local police. Even more challenging was that the Secret Service had on average twenty-five operatives for the entire country between 1875 and 1910, and between 1878 and 1893 that average was well below twenty-five. I could tell you about the early history for pages, but if you obtain a copy of my favorite resource, *Illegal Tender* by David R. Johnson, you'll get a thorough peek at the counterfeiting world and the Secret Service during the nineteenth century. Or you can visit my website, www.crystalcaudill.com, to learn more.

Counterfeit Bills

One thing many readers question is whether counterfeiters really made bills as high as fifties. The answer is absolutely! In my research for this series, I read a lot about the lives of actual counterfeiters. William

E. Brockway was one of the most successful American counterfeiters of the nineteenth century. When they arrested him during the 1880s, operatives found twenty-three sets of steel-and-copper plates used to print $100, $500, and $1,000 banknotes. They also found $350,000 in counterfeit $100 banknotes and stolen government paper used to print genuine currency. Brockway also had a set of half-finished $1,000, 6 percent US bond plates. The man was a genius gone wrong. Though he was arrested several times and watched by the Secret Service all his adult life, counterfeiting proved to be a lucrative crime for him. He died a wealthy man at the age of ninety-two.

Route Cipher

In this story, Colonel Plane is a master at using the route cipher. This was a system the Union army devised to communicate plans to commanders in a way impossible for the Confederate army to decipher. Essentially, it looked like a letter with all the words jumbled out of order. Creating a cipher was a multistep process. First, words with military significance were coded. Then the new message's first word indicated the number of columns needed to decipher it. The coder then filled a grid with one word per column until they reached the end of the row, and then a new row was created.

This continued until the entire message was put into grid form. Additional columns could be filled with null words to add to the complexity of the message. The third and final step to cipher the message was determining the route, for which there were endless possibilities. For example, in a four-column grid, the route might be down column 3, up column 1, up column 4, and down column 2. It really was brilliant.

Time Bombs of the Nineteenth Century

Did time bombs exist in the 1880s? Yes, but not in the form we see today. From what I've been able to discern, the bombs were encapsulated in boxes and relied on gunpowder and other mechanical works beyond my understanding. Also, the timing of the explosion was not an exact science. The earliest timed explosion I discovered occurred on August 9, 1864, in City Point, Virginia. Confederate John Maxwell sneaked aboard a Union supply vessel and planted a time bomb, which he called a "horological torpedo." They initially considered the explosion an accident until Confederate papers were later confiscated and Maxwell's report was discovered.

The Great Floods of 1883 and 1884

Record-breaking floods struck Cincinnati for two consecutive years. The 1883 flood crested at 66.3 feet on February 15, and almost exactly a year later, on February 14, the Ohio River crested at 71.1 feet. The effects were devastating. The flood swept away entire towns and cities from between Pittsburgh, Pennsylvania, to Cairo, Illinois. Food and fuel shortages resulted. People huddled together in flooded buildings. Others took anything they could carry and abandoned everything they'd once known, never to return. This crippled the economy for years, and many businesses and individuals never recovered. At the time of this writing, more than 130 years later, the flood of 1884 is still Cincinnati's second-worst flood on record.

TURN THE PAGE FOR A SNEAK PEEK OF

COUNTERFEIT HOPE

BOOK 2 IN

HIDDEN HEARTS
OF THE GILDED AGE

COMING IN 2023

CHAPTER ONE

Landkreis, Indiana
August 13, 1884

THIS WAS THE LAST TIME. After tonight, she and Oscar would be free from the den of thieves they called family.

Bill's bar mates hooted and hollered as Lu Thorne sidled up to the drunkard and leaned in to kiss his bearded cheek. She filched his coin purse quicker than he could turn his head to catch her lips and left him with a mouthful of hair instead. After months of lightening his pockets, the man ought to know better than to allow her within arm's reach. Still, Bill never failed to be distracted by the low cut of her bodice, bare arms, or ankle baring skirts. Beauty had long been her greatest weapon and biggest curse.

"One of these days I'm gonna get that kiss, Lu."

She tucked the purse into a hidden pocket and stepped away. "Ain't today, sugar."

"Aww, let me have another go. I'll be quicker this time."

"Can't. Ma Frances's rules. Gotta give the others their chance."

"But who'll reward me for my hard work?" Bill's bottom lip pouted as his hands caressed the curve of her waist.

How about his faithful wife or the nine kids he left near starving at home?

She smiled instead of toppling his chair. A lifetime of dealing with men like him told her he'd not learn a lesson from the act. "How about a drink?"

"I suppose that'll do," his gaze swept the full length of her, "unless you want to offer me something better."

Not even if he was breathing his last. "Horace," she turned to the bartender, "pour him a shot from the bottom right." Maybe the cheap stuff would sour Bill's stomach and send him packing. "It'll be on the house."

Horace paused his reach for the bottle. "I don't give free drinks."

Oh, he was a bold one tonight. He knew better than anyone that opposing any member of the Thorne Gang equaled trouble. One word to either of her brothers-in-law and he'd regret that boldness for the rest of his life. Though given the ill-temper Clint was in, Horace wouldn't last the night.

"That so?" She leaned an elbow on the counter and stared him down.

Horace's jaw worked side to side for a moment before he grabbed the bottle and thunked it on the counter.

"Thank you."

He didn't look at her as he filled a glass halfway.

Well did she understand the bitterness of forced compliance, but Horace only had to suffer it on occasion. She'd spent an entire lifetime under the thumb of one master or another. Tonight was no different.

But tomorrow will be.

Lu tempered her smile as Bill gulped his free drink. Membership in the Thorne Gang may not have been a choice, but that didn't mean she didn't have choices. Not now that Walt Kinder offered a way out. She patted Bill on the shoulder and continued her routine of visiting the saloon's regulars.

All she needed was to steal enough to convince Ma Frances she'd done her job, make amends with the women of Landkreis, and keep enough money in her pocket to provide Oscar with a new future. One far from the matriarch's claws. Once Walt got her and her five-year-old son to Newburg, they'd give Walt the slip and disappear forever. Double-crossing the U.S. Marshal was a risk, but testifying against the Thorne family was a surefire death sentence. Her son's only safe future lie in a town where nobody knew them. A place where she could become one of those new creatures Pastor Umbridge talked about and give Oscar the life she'd never had. An honorable one.

Tomorrow couldn't come soon enough.